To Lai

So nice to meet you!

PEDDLERS

A FUTURISTIC LOVE STORY

Let's keep in touch! ♡

love Penny Ann ♡

PENNY ANN

Book one of the Children of Change series

The Greater Reset
Morelia 2023

FriesenPress

One Printers Way
Altona, MB R0G 0B0
Canada

www.friesenpress.com

Copyright © 2022 by Penny Ann
First Edition — 2022

All rights reserved.

1st copyright - Feb 1990

All situations and characters are fictional, and do not reflect events or persons living or dead.

Author Photo: Sean Allman at Lightroom Mobile

No part of this publication may be reproduced in any form, or by any means, electronic or mechanical, including photocopying, recording, or any information browsing, storage, or retrieval system, without permission in writing from FriesenPress.

ISBN
978-1-03-913201-6 (Hardcover)
978-1-03-913200-9 (Paperback)
978-1-03-913202-3 (eBook)

1. FICTION, SCIENCE FICTION, APOCALYPTIC & POST-APOCALYPTIC

Distributed to the trade by The Ingram Book Company

PEDDLERS

PROLOGUE
JUNE 2169

RUNNING FOR HIS LIFE, WITH DEATH ROLLING AT HIS BACK, a young man in a white suit raced for the opening at the end of a large tunnel. He was feeling weak from lack of food, but fear had given him the strength he needed to sprint into a full run. He was not far from the end now and could see endless miles of water beyond.

He could well be jumping to his death.

He dove out of the mouth of the tunnel and found himself sixty feet above the surface of the water. He would need all his diving skills to land him safely. He hit the water beautifully. If only he could have made a dive like that on his aqua finals, he probably wouldn't be in the mess he was in now. He would have been second or third in his class, and Anne would be his wife.

He surfaced, wincing as the water stung the cut over his eye. Off in the distance, he could see Peddlers Island. *How did I get here?* he thought.

HAVANNA

Corey Tusk stood in front of his locker, not seeing the odd assortment of books thrown carelessly on the bottom. His thoughts were on his upcoming aqua practicum that was scheduled in one hour. Closing his locker, Corey walked the length of the hall and entered the Boys' School library. Glancing at the clock, he realized he had only twenty minutes to study before he had to leave for the pool.

The room was well lit with LED lights hanging from the ceiling. Half a dozen boys sat quietly studying at nearby tables, dressed in the gray sweat suits that were supplied to all the Havannians. Besides the vidscreens and vidscanners, the only other pieces of furniture were the tables, chairs, and bookshelves, made of pine wood and particle board. The desks were marked, chipped, and had initials and designs carved into them.

Corey spread out his books in front of him. They consisted mostly of sports journals, rules and regulations, and training manuals for all Havannian sports. There were books on vidgames, first aid for sport-related accidents, and how to avoid injuries, as well as specific exercises for strengthening muscles or toning.

There was no doubt in Corey's mind that he had done extremely well on his aqua written, but the practicum part of the exam could make or break his standings. These next exams were his last hurdle. He knew if he scored well, he could take second or third place at the mating ceremony scheduled for Saturday.

Corey felt confident with the track and field events, as well as the court sports exams. Very few people were in better shape than he was. Years of hard, vigorous exercise had produced a lean and muscular body. He scored especially high on the bicycle relays in a group category, and in high jumping as a singular achievement.

Although Corey often scored well in the swimming events, he was not fond of the water. He hated the feeling of having water in his ears or up his nose. *After this next exam,* he thought, *I will never have to swim again.*

Corey tried to focus his attention on the book in front of him, but his thoughts kept drifting back to last night's first coed function with the girls that were this year's candidates for his graduating class. These were the girls that would be presented to them on the day of the mating ceremony.

His mind drifted to one special girl. Ballroom dancing was a custom that was taught to them in grade school but was only brought up again, in theory, through high school. The day before the dance, Corey had practiced with his mother, Helena, to tone up his rusty feet. It wasn't long before he was sweeping her around the kitchen floor, but it was the dance with Anne Corbett that Corey was thinking of now.

Anne had worn a full-length, pale-blue dress, and Corey could still visualize her firm, supple body and long flowing blond hair. Only on special occasions, such as this, could they wear something other than their usual sweat suits. With Corey's own dark good looks, they made a striking couple as they whirled gracefully around the hardwood dance floor in the Stadium building. Corey was taken in by Anne's beautiful blue eyes, and he loved the way they brightened when she laughed. He knew in an instant that Anne would be his wife.

"You dance beautifully," Corey had said.

"Thank you. I have a good lead," Anne replied as she smiled up at him, thinking he was by far the best-looking guy she had met all night. Standing a foot taller than her, he looked lean and well-built beneath his navy-blue suit. He wore his dark, wavy hair brushed back to accentuate a strong facial structure.

She loved the way Corey looked both masculine and boyish. His face was handsome without being perfect. Anne wasn't sure whether it was his dark-brown eyes that were set too deep or the nose that was slightly too large.

For the first time in Anne's life, she felt herself at a loss for words. Anything she thought to say seemed shallow or pointless. Corey broke the silence by asking Anne what her favorite sport was. Unlike Corey, Anne enjoyed swimming immensely. She was quite animated when speaking of synchronized swimming. Corey pictured her shapely body moving through the water with grace and power.

"I've managed to achieve second standings in the master's swim, topped only by my best friend Becky," Anne proudly announced.

Corey had watched Anne's lips move while she talked, conscious of a strong desire to kiss those soft, sweet lips. He knew his thoughts should be on his aqua techniques rather than on Anne. In three days, they could be wed, if only he could concentrate long enough to pull off a good score.

He flipped his book open to diving techniques now, trying to feign interest. Suddenly the bell sounded, signifying five minutes to the hour. Corey let out a long breath of air, picked up his books, and headed for the pool.

Anne Corbett also picked up her books at the sound of the bell. She had done alright with her homemaker and childcare exams, as well as her cooking practicum. All she had left was her conception and pregnancy exams, which she was well prepared for. Her thoughts drifted to Corey Tusk. She knew they could have beautiful children together.

Anne Tusk. I like the way that sounds, she thought. She knew she shouldn't obsess over one of the candidates because she had no idea who her new husband would be in three days.

Anne reached the classroom and chose the desk next to her best friend, Becky Mullen. The exam room was monitored by TEACHER, the school computer they had all grown to fear and respect. Cheating on a final exam would warrant them a zero. With the mating ceremony so close, no one was willing to take that chance. Even though the women didn't get to choose their mates, it was still important that they scored high.

The TEACHER's five monitoring vidcams clicked on, commencing the forty-five-minute time span to complete the exam. Anne entered all the answers on her digital exam with fifteen minutes to spare. She signed out of TEACHER and retrieved her books from her desk. She left the classroom for the last time, feeling confident. She didn't hang around after school today with her girlfriends, as she had a very important meeting with DOCTOR in the Medicure building. This would be her last appointment before she was married on Saturday.

Corey left the pool feeling exhausted and discouraged. He hadn't scored well on his diving and had been distracted when swimming laps and races. The only thing that might preserve his standing for the mating ceremony was his strokes and precision.

He located his locker and threw his books inside before realizing that this would be the last time he would ever use his locker. Next year, one of this year's grade-school graduates would be assigned this locker, books included, until he had finished his schooling. Corey walked down the polished tiled floors of the corridor feeling exuberant and a little sad.

Although he was excited about graduating, he was unhappy to leave his school of the last six years. Even the hallways held many good memories for him. The weekly duties of sweeping and washing the floors now sparked fond memories, not one of dread.

He ran his fingers along the lockers on his way out of the mahogany front doors. Descending the marble steps, Corey joined his friend Lionel Chaffe, as they had plans to go play mini-golf after their finals today. The streetlights were on, as the light coming in from outside the Dome was dim. The tinted bubble kept out the ultraviolet rays from the sun but muted the sunshine. The streetlights usually kept the Dome quite well lit, except on days when it was cloudy, like today.

Lionel had been Corey's best friend since the eighth grade when he had rescued Corey from the school bully. Unlike Corey's tall, slim build, Lionel Chaffe was short and stocky. His deep-blue eyes, high cheekbones, and square jaw were framed by light-brown hair.

"So how do you think you did on your exams today? I know you were worried about them," Lionel asked, as Corey sat beside him on the steps.

"No problem. I'm willing to bet I'll be among the top three to graduate." Corey wished he felt as confident as he sounded. Now he could only wait to see what the outcome would be. "Hey," he continued, "what do you say we go to the Girls' School today instead of playing mini-golf? There was this girl I danced with last night that I wouldn't mind seeing again before the mating ceremony."

"Are you out of your mind?" Lionel almost yelled. He looked over his shoulder to be sure no one was listening, then continued more quietly, "what if our parents check the computer terminal and we're not registered at Joey's Mini-golf? Or worse, what if BUDDY should catch us in a tabu area and exile us to Peddlers?"

"Come on, Lionel, where's your sense of adventure? Besides, my parents never check up on me, and I don't plan on getting caught. I've long since memorized the camera rotational system." Corey continued before Lionel had a chance to discourage him. "It's better than playing some dumb game of mini-golf. Haven't you ever thought it was strange that they call it mini-golf when there's only one type of golf?"

Lionel groaned. "Don't tell me you're going to sit here and poison my mind with all your rhetorical questions, trying to find flaws in our society. Look, it's called Havanna because it is the perfect society. Stop giving me your theories on how you can make this a better place because you can't. It's all been thought out very carefully. Besides, there's nothing wrong with this place, only with your point of view. Now that's where all the problems lie."

Corey looked away from his friend. Lionel often reacted this way to his enquiries. Although Corey appeared to be watching the other schoolboys leave, his mind was on a similar conversation he'd had with his father the other day. Aloud, he said, "You know, Lionel, you're starting to sound like my father."

"Well, you should listen to him, Corey. Your father is a smart man. He doesn't look none the wear and tear from living in Havanna. You might as well accept life here because there's nowhere else to go."

"Yes, there is." Corey smiled slyly. "We could go to the Girls' School and check out the candidates."

Lionel and Corey took a southbound sidewalk and stepped off at the Forum Skytrain Station. They passed their tattoo codes, located on the inside of their right forearms, over the computer sensor. They then entered the glass-enclosed elevator that could hold twelve. One hundred and twenty feet up, the elevator opened onto a platform.

The skytrain pulled into the station, opening its doors on the opposite side of the train for disembarking passengers. The skytrain had a built-in two-minute delay before the doors would close and the embarking side doors would open. The boys took seats in the back, and the skytrain commenced its short journey to the Courts Skytrain Station.

Five skytrain rails crisscrossed the Dome like a Star. The stations, Stadium, Pool, Courts, School, and Forum, each divided a different section of the Dome. Each section was referred to by a letter: Section M (Medicure) was situated between G (Girls' School) and B (Boys' School), followed by R (Residential) and D

(Girls' Dormitory). Sections D and G were strictly tabu areas for the boys to enter.

They disembarked at the Courts Skytrain Station, took the descending elevator to the main entrance level, and hung back while the other boys headed for the changerooms. The ball courts were outside under the Dome but were fenced off from the surrounding sections.

After the rest of the guys left, Corey and Lionel ran to the corner of the fence leading to the girls' side of the M section, where the fence had been loosened just as Zachary had said it would be. Lionel crawled under and then held it up for Corey. They ran quickly behind the infirmary building that was shadowed by the overhead skytrain station. Lionel flattened his back against the building, breathing heavily.

"My stomach is in my throat."

"Will you keep quiet!" Corey snapped. He could barely keep control of his pulse as it raced wildly in his veins. The last time Corey could remember being this scared and excited was when he took his first dive from the fifty-foot diving board in ninth grade. Taking a deep breath, he remembered he had come at great risk for a purpose. He started for the corner of the building when Lionel grabbed his arm and yanked him back.

"Where do you think you're going? Come on, Corey, enough is enough! Let's go back before we're caught." Lionel knew if his father ever caught him in a tabu area he would get a thrashing, let alone what would happen if BUDDY, the main computer terminal, should discover their whereabouts.

"Relax, man," Corey said, trying to soothe him.

"Relax? Relax? Son of a Peddler!" Lionel yelled before dropping his voice. "I'm going to have a cardiac arrest in a moment, and you want me to relax?" Corey could see his friend was visibly upset. Lionel's face was flushed red with anxiety, and his breathing was shallow and rapid.

"Okay, we'll go back." Corey sighed. "Just hang tight for a minute while I check if the coast is clear." He patted Lionel's shoulder and headed for the corner of the building. Corey fought to keep his breathing under control as he stuck his head around the corner toward the front of the infirmary doors. What he saw then took his breath away.

Anne Corbett arrived for her scheduled appointment with DOCTOR a few minutes early. When the computer voice from the overhead speaker announced her name, she picked up her purse and entered the examination room. She lay down in the Medichair as instructed. Having been through this procedure more than once, she placed her feet in the ankle braces and her head on the headrest before DOCTOR could advise her to do so. Once Anne was in place, the ankle braces closed around her legs while a holding brace moved down to secure her shoulders.

"Examination will now begin," the voice of DOCTOR sounded. It was gentle, unlike the voice of TEACHER, which was strong and intimidating. A mechanical arm, equipped with a built-in laser, X-ray, and ultrasound swung down and positioned itself horizontally across the top of her head. The arm moved slowly down her body until it had reached her toes. Once it had completed its task, unless there were problems, it would swing up and out of the way. The shoulder brace reversed itself while the ankle braces released their hold. The whole operation had taken seven minutes.

"You may get up," DOCTOR instructed. "You are in good health, Anne. No doubt you will make a good candidate." Anne smiled. She liked DOCTOR. He always had something good to say.

"Thank you," Anne replied, blushing.

"This will be your last physical before the mating ceremony. Let me remind you again that the consummation of your upcoming marriage should not take place until you have completed your next menstrual cycle. According to my records, your next cycle will commence in thirteen days. Therefore, depending on the duration of it, you shall be able to consummate your upcoming marriage in twenty-three days. This will ensure the probability that your firstborn will be male. I am sure you are also well informed on the best positions to obtain a male child."

"Yes, TEACHER has made certain of that."

"Very well, Anne. Come in to see me again when you are certain that you have missed your next regulated menstrual cycle. If you get your cycle as usual, then repeat the same procedure the following month. If you are not pregnant in two months, I should like to see both you and your new husband. That is all. Please do not forget to pick up your monthly supply of feminine protection on your way out. Goodbye and good luck."

Anne left the examination room, used her tattoo code to access the supplies dispenser, and placed the items in her handbag. She descended the stairs at the front of the infirmary building and turned to her right. When she reached the corner of the building, she almost walked straight into Corey.

Time stood still for an instant while their eyes met and held, with Anne seeing Corey's dark, sensual brown eyes and he her light, dreamy blue ones. Realization and fear suddenly clouded hers, and she turned and ran.

"Wait!" Corey called out in vain.

Anne fled, lest she be seen talking to a boy out of wedlock. She felt disappointed in herself for not being brave enough to stay and talk with him. She could still hear him calling to her. For an instant, she hesitated, but she knew it was strictly forbidden to meet a boy outside of coed social functions. As tempted as she was, the fear of abolishment to Peddlers spurred her on. Anne couldn't think of a worse fate than that. Peddlers was dirty and disease-ridden. The people were impure and without customs and tabus. Worst of all, she would have to work for the rest of her life, with no chance of returning to Havanna.

She shook her head to clear these unpleasant thoughts and turned her mind to more interesting things. There was something about Corey that made her head spin. She wanted to be with him, to marry him, to have children with him. They would have strong, healthy children, she was sure. Thinking of children made her realize how lucky she was to be the chosen race to breed. She wondered if the Peddlers ever had healthy, normal children. After all, they were the descendants of the Big Three. Who knew what sort of awful diseases and defects they would have!

Anne often wondered what the people were like outside of the Dome. Were they normal, like Havannians? Did they lead the same kind of lives? She tried to talk to her friend about it, but Becky preferred to talk about sports and homemaking. Perhaps Anne could voice these thoughts to her new husband.

Once she reached the door to her dormitory, she passed her tattoo code over the vidscreen. The buzzer sounded that unlocked the door, opening it into a spacious, four-room duplex. She loved the feeling of having the door open only for her. That would all be changing by Saturday. She would have a new home, a six-room house, in the Residential section with her new husband. Again, she allowed herself the luxury of fantasizing about a life with Corey, living with him every day, and having their door open only for them.

Anne knew the dangers of coveting one particular man. She could be setting herself up for an emotional trauma if she was chosen by someone else. If only there were some way she could ensure that Corey would choose her. *Perhaps he had broken tabu to see one of the other girls, and it wasn't me he wanted to talk to...* Warning signals were going off in her head, as she felt her first stirring of jealousy. She had to find some way to get Corey to fall madly in love with her so he would want no one else. *The ceremony is in three days*, thought Anne, frantically. *I must come up with something fast. There's not much time left.*

Lionel grabbed Corey by the sleeve and pulled him back behind the building. He had been shouting at some unseen figure. Lionel held Corey up against the wall by the front of his sweatsuit.

"What are you trying to prove standing in the open yelling your fool head off?" Lionel loosened his grip but steered Corey toward the corner of the fence. Corey's heart was pounding hard against his chest. He had been taken totally by surprise when he encountered Anne looking so beautiful and vulnerable. He couldn't blame her for taking off the way she did. In fact, he respected her for it, but he had wanted nothing more than to take her in his arms and comfort her.

Corey was barely conscious of Lionel leading him back to where they took the skytrain to the Stadium Skytrain Station. This was the closest stop to where they lived in the R section. In the time that it took to reach their destination, Corey's attention was taken up with thoughts of Anne.

At that moment when he had set his eyes on her baby blues, he was lost. He ached for her now as he had never ached for anything in his life. BUDDY had always provided him with everything he had ever wanted or needed, and with the mating ceremony only three days away, it was only natural that he should desire a wife. He knew it wasn't good to harbor feelings for a candidate. It could lead to coveting another man's wife, which was strictly tabu, but Corey could not accept the fact that Anne might not be his. She had to be his wife. BUDDY had always anticipated what he wanted in the past and provided it. He would just have to have faith that BUDDY would provide him with the woman of his choice.

The boys exchanged goodbyes when they reached Lionel's house and Corey continued up the street, whistling and feeling lighter than he had in years. His sister, Tanya, no longer lived with them since she had graduated from grade school. She would live in the D section with the other girls until she was ready for candidacy in two years. Corey wouldn't see Tanya again until he gave her away at her mating ceremony. He figured his sister would be among the first to be chosen due to her striking good looks. She wore her straight black hair in a pageboy, which highlighted her dark, horizontally-shaped eyes. The combination of the hair and eyes was comparable to the pictures of the ancient pharaohs that Corey had studied in Olympic history.

Passing his tattoo code over the vidscanner, Corey entered the front foyer of his home. His mood changed the minute he saw the look on his father's face. Zane Tusk was an attractive man of forty-one with auburn hair and deep laugh lines around his light brown eyes. But Zane's eyes were not smiling now as he confronted Corey at the door. His arms were crossed over his chest, which usually meant he was in no mood for nonsense. It was clear from his expression that he had checked the computer terminal and found that Corey hadn't gone to Joey's Mini-golf. It was rare that his parents checked up on him; Corey usually didn't give them a reason.

"Alright, young man, maybe you can explain to me what you were doing at the Courts Skytrain Station if you weren't registered at any of the ball courts?" Corey glanced quickly at the computer console and was relieved to see that it had been turned off. He didn't want BUDDY to know he had broken tabu. Corey sighed heavily and sank down into the hallway chair. There was no point in lying to his father. He never had before.

"I went to the G section to catch a glimpse of the girls. I'm sorry. I didn't mean any harm by it."

"Sorry?" his father's voice boomed. "Do you realize how much trouble you could have gotten yourself into if you had been caught? Not to mention any of the girls you might have been talking to. I don't want to see you mess everything up when you'll have it all in a few days. I'd like to see both you and Tanya married, with children of your own, so that your mother and I can move on to Dusting."

"I want to see you and Mom retire to Dusting too, Dad. I just get so impatient sometimes."

"Do you think your impatience today brought you any closer to where you want to be?" enquired Zane.

"No." How could he explain to his father about Anne? How could he rationally explain the depth of his feelings for someone he had just met but felt he had known all his life? Could his father understand these things? Could anyone understand how he felt?

"Good things come to those who wait, Corey." If that were true, then all he'd have to do was wait until Saturday. *Yeah, I can wait that long*, Corey thought.

"I guess there are some things in life we learn that aren't taught in school."

"You're a wise boy, Corey, but a bit too inquisitive for your own good. Just slow down and take life as it comes. It's short enough the way it is without trying to rush through it. Don't be in such a hurry to grow up."

"Thanks, Dad," Corey said as he got up from the chair.

The table was set with Pyrex plates, matching napkins, and a tablecloth. The table and chairs were made of fine teak wood and set on varnished hardwood floors. Helena Tusk punched the dinner meal code into the kitchen's computer console. The computer dispensed instant mashed potatoes, dehydrated vegetables, imitation meat (tonight it was crab), and premade dough for buns that took three minutes in the microwave.

Once they were seated at the table, the conversation was kept light. Helena looked at her son adoringly. He had grown into such a fine young man, not unlike his father had been at his age. Although Corey had her dark complexion and hair, he was built like his dad. Zane's hair was graying slightly at the temples now, but his active life playing sports and swimming had kept his body strong and muscular, giving him a more distinguished maturity.

Helena could still remember the day she had married Zane at their mating ceremony. He had been thinner then, but the extra weight now made him look more like a man. He had been third in his class, and she fondly remembered how pleased she was when he had chosen her. She had noticed Zane staring at her during the beginning of the ceremony, and he didn't hesitate once about whom he wanted. It was a great honor to be among the first ten chosen. As Helena ate a mouthful of imitation crab, she was reminded of the great feast BUDDY had provided for the ceremony.

"At our mating ceremony, the women were chosen, then we sat down to a beautiful feast of food. Everything was fresh; the meat, the fruit, the vegetables, and the bread. It was the most delicious meal I have ever eaten. I'm told they serve food like that every day in Dusting. It won't be long now, with you getting married in three days, and then your sister in two years. We'll finally be getting to go to Dusting in nine years." Helena smiled adoringly at Zane.

"Yeah, I can wait that long," he said. His eyes reflected Helena's, full of love and happiness.

Corey was struck by what his father had just said. Had he not thought those same words earlier when he had thought of Anne? Did his father feel the same way about his mother? Would he still love Anne the way his father loved his mom when he and Anne were ready for Dusting?

"Do you suppose you'll still be alive by the time I get to Dusting?"

It was an odd question. No one ever voiced thoughts like that. No one ever dared to question what they had been told. Zane and Helena exchanged worried glances, and then Zane spoke up.

"Well, son, that's a most unusual and uncalled-for question. You know as well as we do that Dusting offers eternal life and peace."

"Well, how do you know for sure? No one has ever come back from Dusting to say that it is true."

"That's enough, young man," his father scolded him. "How could you even doubt its existence? It is written in the customs that this is so. Where do you think everyone is going when they retire to Dusting? Besides," his father continued before Corey could answer, "how else could we get fresh food for the mating ceremony if they didn't bring it in from Dusting?"

"See," Corey retorted, "there's another thing that doesn't make sense. If Dusting is a place of peace and retirement, then who is working to get us food? There are only contaminated waste zones out there. So, you tell me, Dad, where do they get all the fresh food?"

Zane didn't have the answers to Corey's questions. They were questions he had never thought to ask himself. He had never wanted to scrutinize the discrepancies—only to revel in the luxuries that Havanna could and did provide. Zane became furious with his inability to deal properly with the situation.

"How did I ever raise such an ungrateful child? Havanna gives you everything, and you criticize it. You ask pointless questions about things that are totally irrelevant. Maybe you'd rather live on Peddlers? Do you think you're going to find any answers there? No," Zane said, as he slammed his fist down on the table, "we have the main computer center. BUDDY has everything carefully calculated, including dispensing fresh food once a year for the mating ceremony. Would you rather eat your regular dehydrated food on such an important day? I don't know what's gotten into you lately, Corey. Maybe you'll settle down once you're married. It'll do you good to have something better to do with your life than to sit around thinking of useless questions to ask."

Corey didn't say anything. He got up from his seat and headed for the games room to play his favorite vidgame. He couldn't understand why everyone just accepted everything the way it was without questioning the things that didn't make sense. *Don't rock the Dome!* That was their attitude. What made him so different? He realized that he wasn't afraid of being exiled from Havanna like most people were. Corey thought of it as an empty threat, but one that kept people in line.

He tried to focus on his vidgame, but he couldn't concentrate properly. He couldn't shake the feeling that there was something very wrong, even though he couldn't quite put his finger on it.

Helena began to gather the plates and cutlery together to bring to the kitchen. It infuriated her to hear Zane take out his anger on Corey. She dropped what she was doing and turned to her husband.

"Don't you think you were a bit hard on Corey just now?" Her normally gentle voice now held an edge that Zane had not heard in a long time.

"You just don't understand, Helena. I'm doing this for Corey's own good. If he keeps questioning and doubting everything, he'll never become a man."

"You're right. I don't understand. I don't understand why a grown man is frightened by a few harmless questions. Wait," she held up her hand when Zane started to protest, "let me finish. I see nothing wrong with Corey trying to understand the society of which he is to be a part. I do, however, see a grown man who is not man enough to have the courage to question his own surroundings. I think Corey is twice the man you'll ever be."

Zane sat there dumbfounded while Helena picked up the dishes and headed for the spacious kitchen. A few minutes later, Zane approached Helena while she was packing the steam heater with the dirty dishes. He gave her the few remaining objects from the table. The silence between them was deafening.

"Look, Helena, I'm... sorry."

"Don't apologize to me, Zane. Apologize to Corey."

Zane walked up to Helena, encircling her in his arms. "Am I ever glad I married such a smart woman. Has anyone told you they loved you today?" He pulled her closer to him, kissing her softly on the lips. Their kisses became longer. Helena reached up to run her fingers through his hair. Zane dropped his hands to caress her, to move her closer to him. Their hips started to move in unison.

"Oh, sorry," Corey said, as he walked into the kitchen. Zane and Helena parted quickly but reluctantly. Helena smoothed down her clothes while Zane turned to Corey.

"Don't go, son. I want to apologize. I had no right to get angry at you."

"That's alright, Dad. I really do appreciate everything Havanna gives us. I just tend to get angry when I don't understand things." Zane and Helena exchanged knowing smiles.

"Well, it seems to me that you've inherited your father's anger, as well as your mother's common sense," Helena added.

Zane ruffled Corey's hair. "Why don't you go wash up for bed while I help your mother with the dishes? I'll come in and talk to you before lights out." Once Corey left, Zane reached out to Helena. "Now, where were we?" he asked, as their mouths came together once again.

Corey entered the brightly lit washroom. The walls and floors were covered in a light-blue tile with a matching blue towel set. The steam bather, toilet bowl, and sink were royal blue. Corey washed up for bed, trying not to use too much of the daily allotted water so he could leave some for his parents.

He did realize how fortunate he was to have food, water, and everything else he needed, but he just wished sometimes that they could have more. *Imagine*, Corey thought, *if you could drink all the water you wanted. Imagine having so much water that you could leave the tap run while you brushed your teeth.* No. He shook his head. He couldn't imagine it. That would be the ultimate waste.

He supposed it was his greedy nature that got him into trouble. It was that drive always to want more, do more, and have more, including the choice to make more decisions in his life. He knew that if he had Anne by his side, he would never do anything to jeopardize their life together. Maybe his father was right. Marriage and children would probably settle him down. That thought almost scared him, except it meant he would have Anne with him.

He finished in the bathroom and entered his bedroom. The walls were wood-paneled like all the bedrooms in Havanna, with a four-poster bed in front of a small window overlooking the street. Along one wall was his dresser, desk, and chair, with a bureau on the other side. He had just undressed and gotten into bed when his father walked in.

"Ready for your big game tomorrow?" Zane asked, sitting in the chair beside Corey's bed.

"Yes, we're going take the Dome by storm. You're coming, right?"

"Yes, of course. What's on your mind, Corey? You've been very distracted today."

Corey rolled onto his side. "I think I'm in love with one of the girls I danced with last night," he blurted out.

"I see. Does this girl have a name?" Now Zane understood why Corey was acting so strangely.

"Anne. Anne Corbett. She's an angel, and I'll just die if I don't marry her."

"You won't die, but I know how you feel. I was dying inside at my mating ceremony with fear that someone would choose your mom before I could. In retrospect, I don't know what I would have done. Do you really like her that much?"

"Dad, it's like I've known her all my life; like we're already a family. Does that sound strange?"

"No. It sounds like you've found your soul mate."

"Sole mate? Of course! She's going to be my only mate."

"A soul mate is someone that your soul recognizes as being very important to you like your mom is to me."

"Soul mate. Yeah, I like that. Thanks, Dad. Goodnight."

"Good night, son."

Corey had problems falling asleep that night. His thoughts were full of the day's events and with thoughts of Anne. Luckily, Corey had no school tomorrow, or ever again, for that matter.

Soon he would be a married man. He was still awake when the lights automatically turned off at 2200 hours, which was lights out time for all of Havanna.

When the lights came on at 0600 hours the next morning, Corey wished he could have stayed in bed longer since there was no more school, but he knew it was tabu.

Helena came in to kiss Corey good morning, as she usually did on her way into the kitchen. She turned on the computer and punched in the morning meal code. Today's breakfast was instant decaffeinated coffee, instant oatmeal, powdered milk, three-minute microwave muffins, and enough water to mix everything. Both Zane and Helena were seated at the table when Corey came in looking fresh and clean in his school football uniform.

"Good morning," Corey said as he joined the breakfast table. "I hope you haven't forgotten about my big game at 1300 hours?"

"Of course not, Corey. Your mother and I will be there to cheer you on."

Swallowing down his last mouthful of milk, Corey excused himself from the table. Once in his room, he picked up his helmet and his cleats and left the house. As he was walking up the street, he saw Lionel emerge from his home. Corey jogged the short distance while calling out to his friend to wait. It was clear by the bruise on Lionel's cheek that his father, Doug, had checked the terminal yesterday and found that they hadn't gone to Joey's Mini-golf.

On the football field, Corey, as team captain, had his team do warm-up exercises to stretch and loosen their muscles. Lionel Chaffe, Zachary Rhodes, and David Peterson made up the rest of the team, which was called the Panthers. The opposing team, the Raiders, consisted of Christopher Meadows, the team captain, James Hoffman, Orthello Willis, and Shawn Sullivan.

Every year they had the same pre-recorded hype for the game, introducing the elementary-school cheerleaders who would be providing the entertainment at halftime. The only variation was in the names of the teams and their team members. The winners of today's game would each receive a trophy, and all the players would receive a bouquet of flowers.

Flowers were a rarity in Havanna, given only to the players of the football teams, who would present them to their new bride at the mating ceremony. The first half of the game left the Panthers trailing five to ten. The guys left the field feeling exhausted but excited.

Anne Corbett woke that morning when the lights came on and sauntered into the washroom. She removed her cotton nightdress and stepped into the steam bather, which engulfed her like a warm blanket. Hurriedly, she used the shampoo and conditioner from the wall dispensers before her seven minutes were up. The steam stopped suddenly and the heat lamps came on. The heat lamps served two purposes— they dried them off and they added color to their skin, which the Havannians didn't get naturally from the sun.

Returning to her bedroom, she took a fresh sweat suit from her closet and put it on. She brushed her hair on her way into the kitchen, where she turned on the computer and punched in the breakfast code. After she ate, Anne went to the girls' gymnasium to help the cheerleaders get ready for the halftime show. She wondered if Corey was on one of the teams. She didn't know too much about the game. It's funny, Anne thought, that Havanna only taught you things that you personally had to know. She knew all about cooking, cleaning, laundry, and childcare, but knew nothing of all the numerous things that people did.

By halftime, Anne was watching the game with her classmates on the vidscreen of the girls' gymnasium. She had to help the young cheerleaders with last-minute costume adjustments and frayed nerves. She smiled sweetly as the girls ran out onto the field and formed up for their halftime show. She remembered back to when she had been a cheerleader, as all the girls were. It signified the transition from grade school to high school. Even though they were segregated in school from the boys up until the age of twelve, they stayed at home with their parents and their brother. Now all the cheerleaders would take over the rooms in the D section that Anne and her classmates would be leaving on Saturday when they got married.

When the second half began, Anne's eyes lit up when she saw Corey running out to take up his position on the field. He looked so handsome in his football uniform, and he was captain of his team to boot! He was a born leader. Now all she had to do was find a way to lead Corey to herself.

It didn't go unnoticed that Anne had eyes for the Panthers' quarterback. Becky, Anne's best friend, observed the way Anne perked up every time the quarterback was on the vidscreen. Becky Mullen was spirited and zany. Her dark, curly hair fell in ringlets to her shoulders, and she wore large round glasses that almost covered her freckled face.

"I see you have your eyes on that quarterback," Becky whispered to Anne. "He's a real hunk, isn't he?" Anne's heart jumped into her throat. For a fleeting moment, she wondered if Becky was the girl Corey had come to see yesterday.

"What makes you say that?" Anne asked defensively.

"Oh, I just noticed the way you were staring at him with stars in your eyes, and your tongue hanging out." She gestured with her tongue.

"Stop that! You know it's not true."

"Seriously though, Anne. Is that the guy you want to choose you at the ceremony on Saturday?"

"Yes, I do. I think he's wonderful. We talked a bit at the dance, but I was so tongue-tied. I know it's wrong to feel this way, but I'll just cry if he doesn't choose me."

"Well, I'll be! You sound like a woman in love." Becky was envious. She wished she could be in love. It made her sad that she didn't have that special hope for one man. It made her want to do something to ruin the spell that this man seemed to have over Anne, like having Anne's quarterback pick her instead. A small smile formed at the corner of her lips. "Well," Becky piped up, "I think they're all cute." The girls giggled and went back to watching the game.

Zane and Helena were sitting in the stands, proudly watching their son score a spectacular touchdown. Zane was thinking back to his days of football in school. He had been the team captain for the Giants. Watching Corey play now brought back a lot of fond memories.

"He plays football like his old man, wouldn't you say?" Helena smiled, but before she could answer, the crowd jumped to its feet, roaring. The Panthers had scored one more touchdown, with seconds to spare, to win the game.

The post-game ceremony went smoothly. All the boys picked up their flowers, and the winning team took home their trophies. Zane and Helena met up with Corey outside the Stadium building. Once all the commotion had died down, they took him out for his first taste of beer.

Downtown Havanna was in the center of the Dome. East and westbound moving sidewalks ran the length of the strip known only as Main Street. It was the only road in Havanna with a name. Main Street was well lit by LED streetlights. Bars, auto-beauty salons, supply stores, cinemas, and arcades lined both sides of the road.

Corey and his parents entered a bar called Cheerz. It had been predetermined that all the boys from the football teams would gather here tonight to celebrate. Barhopping was popular among some of the Havannians due to a two-drink limit at every bar. At best, a person could get six beers between the three bars in town. The bars opened at 1500 hours and closed at 2100 hours in order to give the people enough time to get home before lights out.

Zane and Helena waited their turn in line for the drink dispenser. They both punched in the code for beer, taking their two drinks at once. They walked back to where Corey sat with his friends and placed the drinks in front of him. The parents of the other boys had not stayed, so with another round of congratulations to the team, a kiss from his mother, and a slap on the back from his father, Corey's parents, carrying Corey's flowers and trophy, left the bar and the beer. Technically, they were breaking tabu, as the boys didn't have their married status yet, which would allow them to get their own drinks, but this had been going on for so many years now that it had become a tradition.

"Well, this is it, guys," Corey proudly announced. "This is our last night as bachelors. Tomorrow, we go for updating, and we'll have our married men's status."

"That means we'll be able to come down here every night and drink." Zachary chuckled. Corey had noticed that Zach had already finished three of the beers his parents had left him. Corey had just finished his first.

"Great touchdown today, Corey," Orthello said. The conversation turned toward football. The boys discussed the game, reliving it, and bringing it back to life. Corey complimented his team on a great game, then excused himself to visit the men's room.

When he was returning, he thought he saw Anne pass by the window. Corey stuck his head out the door, and sure enough, it was her. His heart started pounding. Without a second thought for his beer, he ran to catch up and fell in step with her.

"Are you going to talk to me today?"

Anne's breath caught. She had broken tabu to look for Corey, and now it seemed he had found her. "Yes, I'd like that."

"Good. What shall we talk about?"

"I'd like to congratulate you on your game today. You were great!" They had reached the end of the moving sidewalk. They stepped off, but neither of them made a move in any direction.

"You really shouldn't be here; you know, tabu and all. Why don't I walk you home?" Corey offered.

"Alright." They walked a while in a comfortable silence like one shared between good friends.

"Isn't it odd that we could live so close and yet have never met?" Corey asked.

"It is rather silly, don't you think?" responded Anne.

"I think so. I think a lot of things are rather silly, as you put it."

"Oh? What sort of things?" Anne's heart jumped a few beats in anticipation.

"Well, like our whole marriage system." Corey stopped and looked at Anne. "Are you sure you want to hear this? We could talk about something… safer."

"Corey, I really do find it fascinating to hear different points of view. It's not everyone I can talk to like this."

"Don't I know it." He sighed. "Well, the way I see it, they're going about the marriage system all wrong. I believe people should meet by chance, get to know one another, fall in love, then get married. Not like it is now, where people have a chance to meet once, get married, then get to know one another, and maybe never fall in love."

"I think you're absolutely right. I also feel that people should choose who they want to marry and not just marry who chooses them. There's no equality in our system. The men don't help around the house, and the women never get to leave it."

"This is amazing! Do you know how long I've been waiting to talk about these things with someone? Let's go sit between those trees over there so we can talk some more. It's out of the view range of the rotational cameras," he assured her. Corey took Anne by the hand and led her to a secluded patch of trees under the School Skytrain Station.

"Thank you," she said as she sat down. She looked up at Corey and smiled.

"You know, that smile of yours is going to break forty-nine hearts," he said, as he sat down next to her.

"I don't understand what you mean."

"I mean on Saturday when my name is called and I take you by the hand and make you my wife, forty-nine hearts will break when they see you smile."

Anne couldn't believe her ears. Corey wanted her! Her dreams had come true! She searched his eyes for mockery but found only sincerity.

"Oh, Corey, I can't even begin to explain how happy that makes me. I would be honored to be your wife."

The skytrain pulled into the station, cutting off conversation for the moment. In two minutes, it would pull out again. Corey looked up toward the skytrain.

"I guess we didn't pick the best place to sit and talk."

"It's alright. It gives me a moment to catch my breath."

"You know, Anne, when we're married, I'm going to spend a lot of time with you. I want to get to know you. I want to help you out around the house so we can have more time together. I want to help raise our children. Have you thought about what you want to call our son?"

"I really like the names Taylor and Tyler. I'm not sure which one to choose. Which one do you prefer?"

"I think Taylor Tusk has a good ring to it. What about our daughter?"

"I like the name Meagen."

"Meagen Tusk. No, it just doesn't sound right. It's a bit of a tongue-twister. What other name do you like?" Corey was enjoying himself. Anne seemed to be everything he was looking for. He was sure she would make a great mother, but more importantly, she would be a great wife.

"What about Susan? Susan Tusk. That sounds nice."

"It sounds perfect. It's just too bad we can't have ten kids. It would be great to have ten little Annes to love."

"No, five little Annes and five little Coreys." She laughed. "It would be nice, but it's just a dream. I understand why there must be a perfect rotation of people so that we don't achieve an imbalanced society like Peddlers, but it annoys me that we can't make the choice ourselves about how many children we want. We're not even given the choice of whether we want children at all."

"But why wouldn't you want children?" Corey said, completely bamboozled.

"I don't know. Maybe so I could spend more time with you," she teased. Corey looked into Anne's soft blue eyes, longing to drown in them.

"Anne," Corey ventured, "could I hold you?"

Just then the train pulled out of the station, filling the air with the sounds of the electric engine picking up speed. Corey took advantage of the situation to move closer to Anne. He sat behind her, encircling her in his arms. When the train passed, they sat for a few minutes without speaking.

The relationship with Corey had progressed faster than Anne could have hoped for. He was kind and gentle, and she could talk to him about anything. Everything felt so perfect, but Anne had never felt so scared. She was terrified that something would happen, that somehow, they wouldn't be able to be together.

"Hey, why are you shaking?" he asked, gently.

"Just hold me, Corey. Hold me tight."

"It's alright. Everything's going to be okay. When I was a little boy, I used to get scared thinking that the Dome would collapse, or that we'd run out of food and water. I used to lie awake in my bed at night after lights out, and I could swear I heard people moving about. I used to get so scared that my mother would take me onto her lap and rock me, just like I'm rocking you now. She'd tell me not to worry. BUDDY would take care of everything for me."

Anne stopped shaking and turned to look up at Corey. He bent down and softly kissed her on the lips. Corey pulled his head away and started to apologize, but Anne silenced him with another kiss that left them both breathless. He caressed her face, feeling the contours, committing to memory every line and every freckle.

Anne closed her eyes and let the sensations take her. She could feel Corey's hands moving down her body, touching, caressing, discovering. His mouth was back on hers, this time more urgent and demanding. Their bodies moved as though they had a mind of their own. They lay next to one another on their sides, still kissing and caressing.

"I want you, Anne. I choose you. Do you understand what I'm saying?" Corey said as he moved his hand up her shirt. Anne groaned with pleasure. He slipped off her sweat pants and then reached for his own.

"I don't think we should be doing this, Corey."

"It's okay. We'll be married in two days."

"Married… yes." Then passion ruled out logic and Corey lifted himself on top of her. At first, there was a sharp pain, but soon there was only pleasure. Anne was unrelenting in her desire for Corey. Her hips arched upward, meeting his every thrust. Anne felt pleasure mounting, pulling her tighter until it exploded all through her body. Corey and Anne cried out together, but it went unheard as the skytrain overhead rattled into the station. They lay content in one another's arms, relaxing in the glow of the aftermath. Corey lay on his back with Anne curled around his side.

"I love you, Anne."

Anne moaned and kissed Corey's chest. "And I love you, Corey Tusk."

"Ah, must we be so formal?" Corey reached out and tickled Anne. They giggled and cherished the moment.

"I'm so happy. I never want to leave. I want to stay here in your arms for the rest of my life."

Corey snapped back to reality and glanced at the watchtower. He pulled up his sweat pants. "Come on, sweetie, we've got to hurry. It's half an hour to lights out." He pulled Anne quickly to her feet. She slipped on her sweat suit. They were going in opposite directions from here. Corey pulled Anne into his arms for one last kiss. They parted reluctantly. He brought the back of her hand to his lips for a quick kiss.

"If I don't see you before Saturday, then think of me often," Anne said, as she waved goodbye and blew him a kiss.

"I'll be thinking of nothing else."

Corey got home just in time to brush his teeth and wash up before lights out. He made his way in the dark to his room, where he fell into bed. That night Corey slept like a baby, unaware of any possible repercussions from his actions.

The next morning, Corey slept right through lights on. Helena looked in on her son and found him sleeping peacefully. She didn't see any harm in letting him sleep an extra half hour. It would do him good to sleep off last night's alcohol. She knew that often other people coming in for a drink would give their second drink to the boys on the team. No doubt Corey would also wake up with a hangover.

She made her way to the kitchen, punched in the breakfast code, and was glad to see that powdered orange juice was included with the morning meal. Zane and Helena would gladly donate their juice to Corey's hangover. Zane entered the kitchen looking freshly showered.

"Good morning." He kissed Helena, then sat down to eat his powdered scrambled eggs and imitation ham.

"I took the liberty of giving your orange juice to Corey this morning. I figure it's the best thing for a hangover."

"No problem. Is Corey eating in his room today?" he asked around a forkful of food.

"No. The poor dear was sound asleep, so I let him be." Just then Corey came into the kitchen, looking confused.

"Good morning. I'm sorry, I must have slept through..." Corey was afraid his parents would be upset with him.

"That's alright, dear. I let you sleep. I know I've woken up with a few hangovers in my time. How do you feel?" enquired his mother. Corey thought back to last night. His parents must have thought he spent all night in the bar. A smile crossed his face as he thought of Anne.

"I feel great."

"There's some orange juice for you. Drink it. It'll make you feel better." Corey took a swig of the juice, then dug into his eggs.

"I'm going for my updating today, so the next time you see me, I'll be a man."

"It takes more than just changing your tattoo code to become a man, Corey," his father said. "It means taking responsibility for your actions. It means being in control of your own destiny."

"Uh-huh," Corey mumbled.

"It means learning how to control your emotions. It means treating people with respect. Are you even listening to me?"

"Uh-huh."

Corey was unusually distracted this morning, thought Zane. Normally, he would have jumped at having a serious discussion with his father. He gave up trying to entice Corey into a conversation. No doubt he was not in the mood. Zane stood up to leave the table. "I'll be late for my swim if I don't get going. Corey, leave your night free for a men's night out."

Corey was scheduled for updating at 1000 hours. He rode the skytrain to the School Skytrain Station. He passed his tattoo over the sensor on the vidscreen of the boys' side of the Medicure building. Christopher and Orthello were sitting in the waiting room when Corey walked in.

"Hey, what happened to you last night? We saw you run out of the bar, but you never came back," said Orthello.

"We figured you ran out to get sick and were too embarrassed to come back in," added Christopher.

"Well, looks like you guys got me figured out," Corey responded. He couldn't very well tell them the truth. "Have you been in yet?" he asked, to change the subject. Both boys pulled up their sweatsuit sleeves. There were gauze bandages taped down over their tattoos.

"We're just waiting for Zachary, then we are heading out to play mini-golf. Care to join us in a game, or is football the only sport you're lucky in?"

"Still sore about that, Chris?"

"Not as sore as you're going be when you get out of updating," he chuckled. The computer called out Corey's name. As he was heading toward the office, Zachary came out holding the bandage over his arm.

"Son of a Peddler! I just wish it didn't have to hurt so much."

"Be a man, Zach." Corey and Zachary threw half-hearted jabs at one another as they passed in the doorway.

Corey closed the door behind him. The small vidcam swung toward him as he entered. DOCTOR instructed him to sit in the Medichair, pull up his sleeve, and place his arm in the steel brace. Corey did as he was told. A steel clamp closed firmly around his arm, leaving only the place where his tattoo was uncovered.

Corey remembered Medichair only too well from his dental visits. Even now, he could remember the way it felt when the shoulder and head clamps were moved into place. He wasn't sure what hurt more, the dentistry needles or the lasers they used to implant the tattoo. The mechanical arm swung down and positioned itself directly over his arm. The soothing voice of DOCTOR reached down to him through the overhead speaker.

"Corey Tusk, you are now reaching a new period in your life. It is necessary to change your present status to give you a larger range of computer access. In order to do this, I am required to update your tattoo code. I need only to change one letter. It will not take long, but it will burn a little. Just try to relax. It will hurt more if you are tense."

The mechanical arm moved swiftly and precisely, using lasers to remove the S and implant the letter M in its place. Corey gritted his teeth against the pain. At last, it was over. The mechanical arm swung up and out of the way, while the steel clamps released from around his arm. The whole operation had taken four minutes.

"You may leave now, Corey," said the voice of DOCTOR. "If the tattoo should show signs of infection, then do not hesitate to come back. These things are best treated at the early stages. Goodbye, and good luck at the mating ceremony tomorrow."

Corey grabbed a bandage on his way out and fastened it on his arm. He walked back into the waiting room, pulling down his sweat suit sleeve. The computer was calling in Raymond Neville.

"How does it feel to be a man?" asked Lionel, who had come in while Corey was in the office.

"It feels great, *son*," Corey said, emphasizing the last word.

"You'll only be my senior for a few minutes, so you better enjoy it while it lasts," Lionel joked, but deep down, he always felt that Corey saw himself as his senior. "So, tell me," he asked Corey, "did it hurt?"

"No more than being tackled on the football field by you crazy Lumpkins."

"I heard you heaved your guts last night. Speaking of which, since we don't have the same restrictions and tabus we had as students, we can go for our own beers tonight. I'll teach you how to drink like a man."

"Remember, you're not a man yet. Besides, I promised my father I would leave tonight free for a men's night out."

The computer called out Lionel's name, as Raymond Neville exited the office, trying hard to hide his tears.

"Hey, why don't you wait for me? I have something special I want to show you," Lionel said, as he headed for the office. "Don't go away. I'll be right back." Lionel emerged five minutes later, looking a little pale.

"What do you want to show me?" Corey asked.

"My father said we should go to the observation deck. He said it's really a sight to see."

"Alright! I've always wondered what it was like up there. Let's go."

The boys walked from the Medicure building, around Main Street, to the center of downtown. There stood the observation tower, the tallest standing structure in Havanna. A large clock was visible at the top of the tower. Until updating, the boys had not had access to enter this building. Now they stood proudly in front of it, removing the bandages from their arms, which were still sensitive, and passing their tattoo codes over the sensor on the vidscreen.

The doors to the glass-enclosed elevator opened, and they sat down on the bench that lined the walls. When the doors closed, it circled slowly while climbing the 240 feet up to the observation deck.

The view of Havanna was breathtaking. They could see all its structures below them. At 120 feet, they became parallel with the skytrain stations. It seemed to Corey as though they would go through the top of the roof as they passed the wall, surrounding the Dome, at two hundred feet. When they finally stopped, the doors opened onto a large circular platform. The deck was incredibly bright. Corey and Lionel both took a pair of sunglasses from a shelf just outside the elevator.

The deck was at the very top of Havanna, where the bubble that covered the Dome was no more than ten feet above their heads. There was a railing surrounding the deck, and the only objects in the room were a large plaque mounted in the center of the floor and nine telescopes surrounding it, pointing out toward the horizon. The view from the deck was incredible! The boys ran around, taking in all the sights. The Dome was surrounded by water, but the sight that caught the boys' eyes was the land just north of the Dome.

"Wow, look at that! It must be Peddlers Island," exclaimed Lionel.

"So," Corey said, "it really does exist."

"Did you think they just made it up?"

"Well, up until now, we had only heard of it. We had never seen it. Yeah, I guess I did believe it could have been just a myth." Corey went to one of the telescopes and focused in on the island. All he could see along the shoreline were enormous high-rise buildings. "This is incredible! How many people do you think live there?"

Lionel had also taken up a telescope. "I don't know, but I wouldn't want to live that close to so many people. Hey, Corey, come look at this." Lionel stepped back carefully so as not to lose the positioning of the telescope. Corey stepped up to look as Lionel said, "what do you suppose they're doing?"

The telescope was focused directly on one building. It was a concrete structure with many windows. Corey could see people—thousands of them—in front of the windows, pedaling what looked like bicycles that didn't move.

"Looks like they're pedaling to me." Corey grinned. The boys exchanged glances and simultaneously said, "Peddlers." Corey went back to the telescope. "So, that's how they got their name."

"Hey, Corey, come over here and read this," Lionel called from the plaque in the center of the deck.

"Peddlers Island," Corey read, "was formed after the Third World War when the masses of survivors flocked to the Dome for safety. Due to the risk of spreading contamination and disease, it was forbidden for anyone to enter. Some of the forefathers of Havanna left the safety of the Dome to help create the thriving and productive society of Peddlers, *Population Experiment District 'D', Low Energy Resource System*. From the observation deck, people can be seen pedaling to create electricity for Havanna, as well as for Peddlers Island. This plaque was erected in memory of those who chose to help others less fortunate than ourselves."

"Makes you feel pretty good about living in Havanna," Lionel said, as he looked out over the ocean through a telescope. Corey went back to the telescope fixed on the Peddlers.

"Lionel, how do you suppose there got to be so many people on Peddlers if there's so much disease and contamination? I mean, they all look pretty normal to me."

"I don't know," Lionel said, distracted, "maybe it only affects their brains. That's probably why they work and we study."

"Well, we're never going to meet anyone from there, so I guess we'll never know."

Lionel swung away from his telescope. "That really irks you, doesn't it, Corey?" He went back to his ocean view while Corey read the plaque again.

I'm going to have to bring Anne here, Corey thought. *She would understand. Understand what? My inability to accept what I'm told without proof to be the truth?* Maybe Lionel was right. Corey really had no reason to question what he had been told about Peddlers. At least now he could see for himself that it really did exist. He walked over to Lionel, who was absorbed in watching the ocean.

"See anything interesting?"

"No." Lionel turned to face Corey. "Do you want to go?" Corey took one last look around.

"There is one more thing I'd like to do." Corey gave Lionel a mischievous smile. "I'd like to touch the top of the Dome."

"How are you going to do that?"

"Bend down. I'll climb on your shoulders and when you stand, I should be high enough to reach it." Lionel knelt so Corey could sit on his shoulders, then held on to Corey's legs as he stood up. Corey reached up and touched the top of the Dome.

"It feels like plastic or something."

Lionel let Corey down. "What did you expect it to feel like?"

"I don't know. Harder, I guess. It just seems so fragile."

"If it was harder, it would be too heavy to stay up."

"Yeah, I guess so."

"I don't like that tone of voice, Corey. Let's go before you start getting philosophical on me again." The boys replaced their sunglasses before taking the elevator back down below the wall.

After cleaning her place for the new resident that would be moving in on Sunday, Anne packed a suitcase with all her clothes, except what she would be wearing for the mating ceremony. Last night, she was so sure that Corey would be her husband... but today the fear had returned. What would happen if she had to marry someone else? Would her love for Corey fade? Would her new husband know she wasn't a virgin? Would she be able to love her new husband as she loved Corey?

Anne knew she had to stop this train of thought. She would worry herself sick for probably nothing. She would have to trust that everything would work out. Didn't Havanna always give her what she wanted? Corey definitely seemed confident enough in himself and in what he was doing.

No doubt tomorrow at the mating ceremony it would be just like Corey said. *When his name is called, he'll take me by the hand and make me his wife. We'll move in together, and then Taylor will be born next year and Susan two years after that. Then, when we're fifty, we'll move on to Dusting together.*

Mr. and Mrs. Kravatz, a wonderful, loving couple that had lived next to her parents, would be moving on to Dusting tonight. She was happy for them to be finally retiring. *I wonder why they call it Dusting*, she thought? Surely, they could have come up with a better name than that. Like Haven. It would sound better if they said people retired to Haven. Maybe it meant that they were dusting off their old ways of life. She wondered if Corey would still love her by the time they got to Dusting. Anne realized she would always love Corey, whether she married him tomorrow or not.

Corey went straight home to have his last supper with his parents. It was being served early tonight on account of the retirement celebration. Fifty couples would be honored at the Stadium building before making their journey to Dusting. All the couples that were retiring tonight would be leaving their homes for the newly married couples to move into after the mating ceremony tomorrow. They would bring only their personal belongings with them so that when the newlyweds were assigned their new home, they would be able to move in right away. All the homes in Havanna, with the exception of the girls' dormitories, were identical. This way, the new couples would feel at ease in their new residence.

Corey joined his parents at the dinner table. They were having imitation pork, dehydrated vegetables, instant rice, microwaved muffins, powdered milk, and dried fruit.

Helena looked exceptionally beautiful tonight, with her long dark hair swept up in a bun at the base of her slender neck. She had applied a little makeup, which had brightened up her face.

"You look great tonight, sweetheart," complimented her husband. "What's the occasion?"

"I thought I'd go down to the Dusting ceremony while you take Corey out."

"Do they get fresh food at their ceremony, Mom?"

"No. They'll be eating fresh food in Dusting every day from now on." Looking at his mother, Corey could see why his dad was still very much in love with her. She was a beautiful person inside and out. Come to think of it, Anne reminded him very much of his mother, except in appearance. He was sure she would like Anne very much.

Father and son headed out toward the Forum Station for tonight's big event. Zane wouldn't tell Corey what to expect, only that it would be unlike anything he had seen before. They could see several people starting to gather for the Dusting ceremony being held at the Stadium. The children and the grandchildren of the retirees would all be there, as well as others who would come to observe.

"I went up to the observation deck today," Corey said to his father. "Why didn't you ever tell me about it?"

"It was tabu for me to say anything before you had your M coding."

"So how did there get to be so many people on Peddlers if there's so much disease and contamination?"

"Well, I do believe they treat the air and water with chemicals to keep the contamination down, but no one is really quite sure. It's been over a hundred years since the Big Three."

Corey accepted his father's explanation without question. They had now reached their destination. They queued up behind Lionel and his father, Doug, who was in a conversation with Bruce Stickley.

"I spend more time on the toilet these days than I do on the courts," Bruce was complaining to Doug.

"Have you gone to see DOCTOR about it?" queried Doug.

"DOCTOR said a lot of medical mumbo-jumbo, but what it boils down to is that the problem is inoperable and life-threatening," replied Bruce.

"Son a Peddler! What's to be done?" asked Doug.

"He suggested that I go to Dusting early. As you know, Dusting offers everlasting life and peace, so it can save my life. I'll tell you something, I sure could use some peace from the pain. Looks like I'm scheduled to go next Tuesday, so this will be my last men's night out."

Doug slapped Bruce on the back and said, "Way to go! Lucky you! I wish I could go to Dusting early." The doors opened and the line moved forward.

The Forum had always been off-limits to Corey as a student. There had always been an air of mystery surrounding the Forum. Once inside, he could see some of his classmates being escorted by their fathers to tonight's event. The seats were set at an angle leading down toward a circular field. Lionel and Doug took the seats next to Corey. Zane's friend Ginther Rhodes, and his son, Zachary, took the seats on the other side of Zane.

From what Corey could gather from the conversations going on around him, the event would involve two men, Jude from the class of 2162 and Vince from the class of 2165. Vince was the all-time champion at this event, which was yet to be revealed. Corey did know though that even BUDDY himself wasn't aware of this secret sport. The crowd hushed in silent anticipation, and Corey felt his excitement rising. A man in a black jumpsuit appeared in the center of the field. The crowd broke out in cheers and applause.

"Who's that?" Corey asked his father.

"That's old Thomas Buckineer. He's been the ringmaster since he was twenty-nine. He took over for his father twenty years ago when he retired to Dusting. His son, Steve, will take over next year when Thomas moves on."

"Your attention, please," Thomas's voice sounded out above the noise of the crowd. "Tonight's grand event will take place between our current champion, Vince Novak, and his challenging opponent, Jude Wesley."

Thomas paused while the crowd cheered for their favorite contestant or booed his opponent. Corey was caught up in the excitement he felt building all around him. Nowhere else was there an event that was announced by another member of the community. He felt as though he was sneaking away from the watchful eye of BUDDY.

"Next week, if any of you young men would care to try your luck against tonight's winner, please sign up before you leave. For all you newcomers tonight," Thomas continued, "I'll explain the rules of the game." There was a rustling of whispers and laughter through the crowd while the guys elbowed one another to sign up.

"The rules are very simple." Thomas paused to be sure he had everyone's full attention. "There aren't any." He smiled, as he did every year when the young men went wild upon hearing these words. A sporting event without rules was like reaching Dusting before retirement. Thomas held up his hands for silence. The crowd settled down once again.

"The object of the game is to rope and tie as many of your opponent's limbs as possible within a fifteen-minute time limit. There are no referees in this game. Let's bring out our contestants now."

Two men ran out to the center of the field, both clothed only in loincloths. Their skin was glistening with oils. Thomas held up each man's arm in turn as he introduced them. The crowd responded enthusiastically.

"Let the game begin," Thomas proclaimed, before running off the field. The crowd jumped to their feet, shouting and cheering as the two men on the field circled one another. Corey had never witnessed such an event. The players were rough and fought ruthlessly. They were not above punching, kicking, and biting, causing their opponent to bleed. As unbelievable as what he was witnessing was the crowd of men watching. They were yelling, swearing, shaking their fists, and issuing threats.

Tonight's event made its mark in the history of rope tying. By the end of the fifteen minutes, Jude had managed to tie three of Vince's limbs, as opposed to his one. Although Vince had the strength and the bulk, Jude was wiry and hard to pin down. His agility and speed had won him the new title of the rope-tying champion. It was evident to Corey that both men would be visiting Medicure before the night was out.

"How about it, Corey? Are you going to join up next week?" Zachary asked him.

"No way."

The men started to leave the Forum. Zane decided to go to the Stadium to see if Helena was finished watching the Dusting ceremony. Corey headed back home and quickly washed up for bed. He knew the sooner he got to sleep, the sooner tomorrow would come, and the closer he would be to marrying Anne.

Zane entered the Stadium building, treading quietly across the hardwood floors as he looked for his wife. The ceremony was in full swing. BUDDY was making a speech to the couples retiring tonight. The retirees stood on stage, arm in arm with their spouses. It was touching to see the love pass between the couples as they prepared for Dusting. Zane calculated that there must be around 600, maybe 650 people gathered here tonight. There were predominately more adults than children. People had found that sometimes children who hadn't grasped the idea of Dusting would often cry and so they were left with sitters.

Zane spotted Helena sitting with Martha Brownley, a good friend of hers. Helena looked spectacular tonight. It was easy to see where his daughter, Tanya, had inherited her good looks. He didn't seem to spend as much time as he would have liked with Tanya. He and Helena only visited her every Sunday evening.

Tanya was growing up so fast. In two years, she would be having her own mating ceremony, and then she'd be having her two children within three years of that. Zane was looking forward to having grandchildren soon. Corey would be getting married tomorrow, so he wouldn't have to wait much longer; maybe a year.

He could remember as if it were just yesterday when Corey and Tanya were small children. Corey used to pull Tanya's hair until she cried so loud, that he thought the whole Dome would collapse. So many memories flashed through his head as he made his way to Helena. He thought of the time Corey taught his sister how to dance, and the fun he and Helena used to have playing vidgames with the children. Zane could remember Tanya having a fit when Corey received his first bicycle and she didn't. Zane had taken her swimming to calm her down, promising to let her try the five-foot-high diving board. Zane was smiling with fond memories still fresh in his mind as he took the seat next to his wife.

"It is with great pleasure that we send you to Dusting tonight," said BUDDY's voice through the overhead speakers. "A lifetime has been spent doing what it is you have been chosen to do. You have raised your children in the customs of Havanna, teaching them to avoid tabu and guiding them into parenthood. It is with great honor that we give you the gift of eternal life and peace." The crowd responded with a burst of applause. BUDDY's voice was barely audible over the sounds of people talking and laughing. The couples on stage started a procession out of the Stadium building toward the entrance to Dusting.

Corey jumped straight out of bed and into the steam bather at lights on. Today was the big day! Today he would make Anne his wife! Tonight, they would move into their own home together. Then he could love Anne lawfully. She would be his. He entered his room and started to pack his clothes. He was using the suitcase his mother had picked up for him at the supply store when she had returned the navy-blue suit that he had worn at his first co-ed function. Helena knocked on Corey's door. He quickly pulled on his sweatpants and then said, "Come in."

"You're packing already? Aren't you going to come and eat some breakfast?"

"Are you kidding? I'm saving my appetite for all that fresh food that they'll be serving at the mating ceremony."

"Alright. Call me if you need any help."

"I'm almost done, but thanks." Helena left as Corey was putting the last few articles into the suitcase. He fastened the latch and placed it by the door, then opened his closet and removed the last remaining suit. It was the white tuxedo that his father had worn to his mating ceremony, and his father before him.

Ten minutes later, Corey entered the kitchen where his parents still sat from breakfast, holding hands and talking. From the expressions on their faces, Corey assumed his mother was sad to be losing him today and his father was consoling her. Helena gasped when she saw Corey looking absolutely dashing in his white tuxedo. It was like seeing Zane twenty-one years ago.

"So, what do you think?" Corey turned around for his parents' inspection.

"You're as good-looking as your father was when he wore that suit." Helena smiled at Zane. He put his arms around her and gave her a kiss on the cheek. Helena excused herself from the table so she could dress for today's ceremony.

Zane was already dressed in the traditional black suit for the parents of the newlyweds. Soon Helena returned, dressed in a simple black, V-neck silk dress. She wore her hair down and she had applied makeup to her face. She certainly didn't look like the mother of a son Corey's age. They walked to the Stadium carrying Corey's bouquet of flowers. They met many other parents escorting their son or daughter on the way. The late morning sun filtered down through the Dome, and there was a festive feeling in the air.

Upon entering the Stadium building, they could see it had been divided into two sections. The first had been set up for the actual ceremony, with chairs facing the stage, and the other section had been set up banquet-style for five hundred people.

Everyone intermingled. The young men wasted no time in meeting and talking to prospective candidates, while their parents met up with old classmates. The older brothers of the candidates were there with their wives and children, reuniting with their sisters.

Anne Corbett met her parents at their house before proceeding to the mating ceremony. Her parents had visited her every Sunday night while she was in residence, but it had been the first time she had gone back to her childhood home. Her brother, Tony, and his family joined them as soon as they entered the Stadium. He hugged his sister tight, then introduced her to his wife, Karen, who held their newborn daughter, Ellie, and his son, Matthew, who clung to his leg. Anne scooped Matthew up and whirled him around. It was then that she saw Corey enter with his parents.

With her pulse racing, she stood facing him, bouncing Matthew up and down in her arms. When she saw Corey leave his parents and head in her direction, she handed Matthew back to Karen and excused herself. They met in the middle of the reception area and stood facing one another with smiles on their faces.

"You look great with a child in your arms. Not to mention how stunning you look in that dress." Anne was wearing a beautiful white chiffon wedding dress, edged in lace at the neckline, sleeves, and waist, showing her smooth, flat belly. Her long blond hair flowed around her face like a halo, and an ivory elephant pendant hung around her neck.

"Thank you," she said, as she whirled around, "and you look absolutely dashing. If it wouldn't be considered rude, I'd smother you with kisses this very instant."

"Patience, my dear. We'll have all night for that sort of thing." They smiled at one another.

Becky saw Anne talking with the handsome quarterback from the Panthers. A stab of envy shot through her, and she knew she had to get over there right away. It already looked as though he was falling for her. She walked up and slipped her arm into Anne's.

"Are you going to let me speak with this gorgeous man, or shall I just stand here all day batting my eyelashes at him?"

"Corey Tusk, may I present my friend, Becky Mullen." Becky held out her hand for Corey to take. Her dress had long flowing sleeves.

"Pleased to meet you. We saw you playing football the other day on the vidscreen. You were wonderful!" Becky reached up and kissed Corey on the cheek just as Lionel was walking up to join him. Corey was taken totally by surprise. He had not expected Anne's friend to be so forward. He caught sight of Lionel and thought maybe he could pawn Becky off on him so he could have a few more minutes alone with Anne.

"Ah, Lionel, may I introduce Becky Mullen," Corey said, enthusiastically, then his voice softened, "and Anne Corbett."

"Pleased to meet you," Lionel said to them both.

"Lionel also plays on the Panthers, Becky," Corey said in the hopes of diverting her attention to him, but Becky was too intent on Corey.

So, Lionel thought, *this must be the girl that Corey almost got us into trouble over. She certainly seems enthralled with him. Not as good-looking as her friend though.*

"Would everyone take their places, please." It was the unmistakable voice of BUDDY. People started moving about.

"See you up there, Corey," Becky said, as she left. It was a provocative statement, signifying that he would choose her. Anne was infuriated with Becky. How dare she come on to Corey so strongly? She knew how Anne felt about him! They had talked about it the other day while watching the football game. She looked at Corey. It was apparent by the expression on his face that she had nothing to fear. Before departing, she gave Corey one of her dazzling smiles.

The boys took seats in the first five rows, which were designated for them. Their parents and the wives and children of the candidates' brothers sat behind them. The candidates were escorted by their brothers to their place according to the standing that had been posted outside for reference. Anne was twelfth in the line of the fifty girls standing on stage. The brothers would stand behind them until they were chosen before taking a seat with their wives. The crowd quieted down when the voice of BUDDY came on through the overhead speakers.

"Congratulations, class of 2169. Today's ceremony signifies a new stage in your lives. You now leave the world of study as students, and apply what you have learned in the community, as adults." Murmurs of excitement could be heard throughout the audience. "As adults, it is your responsibility to marry and produce two children, one son and one daughter. Your first child is to be conceived within the following year, by June of 2170. This child must be a male. There are no exceptions to this rule. The next child, a daughter, must be born by August 2172. It is your responsibility to bring up your children knowing the customs and tabus of Havanna.

"As for the mating ceremony, the men will choose a wife in accordance with their own academic achievements, commencing with the man with the highest standing. The woman that you choose will be your mate for life. There will be no changing your mind once you have made your selection. I must also remind you that it is tabu to covet another man's wife or husband. Once you have chosen your bride, step forward for registration and the assignment of your new home. Please then move outside to get acquainted so as not to disturb the rest of the ceremony. Good luck to you all. We will now start with the man who is at the top of his class this year." Anne held her breath in the hopes that it would be Corey. She was more nervous than she thought she would be.

"Would Raymond Neville please step up." There was a burst of applause while Raymond left his seat to approach the stage. He climbed the seven steps and walked straight to the first girl in line. He took her by the hand and led her to the computer console where they ran their tattoo codes over the vidscreen. Corey sighed a breath of relief. He hadn't been aware he was holding it.

"Let it be known," BUDDY was saying, "that from this day forward, Raymond Neville and Barbara Rieker, now Barbara Neville, are husband and wife. Your new home address is R123 on street R51. You may step down." The crowd applauded again while they left the stage. Barbara's brother followed them off.

Alan Silkes was called next. He chose a pretty redhead who had been fourth in her class. William Dey was called third and chose Ilana Stickley to be his wife. She had been thirty-seventh in line. A few people chuckled when he made his choice. It was odd for a man of such a high standing to choose a wife with such a low one. All Corey knew was that he hadn't picked Anne.

"Would Lionel Chaffe please step up." The crowd applauded. Corey gave Lionel a slap on the back.

"Congratulations, Lionel!" Corey said as Lionel was walking away. Lionel looked at the women on the stage. Anne was by far the most beautiful. He suspected that Corey might like Anne, but he had a higher standing, so it was his right and his choice. He took Anne by the hand and led her to the computer console. Anne glanced back at Corey with desperation in her eyes.

Corey jumped to his feet and yelled, "No!" Everyone turned to look at him, thinking, *how dare he dispute the decision of this man? He had no right.* Zachary pulled Corey back down to his seat. Corey's parents were embarrassed by his actions, but Becky was pleased that Anne hadn't been chosen by Corey. Wouldn't that just make Anne envious if he chose her?

Anne numbly ran her tattoo over the computer sensor. Her worst fears had come true. Overhead she could hear the voice of BUDDY.

"Let it be known that from this day forward, Lionel Chaffe and Anne Corbett, now Anne Chaffe, are husband and wife. Your new address is R235 on street R26. You may step down."

Corey was in shock! Never had he expected that Anne would not be his wife. What was he supposed to do, just pretend he didn't love his best friend's wife? He knew he had to do something. Everyone applauded as the couple left the stage, although a few glanced inquiringly at Corey, who sat with his face in his hands. Orthello Willis was called up next and chose the girl with the next highest standing, followed by Peter Farrell, who chose Becky Mullen to be his wife.

"Would Corey Tusk please step up," intoned the voice of BUDDY. Zachary nudged Corey out of his trance. He took a deep breath and walked up on stage. Starting at the end, Corey made his way slowly up the line of candidates. He stopped in front of a girl with jet-black hair and ice-blue eyes. Corey hesitated for a moment then turned back to look at his parents. His mother was smiling and his father was serious. Corey continued to the top of the line, looking over all the candidates. When he reached the front, he looked toward his parents again and wondered if they would support any decision that he made. Corey looked down the line of candidates again, then made his choice. He went straight to the computer console.

He clearly stated, "I refuse to choose a wife on the grounds that it is not a mutual agreement between a man and a woman." There were gasps and expressions of shock and surprise from the crowd. Nothing like this had ever happened at a mating ceremony before.

BUDDY was unrelenting. "Please choose a bride and step forward to the console."

"No, I refuse. The woman I wanted is gone and I shall take no other." Corey stood firm.

"Young man, do you realize the consequences of your actions?" demanded BUDDY.

"Come on! I just want what's fair for everyone. It's not right to marry a woman you don't know, and the women are not given a choice of who they'd like to wed. Why don't you ask the young ladies which husband they would prefer?"

"The previous ladies have already been legally married to their mates. Please choose a bride and step forward to the computer console, or you shall be exiled from Havanna."

"No one has been exiled to Peddlers in a hundred and thirty years," argued Corey.

"This is not an empty threat," boomed the voice of BUDDY. "Now, choose a bride and step forward to the computer console for registration." The place grew deathly silent. Zane rushed from his seat to talk some sense into his son.

"Listen, Corey, I know you liked this girl, Anne, but she's been chosen. Don't be a fool! You won't be the only one to suffer from this decision. Think of the girls. Think of your mother. I can't allow you to do this, Corey."

"You can't allow me? You forget. I make my own decisions. I am a man now." Corey stood up straight and proud.

"Then start acting like one," his father snarled. Zane walked over to Betty Brooke, who was now the first in line. He took her gently by the hand and led her to his son. "Now, take this woman and make her your wife."

"No! I'd rather go to Peddlers than marry a woman I don't love." The girl burst into tears as pandemonium broke out over the entire stadium. People in the crowd were on their feet.

BUDDY's voice boomed out over the commotion. "So be it. Let it be known that from this day forward, Corey Tusk will no longer be a Havannian. He will renounce his birthplace and any connection to it. He shall be exiled to Peddlers Island without hope of returning. No one should have any more communication with this person, or they shall suffer a similar fate themselves. Shun him, as he is now tabu."

Corey couldn't believe it! First, he had lost the woman he loved, and now he had been cast out of his home. This whole system was so unfair! All he wanted was to be with Anne! What was so wrong with that? Well, if this was the way they were going to deal with him, he didn't want to live here anymore. Anger welled up inside of Corey, stronger than he'd ever felt before. At this moment, he wanted nothing more than to be as far away from this scene as he could possibly get. Corey jumped from the stage as BUDDY continued.

"We will take the boy with the highest standings from the next class to graduate and give him the hand of the remaining bride today. Then each boy with the highest standings in each grade will move up one year. DOCTOR will ensure the first woman pregnant will have twin boys. The twin that shows more potential will start school one year before his brother."

Corey's classmates turned their heads away from him as he walked by, but he was too enveloped by his anger and grief to notice. Helena was crying openly when Corey passed by with

Zane two paces behind him. Zane took Helena by the hand and led her from the Stadium. As they left, they could hear the powerful voice of BUDDY over the noise of the crowd.

"Now, to continue with the ceremony. Would Zachary Willis please step up." Corey pushed out through the front doors. All the couples turned to see who the new couple would be. They had heard the commotion in the Stadium but had no idea what had transpired.

Anne was surprised to see Corey by himself. He did not look like a man who had just been married. He looked so angry! Anne's heart went out to him, and she wanted to take him in her arms. He halted at the top of the stairs, looking over the other couples. His eyes stopped when he saw Lionel and Anne. He started down the stairs as the door opened. Corey's parents stepped out, with tears rolling down their faces. Lionel moved Anne off to the side as he saw Corey coming for him. He had never seen his friend so enraged.

"You son of a Peddler!" Corey yelled as he lunged for Lionel. The boys went down, rolling around on the ecograss until Corey was on top of Lionel. He struck out blindly through his rage, landing a punch on the side of Lionel's head. Lionel, being much stronger and more clear-headed, threw Corey off and pinned him down with one hand, while swinging at him with the other. He got three good punches to the face before Zane could pull him off.

"Leave him alone," Zane yelled while throwing Lionel in the opposite direction. Zane pulled Corey to his feet. There was blood running down from his nose and a cut just above his eye. "Haven't you caused enough trouble, Corey?"

Helena ran to him with some tissue and started to wipe his face. "Oh, Corey. What have you done to your life?" sobbed his mother.

Anne started for Corey, but Lionel yanked her back. "Let go of me," she hissed at him. Helena stepped aside as Anne approached. She placed her hand alongside Corey's face. He placed his hand on top of Anne's, sliding it toward his mouth. He kissed her palm. "You've been exiled, haven't you, Corey?"

"Yes." He took her hand in both of his.

"How could you do this? At least we could have seen one another."

"And do what? Pretend we didn't love each other? Pretend we didn't want to hold one other? No, Anne! I could never stand to see you in the arms of another man. It would just tear me up inside. Do you understand what I'm trying to say?"

"Yes." She had been dreading the moment when Corey would come through those doors with his new bride, knowing it would break her heart. Tears were rolling down her face. "Think of me always, as I will be thinking of you." Anne removed the gold chain with the ivory elephant on it and placed it around Corey's neck. It had been given to her as a child by her grandmother. They stared intently into each other's eyes.

Zane stood behind Anne, placing his hands on her shoulders, and gently leading her away. Anne started to sob as Zane brought her back to Lionel, who was trying to process what had just happened.

The doors opened again, and Zachary came out with his new wife. He looked at Corey, then looked away mournfully. He was tabu now.

Zane caught the look and realized that more people would be coming out soon, and it would make it very awkward for everyone to see Corey still here.

"Come on, son, you have to leave." He gave Corey a hug. "I'm going to miss you." Corey's anger was spent. As he gave his mother a last kiss and a hug, he could see Anne over her shoulder. She was looking at him with tears in her eyes. Corey blew her a kiss, which made her laugh and cry simultaneously. Zane took Helena by the shoulders. She was crying so hard she could hardly speak.

"I love you, Corey," she said through her tears. Zane led her away toward their home.

Corey knew where he had to go. They all knew that there were only two places to go once you entered the depths of the Dome. You were either headed for The Highway to Happiness or down

The Road to Ruin. He walked away from the Stadium building, his head and spirits low. His tattoo code would no longer give him access to anywhere but the door leading to Peddlers.

He ran his tattoo code over the sensor outside the door marked EXILE. When the door opened, Corey entered and descended the stairs. The door closed automatically behind him, engulfing him in a dimly lit stairwell. He reached the bottom of the stairs and turned right. Facing him were an underground skytrain and a long dark tunnel in front of it. As soon as Corey stepped onto the platform, the skytrain's doors opened. There was nothing on the other side of it but a wall.

Corey was in no hurry to get where he was going, so he walked the length of the platform. At the tail end of the skytrain, Corey saw another door leading down from the Dome. He made a mental calculation in his head of the layout of Havanna. It dawned on him that this must be the entrance for Dusting. That couldn't be right.

So, pondered Corey, *all this time people thought that they were going to Dusting when in fact they were really on their way to Peddlers? What kind of a sick joke is that to be playing on retirees?* It seemed to Corey that the more he learned about Havanna, the more he didn't want to live here.

The doors to the skytrain closed behind him as he entered it. He could hear the electrical engine accelerating as it started its journey to Peddlers. Along the ride through the tunnel, Corey thought again of the food. *If they were bringing fresh food in from Peddlers, did that mean the food at the mating ceremony was contaminated, or did it mean they would have fresh food in Peddlers?* The skytrain started to slow down. It pulled into another station. He realized it was stupid to assume the skytrain could travel all the way to Peddlers. He would have to go through some sort of airlock first. The doors opened.

Corey got up and left the skytrain. No sooner had he stepped from it when the doors closed and the skytrain started back toward Havanna. Now he stood alone, looking at the entrance of a brightly lit tunnel toward the center of the platform. He walked toward it, mesmerized by the brightness of the light. Corey entered the tunnel and thought, *this can't be right. This tunnel doesn't lead anywhere. It just stops.* At the end was a light brighter than any he had seen before. It was sunlight, pure, unfiltered sunlight. This was not an airlock. This wasn't even closed off from the outside. Then he realized what he had just discovered. If the Dome wasn't closed off from the air outside, then all of Havanna had been contaminated by the air coming in.

That wasn't logical. The only thing that did make sense was that BUDDY had lied to them about the air and the food being contaminated outside of the Dome. Just like he had lied about the retirees going to Peddlers instead of Dusting. What could BUDDY possibly gain by deceiving the people of Havanna? What purpose did it serve?

Corey started down the tunnel. He was glad to be leaving this place and all its hypocrisies. If only there were somewhere more preferable to go than Peddlers. He was lost in thought when he heard a scuffling noise just ahead of him and saw a rat as large as his shoe. Corey had never seen a real animal before. He realized he was more curious than he was scared. As he took a step toward the rat, it scurried on ahead.

"Looks like you're more scared of me than I am of you," he said to the rat. It hustled to keep ahead of him. "Shoo," he yelled. The rat took off over the yellow line that had been painted horizontally across the ground. Just then a blue laser light clicked on. A blinding flash of light appeared and the rat disappeared into thin air. As Corey's eyes adjusted, he could see nothing left of the rat but ashes. What happened to the rat? He pondered.

Overhead, the voice of BUDDY interrupted his thoughts. "LASERS IGNITED. SUBJECT DUSTED."

"Oh shit!" Corey screamed. He realized there was no way out! No one ever made it to Peddlers! No one ever made it to Dusting! Now he understood why no one had ever returned from this place of eternal life and peace. There was nothing left but ashes. Corey felt sick as he thought of all the people who had come down here seeking safety and rest. Lies! It was all lies! He had to warn someone! People had a right to know the truth. He knew he had to save his parents somehow from going to Dusting. Fear washed over Corey as he realized there was no going back. Nor was he going forward. He was stuck in a tunnel of destruction with no place to go and no one to turn to.

The overhead speaker brought BUDDY's voice to him again. "LASERS OFF. SWEEPING CAN NOW COMMENCE." Corey didn't know what sweeping was, but he saw his chance to make a break for the end of the tunnel. He started to sprint.

At the mouth of the tunnel, a large roller dropped down to ground level from its perch, rotating in a backward motion. He was feeling weak from the lack of food, but fear gave Corey the strength he needed to sprint into a full run. He was not far from the end of the tunnel now. He wasn't sure what lay beyond. He could be jumping to his death.

Then Corey could see the water. Endless miles of water. *I hate swimming*, he thought as he looked over his shoulder and saw the sweeper almost on his heels. He knew he could not outrun the sweeper. It would probably knock him down and throw him unconscious into the water.

Remembering a football maneuver, they used when they knew the ball was beyond their reach, he jumped forward, rolled into a somersault, and flew arms first straight out of the tunnel. The sweeper slowed down to throw the dust out before making its way back to its perch.

He now found himself sixty feet above the water and needing all of his diving skills to land him safely. He surfaced, wincing as the water stung the cut over his eye. Off in the distance, Corey could see Peddlers Island. He headed in that direction, floating on his back to catch his breath. The water felt cool and refreshing, much cooler than the water in the swimming pool in Havanna. Overhead, he could see birds flying in the sky.

Corey stopped swimming and started treading water. He couldn't believe what had happened. It seemed like a bad nightmare. He would never see Anne, his parents, his friends, or his sister again. He was no longer a Havannian! How was that possible? Who was he now? The sun was beating down on him, and he could feel it burning his face. He swam the front crawl to keep his body submerged.

He was devastated to be leaving his home and angry to have discovered all the lies BUDDY had told. Corey wondered if he would ever find answers. It would take him time to adjust to the fact that he was no longer a Havannian. He had been sworn to renounce his heritage by BUDDY. He would have to leave everything behind him now, his parents, who had taught him almost everything he knew, Lionel, who had been his best friend, and Anne, whom he loved with all his heart. Wearily, he started the long trek to his new home, Peddlers Island.

The waves increased in size as they neared the shore, and Corey could see them crashing up against a huge wall that appeared to surround the island. He seemed to remember from his view up on the observation deck that the wall only spanned the south end. He started swimming parallel to the shoreline so as not to get pulled in by the tides.

Corey was almost thrown against the wall many times in his attempt to get around it. He followed the wall east, struggling to keep his head above the waves. The wall continued north along the shoreline. It seemed he had been swimming and floating for hours. Just when Corey figured the whole island must be surrounded, the wall suddenly ended. It opened onto a beautiful sandy beach inlet. He reached the shore, exhausted and with no strength even to stand. He lay on his back, breathing heavily.

The sun was setting over the tips of the trees, leaving the deserted beach in twilight. Corey closed his eyes for a moment. He felt dizzy and faint. He held the chain that Anne had given him in his hand. He succumbed to the exhaustion as he drifted off.

PEDDLERS

MOONBEAM RAN DOWN THE SIX FLIGHTS OF STAIRS FROM HIS three-and-a-half-room apartment. He opened the veneer walnut door and stepped out into the early morning sun. He had lived in this neighborhood since moving out on his own seven years ago at the age of fourteen. He no longer noticed the old, decrepit sidewalks nor the large potholes that spotted the roads like freckles. He passed the Nest, a bar that he frequented to unwind from work. It was a Pre-Three structure that people believed had been a house at one time. Moonbeam couldn't imagine anyone wanting or needing that much space.

Most people needed to take the monorails to work, which, although old, ran remarkably well. Line One ran north/south, stopping at every avenue, and Line Two ran east/west, stopping at every second street. Moonbeam had no need of them, though, as he could easily walk the four blocks to work.

He rounded the corner onto the boardwalk, where the sound and spray of the surf pounded against the retaining wall. Thousands of people were making their way into the workhouses. They wore jumpsuits the color of the level they had obtained, most wearing black. He sought out his friends, who wore the same Blue-Level jumpsuit as he did. He was welcomed with handshakes and pats on the back.

The usual crowd was there. Lucky had a small build, blond hair, blue eyes, and was sensitive and sarcastic. He also worked in the hospital.

Bear was large and muscular, with dark hair, a mustache, and black eyes. He was quiet but ambitious. He had a black belt in karate at the Dojo and was a part-time policeman.

Sunshine had a full, hourglass figure, red hair, and green eyes. She was fiery yet patient. She was especially tolerant of the children she taught in school.

Moonbeam, himself, was of medium height and build, with brown hair and blue eyes. He was trustworthy and pragmatic and worked down at the Trade Center. Three days a week he worked out at the Dojo, where he had met Bear, but he was only a green belt.

All these positions within the community were regarded as high ranking. The only way up from the Blue-Level was to wait for one of the Red-Levels to move on, either by retiring or through the point-value system.

"Are you going to do some power pedaling today, Moonbeam?" Lucky asked, as he threw stones over the retaining wall.

"I'm planning on it. I figure if I can pedal hard for six hours today, I just might be able to talk this little lady into joining me for a drink," Moonbeam said, as he pulled Sunshine close to him.

Sunshine was the newest addition to their clique. She had just moved up to a Blue-Level last year when she completed her teaching degree. Moonbeam was continually making passes at her but to no avail. She slapped his hand away playfully, her eyes sparkling like emeralds.

"Stop that, or I may just take you seriously one day."

"Please, I wish you would."

Sunshine had always taken Moonbeam's passes casually, not giving them much thought. He was attractive in his own sort of way, but Sunshine was not yet ready to give up her relationship with Rose. She had met Rose at church after mass one day.

She had noticed her singing in the choir; Rose had a voice like a nightingale. She was a little plump around the hips and thighs, but she had beautiful blue eyes and curly blond hair. "My little cherub" Sunshine often called her.

"Since I can't get lucky in love, I might as well get to work," Moonbeam said, as he headed for the workhouse. They made their way toward the building with the masses. A huge billboard was erected at the entrance of all of the workhouses, stating "Work Hard; Retire Early." There were no set hours, days, or times to work. Everyone worked at their own speed. They received one point of credit for every kilometer they pedaled at the black or entry-level. The Peddlers could live on 150 points a day, which would be approximately five hours of pedaling at a medium speed. Most of the Black-Levels also worked for the sanitation department.

The credits they received were recorded through BUDDY, the main computer, and were deducted as they used electricity or made purchases. If they accumulated fifteen thousand points, they were promoted to a Green-Level, where they would receive two points of credit per kilometer.

They obtained a Blue-Level by completing a degree in any of the chosen professions. Blue-Level was optional and would give them three points of credit for every kilometer they pedaled. The Red-Level was acquired by either promotion or by accumulating five hundred thousand points. Once they reached this level, they were given one row of garden space situated in the Park. Retirement was the last and final step, which was mandatory at the age of fifty, regardless of the level the person had obtained. Retirement could also be reached earlier by accumulating one million credits.

The workhouses ran twenty-four hours a day. An availability vidscreen was visible at the entrance of each floor showing how many unoccupied monocycles were left on that level. If none were empty, they would use the escalators to move up to the next floor.

Today, they found some space together on the seventh floor. The floors were covered with indoor/outdoor carpeting in solid gray. The walls were gray cement, with windows every four feet apart. Suspended from the ceilings were fluorescent lights and an automatic sprinkler system.

Moonbeam chose a monocycle by the window overlooking the ocean with a view of the Dome. The monocycles were mounted to the floor with large bolts, and a computer terminal sat on a desk in front. There were control buttons on the handlebars to manipulate the computer. He ran his tattoo code located on the inside of his left forearm over the console. Automatically, the words "Good morning, Moonbeam" appeared on the vidscreen, followed by the main menu. Moonbeam brought his speed on the monocycle up to thirty kilometers. He was starting slowly but would increase his speed as the day progressed. The day would pass quicker while he studied his spreadsheets on finance on the computer console.

Bear adjusted the tension to high on his monocycle. He had a little difficulty starting the wheel in motion, but once he had gained momentum, he kept a steady speed of fifty-five kilometers. He had calculated that at this rate he was creating about an extra five hundred points a day. Bear had been cycling at this speed for over nine years now but had spent his credits foolishly after he had obtained a Green-Level. By applying himself to a degree in the police force, he managed to increase his credits, and at present, he had already accumulated 427,545 points. He figured it would take him almost three years to get to a Red-Level. *Not bad for someone only twenty-four years old*, he thought, proudly.

He spent most of his evenings at home alone or at the Dojo. He took an occasional lover, but nothing permanent. He preferred to stay single, work hard, and spend less credit so he could retire to the Domed City of Dusting sooner. He was looking forward to relaxing, practicing his karate, or learning to play sports. While he pedaled, Bear studied the updated Undesirable list from the precinct.

After pedaling for a few hours, Lucky finally finished the chapter on natural childbirth. It was used most often these days as opposed to the old methods, where a woman would lie down on her back to deliver her baby.

He decided to head over to the Twilight Bar for lunch before going to the hospital. He turned his monocycle off.

"Done for the day?" enquired Moonbeam.

"Just heading out for some lunch," replied Lucky.

"If you're going uptown, I'll join you," Sunshine said, as she turned her monocycle off and hopped down from it. "I have classes this afternoon, so I might as well grab some lunch beforehand." It was good timing for her, as she had just finished the next level on her vidgame.

"See you around," Bear said as they left.

"Hey, call me later, Sunshine," Moonbeam yelled, as they were walking away. He increased his speed until he was in unison with Bear beside him. They pedaled in silence.

Moonbeam was now reviewing a value system update. Most of it was redundant, causing his mind to wander, which it invariably did, toward Sunshine. He had always prided himself on his logic and ability to see things clearly, but Sunshine confused him. Clearly, she belonged to someone else, so pursuing her was a lost cause. There were plenty of people who had made it quite clear to him that they were available, so what made Sunshine so special? Was it her sparkling green eyes? Was it her cute little upturned nose? Was it the sensuality that emitted from her, or was it the fact that she constituted a challenge for him that he couldn't resist? Moonbeam was sure that must be it. It was the most logical explanation. It wasn't her full, voluptuous breasts or her round, firm buttocks; it was the challenge she represented.

He had all but given up trying to review spreadsheets today. He fixed his gaze out toward the ocean. He loved to watch the waves upon the water. They sparkled like stars under the sunlight. The ocean had a calming effect on him. He could feel the tension leaving his body. *It could also have something to do with the Dome out there*, he thought.

Suddenly, Moonbeam was off his monocycle in one swift movement. He stood in front of the window, staring, waiting. Yes, he had seen someone dive from the Dome. He could see him swimming toward them now. Why would anyone want to leave Dusting? What reason could someone have to leave retirement?

Lucky and Sunshine walked along the boardwalk to the monorail station and passed their tattoo codes over the turnstile to gain entry. They stood with the crowds of other people waiting for the monorail to arrive. "What time do you start work at the hospital today?"

"Not until seven," answered Lucky.

"From seven to eleven?"

"That's right. Why do you ask?"

"I was thinking of inviting the gang over for a drink at my place tonight. I don't know if it will still be going by eleven."

"What? Suddenly, you're rich enough to treat everyone?" Lucky teased.

"No. They can access their own drinks. Why do you insist on taunting me?" Sunshine's eyes narrowed suspiciously.

"Because it bugs you."

The monorail pulled into the station. The crowds merged, fighting their way in or out of the train within the two-minute time limit. The monorail whistle blew to signal that the doors were closing. Sunshine found a seat by the door, but Lucky had to stand. Within the next three stops, a few people got off, but more got on. The monorail was thirteen cars long and traveled at fifty kilometers per hour between stations. Lucky was crammed into the corner and had to fight his way to the doors to disembark at the Fifth Street exit. They held hands in order to stay together through the bustling downtown crowds. Fortunately, the Twilight Bar wasn't far.

From the outside, the bar looked like many of the other rectangular cement structures in Peddlers, except this building had hand-painted windows with ocean landscapes during twilight hours. They entered the bar and waited for their eyes to adjust to the darkness.

They took in the colored flashing lights, the vinyl-covered chairs, and glass-topped tables. In the center of the room was a lacquered oak floor stage with striped red-and-white poles in each corner. Sunshine and Lucky took seats in front of the stage, and a Black-Level server approached their table.

"Hi. What can I get for you?" he asked, with a smile.

"I'll have a cheeseburger and some red house wine," said Sunshine.

"And I'll have a big burger and the same wine," Lucky decided.

"Great. I just need to see your tattoo codes." The server scanned their tattoos with the portable computer terminal. The computer automatically deducted the credits from their points. The server flaunted a beautiful smile.

"Relax and enjoy the show. It should be starting in a few minutes. I'll be back in a flash with the stash."

"What a character!" Sunshine commented when the server left. The music started to play a familiar tune. Three men and three women ran out from the audience toward the center of the room. The women jumped up on the stage, twirling around the poles, while the men did a handspring onto it. It was such a spectacular entrance that the audience applauded with approval.

The dancers were dressed in beautiful costumes of black or green. The men wore a one-piece bodysuit that was open in the front and back. Tassels hung from bands around their wrists, their triceps, and just above their knees. They wore no shoes on their feet.

The women wore two-piece suits with tassels across their breasts and hips. They also wore a band of tassels around their thighs and heads. Their toenails and fingernails were painted the same color as the suit they wore. The dancers paired off. Erotic dancing was more than just a dance, it had become an art form. It held the audience captive as the couples moved rhythmically and sensually to the music.

Lucky hardly noticed the food the waiter had placed in front of him; he was intent on the figures of the two men as they danced to the left of the stage. Their bodies moving together, then apart, then together again, tempting, teasing, building up the sexual tension between them. The power struggle was exciting, almost violent, as they each tried to dominate the other.

He diverted his attention to the center of the stage, where the other man and one of the women danced. Each set of dancers was a work of art in itself. The beauty of motion was enticing. The contrast between the male's large, muscular body and the slender, graceful form of the female's body was spectacular. The masculine spirit seeking love and acceptance. The feminine spirit seeking strength and discipline. Their dance was the romantic union of two great spirits.

Lucky shifted his attention to the last couple, who were on the right of the stage. He had to admit, even to himself, that when a woman's body was beautiful, it was outstanding. Gracefully they moved, like the branches of a willow tree gently blowing in the breeze, seeking, finding, retreating. They portrayed emotions like the colors of a rainbow. Caught in their lover's dance, every action caused an equal and opposite reaction. It was clearly a dance of pleasure and pain.

When the music stopped, the couples froze for an instant in a position that conclusively stated the mood they were trying to portray. The crowd was on their feet, cheering and applauding, showing their appreciation to the volunteers on stage. Sunshine and Lucky took their seats again while the dancers moved off. Sunshine had finished her cheeseburger, whereas Lucky's burger sat untouched.

Moonbeam turned quickly from the window while reaching over his monocycle to turn off the computer console.

"What's up? Where are you going?" asked Bear, as he also stopped pedaling. Moonbeam reached over and turned off Bear's computer.

"Come on, I'll brief you on the way."

They ran down the escalators two steps at a time. Leaving the front door of the workhouse, Moonbeam ran for the retaining wall. He spotted the figure in the water about a mile out from shore. "Look, out there!"

Bear followed the direction Moonbeam was pointing. All he could see were the waves on the water. "What am I supposed to be looking for?"

"There is someone in a white suit swimming toward us." Bear sighted the figure instantly. "Listen, I know this sounds farfetched. If I hadn't seen him dive from the Dome, I probably wouldn't have believed it myself. But he dove into the water! No one pushed him. He wasn't thrown. He jumped of his own accord! Now, you tell me, who would leave Dusting to come here?"

Bear played with the corner of his mustache while he contemplated the issue. "You know, of course, that it is my duty as a police officer to report this to BUDDY."

"Bear, you wouldn't! If the Men get a hold of him, we'll never know who he is or what it's like in Dusting."

Bear placed his thumb and his forefinger in his mouth, producing an ear-splitting whistle. Moonbeam grabbed Bear's hand.

"Don't. It will draw unnecessary attention. There's nowhere for him to enter Peddlers, except by the beach."

"Shouldn't we find a way to help him from the water?" Bear was starting to feel Moonbeam's excitement.

"There is no way. We'll have to wait until tonight, and hope he makes it to the beach. Come, we have lots of plans to make."

Sunshine left the monorail at Fifteenth Avenue where the Basic School for ages four to nine was located. The school was an old warehouse converted from a seven-floor building, close to the residential area. This location was favored for the small children because it was next to the Park. It kept the children out of the downtown area and away from the hospital. The lowest grade, age four, was placed on ground level. The next grade, age five, was taught on the second level, and so on. The gymnasium was on the seventh floor.

The Finishing School, for ages ten to fourteen, was located north of downtown, near the Church. There, the older kids learned the fundamentals of their society and could start building interest in a career in any profession. When they reached the end of their schooling, they immediately became part of the working class. They would start to pedal for credits, obtain their own apartments, and have access to all the bars.

Sunshine entered the Basic School and headed immediately to the teacher's office on the ground floor level. Everyone coded in with BUDDY upon commencing work. It didn't give them any extra credits, but the community time converted into bargaining chips at the Trade Center. There were three shifts of students—morning, afternoon, or evening—depending on when it was more convenient for the mothers. Sunshine entered her tattoo code and headed for her homeroom class on the fourth floor, which started at three o'clock.

Small children darted about in the hallways, screaming, playing, or laughing. Up ahead, Sunshine saw seven-year-old Billy pulling his little sister's ponytail. He was a problem child who constantly interrupted her classes with snide remarks and childish games. His mother, Rainbow, was a card dealer at the casino bar called the Owl Club. Rainbow usually slept during the morning, worked in the afternoon, and pedaled late at night. Sunshine often saw her picking up Billy and his four-year-old sister, Daisy, after school. Rainbow would feed her children, put them to bed, then head out to pedal.

Some of the mothers, especially those with more than one child, would often take their second job with the Church, where they were only required to work three days a week. Most mothers, though, became teachers so they would be working the same hours that their children were in school. It also gave them more chips with which to barter.

"Let go of your sister," Sunshine said while pulling Billy by the ear. Billy admired Sunshine. She was much stricter than most of the adults. She reminded him more of his mother. Neither of them would let him get away with anything. Billy had come to expect a slap to the head as a sign of affection. Even negative attention was better than none.

"Don't do that to me," whined Daisy. She slapped her brother on the back before running away down the stairs to her homeroom.

Sunshine and Billy walked to room number sixty-five. There were seventeen classrooms on every level, plus a teacher's lounge. Most of the other kids were already seated or playing on the chalkboard. The classroom had a capacity of fifty children. When Sunshine entered, they all ran to their seats.

Each desk held a laptop computer. The children entered their code number manually into the keyboard along with a password, until they were given their tattoos at the age of twelve. Sunshine erased the chalkboard while the kids settled down. She turned and stood behind her desk.

"Good afternoon, class," she said, with a broad smile.

"Good afternoon, Sunshine," they all said, in unison.

"Alright, children, please turn your computers on. Yesterday we finished lesson fifteen, so let's review just what it was that we learned. Can anyone tell me..." The children had started running around the room. Billy and Toad were having a fist fight while others stood around cheering. Some of the girls were braiding each other's hair, and others talked among themselves. *Yes*, Sunshine thought, *this was going to be another typical, hectic day at work.*

Moonbeam and Bear sat in the kitchen at the pine table ensemble that was the norm for apartments in Peddlers. The walls were painted a pale yellow over the stucco, with Venetian blinds on all the windows. Moonbeam's kitchen held the standard appliances: a microwave, a compact fridge, a garbage compactor, and a food dispenser. They sat with colas in front of them.

"It's very important that he has somewhere to live," Moonbeam was saying, as he jotted down notes on a vidpad. "He can stay here with me until we find somewhere more suitable."

"It's too bad he can't be issued an apartment through BUDDY. It would sure simplify things if he had a tattoo code."

"Bear, I know you're trying to be helpful, but we can't waste our time on 'ifs.' Food will be easy enough to attain, but it sure is going to run down my credits awfully fast if I support him fully. Therefore, we're going to have to let other people know so that everyone can share the responsibility of food and drink."

"Do you think that's a wise move? The more people who know about him, the greater the chance that BUDDY will discover his whereabouts and send him back to Dusting."

"You have a point."

"I don't know, Moonbeam. I think for the time being we should keep it to ourselves. Let's find out who he is first."

"Agreed! We still haven't discussed clothing and transportation. How will he work? What if he should get sick?"

"Do I detect an if?" Bear mocked. Moonbeam ran his hand through his hair. "I think it's time we got going if we want to be there when he reaches the shore," Bear said, decisively while getting up from the table. Moonbeam switched off the lights on his way out the door.

They walked a block north to the Monorail Station at First Avenue. The platform was full of the rush-hour crowds, all pushing to get to the front. A monorail pulled into the station, filled up with people, then moved on. Moonbeam and Bear shuffled in a little closer.

"Damn the Men! How many monorails will go by before you figure we'll get on one of them?" Moonbeam asked, impatiently.

"You know how it goes. The chances of us being delayed are equally proportionate to the urgency of our trip."

"Somehow I knew you were going to say that."

Another monorail pulled in, filled up, and moved on. This time they moved right up to the front of the platform. Moonbeam felt like a man on an important mission.

As another monorail was approaching, a man in his early twenties accidentally slipped from the platform and onto the tracks below. The monorail conductor immediately applied his brakes, but not quick enough to avoid hitting the man. Gasps and screams could be heard among the crowd. Accidents like this happened more often during rush hour than any other time.

When the monorail had come to a full stop, the doors opened to disperse its passengers. The conductor turned off his engines to signify that this line was closed until further notice. He would have to inform the police, who would pick up the body and bring it to the hospital for identification and disposal.

Moonbeam and Bear now found themselves at the end of a long procession of people heading back out through the doors. This was the fourth time this month that an accident had happened.

"Bear, you've cursed us with that saying of yours."

"It's not really mine," he replied, as they slowly shuffled forward. "It's Murphy's Law."

"Well, I believe more in Phillip's Law," stated Moonbeam.

"Who's Phillip?" enquired Bear.

"Phillip was a great philosopher who died during the Waste War. He believed that Murphy was an optimist."

They broke out laughing, much to the dismay of the horror-stricken people around them. Out on the streets, most people were milling about or walking east toward downtown. The night was just falling as they left the Monorail Station.

"Well, Moonbeam, we can spend an hour and a half walking to our destination, or we can make it in about thirty minutes if we run."

"Last one there is in despair," said Moonbeam, as he took off running, dodging pedestrians along the way. It wasn't long before Bear was jogging in step with Moonbeam heading east toward the Park located at the end of Seventeenth Avenue.

Lucky returned from bringing a patient to the last remaining Medichair. He checked the emergency waiting room to find an older woman who had cut herself, requiring laser fusion, and a young man who had developed a rash.

It was slow for a Saturday evening. Most of the Medichairs were still occupied with patients from the afternoon rush. The hospital was a six-story brick structure west of downtown. Every floor, or department, had a maximum of ten Medichairs. Lucky worked on a rotational system, working six days on then three days off. Every day he would work in a different department, starting with emergency on the ground-floor level. Working up from there, the following days he would work in maternity, pediatrics, cafeteria and laundry duties, pre-op and post-op, and on his last day, psychiatry. Medichair took care of all their needs, including taking blood samples, operating, diagnostics, and administering drugs.

Lucky walked to the nursing station, where Holly sat reading a romance novel. Holly was a mother of three children, ages six to ten, who often worked the same shifts as Lucky. She was an obese woman in her mid-forties with coal-black eyes behind her brown-framed glasses. She wore her black-and-gray-streaked hair pulled into a tight bun at the top of her head. Her mouth was no more than a straight line cut across her face. She was lazy and bossy. Her abrasive manner made her unpopular with her fellow workers. She looked up over her vidpad when she saw Lucky approach.

"Quiet night," she commented.

"That's good for you. You can sit on your ass without feeling guilty." Lucky insulted her constantly. More often than not, she responded with gales of laughter. They all wore Blue-Level jumpsuits except for the department heads, who wore the Red-Level ones. The vidphone rang next to Holly. She closed her vidpad, slid it under a shelf, and pushed the receiving button that gave her both visual and audio.

"Good evening, Peddlers Hospital."

Sunshine's worried face appeared on the vidscreen. "Yes, hello. May I please speak with Lucky?"

Holly disconnected the audio while passing the vidphone to Lucky on the other side of the counter. "Make it quick, Romeo. This is not a dating service."

"It's a good thing that it's not, Holly. You'd have to disconnect the visual!" retorted Lucky, sarcastically. He put the audio back on. "Hello, Sunshine. Party in full swing?" he asked, as he gave Holly an antagonistic grin.

"No, that's the problem. I can't seem to get a hold of either Moonbeam or Bear. I've been calling their places since seven o'clock. They should have been back by now. I know that neither of them was working tonight at their other jobs."

"I wouldn't worry about it, little one. They've probably gone to the Nest for a glass of wine."

"That's what I thought too, so I called. Neither of them has been in all night." Sunshine sounded anxious.

"Maybe they've gone to another bar for a change." Lucky was starting to wonder. It was odd for either of them to disappear like this, let alone both of them.

"I've thought of that too, but you know how Bear likes to save his money and stay home."

"Sunshine, Sunshine, Sunshine, did you check the Dojo?"

"Oh my gosh! No, I didn't! You know, they're probably there." Two policemen entered the hospital emergency department with a body on a gurney.

"Hey, sweetheart, I have to run. The police just brought in a body. And no, it's not someone we know."

"Thanks a lot, Lucky."

Lucky disconnected the line to speak with the police. He checked the body on the gurney, then relieved them of their responsibility after obtaining the facts. Even the corpse would have to visit Medichair before being brought to the disposal chute. Every floor had a disposal chute on the back wall of the building. No one knew where it led, but no one was curious enough to find out. He placed a sheet over the unsightly form of the dead man and put him in an unused room for the time being. There was no rush to get him to the Medichair now. When Lucky returned to the nursing station, Holly put down her vidpad.

"Where have you been?" she yelled. "There are four available Medichairs and a lineup in the waiting room."

"Sorry," Lucky said, "I must have left my other six arms and legs at home." He headed for the waiting room, with Holly's laughter echoing down the hall.

Moonbeam and Bear stopped jogging by the Basic School. They could see the children in their classrooms working in front of their computers. Just as they were passing the Dojo, the monorail pulled into the station. "Well, it's about time the monorail started running again."

"The monorail is a bit too late to help us," commented Bear.

They used the bridge to enter the Park. Moonbeam stumbled on a root in the ground. It was pitch black now, so visibility was poor.

They found four men turning out the pockets of a man curled up asleep on the shore. Bear recognized them immediately from last night's hot sheets at the precinct:

Eagle, the leader, bald with blue eyes and thought to be armed. Rocky, blond hair, brown eyes, dropped out of school at the age of eleven. Wolf, dark-brown hair, light-brown eyes, son of the High Priestess. Lastly, Spud, red hair, blue eyes, fifty-seven points of credit, was last seen escaping from the hospital after being pronounced mentally unstable.

There had been reports of robberies in the Park for two weeks, but they couldn't catch them in the act. Bear saw them now holding the man in the white suit down and punching him in the face.

None of them saw Bear coming as he tackled two of them to the ground. With two quick shots to the face, both men were out cold before they knew what hit them. It was times like this that Bear never regretted his decision to learn karate.

Moonbeam used his karate skills to incapacitate the other two. Bear removed a chain link from the pocket of his jumpsuit. He threaded the loop at the back of their jumpsuits with the chain and fastened it with a lock. Rocky came to, rolling onto his side, moaning.

"Alright, guys, on your feet," Bear commanded. He shoved the men, now chained together, in the direction of the Police Station.

"Thank you," said the young man as he gained his feet. "My name is Corey. Corey Tusk." He extended his hand in greeting. The men shook his hand while making introductions.

"I'm Moonbeam, and this is Bear."

"Moonbeam," Bear said in hushed tones, "why don't you take Corey to the hospital while I take these scumballs to the Police Station. It's off to the C Zone for these guys. I'll meet up with you later."

"Right. We're going to have to walk." Moonbeam turned to Corey. "If you'll come with me, we'll see to your wounds."

Corey hadn't even noticed that he was in need of medical attention. He tenderly touched his eye where it had been ripped open again. He followed Moonbeam out of the Park.

"Are we really going to the C Zone?" Spud asked anxiously.

"No, we're going to a tea party. What do you think?" answered Rocky, sarcastically. Eagle and Wolf followed along, but Spud tried to make a break for it, unsuccessfully, as the other three men landed on top of him. Bear pulled them back to their feet. Once standing, he slapped Spud across the face.

"One more smart move out of you, and I'll make sure you don't make it to the C Zone in one piece. Now get moving."

They left the Park, walking by the Basic School and the Dojo. As they approached the Police Station, a few of Bear's friends cheered and congratulated him. Bear brought the Undesirables up the five steps into the building. Garnet, the police chief, was waiting at the top, dressed in his Red-Level jumpsuit, holding the door open. He gave a low whistle when he saw who they were.

"Even on a night off, you're right on the ball." Garnet often teased Bear about being ambitious enough to want his job as head of the police department. "So, this is the notorious Eagle and his band. Where'd you find them?"

"They were harassing a citizen in the Park when I happened on the scene. I then apprehended them and brought them here."

"That's all you have to report? No injuries?"

"No injuries."

"Bear, I'm impressed. This will go very well on your record." Garnet smiled at him. It wasn't often Bear apprehended Undesirables without roughing them up a little first. Removing the key ring from his hip pocket, Garnet opened the lock on the chain and shoved them into a retaining cell.

"If that's all, I'll be on my way," Bear said, impatiently. He wanted to get to the hospital quickly. Garnet closed the door behind Eagle and turned to face Bear.

"What's your hurry? You don't want to stick around and give me all the gruesome details?"

"Actually, I'd love to, but I have a previous arrangement."

"Ah, have someone waiting for you? Don't let me keep you then. You're only young once." Garnet gave him a wink. Bear headed for the Fourteenth Avenue Monorail Station.

Moonbeam led Corey straight up Fifth Avenue to the hospital. Corey was feeling a kaleidoscope of emotions that all mixed together to make him feel a kind of nervous tension. While they were passing the Dojo, Corey could see people inside all moving in unison, making strange choppy motions with their hands and feet.

"What are they doing in there?" Corey asked.

"They're learning karate. It's an excellent form of self-defense, as I'm sure you saw earlier tonight."

"Is that what you were using on that big guy… karate?"

"Yes. By using the full force of my body weight rather than just the muscles in a single limb, I was able to hit him many times harder. Karate also shows you how to use your opponent's force of motion to your own benefit."

"I'd love to learn this sport. It fascinates me."

Moonbeam didn't feel it was necessary to correct him by saying karate was not a sport. It was an art. They had passed the Police Station and the Trade Center and the monorail passed by them. People openly stared at the suit that Corey wore. The Peddlers didn't have white clothes. Moonbeam contemplated going to Bear's place to pick up a jumpsuit but realized he was closer to the hospital. He would have to try and keep him out of sight.

"How interesting! You have your skytrains on the ground. Why did we walk instead of taking the skytrain?"

"Oh, the monorail. We didn't take it because you don't have a tattoo code."

"Yes, I do." Corey stopped walking and pulled up the sleeve on his right arm. He winced in pain, as the new letter on his tattoo had become infected, causing the arm to swell.

Moonbeam held Corey's arm. He couldn't make out the markings on the arm. "This tattoo is on your right arm," he observed.

"So, where is it supposed to be, planted on my forehead?"

"No, I'm sorry. I only meant that we have our tattoos on our left arms. It's just different to see it on the right."

The door to the Twilight Bar opened, filling the night air with sweet melodic tunes. A couple of women left the bar arm in arm, laughing as they walked toward the monorail. Corey tilted his head, listening to the unfamiliar sounds of the music. He had never heard anything like it before.

"What kind of music is that?" he enquired.

"It's music. Music is music. Don't they have music in Dusting?"

Corey stopped dead in his tracks. He turned to face Moonbeam. "How did you know I came from Dusting?"

"I saw you jump from the Dome myself," Moonbeam said, uneasily.

"No one must know where I came from. Is that understood?"

"Yes. Bear and I are the only two that know."

"Then let's keep it that way." A man walked up to Corey and reached out to feel the fabric of his white suit.

"Leave him alone," Moonbeam said while pulling Corey away from the man. Moonbeam tried to keep Corey walking in the shadows, away from the streetlights. As they approached the entrance of the hospital, Moonbeam motioned for Corey to stop.

"Wait here for a moment while I look for a friend of mine who works here. I'll be right back." Corey watched as Moonbeam's back disappeared into the building. Peddlers was sure a lot different than he expected. In some small ways, it reminded him of home, and yet it was so unusual, so unfamiliar, and so crowded!

As Corey stood there, exhausted, waiting for Moonbeam, he couldn't get the image out of his mind of the lasers dusting the rat. How was he ever going to warn his family and friends? There was definitely no way back into the Dome from the way he came out. Was there no way back in at all? Was he destined to know the truth and not be able to share it? Corey hung his head as he realized that he had been made to promise to renounce his heritage. Life was so unfair!

Lucky had been busy all night with minor casualties. Earlier in the evening, a few people had fainted due to the accident at the monorail. The waiting room was now empty. Lucky had just brought the last patient to one of the Medichairs. He escorted another patient, Sunflower, from the only Medichair that had been, until now, occupied.

"Good night," Lucky said, as he waved to Sunflower. He glanced at the monitor at the nurses' station. He saw Moonbeam pass by Sunflower in the waiting area. A broad smile crossed his lips as he headed into the waiting area himself.

"Lucky, I'm glad to see you're still working," said Moonbeam, as he gave Lucky a hug and a slap on the back. "I have someone… a friend, just outside, who's in need of medical attention."

"Well, bring him or her in. We're not very busy tonight, so you won't have to wait."

"See… the problem is…" Moonbeam wasn't sure what to tell Lucky. He had sworn that he wouldn't tell anyone where the man was from, but at the same time, he had never lied to his friend before.

"Moonbeam, you sly devil," Lucky said, with a lopsided grin. "I never knew you were into S-& M. No problem; my lips are sealed." He pulled an imaginary zipper across his lips.

"No, no, it's not like that." Moonbeam let out a long breath of air. "He hasn't got a proper tattoo code."

"That's impossible. Everyone in Peddlers has a proper tattoo code." Moonbeam didn't reply. He only raised his eyebrows.

"Oh, you mean he's not from Peddlers. How exciting! Well, where did he come from then?"

"I can't tell you that."

Lucky's eyes narrowed suspiciously. "He's not one of those soldiers from Mensis, is he? Because if he is, he can just turn around and go right back where he came from."

"I assure you, he's not a Men. Can you help him or not?"

"If he hasn't got a tattoo code, it's going to be awfully difficult to treat him." Lucky started to hum.

The doors automatically opened. They swung around to see Bear leading Corey into the waiting area. Bear had met up with Corey standing outside the hospital. Lucky looked at the clothes Corey wore and the gold chain that hung around his neck. He walked around him as though inspecting merchandise. He took in the cut over Corey's eye, the bruise on his sunburned cheek, and the scrapes on his hands.

"He hasn't got a tattoo code," said Bear authoritatively. Moonbeam gave Corey an almost imperceptible shake of his head to let him know not to mention his tattoo.

Corey noticed that all three of these men wore blue outfits, unlike the men on the beach, who had worn black, like the one Thomas Buckineer wore at the men's night out in Havanna. "Look, I'm sure if I could just find someplace to sleep and something to eat, I'll be fine by morning."

"There isn't anywhere for you to stay at the moment, except with me," Moonbeam stated.

"Yes, there is!" said Lucky, snapping his fingers. "Why didn't I think of this sooner? There's a man who died tonight at the monorail station..."

"Yes, we know. We were there when it happened," Moonbeam said.

"It's perfect. This guy can take his place. I'll give him the dead man's tattoo number," said Lucky.

"My name is Corey."

"Corey, what an odd name. Well, soon enough, you'll have a new name. I'll go and get the number so that we can leave."

"Can't you do it here with Medichair?" asked Bear.

"No. The same tattoo number cannot be inscribed twice," Lucky said over his shoulder on his way out the door. The three men took seats in the waiting room. Corey got up and paced the floor.

"What did he mean by take his place?" enquired Corey.

"He meant just that. You can assume the other man's life. Will it bother you to have the tattoo code of someone who died?" Moonbeam asked.

"Is it necessary for me to have one?"

"Yes. It's the only way that BUDDY will let you have access to credit."

Bear sat quietly listening to the exchange between them. Corey was only slightly surprised to hear that BUDDY controlled their society as well.

"What is credit?" asked Corey.

"Credit is something we need in order to live," replied Moonbeam.

"Perhaps we have another name for that in Ha… I mean, where I come from." Corey was trying hard to understand what they were attempting to tell him.

"We use credits to eat, to drink… basically anytime we need to access the computer," answered Moonbeam.

"How do you obtain credit?"

"We acquire credits by pedaling. The more we pedal, the more credits we get. We're lucky to have a job and contribute to society," Moonbeam recited.

Corey realized then that the Peddlers were not only required to work, but also had to pay back credits for everything they needed to live. They paid for the very things that Corey had always taken for granted.

"What about Medicure? Do you have to pay for medical treatment?"

"Yes. Credits are deducted according to the severity of the case. Only children don't pay for medical," added Moonbeam.

"That's absurd!"

"That's the way it is," Bear said.

Lucky had almost forgotten the body that he had placed in one of the exam rooms. He went in and closed the door behind him. Removing his vidpad from his back pocket, he copied the code #M049-245 from the tattoo on the dead man's left forearm. Rather than bringing the man to Medichair for identification and recognition of his death, Lucky wheeled him straight to the disposal chute. He opened the door at the base of the wall, placed the body on the floor, and gave him a push down the chute. Lucky could hear the body hitting the sides while it fell. Normally he closed the door right away, but today he wanted to make sure it went all the way so no one would find it. He saw a blinding flash of light, sort of bluish in color. He closed the door and wheeled the stretcher back to the nursing station.

"Are you going to leave these people sitting in the waiting room all night?" Holly asked when she saw Lucky. He took a quick look at the vidscreen while he punched in the man's tattoo code and saw that no one new had come in.

"They're waiting for me. I have a very urgent matter to attend to. Would you mind taking the laundry to the elevator before the next shift arrives? That's not too much work for you to do in one night, is it?" Lucky asked, patronizing her, while he backed out of the computer vidscreen.

"I'll certainly make sure the next shift knows to do it," Holly said, before returning to her vidpad.

Lucky entered the waiting room. "All set," he said. The others got to their feet and followed him out.

Once on the street, Lucky headed west along Fifth Street. Not too many people were out in this section of town this late.

"From now on, your name is Cobra," he said to Corey.

"Where are we going?" asked Moonbeam.

"There's this guy I know on Second Avenue. He deals in all sorts of Pre-Three hobbies. If anyone can help us, it'll be him. His name is Chip."

"What are Pre-Three hobbies?" enquired Corey.

"Hobbies were like creative pastimes people used to enjoy before the Waste War."

"Just leave it to the Trivia King to be well informed on every topic under the sun!" Moonbeam mused.

"That's Trivia Queen to you," bantered Lucky. Everyone chuckled except Corey, who hadn't understood the joke.

Corey felt like an outsider with his new friends. He didn't understand their ways, their words, their attitudes, or their humor. He was feeling more homesick than ever.

Bear and Moonbeam walked on either side of him while Lucky walked a pace in front. They surrounded him in a protective manner that made Corey feel trapped. They kept to the side of the street with no lights overhead, passing many people. Most of them moved out of their way, not bothering to look too closely as they marched by.

When they reached Chip's place, Lucky went alone to the sliding door on the first-floor balcony. The door opened, revealing a small man with long auburn hair. He wore a Green-Level jumpsuit. Corey estimated that Chip must be in his late twenties or early thirties.

Lucky and Chip embraced, holding onto one another longer than necessary. With his arm around Chip, Lucky led him to meet his friends and introduced everyone. Moonbeam and Bear were startled as Lucky introduced Corey by the name Cobra, but it was necessary to keep his identity quiet for the time being.

"Come inside." Chip led them through the sliding door. They stepped into a comfortable but cluttered apartment. Chip picked up some books, cards wrapped in a silk cloth, and a crystal ball that littered the sofa. "I apologize for the mess." He made his way to the kitchen and returned with five beers.

Corey took his with a "thank you" to Chip, who eyed him, amused. When Corey couldn't figure out how to open the can, Chip took it from him and flipped open the tab.

"You're not from around here, are you?"

An uncomfortable silence filled the air.

"Hey, Chip," said Lucky, "do you still do tattooing?"

"From time to time," he answered.

"Cobra needs this number tattooed on his arm. Would it be possible to get it done tonight?" Lucky handed the vidpad to Chip, who looked at the code and then back at Lucky.

"This is an active number." He tried to hand the vidpad back.

"Not anymore. The guy who owned it is dead."

Chip inhaled deeply. "First of all, it is illegal for me to tattoo a code number. One little slip and BUDDY will find out the first time he tries to use it. The police will be all over this place with a fine-tooth comb." Chip shot a quick look at Bear, who was sitting on the sofa next to Moonbeam.

"Secondly," he continued, "how am I to be sure you didn't knock this guy off just for his code? I don't want to be an accessory to murder."

"We didn't knock the guy off. He slipped in front of the monorail. You're not the only one with his butt on the line. We've all taken risks to help Cobra. I've committed myself by disposing of the body without reporting it to BUDDY, and Bear stands to lose more than all of us if anyone else finds out."

"So why all the risks?" Chip asked.

"Because... he is from the Domed City of Dusting," Moonbeam blurted out while jumping to her feet. "I can attest to it." The men in the room were silently staring at Corey. Lucky's mouth hung open. Bear played with the tip of his mustache

"Why didn't you tell me this before?" Lucky accused.

"Would you have done anything differently?" asked Moonbeam.

Corey took a deep breath then said, "Since everyone else has put their butts on the line, I might as well too. This must be kept strictly between us, though. All the trouble started when I met Anne." Corey explained his situation to his new friends.

"You mean you're still a virgin?" asked Lucky, incredulously, after Corey had finished talking.

Moonbeam elbowed him in the side then leaned forward on his seat. "You think BUDDY here is the same one as the one you have there?"

"Yes, I do. It's the same. I'm sure of it," replied Corey.

"This is unbelievable! I can't believe Dusting is a myth," opined Moonbeam.

"So, there's not much point in me, or any of us, pedaling our little hearts out to get to Dusting quicker," Bear stated. "What a waste of years, and I'm so close. I didn't realize it meant so close to dying."

"You know," said Lucky, "it's funny what you said about the blue laser lights in the dusting tunnel. When I put the body in the disposal chute tonight, I saw a flash of blue light when it reached the bottom."

"Well, at least we know no one will find him," Corey said.

"Let's get your tattoo implanted before BUDDY finds you, then." Chip got up and signaled for Corey to follow him. He led Corey to the back bedroom where his tattooing equipment was set up. Chip called Bear into the room while he looked at the tattoo number Lucky had given him.

"Would you mind doing the honors?" Chip asked Bear, motioning for him to pedal the tattoo machine. Bear climbed onto the makeshift monocycle to produce the necessary electricity. Corey sat in the chair beside the machine. Chip shaved Corey's forearm and swabbed it with a disinfectant. He picked up his tattooing needle, then sat across from Corey.

"I'm sorry, but it's going to hurt." Chip started with the letter M. The pain was bearable. Not as bad as the lasers that DOCTOR used. It did, however, take a lot longer.

By the end, Corey was feeling faint and nauseous. He was glad when Chip told Bear to stop pedaling. Chip covered it with a gauze bandage and regretted not having any healing ointment. Corey sat on the sofa in the living room next to Lucky. His arm throbbed with a dull pain.

"We should keep this information between the five of us. If the Mensis find out we know the truth about Dusting, our lives will be in danger." Chip looked around the room at the faces of the other men. They all gave a nod of consent and then stood to leave.

At the doorway, Corey shook Chip's hand. "Thank you. I owe you one for the tattoo." The four men walked to Fifth Street, where Bear and Lucky would take their monorails home.

"Good night, Cobra."

"Good night, Bear. Please, call me Corey." Bear nodded.

"Do you really only get one mate for life?" asked Lucky.

"That's right." Corey smiled.

"You don't find that to be selfish?"

"No, not at all. I find it stable and secure but not selfish." *How could it be selfish?* he thought.

"I just find that strange. Good night, Corey."

"Good night, Lucky." Moonbeam and Corey continued toward Moonbeam's place.

"Don't take Lucky too seriously. Sometimes he can be insulting, and not always intentionally," explained Moonbeam.

"Relax. It takes a lot more than that to offend me."

They climbed the six flights of stairs to Moonbeam's apartment. Moonbeam opened the door and switched on the lights.

"You don't need your tattoo code to unlock your door?"

"No. Everyone's apartment is the same, so who would want what I have?" Moonbeam ordered up a big burger and a cola for Corey on the food replicator. Corey ate ravenously while Moonbeam washed up for bed. When he returned from the washroom, Corey was trying to figure out the garbage compacter.

"Interesting device you have here. In Havanna, we put our garbage in plastic bags and send them down the garbage chutes." Corey followed Moonbeam down the hall to the bedroom.

"The bathroom is here if you'd like to wash up."

"Thank you, I would. How much water is left?"

"What do you mean? There's lots of water. Use as much as you want, just don't drink it." Corey entered the bathroom. It was smaller than the bathrooms in Havanna. He noticed that instead of a steam bather, they had an open tub. There were no dispensers on the walls for shampoo and conditioners. Instead, they had bottles boasting the same products. Corey couldn't believe that he was really allowed to use as much water as he wished. It was a dream come true, of a sort.

Corey turned the water on, adjusting it to the perfect temperature. With a face cloth, he dabbed the cut over his eye and washed the dry blood from his fingertips. He couldn't find the heat lamps to dry off, so he just shook the excess water from his hands and returned to the bedroom.

"Could you please turn out the light in the bathroom?"

It was more of a command than a question. Corey went back and found the light switch that turned it off.

"Don't your lights go off automatically at lights out?"

"No. Here we pay for all the electricity we use. Could you put out the bedroom light on your way to bed too?"

"Sure, no problem." Corey switched off the light and crawled into bed next to Moonbeam.

"You know, I've never slept in the same bed as anyone before."

"That's nice," Moonbeam said, sleepily. "G'night, Corey."

"Good night, Moonbeam."

Moonbeam opened one eye. "You've never slept in the same bed as anyone? Not even when you slept over at a friend's place?"

"Why would I want to sleep at a friend's place when I have my own place?" Corey couldn't understand the logic in that.

"Never mind. Just go to sleep," mumbled Moonbeam. Corey lay awake, listening to the sounds of Moonbeam sleeping. Even though he was exhausted, Corey found it difficult to fall asleep. He was worried about his parents, mad at Lionel, and missing Anne. Inside he felt hyper like he'd rather be up running than going to bed. His mind kept going over and over the events of the day in an endless loop of insanity. Corey didn't know how long he tossed and turned before he finally drifted off.

The next morning, Corey woke up in pain. Both his forearms were on fire. One hurt from the newly planted tattoo, and the other hurt due to the infection. Corey tried to sit up, but his stomach muscles were sore and bruised from the beating he had gotten on the beach. He lay back down for a moment, then tried to sit up again. He finally managed to perch himself on the edge of the bed. As soon as he was upright, his head started to pound.

Moonbeam walked into the room in his underwear and pulled open his clothes closet. "How are you feeling this morning?" he asked, as he pulled on his Blue-Level jumpsuit.

"Not very well, I'm afraid." Corey's face contorted in pain as he attempted to stand.

"I think you ought to stay in bed, Corey." Moonbeam gently pushed him back down. "It'll do you good to rest."

"Isn't it tabu to stay in bed after lights on?"

"What do you mean 'taboo'?"

"Tabu. Forbidden."

"No, there's no curfew about staying in bed if you're not feeling well. Everyone is pretty well free to do what they want. There are no set hours to work or sleep. You can sleep all day and work all night if you want." Moonbeam fluffed up Corey's pillow for him. "You just relax and go to sleep. If you're hungry later, punch in your tattoo code manually." Moonbeam slapped himself on the forehead.

"What's wrong?" Corey asked, sitting up.

"I just remembered that you can't punch in your code unless you have your password. I don't know what Cobra's password was, so you won't be able to get computer access until your arm heals."

"Don't worry about it. I don't feel like eating, anyway. I ache too much to think about food."

"I'll work something out for you. I have to leave now, but I'll be back in a few hours, so make yourself at home."

"Thank you, Moonbeam," Corey said before Moonbeam left the room. He lay down on his back. His whole body ached with every move. *I must be dying,* Corey thought. *I probably don't have any of this so-called immunity that my father was telling me about.* It wasn't long before he fell into a fitful sleep. He dreamed he was running in a tunnel, with a blue laser light close on his heels. Overhead he could hear the voice of BUDDY laughing.

Moonbeam rounded the corner to the boardwalk. Lucky and Bear walked up to meet him, and Moonbeam gave them both a high five in greeting.

"How is our new friend today?" asked Lucky.

"He's not feeling too well. I left him at home to rest."

"Is it anything serious? Is there something I can bring for him from the hospital?"

"His arm is sore, no doubt," commented Bear.

"It's nothing a little rest won't cure," Moonbeam assured him. "I'm going to work from three to seven at the hospital, so I'll drop by when I'm done. In the meantime, if Corey needs anything, call me."

"Lucky, you're starting to sound like a mother hen." Moonbeam laughed while ruffling Lucky's hair. Lucky smoothed his soft blond hair back into place. He looked up to see Sunshine heading toward them.

"What are we going to tell Sunshine?" Lucky asked.

"Nothing. There's nothing to tell," answered Moonbeam.

"Hi," Sunshine said, giving Moonbeam a big hug. "Did you guys have fun at the Dojo last night?"

"The Dojo... ah yes, the Dojo." Moonbeam realized Sunshine must have thought they went there when she couldn't get a hold of them. "We had an interesting brawl, alright. Didn't we, Bear?"

"You could call it that," he replied. They all started walking toward the workhouses.

"How come everyone is acting so weird today?" enquired Sunshine, suspiciously. Her eyes shifted to all three of them.

"We're always weird," joked Lucky. Sunshine let it go at that. They would tell her, sooner or later, what they were up to.

They followed the crowd into the workhouse. Today they found monocycles together on the eighteenth floor. Moonbeam and Sunshine took the two seats behind Bear and Lucky. They settled onto their monocycles and tapped into their computers. Sunshine noticed that all three of them chose Dusting today, which was never one of the more popular topics among her friends.

"What is this? Has everyone decided to retire all of a sudden?" Lucky and Moonbeam escaped out of their topic quickly, like children caught with their hands in the cookie jar. "Are you hiding something from me? I want to know what it is right now. Do you hear me?"

None of the guys made a move to speak. They acted as though they hadn't heard a word she said. Sunshine turned off her monocycle and fled in tears. She took up another monocycle on the other side of the room.

"This is crazy. We're going to lose one of our best friends because we can't tell her the truth." Moonbeam ran a hand through his hair.

"Tell her that Corey is your new boyfriend," offered Lucky.

"She'll never go for it."

"All we really know is that he is a fugitive from Havanna."

"Bear, I'm shocked that you could say such a thing." Lucky shook his head back and forth.

"Knowing where he came from and how he came to be here had no bearing on the fact that BUDDY exiled him. It only proves that he had become too powerful," insisted Moonbeam.

"When I exile Undesirables such as Eagle, I don't do it because they have become too powerful. I do it because they broke curfew."

Bear continued to play the devil's advocate. "Corey was exiled because he broke the rules."

"Corey didn't do anything wrong!" Lucky said in Corey's defense. "He was speaking out for free love. We all would have done the same thing in his place."

"He has also been the only person to make it through the dusting tunnel alive," Moonbeam added. "It was his destiny to survive. It is fate that has brought him here."

"We only have his word that all this is true," Bear insisted. "It was pure luck that he survived the swim."

"This still doesn't solve the problem about what we are going to tell Sunshine," Moonbeam said.

When the guys turned off their monocycles at two o'clock, Sunshine had still not come back to join them.

"I'm going home for lunch," said Moonbeam. "You're both welcome to join me." By the time they made their way across the room, Sunshine had already left her monocycle.

They walked in silence to Moonbeam's apartment, then climbed the stairs two at a time in a mock race. Moonbeam quietly opened the door and stepped inside. The blinds were still drawn from last night. Moonbeam crossed the living room and pulled the blinds up. Sunlight flooded the room. The three men walked into the kitchen and pulled chairs up to the table.

Corey joined them in the kitchen, wearing one of Moonbeam's old green jumpsuits. They ordered up lunch, then continued their previous conversation.

"Let's get back to what we should tell Sunshine. I know we made a vow to keep this information quiet, but we have to get our story straight." Moonbeam said between mouthfuls.

"Why do we have to say anything?" enquired Bear.

"Because she is our friend. She also knows us well enough to know that we just didn't become best friends with someone overnight. And she's smart enough to figure out that Corey's not from around here."

"So, tell her I'm not from around here," suggested Corey.

Moonbeam looked at Corey as though he'd lost his mind. "Where do you suppose we can tell her you're from, then?"

"There must be some other places in this world besides Havanna and Peddlers," Corey joked.

"Only Mensis, and you wouldn't want to admit you are from there!" Lucky stated.

"Mensis? How come I've never heard of this place before? Where is it? What are the people like there?" Corey was floored. He had never really expected that there were other people living not far from here. He had only ever heard of Peddlers. How was it that these people knew of Mensis and the Havannians did not?

Bear spoke up. "No one really knows where they live, or cares, for that matter. They come into Peddlers periodically to take the prisoners to the C Zone or fix the monorail if it breaks down. That sort of thing."

"They are ruthless people! They have no respect for the people of Peddlers. In my opinion, they're just as bad as the Undesirables that we send away." Lucky was fuming, as he always did when he thought or spoke of the Mensis soldiers. "Sometimes they take people away too, with no warning, no reason, and no explanation. They ride in on horses, wearing these shiny, silver suits that make them impossible to injure. They just scoop people up with nets and take them away."

"Where do they take them?" Lucky just shrugged in answer to Corey's question. "Well," Corey continued, "how do they get in and out of Peddlers?"

"They have the key to the gate. There's an electric fence surrounding Peddlers where there is no retaining wall. They come in and out from there," Moonbeam explained.

"So, you're imprisoned on the island."

Bear started to chuckle quietly to himself. "Peddlers is not an island. It's on the tip of the mainland."

"I would hardly say we're imprisoned. The fence keeps us safe. The land beyond is forbidden territory," Lucky informed Corey.

"Safe from what? If the Mensis have the key, then you're hardly safe. If the land beyond is forbidden to you, and there is nowhere else to go, then wouldn't you consider that imprisonment?"

Lucky started to hum. Bear sat playing with the corner of his mustache. Moonbeam sat staring into space. Corey wasn't sure if they were hiding something or had never realized their predicament.

"We're safe from the wild animals that are believed to still roam," Lucky weakly replied.

"Sounds like bollocks to me," Corey stated. "Why is the land forbidden? Because there are wild animals? It sounds to me like you're not really free to do what you want."

"Well, we're free to do what we want inside of the fence. And if the Mensis soldiers are any indication of what other people might be like in the forbidden area, then I'm glad we're safe in here." Lucky stood from the table to perch on the side of the kitchen counter.

"Do you know for a fact that the people are all like the soldiers? Has anyone ever ventured beyond and back? Has anyone considered why it's a forbidden territory?"

"Why do you have to question everything, Corey? Why can't you just accept what we tell you?" Lucky retorted.

"If I had accepted what BUDDY had told me in Havanna, then I would have never learned the truth. It seems to me that BUDDY is leading you on, too. I just want to understand what is going on. Is that so wrong?" Silence filled the air.

"Damn the Men! This still doesn't help us decide what we are going to tell Sunshine." Moonbeam was getting irritated. Every time he brought up the topic of Sunshine, they would end up arguing about something else.

"What about the C Zone you spoke of? Couldn't we say I've returned from there?"

"Corey, you're a genius. That's brilliant!" Lucky clapped his hands and pushed off the counter. "Now we've settled that problem, I can go to work feeling better."

"I'm going to be late for work if I don't get going too. Are you going to stay with Corey until I return, Bear?"

"Sure. I'd like to discuss the C Zone with him." Bear and Corey walked Lucky and Moonbeam to the door.

"Oh, how's your new tattoo doing today?" asked Lucky.

"It's sore."

"I'll see if I can get something to bring back for you. I'll call Chip. He knows a lot of home remedies." Lucky followed Moonbeam down the stairs toward the monorail, glad to have an excuse to call Chip again.

Moonbeam disembarked from the monorail heading toward the Trade Center, which was bustling with activity. When he arrived at work he approached Bunny, a young woman he knew who always worked on the ground-floor level. She had short, red, spiked hair and deep brown eyes under long, thick lashes. She was serving an older gentleman in a Red-Level jumpsuit who was more interested in a date with her than the value of his trading chips. She sighed with relief when she saw Moonbeam arrive.

"Boy, am I glad to see you. What a day this has been! If you don't mind, I'll leave you with Gopher here," she said, indicating the older gentleman, "and I'm going to get out of here before I scream."

Moonbeam took his place behind the trading counter and ran his tattoo over the console. He looked up to see a line forming behind Gopher. Moonbeam let out a long breath of air.

"Get used to it, honey. It hasn't let up all day." Bunny smiled tiredly at Moonbeam before signing out for the day.

"How may I help you?" Moonbeam extended his greetings to Gopher.

"I received these trading chips for sixteen heads of lettuce that I brought in yesterday. I would like to know if I have enough chips for five tomato seeds." Gopher's voice rasped when he spoke. It made Moonbeam want to clear his throat. He resisted the urge and scrolled through the value system reference vidscreen. He opened the page under T for tomatoes and scanned down the list.

"You would need fifteen points in trading chips for the tomato seeds, and you have…" Moonbeam quickly counted the value of the chips. "Yes, you have more than enough for the seeds. Would you like to make the exchange today?" he asked while looking up from the vidscreen.

"No, thank you. I'll wait until tomorrow morning." Gopher collected his chips and placed them back into his pocket. Moonbeam knew he would return tomorrow when Bunny was back on shift.

The next person in line came forward. Sandpebble was a regular at the Trade Center and a favorite of Moonbeam's. He always had interesting new ideas or inventions. Sandpebble wore a Black-Level jumpsuit, which was straining against his massive frame. His long hair was strawberry blond, as were his beard and mustache.

Moonbeam often felt sad that Sandpebble, ingenious as he was, had never progressed past the Black-Level. He preferred to spend his time working on his new inventions rather than pedaling in the workhouses. Like some in Peddlers, he lived mainly off the point value system. They would take their goods, crafts, or food to the Trade Center, where they would be evaluated and given points in the form of trading chips. They could use these trading chips to buy other items. Rather than pedaling for credits, they found other ways to make ends meet. Moonbeam worked as a barterer for the items people brought in. He also calculated the value of the chips by the amount of community time they had acquired.

"Good afternoon, Sandpebble. What can I do for you today?"

"I've invented this new device that freezes food within a matter of minutes. It works much in the same way a microwave oven operates to heat food but in reverse. The microcomputer matches the harmonic wavelengths of the molecules within the food and then counters the resonant frequency with the exact opposite wavelengths. This procedure reverses the molecule's vibration, thus creating… oh, never mind." It was obvious from the expression on Moonbeam's face that he wasn't understanding a thing he said.

"That's great! Can you show me how it works?" *He's done it again*, thought Moonbeam. *Sandpebble has come up with another incredibly inventive device.* Sandpebble brought the small square box to the electrical outlet beside the counter. While he was plugging it in, Moonbeam went to the storage area and brought out a cabbage head. He knew they would never be able to sell the cabbage; it had seen better days. All the food was stored on the ground-floor level due to its popularity. Moonbeam had to push his way through the crowds that had now gathered to witness this new and interesting device.

Handing the cabbage to Sandpebble, he stood back and watched as he stuffed the head inside the box. Sandpebble closed the glass door, turned the dial to two minutes, then pushed the start button. The box started to hum while white smoke clouded the window. When it stopped, he opened the door. The white smoke escaped, revealing a frozen cabbage head. Moonbeam motioned Sandpebble back to the counter amidst the applause from the surrounding crowd.

"Very effective!" Moonbeam nodded his approval. "Is this the only size it comes in?"

"If there is a demand for this kind of machine, I'm sure I could build it in any size," Sandpebble said, confidently.

"The problem is, we don't have a demand for such an item at this point in time. It may take a while before the value of this invention will increase. What do you call this new device of yours?" Moonbeam looked up from his vidscreen.

"I call it a Chiller."

Moonbeam started looking up information to help him calculate its value. Sandpebble purchased food in trade for his new invention. Moonbeam advised him to keep making his Chillers. The more there were, the more valuable it would become through popularity.

The hours flew by as endless lines poured through the Trade Center. Moonbeam was relieved to see his replacement come in at seven. He gladly relinquished his post and headed home.

Lucky had been working in the maternity ward all day. Much to his dismay, so was Holly. Maternity was one of the few wards that demanded the constant attention of the medical staff. This meant that Holly had to work as hard as the rest of them on this floor. Unfortunately, it made her incredibly irritable, causing her to lash out at anyone within earshot.

Lucky left the delivery room, exhausted. It seemed that all the women had decided to wait until after three to deliver their babies. He removed his blood-stained smock, dropping it in the laundry chute. He walked to the nurses' station and pulled a fresh smock from the shelves below. He quickly dialed Chip's number on the vidphone. It rang twice before Chip answered.

"Hello."

"Hi, Chip, it's Lucky. Turn on your visual."

"I'd rather not, if it's all the same to you," Chip replied, hesitantly. "I haven't any clothes on."

"No problem." Lucky chuckled. "I was just wondering if you knew of some home remedy we could use on Corey's arm."

"If it's starting to infect, then you could make a bread poultice. Just boil some milk, dip in some bread, and apply it to the infection. It'll draw out the poisons."

Lucky could see Holly heading toward the station. She came waltzing into the room, looking tired and dirty. She had not bothered changing her smock since the beginning of work.

"That's great, Chip. Thanks for the advice. Got to run." Lucky disconnected the line, but not before Holly saw him.

"I can't believe this," Holly yelled. "I'm working my ass off in the delivery room while you're on the vidphone making plans for your social life."

"Jealousy will get you nowhere, my dear." Lucky flashed her a smile on his way to the recuperation room. Inside, there were forty beds lining each side of the walls. Half the beds were occupied by either women waiting to deliver or women with newborn infants.

The natural childbirth position used Medichair's supports to hold the woman in a squatting position so she could use her energies for pushing and breathing. This position used gravity to its advantage and eased some of the pressure by placing the uterus at the proper angle for delivery. Usually, a basin of warm water was placed below the woman so the child could be born into it. Without the quick drop in temperature, the baby would be less likely to suffer the trauma of childbirth.

Lucky always found maternity and pediatrics the most challenging wards to work in. It wasn't that he didn't enjoy the work. On the contrary, he would come in even on days off to bestow copious amounts of attention on the babies. The challenge was trying not to get too attached to the precious babes.

He removed a baby bottle from the supply shelf and discreetly asked a few of the women he knew well if they could spare some milk. The women consented happily, even though it was an unusual request. Once the bottle was full, he brought it back to the nursing station, hiding it under the smocks. Lucky knew Holly wouldn't look there, since there were only ten minutes left to their shift.

Corey and Bear sat down to discuss the C Zone once Moonbeam and Lucky had left.

"The C Zone is a place where we send the Undesirables. I say we, because it is my job, as a policeman, to apprehend them."

"I was wondering about that last night. Was it only last night that I came here? It feels longer than that. I've learned so much and gotten to know so many people in such a short period of time. Sorry, continue with your story."

"As you know, the Men pick the criminals up and herd them out still chained together. The C Zone is a labor camp. Exactly what they do there, I don't know. Use your imagination. No one has ever come back, so you can say what you want."

"Never? What do you suppose the C could stand for? Do you think it means contamination?"

"What kind of contamination?" Bear asked.

"We were told in Havanna that Peddlers was in a contamination zone. Actually, everywhere outside of the Dome was contaminated. Is it true that you still have contamination and disease here?"

"The water's not potable, not that you can drink salt water anyway. The food and the air are fine. There hasn't been any disease around since Medichair was installed. That would have been before my time."

"So, I'm not going to get sick or anything like that?"

"Hell, no. They came up with an antidote to most viruses just before the Waste War ended."

"Have you been inoculated?" Corey asked Bear.

"Yes. I remember as a child there was an outbreak of Metry. It was a mutant virus originating from the SARS virus. The Mensis soldiers came in to set up makeshift medical centers to inoculate everyone from the new strain. The soldiers treated everyone roughly. It was like they were helping us because they had to and not because they wanted to."

"I've been inoculated, too," Corey said, as he got up to pour himself a glass of water from the sink. Bear jumped up and took the glass away from Corey.

"This is the bad water. I'll order you up some water."

"Don't you have to pay for everything that you order up?"

"Yes. It is deducted from the points we acquire by pedaling." Bear handed the glass of water to Corey.

"Then you have to pay for clean water? Doesn't that seem unfair to you? Drinking water should be free."

"Maybe, but it is a rare commodity around here."

They sat down again at the table. Corey's body was feeling better, but he was still sore in places.

"Tell me more about Havanna. What's it like there? What did you do?" Bear still wanted to believe he would go there one day. He wanted to believe Dusting represented life, not death.

"We played a lot of sports. I don't know. It seems I was always busy. Other than playing sports and vidgames, I really can't remember what else I used to do."

"Is it nice there?" Bear enquired.

"Sure, it's nice. Trees line the streets, and the houses are surrounded by ecograss. We have a skytrain and an observation deck." Just talking about Havanna made Corey feel homesick, even though he knew he could never return.

"An observation deck?"

"The view is incredible! We can see Peddlers and all the people pedaling. There's a plaque up there that says that the Peddlers produce electricity for Havanna, as well as for itself."

"How can that be? We hardly pedal enough electricity to survive on from day to day. Even still, it costs us a fortune to use it."

"I wouldn't be surprised if it was all lies. The whole place is shrouded in hypocrisy. It makes me so angry when I think of it. I'd love to see the whole system come crashing down."

"Maybe if everyone stopped pedaling it would," Bear said to lighten the moment.

"That's it, Bear! That's what we've got to do! We've got to get everyone to stop pedaling!"

"I was only joking," Bear smirked.

"Well, I'm not," Corey insisted. If he couldn't help his own people in the Dome, the least he could do is help his new friends in Peddlers.

"It's impossible. If the people don't pedal, they don't get any credit. Then how are they supposed to eat and drink?"

"I'm working on that."

That evening when Moonbeam walked into his apartment, he found Lucky and Bear sitting on the sofa in the living room. The curtains were drawn and all the lights were on. They sat with their dirty shoes up on the redwood coffee table. Next to them, leftover food morsels had fallen and had not been picked up. Empty cola cans littered the floor.

"What the hell is going on here?" Moonbeam could feel his temperature rising. "I work hard for my credit. I don't need you guys wasting it." He handed two candles to his friends while he crossed the room to switch off the overhead lights. "Where the hell is Corey?"

"He's taking a bath," replied Bear.

"Wonderful!" Moonbeam said, sarcastically. "That'll use up about twenty credits, I'm sure. Why the hell don't you guys start pitching in and spending your own credits?" Moonbeam walked back to the sofa. "While you're at it, why don't you go mess up your own apartments?" He bent down to pick up the cola cans.

"Here, let me get that." Lucky jumped to his feet, taking the cans from Moonbeam, and followed him into the kitchen. Moonbeam ordered himself some food while Lucky packed the garbage compactor.

"You want to tell Corey to save the bathwater? I really need to relax in a tub for a while."

"Sure thing," Lucky said. He headed down the hallway, passing Bear, who was on his way to join Moonbeam in the kitchen. When Lucky reached the bathroom, he saw Corey had a towel wrapped around his waist and was using another one to dry his hair.

"Moonbeam wants you to save the bathwater for him." He saw that both of the tattoos on Corey's arms were red and swollen. "You're going to have to do something about the infection in your right arm."

"Don't I know it. It hurts like a bellyflop!"

"Stay here. I'll be right back." Lucky sauntered off back into the kitchen, returning a few moments later with a burger and the milk he had brought from the hospital.

"Oh, no thanks, Lucky, I couldn't possibly eat another bite."

Lucky just chuckled. He placed the bowl of hot milk that he had warmed up in the microwave on the vanity. Removing the bun from the burger, he soaked the bread in the milk.

"Hold out both of your arms," Lucky commanded. He placed the soaked bread over each tattoo. Corey sucked in his breath against the pain the heat created, and then Lucky taped two gauze bandages on Corey's arms. "I'll put the rest of the milk in the microwave for you." Corey followed Lucky into the kitchen.

Sunshine entered the apartment unannounced and joined them in the kitchen. She had decided that if the boys wanted their secrets, they could have them. She didn't want to lose their friendships over something ridiculous. Moonbeam jumped up to greet her.

"Come on in. There's someone here we would all like you to meet. He's a new friend of ours. Corey, this is Sunshine."

Sunshine's heart jumped to her throat as Corey's intense, chocolate-brown eyes met hers. She took in the hairless chest tapering down to a slim, muscular waist. An ivory elephant on a chain hung around his neck and a white towel was tightly bound around his square hips. The towel was splitting slightly open, high on the left thigh, revealing strong, powerful legs. Two bandages were taped to his forearms.

"Pleased to meet you," Corey said, extending his hand toward Sunshine. He brought her hand to his lips, kissing the back of it softly. "Excuse me while I put on something more appropriate."

He left the room thinking that life was starting to get more interesting. The combination of the green eyes and red hair together with that body was enticing. Yes, things were more interesting, indeed. He dressed in a Green-Level jumpsuit and brushed out the waves that had gone wild on his head. When Corey entered the living room where they now sat, Lucky was just leaving.

"Well, I'd really love to stay and chat, but I have the early shift in pediatrics tomorrow morning." Lucky started for the door, with Bear following him out.

"I'm on my way too. I'll see you tomorrow." Bear closed the door behind him, leaving Corey and Sunshine in the living room while Moonbeam cleaned up the kitchen.

"Moonbeam tells me you're from the C Zone." Sunshine knew she should be getting back to Rose, but couldn't resist wanting to get to know this strange, sexy man. She couldn't remember the last time she was so attracted to a male. There was something different about him. *He's confident with himself,* she thought, *even a little arrogant, but his eyes are kind and gentle.* They looked as though they were capable of expressing a lot of love. She knew Corey was speaking, but she hadn't heard a word he said. "I'm sorry, you were saying..."

"I just got back last night. It's a rough place."

"It must be," Sunshine said, while softly touching the bruise over Corey's eye. She was struggling internally with her emotions. She wondered what it would be like to have a relationship with Corey, knowing he was once an Undesirable. Something in his eyes said he would never hurt anyone, and yet the truth spoke for itself. He was only a Green-Level but carried himself as though he were a Red. *With his good looks, he must have had hundreds of lovers, so why would he be interested in her?*

He cleared his throat and moved to the chair opposite the sofa as Moonbeam came back into the room. Sitting next to Sunshine, Moonbeam started to tell them of the incredible invention Sandpebble had come up with that afternoon.

Looking at Sunshine sitting there in her Blue-Level jumpsuit, Corey couldn't help comparing her to Anne, even though they were nothing alike. Anne was blond-haired, blue-eyed, slim, and intelligent. Sunshine was a red-haired, green-eyed, full-figured woman who was incredibly sexy. Was it possible, he wondered, to be attracted to two very different women?

"What did you say he traded his ice maker for?" Corey was suddenly aware of what Moonbeam was saying.

"He traded it for food. Sometimes Sandpebble will trade for new materials with which to work, but for the most part, he takes food."

"You said once that they get food from the Park, right?" Corey's mind was suddenly working hard trying to figure out how to feed everyone without pedaling for it.

"How long have you been gone for?" Sunshine teased. Corey smiled coyly at Sunshine.

"Too long, I suppose."

"I've been gone too long myself," she said, rising to her feet. "I must get back home." They both walked her to the door. Corey took her hand in his, holding it gently.

"It was a pleasure meeting you. I do hope to see you again." He kissed her hand again then let it go.

"We'll definitely be seeing each other, believe me. Good night, Moonbeam. Thanks for an enjoyable evening." She gave him a hug and a kiss on the cheek then left with a quick glance over her shoulder toward Corey.

"I want to know everything about that girl, Moonbeam," Corey said after Moonbeam had closed the door.

"Forget it, pal. She's living with a girlfriend and she's not interested in men."

"Funny, that's not what her eyes were telling me tonight."

Moonbeam laughed. "That's just the way her eyes are. They can be very deceiving."

Corey couldn't believe his ears. Could such a beautiful woman not care for a man? "Perhaps she's just never met the right guy," he voiced, aloud.

"Don't hold your breath, and you can get in line behind me. Now, if you're looking to get laid, I know this woman who is always eager to please."

"No, thanks." Corey couldn't understand how casually the Peddlers seemed to take their relationships. Were there really women who would sleep with a man and not want to marry him? Were they lacking mating customs altogether?

Corey thought how ironic it was to be able to have the freedom now to fall in love with a woman before marrying her, but the woman he had wanted was no longer available to him. He thought of Sunshine. *Would she make him a good wife? Could he actually marry a Peddler woman?* He chuckled to himself. The idea seemed so absurd, and yet was he, not a Peddler himself now?

His laughter died in his throat as the reality of his situation dawned on him. He had always been so proud to have been from Havanna, and now he was a mere Peddler. His heart ached for Anne. As much as he would like to get on with his life, he knew he never would until he could get Anne out of his head and heart.

Walking into the bedroom, he removed his jumpsuit and fell into bed. He pulled the covers up to his chin protectively. He fell asleep feeling small and insignificant.

Moonbeam headed toward the washroom. The bathwater was much too cold to bathe in now, so he settled for a sponge bath. He brushed his teeth, then turned out the light. Corey was already settled in bed when Moonbeam entered the bedroom carrying a candle. He set it down beside the bed, blew it out, then climbed in. "Good night, Corey."

Moonbeam woke Corey up early. He had already bathed and dressed in a fresh Blue-Level jumpsuit. Corey sat up in bed, stretching his muscles. After washing up, he joined Moonbeam in the kitchen for breakfast. Corey had removed the bread poultices from his arms, noticing that both tattoos looked better. The infection on his right arm was almost gone.

"Why don't you try out your tattoo code today, Corey? It may just work," Moonbeam urged.

Corey stood in front of the kitchen computer console and ran his left arm over the vidscreen. In the top left-hand corner were the words "Cobra's function list."

"Alright!" said Moonbeam, who had been looking over Corey's shoulder. "Now access the personal information category."

The next vidscreen provided Corey with all the information he needed about his new identity. Cobra had been born in 2146, which meant he had been twenty-three years old. He was a Green-Level in his last semester of school to become a gymnastics teacher. Cobra had accumulated 12,567 points of credit, but only had sixteen hours of recorded community time.

"I don't think the community time will convert to too many trading chips," Moonbeam said. "I'll check on it when I go to work today. How would you like to come in and see how the Trade Center works?"

"Sounds great. I'll go with you after pedaling today."

"Are you sure you're feeling up to it? You have enough credits to keep you going for a while."

"No, I would prefer to work. It's time I start my new life as a Peddler. My father used to tell me that I need to take responsibility for my actions. Seeing that my actions brought me here, I don't see any reason why I should be treated any different than anyone else."

They continued to read the file. Cobra lived on Fourth Street, the same as Moonbeam, but his crossroad was Sixth Avenue rather than first. Corey would now be living five blocks from Moonbeam. Lucky was about three long blocks from Corey.

He escaped from that vidscreen and chose the food menu. From there he ordered up an egg muffin and some water. Corey longed for the meals they used to get back home. He would have loved to have some coffee and oatmeal with a glass of orange juice. Funny how he had once thought that the fresh food had come from Peddlers. Corey ate his muffin unenthusiastically, realizing that he was no closer to knowing where the fresh food came from.

After eating and dressing, Corey and Moonbeam headed out to the workhouse for Corey's first day of pedaling. Sunshine and Bear were already there waiting for them when they arrived. *Sunshine looks even better today than she did last night*, Corey thought. He didn't kiss her hand as he had yesterday. He did not want to bring any unnecessary attention to himself. Moonbeam suggested they go in before the crowds, so he could refresh Corey's memory on how to use the monocycle controls. Being among the first few to arrive, there were still plenty of seats on the first floor.

"How many floors are there?" Corey asked Moonbeam.

"Twenty-five," he answered. "There are two hundred monocycles on each floor, so there can be a maximum of five thousand people per workhouse. Of course, not everyone pedals at the same time. There are many workhouses, so there's lots of room for an increase in population."

Bear and Sunshine took seats behind Corey and Moonbeam. Corey looked longingly toward the Dome through the windows on the other side of the room. He had only been gone for two days, but it already felt like a lifetime.

"Alright, Corey, pass your tattoo code over the vidscreen to start it up," instructed Moonbeam. Immediately, the words "Good morning, Cobra" appeared on the vidscreen, followed by the main menu. Moonbeam explained how Corey could choose categories in the entertainment or educational menus.

"Yeah, yeah, I got it," Corey replied.

"Now, you don't have to choose anything, but the time passes quicker when you take your mind off the pain in your legs."

Corey started to pedal his monocycle. It felt odd to be cycling but not moving. "What's this lever down here?" he asked, indicating a lever on the bar below the seat.

"That's to adjust your tension higher or lower."

"You mean like changing gears?"

"Corey," Moonbeam whispered, "maybe you ought to stick to the terminology that we use here."

"Right. So how fast can these bikes go?"

"The monocycles can go as fast as you can pedal. This dial over here," Moonbeam indicated the meter to the left of the vidscreen, "shows you how many credits per hour you're accumulating." Corey adjusted the tension as he pedaled to its limit until he was doing fifty-five credits an hour.

"Hey, Bear, come and check this out," Moonbeam called out.

Bear stood behind Corey with his mouth hanging opening as the meter raised even higher. Corey was now doing fifty-six, fifty-seven, fifty-eight. Corey lifted his feet from the pedals and they continued to spin, slowly decreasing in speed.

"Damn the Men!" Bear exclaimed. "He's gaining credit without even pedaling." He returned to his monocycle to test out this new technique. It had never dawned on Bear to experiment with the monocycle. He had always pedaled as he was taught: slow and steady.

"Well, it looks like you've got the hang of it." Moonbeam left Corey to take up his own monocycle. By the time Lucky arrived at eleven thirty, after his morning in pediatrics, half of the first floor of Peddlers was using Corey's new technique.

"What's gotten into everyone?" Lucky said as he approached his friends.

"Corey has started a new trend. You pedal like crazy, then stop. The computer continues to calculate credit because the wheels are still turning." Sunshine beamed proudly. She was becoming more infatuated with Corey as the day progressed. He was not only creative, but he often made her laugh with his choice of words or his strange outlooks on life.

Lucky couldn't find a monocycle near his friends, as the first floor rarely had vacancies. He stood there watching them pedal.

"Why don't we all stop for the day and do something exciting?" suggested Corey. He switched off his monocycle and turned to face the others.

"I've got to go on patrol this afternoon," Bear said. He continued to pedal.

"I'd love to, but I really need the credit. I've been spending it a bit foolishly lately," Lucky apologized.

"I have a class at three," Sunshine fretted. She would have loved nothing more than to spend some time with Corey.

"I work too. Remember, you're supposed to come with me to look up the value of your trading chips." Moonbeam turned off his monocycle and jumped down.

Corey nodded. It seemed to him that the Peddlers didn't know how to have fun. Everything was work, work, work. It was fun to pedal for a few hours, but Corey couldn't imagine wanting to rush off to another job right away.

"That's it," he said. "Tomorrow, no one is to work in the afternoon. I'm going to show you how to have some fun. I want everyone to be in the Park at one o'clock, and I don't want to hear any ifs, ands, or buts. Is that clear?"

They all stared at Corey, speechless. Although Sunshine often resented being told what to do, she was thrilled by Corey's power of authority. It was exciting to be around someone with so much charisma. It somehow made her feel more confident in herself like she could do anything. The others all agreed.

Lucky figured he could switch with Cliff, who had the earlier shift in cafeteria duties tomorrow. There was no way he was going to sit this one out. Bear had plans to work out at the Dojo, but he could postpone it until later. Moonbeam would tell his department head today that he would be unavailable for work tomorrow afternoon. As long as they had twelve hours' notice, they could get someone else.

Corey and Moonbeam bid their friends farewell and walked along the boardwalk to the First Street Monorail Station. Corey followed Moonbeam into the station, passing his tattoo code over the turnstile to gain entry. He had almost used the tattoo on his right arm through force of habit. It would take him a while to adjust to his new code.

The monorail was crowded with the lunch-hour rush. Corey had never seen so many people pushing and shoving their way to the trains. One train pulled in. People fought their way in and out in the two-minute time limit before the whistle blew and the doors closed. Corey and Moonbeam fought their way closer to the edge of the platform, trying desperately to stay together.

Another train pulled into the station. Corey and Moonbeam both got on but were separated in the process. The pushing and shoving of the crowds made Corey yearn for the space and freedom he had always taken for granted. He felt stifled and pressured by the close proximity of all the people. Corey's breathing became shallow and more frequent.

Moonbeam sensed Corey's discomfort within the close confines of the monorail. He managed to attract Corey's attention and gave him a reassuring smile, which seemed to relax him long enough to complete their trip. Corey followed Moonbeam out at the Fifth Street Station. He was glad to be back outside, away from the crowds. They walked north along Twelfth Avenue.

"Let's head over to the casino for lunch," suggested Moonbeam.

The Owl Club's flashing neon sign stood out amongst the drab-looking apartments on either side. It was a white stucco Pre-Three structure with a blue-shingled roof. It dulled only in comparison to the Church across the street. The geometric design of the Church, with its stained-glass dome and large brass bell, was the most spectacular building in all of Peddlers.

"What's that?" asked Corey. Moonbeam gave him an odd look.

"It's a church. A place where we go to worship God."

"Oh," Corey said, as he scratched his head. He wondered if he'd be allowed in even though he didn't know what "worship" was. Moonbeam held the door of the casino bar open for Corey. They walked into a brightly lit room decorated in a variety of pastel colors.

Moonbeam guided Corey to the service bar where they each picked up a burger and some wine. Corey tasted the sweet, fruity wine and smiled with approval. From their table, they could see the blackjack table. Rainbow was dealing hands to the four people who had come to challenge the table.

"Do you want to try a hand or two?"

Corey finished his burger and wine. "No, it doesn't interest me at all." They got up and placed their plates in the giant garbage compactor. Moonbeam led Corey over to the crap table. It was quiet around the table, with only one older gentleman dressed in a Red-Level jumpsuit. Moonbeam recognized Gopher right away. Beside him sat a young woman in her early twenties who was laughing at something Gopher had said. In front of him sat a large pile of trading chips.

Moonbeam and Corey sat across the table from Gopher and his companion. The crap table attendant placed a free wine in front of them. He was of a medium build with brown hair and eyes. "Hi. My name is Chuckles. Welcome to the crap table." He smiled pleasantly at them. "I haven't seen you guys in here before. Are you familiar with the game?"

"No," replied Corey. He leaned forward and placed his elbows on the table. There were pictures on the board of the four card suits, as well as a star and a square.

"The way the game is played," explained Chuckles, "is that you bet what design or designs you believe I can roll." He held out the dice for Corey to see. "These dice have the same designs as the board. If I roll even one design the same as your bet, you win. You receive an extra chip back for every bet placed. Would you like to give it a try?"

Moonbeam dug into his pocket and pulled out his trading chips. He handed a couple to Corey, then placed one on the spade and one on the star. Corey placed both of his chips on the heart.

"Are you sure you want to put both your chips on the same design, Corey?" Moonbeam asked.

"I wouldn't put them there if I wasn't sure."

Chuckles gave the dice a hearty shake, then let them drop on the table. The dice rolled around and stopped on the star and the heart.

"Alright," Moonbeam yelled, as he slapped Corey on the back.

"We have a winner," Chuckles called out. He gave Moonbeam back his two chips and handed Corey his two chips, as well as two more. Corey handed back the chips that Moonbeam had originally given him. He then placed both on the star. Moonbeam placed both of his on the spade. Chuckles rolled the dice again. This time they came up with a diamond and a star. Moonbeam lost his chips, but Corey gained two more. Gopher and his friend applauded Corey's good fortune.

"We have another winner," Chuckles shouted. Corey placed all four of his chips on the club. Moonbeam placed two chips on the club as well. A few more people came around to watch as Chuckles threw the dice again.

Corey heard the yells and hollers before he saw that the dice had come up a club and a star. Now he had eight chips to play with. Moonbeam slapped Corey on the back.

"Thanks! I just won two more chips. Now I've broken even."

Some other people were placing their chips on the board now. Corey placed four on the square, and four on the diamond. Moonbeam chose the square and the star. Gopher waited until Corey had finished choosing, then placed six chips on each of Corey's selections. Chuckles rolled the dice. The dice stopped on the diamond and the square. Corey now had sixteen trading chips. He had also won a small fortune for Gopher.

"We have more winners," Chuckles yelled out. More people were drawn to the table.

"This is great! What are you going to choose now?" Moonbeam asked Corey. His eyes were bright with excitement and greed. Moonbeam had never seen anyone win so consistently before.

"I'm not choosing anymore. I've won enough, and the odds have just run out." Corey vacated his seat at the table. Gopher grabbed Corey by the arm.

"I'd like you to have these as a token of my appreciation," Gopher rasped, as he handed Corey four more chips. Before Corey could refuse the offer, Gopher had disappeared into the crowd that now surrounded him. People reached out to touch him, then moved on back to their games. Once again, Corey felt trapped by the crowd. He pushed his way out toward the door. Moonbeam followed him out to the street.

"What's gotten into you? Those people were only touching you for good luck. It's considered an honor."

"I'm not used to crowds, and I don't like being grabbed." Corey started walking back toward Fifth Street. Corey knew that the Peddlers were not disease-ridden, but he still wasn't comfortable being so close to so many people. They walked in silence until they reached the Trade Center.

"This is where I work," Moonbeam proudly announced. He opened the door. Corey stood outside, staring up at the tall building made of chrome and glass. Several people pushed passed them on their way in or out. An older woman in a Red-Level jumpsuit caught Corey's eye. She was struggling with a large pail of lettuce heads on her way in. Corey grabbed the pail from the woman.

"Here, let me help you carry this," he offered.

The woman looked up at Corey with a strange kind of wonder in her eyes. "Do you work here, young man?" she questioned him.

"No, I don't."

"Then why are you helping me? What do you want?" She narrowed her eyes suspiciously as they walked through the Center to take her place in line.

"I don't want anything. I saw you struggling with the pail, and I thought perhaps you could use some help." He placed the pail next to the woman as she stood in line. When Corey turned to leave, the woman restrained him with a hand on his arm.

"Please don't go yet. This is the kindest thing anyone has ever done for me. I want to thank you." She placed five trading chips into Corey's hand.

"I'm sorry. I cannot accept this."

"But you can and you must... I insist," she said, closing Corey's hand around the chips. She held his hand in her own. "It is because you didn't expect a reward that I give it to you freely."

"Your appreciation is its own reward. I have no need of your chips." Corey smiled down at her.

"You're an angel, but don't insult me by refusing my gift to you." Her blue eyes sparkled like sapphires. "Now, take the chips and be on your way."

Corey lightly kissed the back of her hand, then went to join Moonbeam.

"Was Lily giving you a hard time?" he asked Corey.

"No, on the contrary, she was quite enthralled with me." Corey held out his hand to show Moonbeam the chips Lily had given him.

"I've never seen anyone give their chips away to someone else without some sort of trade. Yet today, two people have given you chips for what seems like no apparent reason."

"I'm sure they had their reasons," Corey replied.

"I know you don't like crowds, but the Trade Center is always this busy." Moonbeam made a sweep of the room with his arm.

Lined up in front of all the available barterers were people from the four colored level groups, but mostly the Red-Level. Moonbeam led Corey through the building, explaining how the

Trade Center worked. He brought Corey to the upper-floor levels where items were displayed by category. Above the display floors were the offices of the Red-Level executives. On the eighth floor, Moonbeam ran into Sandpebble carrying a box.

"Hi, Sandpebble. What are you doing in the book department?"

"Trying to trade in some bookmarkers I made for a few books. I want to start learning about gardening."

"Gardening? Only Red-Levels get gardening space."

"Yes, I know, but I thought I would try to grow something in a bowl inside my apartment. I can get some soil from the Park and trade for a few seeds. I know it's not a custom, but it's worth a try if I don't get caught."

"That's what I like about you, Sandpebble. You're always thinking of inventive things to do. I'd like you to meet a good friend of mine." Moonbeam beckoned Corey forward. "This is the fellow I was telling you about last night that invented the ice maker."

Corey shook hands with Sandpebble. "Pleased to meet you. My name is Corey."

"Any friend of Moonbeams is a friend of mine. The name is Sandpebble, and it's called a Chiller, not an ice maker. Do you do much reading, Corey?" Sandpebble reached into the box of bookmarkers he had made. He handed one each to Corey and Moonbeam. They were solid-colored markers in blue with an arrow pointing outward.

"What is this arrow for?" Moonbeam asked him.

"Have you ever been reading a book then put it down only to discover later you forgot where you were? Then you read both pages over again to find out you were on the last paragraph of the second page? Now, with this book marker," Sandpebble continued, enthusiastically, "all you have to do is place the arrow at the last sentence that you were reading. When you pick up the book again, you know exactly where you were. It's a real time saver."

"That's great! Thank you," Moonbeam exclaimed.

"What line of work are you in?" Sandpebble asked Corey.

Corey hesitated for a moment, not sure what to say. "I'm... studying to be a gymnastics teacher." He remembered reading that on Cobra's profile.

"You certainly look to be in good enough shape for it. I used to love going to gymnastics as a child."

"Do you still keep physically active?"

"The only active thing I do these days is run back and forth to the Trade Center with new inventions."

Corey turned to look at Moonbeam before he said to Sandpebble, "meet us in the Park tomorrow afternoon at one. I kid you not, you'll have the time of your life!"

Sandpebble looked at Corey with renewed interest. "Thank you, I believe I will. I must run now, but I'll see you in the Park tomorrow at one," he confirmed, before heading out. He was intrigued by Corey's kind offer to join him in some fun. Sandpebble realized how few friends he had. He had always been too busy working on some new invention to notice how lonely he really was. He placed his box of bookmarkers on the counter in front of a trade barterer.

Moonbeam and Corey made their way back down to the first floor. It was still as busy as ever. "I've got to take my place behind the counter now. Look around and see if there's anything here that interests you. You certainly have enough chips to barter with." Moonbeam slapped Corey's back with affection, then left him.

Corey had twenty-five trading chips in his pocket. He walked around from floor to floor looking over items. On the fifth floor, he purchased an inner tube for a monocycle wheel. On the sixth floor, he bought a toothbrush and paste. He went back down to ground level with his wares and looked over the assortment of food displayed on a table. He reached out to pick up a fresh ripe tomato. One of the barterers grabbed Corey's hand.

"This is the display table. If you'd like to purchase some tomatoes, then line up like everyone else." He released Corey's arm. Corey looked at the long lines of people and decided against waiting. He would go to his new apartment instead. Moonbeam was too engrossed in his work to notice Corey leave.

Once outside, Corey inhaled fresh air into his lungs before entering the Monorail station heading west. He remembered the address as 1-C, 645 Fourth Street. The 6 represented the crossroad and the 45 the building number. The 1-C meant he was on the first floor—apartment C. Corey opened the door to his new home. It resembled Moonbeam's and Chip's places in every way except that Cobra seemed to collect all different forms of artwork. There were statues, drawings, and needlepoints of various animals, people, and landscapes.

Dropping his Trade Center bag on the coffee table, Corey crossed the room to the window. He pulled open the blinds to discover a balcony off his living room. The kitchen was a little messy but otherwise clean. Walking down the hall, he checked out the bathroom and the bedroom. In the bedroom closet, Corey found half a dozen Green-Level jumpsuits. He lay down on the bed, trying to feel at home here in his new surroundings.

Corey knew he was fortunate to have made some good friends so quickly, but he felt lonely for the friends and family he had left in Havanna. His heart felt heavy and just the thought of Anne threatened to bring tears to his eyes. "Son of a Peddler!" he swore aloud as he swung his feet over the side of the bed. He would have to stop thinking of the past. He had a new life now, and he had to make the best of it.

He returned to the living room and picked up the inner tube from the bag. He went into the kitchen and searched through the drawers until he found what he was looking for. He picked up a kitchen knife and cut the tube in half. From the same drawer, he extracted some thread and a needle. Corey sewed up one end of the tube. Saving himself about eight inches, he cut the rest of the tube off. He filled up the tube with an old Black-Level jumpsuit, then sewed up the other end. When he was done, he had a makeshift football.

Sunshine was waiting for Moonbeam when he got off work at seven. She almost missed him in the commotion of the downtown crowds. She fell in step beside him while tucking her arm in his. Moonbeam looked startled for a second then smiled.

"Well, if it isn't my favorite gal." He held the hand that was cradled at the crook of his elbow. "What brings you here?"

"I'd thought we'd get the gang together for a drink."

"Sure." Moonbeam couldn't believe his luck. After what seemed an eternity, Sunshine was finally starting to pay more attention to him. "I don't think that Bear will be joining us. He's going to the Dojo after work, and you know how he is about going out to the bars."

"Yes, I know," replied Sunshine. "What about Corey?" Sunshine tried to make her voice sound casual, but it sounded funny even to her. Moonbeam didn't seem to notice or didn't let on if he did.

"I'll give him a call when we get inside." He held the door of the Twilight Bar open for Sunshine.

"I'll use the vidphone to call Rose while you talk to Corey."

They placed their calls side by side on the communal vidphones. The club was noisy, which made it difficult to hear the person on the other end of the line.

Rose refused to come to the bar. They had another one of their bitter arguments about jealousy. Sunshine was angry when she disconnected the vidphone. Rose always had some convenient excuse not to meet her friends. She always managed to make Sunshine feel guilty about having some fun. "To hell with her!" Sunshine mumbled under her breath. She vowed not to let Rose's sour mood spoil her evening.

Moonbeam disconnected the vidphone and walked to where Sunshine was waiting. He knew better than to ask her how her conversation with Rose went. It was written all over her face.

"Corey will be down as soon as he can, and I couldn't get a hold of Lucky." Moonbeam placed his arm around Sunshine's shoulders, leading her to a table. The loud music and flashing lights did little to elevate Sunshine's mood. The server came by and took their order, swiping their tattoo code numbers on the portable.

Moonbeam couldn't stand to see Sunshine's beautiful face looking so melancholy. "Would you like to dance?"

Sunshine looked up into Moonbeam's expectant face. If he only knew how she treasured their friendship. He never pressured her or taunted her when she was down. "No, thank you."

Moonbeam took Sunshine's hands in his own. "Do you want to talk about it?"

"No. I'd rather talk about anything but."

"Alright," he said, as he let go of her hands. "What do you think of Corey?"

Sunshine's face visibly brightened. She sat up straight with her green eyes sparkling. "I think he's wonderful! He's funny and fun to be with. He's unlike anyone I've ever met. I couldn't imagine Corey ever being an Undesirable."

Moonbeam suppressed a smile. *If only she knew the truth*, he thought. Although he was apprehensive of her enthusiasm, he couldn't help sharing her point of view. There was something very special about Corey. "He's one of a kind," Moonbeam agreed.

"He's the kind of guy who could turn me straight. You know what I'm saying," Sunshine confessed. "I know that sounds odd coming from me, but it's the way he makes me feel. I want to hold and comfort him like a lost child, but at the same time, I feel empowered." Sunshine fell silent, fearing she had said too much.

Moonbeam's heart felt heavy in his chest. All his illusions and visions of grandeur with Sunshine came crashing down around him. He realized then that Sunshine was using him to reach Corey. He knew then that Sunshine would never feel the same way about him as he did for her. He would have to be satisfied with being her friend. Moonbeam pushed his feelings aside in order to help Sunshine sort through hers.

"It sounds to me like you're really hung up on the guy."

It was as if Moonbeam had been reading her mind. Sunshine looked up with a helpless look in her eyes. "What am I going to do, Moonbeam? I love Rose so much… even though she infuriates me to the point of destruction." She inhaled and sighed deeply. "Corey's new and exciting. He's so much a man and yet so much a boy. I think half the attraction I feel for him stems from the fact that he seems unattainable. It appears he doesn't need anyone, and yet he's vulnerable as hell. Rose, on the other hand, needs me too much. It's almost suffocating."

"You can't live your life for her, Sunshine. You should know that better than anyone. If your relationship with Rose causes you more heartache than pleasure, you have to let it go. You can't hang on to a sinking ship because you're afraid to swim. When the time comes to move on, do it. Sometimes we have to let go of someone we love because they're toxic to us." Silent tears ran down Sunshine's face.

"You're the best friend I have, Moonbeam. I don't know what I'd do if I didn't have you to talk to. You always seem to know the right things to say." The server brought their drinks to the table. Sunshine took a long gulp of the sweet, cool wine. The liquid seemed to revive her some. She wiped the tears from her face and forced a smile.

Moonbeam ruffled her hair affectionately. "I don't have all the answers, Sunshine. You have them. Just look deep inside yourself and you'll find all the answers you've ever wanted to know."

"How is looking inside going to tell me if Corey likes me?"

"Do you like him?"

"Of course, I do."

"There you go. Like attracts like. Now, what you two do with those feelings is entirely up to you. Speak of the devil…" Sunshine turned to see Corey approaching the table. "I see you found the place alright." Moonbeam pulled out the chair beside him for Corey.

"No problem. Your directions were right on." Before Corey sat, he gave a half bow in greeting to Sunshine. "Pleased to see you again, Sunshine. You look lovely tonight."

"Thank you." Sunshine's blushing face went unnoticed in the dim of the lights. The server was immediately at Corey's side. "Can I get a wine for you?"

"Yes, and bring another one for my friends."

"Can I see your code please?" enquired the server, as she reached for the portable.

"Why, is something wrong?" Corey looked alarmed. Moonbeam laughed to cover the awkwardness of the moment.

"My friend's a real joker. How else are you supposed to pay for your drinks if you don't show your code to the server?"

Corey started to lift the sleeve of his right arm, then switched to the left. The server swiped his number. "The show will be starting in a few minutes." The server smiled at Corey, then left.

"Wow!" Corey said as he looked about the room. "I've never been in such a flamboyant place." The music was pounding out tunes unfamiliar to Corey's ears. He sat mesmerized by the flashing-colored lights around him. People sat at tables or stood around talking and laughing. How different this place was from the bar Cheerz in Havanna.

"What do you have planned for the Park tomorrow, Corey?"

Corey turned at the sound of Moonbeam's voice. He saw both his companions watching him with undisguised curiosity. "A football game," he answered simply. The server placed three more glasses of wine on the table. Corey took his and lifted it to his lips.

"How is the game played?" Sunshine asked. Just then the music increased in volume and the stage lights came on.

"You'll find out tomorrow," Corey yelled over the music.

Bear left the Police Station and headed for the Dojo next door. He was uptight about his day's work at the station. He had been on patrol through the Park when he saw some teenage boys fighting. Bear realized as he had gotten closer that one boy was holding a knife to the other one.

When Bear had called out to them, the dark-haired boy turned his knife on Bear. With a natural instinct built into him from his karate training, Bear kicked the knife from the boy's hand. It had been too quick for the boy to react, and as a result, Bear had broken the kid's wrist.

After bringing him to the hospital, Bear was stuck filling out reports on the computer for the rest of the night. He was uptight about the number of casualties on his record. Bear knew if he didn't take more care in handling people, he could be thrown off the force. He bowed at the entrance of the Dojo before removing his shoes. He carried them to the shoe shelf, removed a black cloth belt from the belt cabinet, and tied it around his waist.

The Sensei entered the Dojo, removed his shoes, and wrapped a black belt around his Red-Level jumpsuit. He nodded at Bear as he made his way to the front of the room. Behind the Sensei stood the painted symbols of yin and yang. The wooden floors were coated in wax, giving them a shiny luster. There were long windows encircling the room. The Sensei would severely reprimand anyone whose attention strayed to the outdoors during their session.

He clapped his hands, signaling the beginning. The Peddlers lined up according to the color of their belts, as opposed to the color of their jumpsuits. The Sensei bowed to the class as a gesture of greeting. They returned the bow in unison before dropping to their knees. There were a few minutes of silence as they all used this time for meditation. Concentrating on their inner strength, they prepared mentally for the discipline and commitment it took to learn this martial art.

Bear cleared his mind and emotions of today's events. He focused his attention inward, channeling his energy toward the center of his body. This was the point, according to the Sensei, that was the balance of our gravity.

After a few minutes, the Sensei lifted his head, calling out in Japanese. The group jumped straight from their knees to their feet in one swift movement. They stood relaxed, with their arms at their sides.

"HUH," Sensei yelled. The Peddlers stepped together into their stance. They stood with their feet apart, one diagonally in front of the other. Their hands were balled into fists, one elbow bent at their side, the other straight out in front of them.

In unison, they performed their movements while the Sensei counted in Japanese. The only music by which they moved was the swishing of their jumpsuits. The voice of the Sensei counting was the words to their song. They moved together to this traditional ancient art as though they were one spirit.

The dancers in the Twilight Bar ran around the tables, jumping and flipping up on the stage. The crowd applauded. Corey watched them with fascination. He had only ever seen ballroom dancing, but this dance was different. It was exotic and exciting. Each duo of dancers had its own style.

Corey could feel himself grow excited as the dancers seductively moved to the music. He looked at the other people in the bar. All around him couples were kissing or holding one another. Corey realized that the people clung to each other in the same way as the dancers.

When the dance was over and the music had returned to the normal decibels, the people stopped applauding. The dancers left the stage, talking with some of the customers.

Corey leaned over to whisper in Moonbeam's ear. "Does everyone dance like that?"

Moonbeam broke out laughing. "I don't mean to laugh at you, Corey, but it just struck me as funny. The answer to your question is 'no'."

Corey caught sight of Chip walking toward them on his way out the door. He was accompanied by a man who limped, and whose Red-Level jumpsuit clashed with Chip's green one.

"Hey, Chip," Corey yelled out. Chip headed toward Corey with a smile on his face.

"Hi, Corey. Hi, Moonbeam," he said, touching their shoulders. "Is that… Sunshine?" he cried enthusiastically. He went around the table to embrace her. "I haven't seen you in ages. How have you been?" He stood back to look at her.

"Great!" replied Sunshine. She hadn't seen Chip since she left her old workhouse on Second Street. "Are you still doing ten-hour shifts on the monocycle?"

"Are you kidding? I couldn't keep up that pace anymore." Chip returned to where he had left his friend standing. "I'd like you to meet my friend, Limpy."

Limpy shook hands with Corey. "My name really isn't Limpy. It's Fireball, but since I hurt my leg, people have been calling me Limpy." He shook hands with Moonbeam and Sunshine as well.

"Chip, why don't you and Limpy come to the Park tomorrow at one? A few of us are going to get together to play some football," Corey offered.

"Football? I don't believe I've heard of that game before."

"We used to play it in the C Zone." Corey gave Chip a wink.

"Right. Sure, it sounds like it might be fun."

"Great, we'll see you there then."

"Are you heading home now?" Moonbeam asked Chip.

"Yes, I am."

"Wait for me. I'll ride the monorail with you." Moonbeam got up from the table. "You'll have to excuse me," he said to Corey and Sunshine. "I've had a long day and I'm tired." He squeezed Sunshine's shoulder affectionately, giving her a knowing look. He would give her some time to get to know Corey better without him around.

Corey stood and offered his hand to Moonbeam. After they had left, Corey took the seat that Moonbeam had occupied. Sunshine was nervously playing with her drink. Corey wanted to strike up a conversation with her, but couldn't think of anything they might have in common.

"Have you known Chip for very long?" Sunshine asked.

Corey felt himself in a dilemma. He had always prided himself on being honest with people, but now his honesty could cost him his identity. "Not long, but I'd rather talk about you. What kind of classes do you teach?"

"I'm an English teacher in the Basic School."

"Do you enjoy your work?" Corey loved the way her eyes sparkled.

"Yes, I do. Sometimes the kids can be a real handful, but for the most part, I enjoy being with them. I find I learn a lot about myself through them." Sunshine reached up to move a piece of hair that fell down over Corey's forehead.

Corey caught her hand and held it to his cheek. "I have a feeling you would be wonderful with children. Have you ever thought of having children yourself?"

"Yes, I've been thinking about it a lot lately."

"You know you need a man in your life if you want children." Corey's eyes met and held hers.

"It's been a long time since a man has attracted me."

"Do I attract you?" Corey's voice was husky.

"Yes," she answered honestly. Corey smiled. He knew he was right. Sunshine had just never met the right man. Moonbeam had been so sure that she wasn't interested in men. Corey knew he was not ready for such a step. The thought of Anne still burned deep inside him. He wanted a wife and children one day, but it would take time before he was ready. In the meantime, he decided not to lead Sunshine on. He let go of her hand.

"Sunshine, you're a sweet girl, and I'm sure you'll find a husband one day who'll give you the children you want," Corey said gently.

She felt like such a fool. She turned her head away as Corey signaled the server for another round, so he wouldn't see the single tear rolling down her face for a dream that would never be.

Corey woke with a wicked hangover pounding in his head. His thoughts drifted back to last night. He knew he had drunk a lot of wine, but he hadn't felt he overdid it. A wave of pain coursed through his head as he sat up. He would have to be more careful with the amount of wine he consumed. Corey couldn't even remember how he got home. He ran a bath, but it smelt of ocean water, so he poured some shampoo in under the flow to scent it. Bubbles foamed to the top of the tub, reflecting the colors of the rainbow. Corey stepped in and then turned off the faucets. He stretched out, totally submerged, with his arms floating lightly by his sides.

Corey remembered dreaming of Anne last night. The dream had seemed so real, as though she were there with him. He played with the elephant chain hanging around his neck, his heart heavy in his chest.

He thought back to the day of his mating ceremony and could distinctly remember the look on Anne's face when she had given him the necklace. There had been so much love and an equal amount of sorrow in those brilliant blue eyes. Corey's heart skipped a beat as he thought of the love he had lost.

He pulled the plug and stepped from the tub. He grabbed a towel from the rack and began briskly drying himself as if he could wipe away the thoughts of the past. He walked to the bedroom and pulled a fresh jumpsuit from the closet. He realized he would have to hurry if he wanted to be on time to meet his friends for work.

Bear and Moonbeam occupied two monocycles on the top floor. They had waited around for Corey and Sunshine, but neither of them had shown up yet. It was agreed that they would meet on the twenty-fifth floor if ever someone was late. There were always monocycles available on this floor.

Moonbeam knew Lucky was at work because he had stopped by his place earlier this morning to pick up Corey's white suit. Lucky was on cafeteria duties at the hospital today, which meant he was also responsible for laundry. He explained to Moonbeam that it would be easier for him to wash Corey's clothes at work instead of at the cleaners. This way no one would see the suit besides himself.

Bear settled onto his monocycle and adjusted the tension as he pedaled. He found it made it easier to pedal while increasing speed. He accessed the Undesirable list and committed the two new names to memory.

Moonbeam was still apprehensive about his friends' absence. It was not like Sunshine to miss a day at work or arrive late. Should he call her at home to see if she was alright? Did she have another quarrel with Rose? Maybe she was doing an early shift at work so she could have the afternoon free? He decided to wait until one. If she was not at the Park, then he would call her.

Corey didn't seem to be the type to miss work either, but Moonbeam wasn't sure. He had insisted on being treated the same as any Peddler, but he wasn't like them. Perhaps he needed some time to get accustomed to his new place. While Moonbeam contemplated the situation, he challenged the computer to a game of backgammon.

Spotting Sunshine just as she had entered the workhouse, Corey ran to catch up with her, with his makeshift football tucked under his arm. The running didn't make the pounding in his head feel any better. They arrived at the top floor, spotting Bear and Moonbeam by the windows facing the ocean. They made their way over.

"Hi," Sunshine said, startling Moonbeam. "We figured you'd be up here when we didn't see you outside."

Moonbeam and Bear exchanged curious glances while Sunshine and Corey took up monocycles behind them.

"I just love the view from up here," Corey said while staring out at the endless horizon of water. He brought his speed up to forty kilometers per hour, then looked out toward the Dome shining like a silver sphere in the midst of the ocean. Strangely enough, Corey didn't feel the same sense of longing toward Havanna as he had yesterday. He was starting to view even the attitudes of the Havannians as shallow and selfish. They took everything for granted that these hard-working Peddlers paid to obtain.

They never thought to help one another in the ways the Peddlers did. He could never see Lionel working at Medicure, or his father slinging beer. They would say, "I'm a Havannian. I don't have to work." *Why should these hardworking Peddlers waste their time pedaling electricity for Havanna? The Havannians should pedal for their own electricity.* Corey was starting to wonder if maybe in an indirect way he was sent here to help the Peddlers. They couldn't see how the Havannians took advantage of them every day. They didn't receive the same benefits from BUDDY as the Dome did. It wasn't fair.

"Do you realize that thousands of people in the Dome are benefiting from the work that we're doing right now?"

Sunshine looked over at Corey. "How are they benefiting?" she asked.

"They're living a life of luxury while we pedal our asses off. They don't give a shit about us. Why should we give a shit about them?" Corey's face was set in an angry scowl.

Sunshine couldn't believe Corey's attitude. The whole point was to work hard now so they could retire to the Domed City of Dusting. "Corey, I think you're being unreasonable. How do you know what they think, anyway?"

"Corey…" Moonbeam said cautiously.

"Alright, alright. It just pisses me off. I think people should learn the truth whether they like it or not. I don't know how you two can keep pedaling so diligently with what you know."

"Know what?" asked Sunshine.

"What else are we supposed to do?" Moonbeam questioned.

"Know what?" repeated Sunshine.

"Stop pedaling," Corey suggested. Sunshine stopped pedaling while the men continued.

"We went over this the other day, Corey. It just wouldn't work," Bear added. "There's nothing we can do."

"Went over what?" insisted Sunshine.

"Bollocks," Corey yelled. A few people glanced over in their direction. He lowered his voice. "If you don't help yourselves, no one else is going to. You're being taken advantage of and you don't even realize it."

"Great!" Moonbeam said sarcastically. "If we don't pedal, the only place it will leave us is out in the cold."

"Like you guys are leaving me in the cold? You have me totally lost with this conversation," stated Sunshine. "What the hell are you talking about? Who is taking advantage of us? What does it have to do with Dusting?"

"Now look what you've started, Corey," sighed Moonbeam.

"I think she has as much right to know as anyone."

"Will you guys stop talking over me and speak to me?" demanded Sunshine.

"There's a lot of things you don't know about Corey. Things that we all took a vow to keep secret." Moonbeam directed his last sentence to Corey with reproach in his eyes.

"You're right. I'm sorry. I should never have brought it up in front of Sunshine." Corey went back to silently staring out the windows while he pedaled. He decided he would try to complete Cobra's gymnastic exam. It would do him good to take his mind off Havanna.

"Is this what you've been hiding from me?" Sunshine asked.

"Yes," replied Moonbeam. "I'm sorry, Sunshine, but we can't break our vow. You'll just have to trust us, and I promise you'll be the first one to know when the time comes. Can we count on you to keep this quiet?"

"I don't even know what it is I'm supposed to keep quiet about." Sunshine resumed pedaling, inwardly pouting.

"Good." Moonbeam had been afraid Corey had said too much.

Sunshine tried to recall what they had been talking about. Corey must have learned something about Dusting while he was in the C Zone. What could he know that would make people want to stop pedaling? Surely if they stopped pedaling, they would die. They wouldn't have food, water, or electricity. She would wait until she could talk to Corey alone, then she'd ask him about it.

Lucky filled up the order counter with the tray of burgers, fries, hot dogs, and the chicken fingers that he had brought up from the back. The supplies were kept well stocked during meal rushes. During off-hours, the meals were ordered up on demand. The hospital had its own code for ordering food for patients. The hospital staff was still required to order under their own tattoo codes.

Once the tray was full, Lucky checked his watch. It was ten forty-five. He had just enough time to collect Corey's suit, he thought, as he passed by Holly collecting trays from the tables. Yesterday had been a nice change in pediatrics without Holly's presence.

He had been working with Cliff, a man in his early forties, who was very gentle and caring with the children. Lucky enjoyed working with him, as he was not only co-operative and helpful, but he would also often invite Lucky back to his place after work. Yesterday had proved to be no exception.

Lucky entered the laundry room just as his load in the dryer stopped. He pulled Corey's suit from it, laying it over the pressing board. He folded the bedsheets that had been in the dryer and pulled out the rest of Corey's clothes, placing them atop the suit.

He opened the washer, pulled out sheets, and stuffed them into the dryer. Holly poked her head in.

"There's a vidcall for you. It's Cliff. I think he wants to trade shifts with you tomorrow."

"I'll be there in a minute. I just want to finish up here."

"I didn't walk all this way for nothing. Go get your vidcall. I'll finish doing that."

He hurried from the laundry room to the nurses' station. Cliff's face was visible on the vidscreen. Lucky accessed the audio. "Hi, Cliff, what's up?"

"Nothing much. I hope I'm not disturbing you. I wanted to catch you before you went off shift."

"I can't talk too long. I have a few more things I have to do before I'm done."

"I was just wondering if you'd like to come over tonight for supper. I bought some fresh tomatoes today."

"Sure, I'd love to. I'll see you later." Lucky disconnected the line and hurried back to the laundry room. He breathed a big sigh of relief when he returned and found that Holly had not discovered the white suit. He had no idea how he would explain its existence. He pressed the suit quickly, then wrapped it in a linen sheet, along with Corey's shirt and underwear.

Lucky stopped by Corey's place on his way home. He entered the apartment with the suit over his arm and removed the hospital sheet. He hung the suit in the closet next to the Green-Level jumpsuits. The rest he placed on the shelf overhead.

At noon, Corey turned off his monocycle and hopped down. "Let's go, guys," he called to his friends. They quickly stopped pedaling and followed him out.

"Why are we leaving so early?" Sunshine asked while trying to catch up to Corey.

"Don't you want to eat before we play?" he asked.

"Why don't we go to The Nest? It's not far from here," suggested Moonbeam.

"I don't know. Why don't we?" teased Corey.

Leaving the boardwalk, they headed for The Nest on the corner of Second Avenue. They entered the old colonial-style structure just as the next show of female dancers was starting.

They sat at a table by the door, as the bar was pretty full with the lunch hour crowd. A server took their order once they sat down. Sunshine insisted on paying for Corey's lunch to celebrate.

Earlier, Corey had whizzed through the final exam for his gymnastics degree. It had been surprisingly easy. The years he had spent learning sports and doing exercises made this exam seem like child's play.

After lunch, they left The Nest for the Park. The sun was shining brightly overhead as they walked the two blocks to the monorail. Corey was in a great mood. His spirits were high from scoring extremely well on his exam and being in the company of good friends. His head had stopped pounding, his mood had improved, and he loved the warmth of the sun on his skin. People no longer looked at him strangely as he walked down the street.

They entered the first monorail that pulled in. Corey chased Sunshine around the monorail car, trying to pull her hair. Sunshine laughed and squealed, playfully fighting off Corey. Moonbeam and Bear sat and laughed at Corey's crazy antics.

They were all in a festive mood by the time they reached their destination. The Park was in a flurry of activity. Children ran around the playground, swinging and climbing on the monkey bars while their mothers strolled with their babies in carriages up and down the walkway. Teenagers rolled around the grass, tickling and play fighting, and lovers walked arm in arm or sat under the elm trees. People lay on the beach taking in the sun, while children swam in the water by the shoreline.

As they approached the gardens, Corey was awed by the food growing out of the ground. Only the Red-Levels could be seen in the garden pulling weeds or picking food. He watched them for a while before spotting some flowers growing wild. Corey ran over to the little yellow flowers, bending to pick them. He inhaled the scent, noticing that they were not as aromatic as the flowers he had received from the football tournament. Corey gathered some in his hand to present to Sunshine.

He held the flowers behind his back as he approached his friends. He stood in front of Sunshine, then extended his hand. "These are for you," he said, proudly.

"Corey... how sweet," she said, "... dandelions." His friends broke into laughter. Corey laughed along with them.

By one-fifteen, Lucky, Chip, Limpy, and Sandpebble had joined them in the center of the Park. They spent a few moments getting acquainted before Corey asked them all to sit. They settled themselves on the grass while Corey stood.

"It seems we're short one guy," he stated. "We need four guys on each team."

Moonbeam quickly surveyed the group. "It's alright. There are eight of us."

"Football is a rough game; too rough for women." *It was unheard of for a woman to play football*, Corey thought. Aloud, he said, "They're just too delicate."

Sunshine was on her feet, her face flushed with anger. "How dare you patronize me?" she yelled. "I'm just as capable as anyone here. You think I'm delicate? I'll show you delicate!" Sunshine leaped on Corey, bringing him down hard.

Corey was taken by surprise. Sunshine now sat on him, pounding her fists against his chest. He rolled her over in one swift movement, pinning her on her back.

"Let go of me, you bastard," she hissed.

Corey started to laugh. "Well... you certainly talk like a football player." He pulled Sunshine to her feet. "Okay, you can play opposite Limpy."

Once she had settled down on the grass again, Corey described the object of the game. He went over the rules and set boundaries. "This is not a real football, of course, but it will have to do," he said, holding up the inner tube. "Sandpebble, Chip, Limpy, and I will play against Bear, Moonbeam, Lucky, and Sunshine. The first thing we have to do, though, is warm-up exercises."

Corey went through some basic exercises with them, helping them to stretch their muscles. Sunshine and Limpy were the first two to show signs of fatigue while doing jumping jacks. Corey would follow the strenuous exercises with stretching.

"I thought this was supposed to be fun," said Lucky, breathing heavily.

Corey gave them a five-minute rest before starting the game. While the others were resting, Corey took Moonbeam aside to teach him how to throw the ball. Once he had gotten the hang of it, Corey called them together to start the game.

The first half of the game was disastrous, in Corey's eyes. Everyone fumbled the ball in their attempts to catch it. They all alternated positions until they found one that was suitable for them. Limpy was now the quarterback for Corey's team, as he couldn't run well.

Moonbeam had collided with Lucky once as they both tried to catch the ball at the same time. Sunshine jumped on Sandpebble's back in an attempt to bring him down, and he piggy-backed her half the length of the field to score the first touchdown of the game. While Moonbeam was quarterback, he side-stepped Limpy, running in the first touchdown for his team. The Peddlers were having fun, laughing and horsing around.

Although Corey was fiercely competitive, he kept his anger and frustration in check. He couldn't expect them to be professionals in their first game. The whole point was for them to have fun, which was exactly what they were doing.

By this time, a crowd had gathered to watch. The crowd cheered and hollered, even though they didn't know the rules of the game.

Limpy threw the ball to Chip, who fumbled it off his chest. Corey caught the fumble not a foot from Chip when Bear came at them and took them both down. Corey and Bear fell on top of the little guy. They got up and pulled Chip to his feet. Corey was afraid they may have hurt him.

"I just love this game!" Chip exclaimed, while running back to the line of scrimmage. Bear gave Corey a shrug before joining his team. A man in a Black-Level jumpsuit approached the huddle of Moonbeam's team.

"Hi, I was just wondering if I can join the game?"

"I don't think there's room for any more," replied Moonbeam. He shot a quick look at Sunshine. She had gone suddenly pale, thinking she was no longer needed. "I'll ask my friend." Moonbeam walked over to Corey and explained the situation.

Corey walked over to the stocky young man who now stood in their huddle. Corey looked from the stranger to Sunshine then back to the stranger. "I'm sorry, but we have all the people we need for this game. Maybe another time, okay?"

"Sure thing. I just thought I'd ask."

Sunshine smiled from ear to ear as the man left the field.

Corey managed to score another touchdown for his team before they quit for a break. Through playing together, they forged a bond that went beyond the ties of work. It strengthened the existing friendships and connected them to the others they had just met today.

Sandpebble felt as though a dam inside of him had burst. He was no longer guarded and defensive as he had always been with people. His fear of rejection had kept him sheltered for too long. He felt freer today than he had felt in all his life.

Bear looked at the odd assortment of people that Corey had successfully brought together. It reminded him of his nights in the Dojo, except this was more fun. The same feeling was there, though—the feeling of pulling together for one sole purpose. Like karate, even if you lost, you still won.

Limpy surveyed the young people around him, enjoying their spunk and enthusiasm. He had been afraid he would not be able to keep up. Since he had hurt his leg, he stayed away from strenuous activities. He realized from playing ball today that he was not as disabled as he thought he was. This knowledge filled his soul with renewed hope. No longer would he be the permanent fixture sitting on the sofa, wallowing in self-pity. From now on, he was going to live again.

Sunshine stretched out on the grass, feeling happy. Through her spat with Corey earlier, she realized she had never felt truly accepted by men as an equal. It dawned on her that they all accepted her for who she was. It was just her own insecurities that she needed to face.

Lucky was glad Corey had insisted they play football. He had no regrets about trading shifts with Cliff. He wondered if he should cancel his supper with him tonight. Seeing Chip again stirred up a lot of fond memories. He couldn't remember now why he and Chip ever broke up. They had been so happy together. Chip didn't seem to be too serious with Limpy, so maybe he wouldn't mind rekindling an old spark.

Moonbeam was surprised by how good he felt now that he had given up his illusions about Sunshine. He felt as though the weight of the world had been lifted from his shoulders. He knew he should have been mad at Corey for stealing Sunshine's heart, but instead, he felt grateful. *It's time for me to get on with my life*, he thought. *No more chasing rainbows.* In a strange way, he now felt more comfortable with Sunshine, like a big brother.

Chip was having the time of his life. He hadn't noticed when his life had become stagnant and boring. It wasn't until Corey had come over to his place a few days ago that he perceived how out of touch he had become. He had fallen out of touch with himself, his friends, his hobbies, and even his dreams. *It's never too late to set things straight*, he thought. His eyes strayed toward Lucky.

Corey sat back, studying his array of new friends. He had grown quite fond of the Peddler people. He knew he would always feel that subtle difference between them. After all, he was a Havannian. It became clear that this attitude was what he most hated about himself. How was it he could not shed the deceptions of the past? Was he as much a victim of his upbringing as these people were? Corey vowed to try harder to accept his faults and strive to change them. He knew he could start by trying to be less competitive.

"Halftime is over," Corey said, jumping to his feet. "Let's get this show on the road."

They continued with their game. This half of the game went smoothly, as they improved with experience. The crowds that had watched the first half had stayed around to see them play again. They cheered and applauded as Chip made his first touchdown of the game. This brought the score up, fifteen to five for Corey's team. Moonbeam threw the ball to Sunshine. It bounced off her chest and landed on the ground.

"Okay, we're going to go for the same move," Moonbeam said once they were back in their huddle. "They'll never expect us to use the same move twice. Bear and Lucky, I want you to swing to the left. I'll fake the pass, then pop it into Sunshine's direction."

"Maybe you shouldn't," Sunshine spoke up. "What if I drop it again?"

"You won't. I know you won't," assured Moonbeam. "You almost had it last time. Just hang on to it. You'll already be behind the line, so all you have to do is catch it."

They broke out of their huddle. Corey took off toward Bear when Moonbeam faked the ball left, leaving Sunshine uncovered. Moonbeam then threw it to Sunshine just as she turned around. When Sunshine opened her eyes, the ball sat in the crook of her arm. Cheers and squeals could be heard from the crowd. Bear scooped Sunshine up onto his shoulders, carrying her back to the huddle.

The next time Moonbeam's team had the ball, he passed it to Bear. Bear caught the ball, tucked it under his arm, and ran screaming like a madman down the field. No one bothered to get in his way. Fun was fun, but that would have been suicide.

The score was now fifteen all. In their fatigue, they agreed that the next touchdown would be the last. Corey's team made their way down the field. On their last down, in his eagerness to win the game, Limpy overthrew the ball. Corey sprung into a somersault, using his momentum to fly through the air. With his arms straight out in front of him, he caught the ball just over the goal line. Moonbeam threw his arms up in the air in a helpless gesture while Lucky rolled his eyes.

"Yahoo!" Limpy yelled. He threw his arms around Chip and laughed. The score ended twenty to fifteen for Corey's team. The surrounding crowds applauded, then moved on to other things. The eight of them stood there hot, tired, dusty, and completely happy. Sunshine's hair was disheveled, and one sleeve hung by a few threads on Chip's jumpsuit. They broke into laughter as they collapsed on the grass.

"Let's go for a swim," suggested Lucky.

"Last one there is in despair," Moonbeam called over his shoulder as he sprinted for the water.

They all took off running for the beach. Corey hung back with Limpy, who had run enough for one day. Moonbeam was the first to reach the beach. He dropped his jumpsuit and dove butt naked into the shallow waters. Everyone else followed suit. When Corey reached the beach, his friends were already in the water, splashing and having fun. Corey noticed the heap of jumpsuits on the sand by his feet. He laughed and shook his head.

"Hasn't anyone heard of bathing suits?" Limpy gave him a strange look as he also removed his jumpsuit. Corey noticed that none of the other Peddlers on the beach wore their jumpsuits either. Corey chuckled and dropped his suit.

After their swim, they dressed back into their jumpsuits. It was bright and warm in the late-afternoon sun, so they started to walk back into town. By the time they reached the end of the Park, Limpy and Chip decided to take the monorail home. Limpy had done more walking and running today than he had in a while. They bid their new and old friends farewell, then took the monorail heading west. The rest of them walked arm in arm down the street, singing and dodging potholes. Corey didn't know the words to their songs, but he enjoyed the catchy tunes.

"There's music in my head crying out to be heard. I don't know how to say it, it won't come out in words..." they sang. When they reached Fourteenth Avenue, Sunshine called out for everyone to stop.

"I have to get home before Rose disowns me. I've had a wonderful time, Corey." Sunshine gave Corey a big hug.

"Hey! Where's mine?" Moonbeam pouted.

"It's right here, silly," she said, hugging Moonbeam. "I might as well hug everyone while I'm at it." Bear encircled her in his arms, lifting her from her feet with his squeeze.

"I hope you're not going to be a stranger," she said to Sandpebble while extending her hand.

"No way!" Sandpebble ignored the hand and scooped her up in his arms.

"I'm not even going to talk to you," she teased Lucky.

"Come here," he said. He pulled her close to him while gyrating his hips. Sunshine slapped him playfully as the other guys laughed. They were still chuckling after Sunshine left, and continued on their way.

They noticed many people on the streets enjoying the beautiful day. Children were playing hopscotch and adults stood or sat in front of their apartments, talking with their neighbors.

Suddenly it seemed to Corey that everything stood still. The children stopped playing and the adults stopped talking. There was a moment of quiet, like the calm before the storm. Then everyone was running in all directions. Mothers were calling for their children and people were ducking into their apartments. Corey could hear a rumble like the sound of thunder. He looked to the skies. They were as clear and as bright as they were a moment ago.

"Let's go, Corey," Bear yelled, as he yanked Corey by the sleeve. Corey stood immobilized. He couldn't understand what was happening. His friends ran for the Police Station across the street. In the distance, he could see a dust cloud heading his way.

As it grew closer, Corey could see men in silver suits riding on huge beasts. He stood there in awe of the power and beauty of the horses. These must be the Mensis soldiers that he had heard about. He had never seen anything so intimidating in his life. Sandpebble ran back out to grab Corey. One of the soldiers pointed in their direction.

"Come on, Corey," Sandpebble urged. As the soldiers closed in on them, Sandpebble made a break for the station.

Russ Fletcher spotted a man with red hair. They had already checked Sandpebble's place of residence but to no avail. All they knew was that he wore a black uniform and had red hair. It was like looking for a needle in a haystack when they were sent to look for one particular person. He didn't know why they wanted this man, but his instructions were to bring him back alive. He knew he stood a good chance for promotion if he was successful in his mission.

"Look over there," he yelled. He pointed to the man with the red hair. Russ spurred his horse on while readying the net. *Stupid fool*, he thought, as he saw the man dash across the street. "You're mine."

Russ brought the net down over Sandpebble while halting his horse. He jumped down and fastened the net around him.

"What is your name?" demanded Russ.

"Sandpebble," he said, shakily.

"We've got him," Russ called out to the other soldiers who had caught up to him. He knocked Sandpebble out with a punch to the head. He just might get that promotion after all.

Corey watched the red and silver-clad soldier trap Sandpebble in the net. He wore an armor plate on his chest and an armored helmet on his head. Two crescents of steel extended out over his cheeks. What right did these men have to just take people away? The right of might? What did they want with Sandpebble? Where were they taking him? How come no one was stopping them?

"Put that man down!" Corey ordered. Russ had just finished hoisting Sandpebble over the back of his horse. He quickly mounted his horse, then turned to stare down at Corey.

"What's it to you, Peddler?" he spat.

"I said, put him down." Corey didn't like the way the soldier talked down to him. Russ laughed. He steadied his horse with the reins in one hand and pulled out his revolver with the other. He aimed the barrel straight at him. Corey had never seen a gun before, so was not frightened by the soldier's actions.

"I should shoot you right where you stand." Russ switched off the safety and cocked the gun.

"How do you sleep at night?" asked Corey.

"What?" Russ screwed up his face. His coal-black eyes clouded in confusion.

"How can you live with yourself when you treat people the way you do? Don't you have a conscience?"

"Oh, for fuck's sake!" Russ rolled his eyes. "Let's get out of here," he called over his shoulder. Russ fired a shot in the air and rode off with Sandpebble slung over the back of his horse. The horses' hooves on the pavement were the only sounds as they headed out through the Park.

Moonbeam, Bear, and Lucky joined Corey back on the street.

"Are you crazy?" scolded Lucky. "They could have killed you." They watched as the dust cloud receded.

"Some help you guys were, running away like cowards." Corey turned to Bear. "You're a police officer. Why didn't you stop them?"

"They are outside my jurisdiction, and I'm not that fond of death," Bear retorted.

"But you're fond of watching your friends being taken away? I can't believe no one did anything!"

"What could we do? They have guns," Moonbeam stated.

"We warned you that they take people away," Lucky added.

"They only take them away because you let them." Corey was angry with the injustice of the situation. It seemed to him that the Peddlers were no better than the Havannians. Neither of them had the guts to change things.

"Sandpebble wouldn't have been taken if you'd only had the sense to take shelter. He wouldn't have been standing in the middle of the street like an open target," argued Lucky.

"Bollocks!" Corey yelled. "They were looking specifically for him, by name."

"Why would they be looking for Sandpebble?" asked Bear. "He's just a Black-Level, and he's not even on the Undesirable list."

"It doesn't matter," Moonbeam said, sadly. "There's nothing we can do for him now."

"Yes, there is. We could go after him," Corey suggested. "That many horses should leave an easy trail to follow."

Lucky let out a nervous laugh. "You can't be serious!"

"I'm very serious, and I'll go with or without you." Corey looked at each one of his friends. They avoided eye contact with him. "Fine! I don't need cowards with me, anyway." Corey stormed off toward his apartment. He was already thinking of the provisions he would need.

Sunshine walked up the two flights of stairs to the apartment she shared with Rose. She was in a great mood from her day in the Park. She wondered if Rose would be in since she was not normally home this early. She opened the door and stepped into a quiet apartment.

Rose must be out at the Church, she thought. She walked into the living room and pulled up the blinds. The sunlight flooded in, and she stood in the warmth of the rays, looking out toward the street to watch the children play hopscotch.

Turning from the window, she headed for the kitchen. Just then she heard noises coming from the bedroom. She realized Rose was home after all, and probably singing to herself. She walked down the hall, threw open the bedroom door, and found Rose in bed with another woman. Too shocked and angry to speak, Sunshine slammed the door and headed out of the apartment. She ran down the stairs while tears streamed down her face. How long had this been going on? Sunshine felt anger and betrayal urging her faster down the stairs. Once on the street, she wasn't sure where to go or what to do. She found herself heading downtown in the direction of Corey's place.

Sunshine knocked on Corey's door. She didn't want to just walk in and discover that he wasn't alone. She quickly wiped the tears from her face as she stood there waiting for Corey to answer.

After Corey had stormed off and Lucky left for his dinner date, Moonbeam and Bear headed to the Twilight Bar for supper. They sat at a quiet table in the back, silently chewing on their burgers and drinking their wine.

"I feel like hell!" Moonbeam declared. He was feeling guilty for not offering to accompany Corey on his journey to Mensis. It wasn't that he didn't like Sandpebble, but it was just too risky. He wished he had half the courage that Corey had.

"I know what you mean. I really feel like I could use a good workout at the Dojo. Maybe it'll help me to channel some of this anger I'm feeling." Bear was still angry at Corey for calling him a coward. Wasn't he the one who came to Corey's rescue on the beach Saturday night? A coward would have stood by and watched or run away… just as he ran away when the Mensis took Sandpebble. Bear's heart felt heavy. *Corey was right*, Bear thought, *I was a coward.*

"I was thinking more along the lines of getting completely inebriated and falling into the arms of a beautiful woman."

"Suit yourself, but I need something more physical," Bear commented dryly. He finished the last of his wine, then pushed his plate away. Moonbeam felt that familiar pang of guilt, as he always did when he felt he let someone down.

"Alright! I'll go with you. God knows I don't deserve a beautiful woman right now."

They dropped their paper plates and plastic cups in the garbage compactor before heading out. They walked the three blocks to the Dojo, as there was no monorail in sight.

Corey came home and wrote out a list of the things he would need. He was searching for them when he heard a knock on the door. He figured it was probably the guys coming back to join him in his quest for Sandpebble. He dropped what he was doing and headed for the door.

"Hi," Sunshine said, as Corey opened the door. "Can I come in?" He stepped aside to allow her to pass. He was surprised to see Sunshine instead of one of the guys.

"Sure." He closed the door behind her. He looked closely at her and noticed she had been crying.

"So, you know," Corey remarked. He didn't expect that word of Sandpebble's abduction would get around so fast.

"Yes, but how did you know?" *Could it be possible that everyone knew what was going on but her? Are we always the last ones to see the illusions in our lives?*

"I was there when it happened." It dawned on Sunshine that they must be speaking of different things. Corey had been with her all day.

"I was thinking about what happened with Rose. Is that what you were talking about?"

"No." He motioned for Sunshine to have a seat on the sofa. "The Mensis soldiers have taken Sandpebble away."

"Oh my God!" Sunshine crossed herself. "I don't know how much bad news I can handle in one day."

"Why? What else has happened?" Corey leaned forward in his chair.

"It's... it's..." Sunshine couldn't hold back any longer and burst into tears. Her body shook up and down as she cried. Corey sat on the sofa next to her and placed an arm around her shoulders. Sunshine leaned into him, letting out all the grief in her heart.

"Shh... it'll be alright," he soothed while stroking her hair. Her sobs subsided enough for her to speak.

"I found Rose in bed with another woman." He had never encountered a situation like this before and wasn't sure what to say, so he remained silent.

"It's funny, you know because I was thinking of leaving her. I really should be glad this happened, but I just feel so confused. I feel she has betrayed my love, and yet... I don't even feel like I love her anymore. Does this make any sense to you?"

"The question is, does this make any sense to you?" Corey walked to the kitchen to get Sunshine a tissue. She took it and blew her nose.

"You know what makes me mad?" Sunshine continued. "Rose used to get angry every time I even mentioned someone else. She was jealous of my friends even though they were male. She used to make me feel guilty when I went out with them, and I wasn't even doing anything wrong."

"Jealous feelings are often inspired by feelings of guilt or insecurity. Perhaps she would get angry at you to divert attention from herself. Who was it that said that those who accuse others of something are generally guilty of it themselves?"

She had been so blind. All the guilt trips Rose had laid on her were just covering her own indiscretions. "Maybe you're right. I don't know anymore. The only thing I have to worry about now is a place to stay."

"Well, don't worry, then. You can stay here for the time being. I won't be using this apartment for a while, so you might as well live here."

Sunshine thought for a moment that Corey wanted her to move in with him. She couldn't think of why Corey wouldn't be using his place unless he was moving in with someone else. "Where are you going to be staying?"

"I don't know. I'm going to look for Sandpebble."

"Oh no, Corey! You can't do that! The land beyond Peddlers is forbidden. If the soldiers catch you there, they'll kill you."

Corey figured if the Peddlers were too scared to venture into the forbidden territory, then it must hold some secrets.

"I can't just sit here and pretend nothing is wrong. They took away a friend of ours today. Doesn't that mean anything to you?"

"Sure it does! This news saddens me, but I'm not going to run off and try to save the world."

"I'm not trying to save the world, just one friend." Corey walked into the kitchen where he had placed the items on his list. Sunshine followed him in.

"What are you doing?" she asked.

"I'm collecting some things together that I think I may need." On the table, Corey had placed a few candles, a box of wooden matches, a large kitchen knife, and a blanket. He would have to pick up some food on his way out. Corey had planned to leave in the morning but decided to leave tonight since Sunshine needed a place to stay. "All I need is a way to carry all this stuff."

"Why don't you use your backpack?" suggested Sunshine. "You do have a backpack, don't you?"

"I'm not sure."

She walked to Corey's bedroom and pulled open his closet. On the top shelf sat a dark-blue backpack. She pulled the pack from the shelf, not even noticing the white suit that hung in front of her.

"Here," she declared triumphantly, holding the pack out to Corey. He started to fill it with the items from the table. When he was done, he closed it up. "I still can't believe you're actually going to do this."

"Believe it," Corey said while pulling the pack on. "Do you have any trading chips with you?"

Sunshine unzipped her pocket and came out with a handful of chips. "This is all I have."

"Can I trade you the chips for my credits?"

"No, you can't. I'll give you the chips as payment for the use of your apartment." Sunshine placed the chips in Corey's hand. He slipped them into his pocket.

"You're a doll." He gave Sunshine a big hug and headed out the door.

"Take care, Corey," Sunshine said, as a tear rolled down her face. Her whole world was falling apart in the blink of an eye, and she had no idea if she'd ever see him again.

Corey walked the two blocks to the Trade Center. While he was passing the Twilight Bar, he noticed an unkempt, Black-Level Peddler woman wearing dark glasses and holding a walking cane. Her hair was a tangled nest of brown and gray, and her jumpsuit was wrinkled and stained. She had a cup in front of her and was begging for trading chips. Corey dug into his pocket and pulled out a few chips. He dropped them into the cup.

"Bless you," came the quiet voice, as her eyes tried to find her benefactor.

"You're welcome," replied Corey. "What's your name?"

"Rain. Rain, Rain, always in pain. You talk funny."

Corey chuckled. "I suppose I do."

"I'm blind, you know," stated Rain.

"Yes, I gathered that," replied Corey, with a smile.

"Sorry, I don't talk much. I mean, no one talks to me. Have a nice day."

"You too, Rain." Corey started to move on.

"The one you seek is fine, but he's not the one you'll find," Rain prophesied.

"Excuse me?" Corey turned back. "What did you say?"

"I see. I see things others don't. Many adventures for you. Goodbye."

Corey shook his head and carried on. He was pleased to see that there were no lineups at the Trade Center. He approached the first barterer at the counter and bought as much fresh food as he could with the remainder of his trading chips. The barterer was helpful in suggesting berries, tomatoes, and carrots. Corey also purchased a large container of fresh water. He had difficulty closing his pack once all the food was inside. He thanked the barterer for his help and headed out, taking the Ninth Avenue monorail to the Park.

Crossing over the bridge that led into the Park, Corey noticed how dark it had become. Clouds had moved in to block out the light of the moon. He stumbled once or twice while making his way through.

He followed the shoreline to the northernmost tip of the beach. He could just see the outline of the fence that surrounded Peddlers. Short of stepping through the water, there was no way through the fence. At least not that he could see in the dark. Corey decided the best thing for him to do was to wait until morning when he could see where he was going.

The conversation he had had with Sunshine came back to him. He had told her he wasn't trying to save the world, only one friend. In reality, he would prefer to be saving everyone from the control of BUDDY. He felt utterly useless to help those he loved in the Dome, but perhaps, as compensation, he could save just one new friend.

Dropping his backpack on the ground, Corey removed his blanket, spread it out in the sand, and ate a handful of berries. He had never slept outside under the stars before. He was actually quite excited about experiencing it. He removed his shoes and pulled his blanket around him. The sky was covered in thick gray clouds, and he realized he couldn't see any stars. His excitement soon dissipated, and he grew tired. He put his food away and fell into a restless sleep.

It was late by the time Bear and Moonbeam left the Dojo. Their session in karate had bolstered their spirits.

"You're right, Bear. I feel much better now."

"Are you heading home right away?" asked Bear.

"I was thinking of heading over to Corey's place. I've been thinking about what he said, and I know he's right. I should have offered to go with him. I want to drop by and see if it's not too late. What are you going to do?"

"Hell! Someone has to babysit you guys." Bear gave Moonbeam a brotherly hug before they made their way to Corey's apartment. They knocked and walked in, surprised to see Sunshine sitting on the sofa. She was toying with the inner tube they had used that afternoon. A heap of used tissues sat on the coffee table in front of her.

"Hi," she said, getting up. "What are you doing here?"

"Looking for Corey. What are you doing here?" Moonbeam knew Sunshine liked Corey, but he had not suspected that things had progressed this far.

"Rose and I broke up tonight. I just got off the vidphone with her now. I'll be going by tomorrow to pick up my things."

"Geez! I'm sorry to hear that," Moonbeam sympathized. "It still doesn't explain what you are doing here, though."

"Corey said I could stay here while he was away. Did you know that he's going to look for Sandpebble?"

"Yes. Is he gone already?" asked Moonbeam.

"He left a couple of hours ago."

"Damn the Men, Bear. He could be anywhere by now."

"Will he ever come back?" Sunshine asked, anxiously.

"I don't know." Moonbeam put his arm around Sunshine and pulled her in for a hug. "I don't know."

WILLOWDOWN

All around him was nothing but barren land sparsely covered with sagebrush. Corey walked along the shoreline to avoid getting lost. A couple of hours later, he could see the outlines of a forest. It stood out lush and green in the distance.

The farther Corey got from the shoreline of Peddlers, the lonelier he became. He realized he hadn't seen a single person since he had arrived on the beach last night. He had bypassed the fence this morning by wading hip-deep through the water around it. It was an odd feeling to be out of contact with other people. In Havanna, Corey always had his family and friends around him. He never had to be alone.

Fear rose inside him, sending shivers up his spine and prickling the hairs on the back of his neck. He quickly glanced behind him, as if expecting to find something or someone creeping up on him. Corey broke out in a cold sweat. He had no idea what he was suddenly frightened of, but he knew he had to keep moving. He had to outrun his fear.

Rain started to fall, so Corey sprinted for the woods. He would seek shelter under the trees. By the time he reached the entrance to the woods, he was soaked through to the skin again and panting heavily from exhaustion. The woods provided him with shelter from the rain, but not from the demons that haunted him.

"Son of a Peddler!" Corey exclaimed. Somehow, by speaking aloud, he didn't feel so alone. He forced happy thoughts into his head to drive away the fear. Looking around him, he realized he had never been in a real forest. He stepped off the path and picked his way over and through rocks, bushes, and stones to sit on an old stump of a tree. He was fascinated by the rings in the center of the stump.

That's when he noticed the fresh blueberries on the bush beside him. He picked a handful, then sat again to eat them. It seemed strange to find himself sitting alone, eating fresh food when a week ago he was eating dehydrated food in Havanna. It felt like years since he had been exiled.

His mind drifted to Anne. He wondered what she was doing. Was she thinking of him? Was she happy with Lionel? A stab of pain shot through his heart as he thought of Lionel loving Anne. Corey placed his head in his hands. *What was he doing here,* he wondered? He should be back home with Anne, having children, and playing sports. That was what he was trained to do, not running after lost Peddlers. Corey looked toward the sky through a break in the thick branches overhead.

"What am I doing out here? I'm freezing my butt off… for what? For what?" Corey screamed to the skies. He let his head drop and then got to his feet. There was no point in feeling sorry for himself.

Corey followed the trail leading through the woods. He wasn't sure if it was natural or made by humans. It wasn't straight like the streets were, but it looked like a path. There were footprints in the dirt, but not human prints. Could there be wild animals about? He quickly turned and looked around him. The fear was back again; that nameless trepidation that gripped the back of his neck.

Without a second thought, Corey started running through the forest. Branches grabbed at him as he ran, and strange birds made haunting noises from the trees. Roots in the ground sprung up to trip him. The trees grew larger, threatening to close in on him. He realized he had lost sight of the shoreline completely. The deeper he ran into the woods, the more lost he became. He leaned up against a tree to catch his breath. It wouldn't do him any good to panic. He had to pull his thoughts together so he could think rationally. The first thing he had to do was calm down and realize he was lost. Once this was accomplished, then he could try to figure out a solution.

Taking another deep breath, he held it for a minute as he listened to the sounds around him. He could hear running water. How, he wondered, was it possible when he was nowhere near a water faucet? Corey followed the sounds of the water off to his left.

The forest opened up to a stream of running water crossing his path. Corey stood in disbelief, watching the waves rippling over the rocks in the stream. *This might be the most beautiful thing I've ever seen*, he thought. The stream wasn't very deep, but it was clear and fresh. Kneeling on the bank, he cupped his hands, bringing the cold, clean water to his lips. It was not salty like the ocean water. Corey drank greedily from the stream. Once his thirst was quenched, he stood to survey his new discovery.

Should he follow the stream up or down? Or should he step over and continue forward? He scratched his head absentmindedly while contemplating a decision. Corey remembered his father telling him that it didn't matter what he chose to do, so long as he made a decision. He decided to head upstream.

The underbrush was worse here, causing Corey to step into the stream a few times. He came to a small bridge and decided to cross it and follow the path through the woods, as he could see daylight in the distance. He felt lighter now that he had found his way out of the forest. He whistled as he walked.

Leaving the woods, Corey stepped into a beautiful pasture of flowers. He recognized the flowers as the ones he had received at his football tournament in Havanna. The pasture was covered in the colors of a rainbow. Corey went from flower to flower, smelling the different types.

The land sloped gently up into a hill. Corey climbed to the top of it. His runners were still wet from the stream and the dew from the pasture. His right shoe rubbed up and down over his heel, causing it to blister. The clouds dispersed, allowing the sun to shine down. He turned his face to the sun, enjoying the warmth.

Looking around, he could see the pasture of flowers below him and the woods in the distance. Corey swung around to the left to see there were more trees, and to his right was the ocean, shimmering brightly in the sunshine, but he only saw the town that lay out before him to the north.

"I've found it!" exclaimed Corey.

The town below seemed like an awfully quiet place. He knew he was still quite a distance from it, but he didn't see any movement or signs of life. He started down the hill, leaning slightly back to avoid tumbling forward.

The closer Corey got to the town, the more it dawned on him that it must be empty. At the entrance, a large wooden sign hung down between two posts. "Willowdown," he read. He walked through the town cautiously, alert for any signs of danger. Tumbleweeds rolled down the vacant streets, and old signs creaked in the wind. The modest-sized wood houses were old and falling apart. Corey stopped in the center. He had found a ghost town.

"Tavern," Corey read on the sign over a storefront. He walked in to investigate, pushing through the swinging front doors. The hinges squeaked, echoing loudly in the empty hall. He stood in the doorway to examine the glass-enclosed bar and the big wooden booths along the wall. There was a stage with an old torn net hanging in front of it. His footsteps disturbed the silence as he crossed over the worn-out dance floor. Corey sat on the stool in front of a large… desk? He reached out to touch it. The keys gave way with very little effort to produce a musical note. Corey started to laugh as he continued to press down different keys. The sign on the instrument read "Steinway."

"Thought I heard someone in here." Startled, Corey spun around to see an old man supporting himself on a wooden cane. His hair was completely white, as were his beard and mustache.

His skin was wrinkled, and he wore an old three-piece suit with a stained white shirt. His friendly blue eyes shone young in his face.

Corey had never seen someone so old before. Was it possible for people to grow this old?

"Where did you come from, my son?" asked the old man.

"I was lost in the forest," Corey stammered.

"It's been so long since I've seen a new face." His eyes narrowed, piercing into Corey's. "You wouldn't be running away now, are you?" His voice was strong and gruff.

"No. In fact, I'm not really sure where I am."

"Well, this here is Willowdown. My name is Luther. Luther Saxon, but you can call me Lu."

Corey shook Lu's shaky hand. "My name's Corey."

It was nearing the end of the day as Luther brought Corey back to his house. It was a western-style design in red-painted wood. It was in fairly good condition compared to most of the other houses in town. Inside it was cozy and warm. There was a wood-burning furnace in the center of the room, casting off a tremendous amount of heat. There were no walls separating the bed from the tub, nor the stove from the sofa.

"Have a seat on the couch," Lu instructed. "I'll just be a moment." He took down a copper kettle from the wooden shelf above the kitchen sink. He filled it with water and placed it on the furnace. Luther then lit some candles to lighten the room.

Corey was stifling with the heat. He unzipped his jumpsuit and removed his socks and shoes.

"Sorry about the heat in here," Lu apologized, "but at my age, I need it. My arthritis acts up in the cold."

"No problem. Do you mind if I ask how old you are?"

"I'm eighty-six last March," Luther replied, proudly.

"Eighty-six? I didn't know people lived that long."

Luther looked at Corey and said, "You're not from around here, are you?"

Corey looked at Lu and said, "A week ago…"

Corey could hear pots and pans rattling in the kitchen and smelled coffee perking. He opened his eyes to see Luther cracking some eggs into a frying pan.

"Good morning," Corey called out while sitting up on the sofa. He had slept in his jumpsuit last night. Luther didn't seem to hear him. He walked barefoot over the warm wooden floors. Lu had stoked the fire before starting breakfast. "Good morning," Corey repeated.

"By golly, I can't remember the last time someone wished me a good morning." Luther was scrambling eggs in a pan. "I thought I'd never hear those words again."

"What are you cooking?" It seemed odd to see a man cook. Corey knew Luther didn't have a wife to cook for him, but it seemed odd all the same.

"Eggs, my boy. These ones here are goose eggs. I picked them up a few days ago while I was down by the stream. I've got some coffee on the furnace if you'd like a cup."

"Don't tell me you found the coffee lying around too?" Corey took the mug that Luther offered him and poured himself a cup from the pot.

"Hell, no! I've been eating all the food that people left behind when they went to Peddlers. The coffee you're drinking now is the last jar of coffee grounds in town. It may taste a bit stale, but by golly … coffee's coffee."

Corey leaned up against the kitchen counter watching Luther cook the eggs over the wood-burning stove. He cupped his hands around the steaming mug. "Why did the people leave here to go to Peddlers?"

"After the war, there was a lot of confusion and sickness. They needed food and medical attention. There weren't enough people here who were willing or knowledgeable enough to make it work. I guess they figured they would have it easier in Peddlers." Luther spooned the eggs onto two plates and handed one to Corey.

"Thank you," Corey said, as he sat on the sofa to eat. They were the best eggs he had ever eaten.

"If I'm not mistaken," resumed Luther, "Peddlers was just being built then. The people assumed that they would be able to live in the Dome. Of course, that wasn't possible, because there was no room for all those people. Once it was safe for the Mensis to leave their fallout shelters, they set up a system for the people. They provided them with medical care and food, but knew they couldn't support them fully as they did the Dome."

"So, it's the Mensis who control BUDDY?"

"I don't know who BUDDY is. I do know that they set up the young people and children in the Dome before the war. They were trying to ensure that there would be survivors if things turned bad. That's the way it was told to me as a child." There was something else he had been told about the Dome, but he couldn't seem to remember what it was. Somehow the image he had of the Dome didn't seem to fit with what Corey had said last night.

"So why didn't they let the people out of the Dome after the Waste War?" Corey asked.

"There wasn't a need to. Other people had survived, and they didn't need to integrate more people. Why leave the Dome empty when everything was running so smoothly?"

"What about the lies, the lack of fresh food, and Dusting? Is it fair to leave the people of Havanna living in ignorance?"

"Ahh... these were the same questions I had at your age. Things got pretty bad after the war." The old man entered the living room and took a seat next to Corey.

"I didn't like the way they were handling things back then. I was just a young man, of course, but I remember it well. I never thought it was fair the way they treated the Peddlers. I wanted to change things. I was full of these ideas on how I could make Peddlers a better place. Of course, changes are made from within, not from without. I had a violent argument with Nick Henniger.

He was President at the time. I imagine he's handed down his position to his son, Curtis, by now.

"I guess a young buck like you wouldn't know that sort of thing. Well, like I was saying," the old man continued, "after that argument, I fled for my life. I wandered around for a few days, not knowing where to go or what to do. I didn't want to live in Peddlers, but it did seem to be a more favorable decision than going back to Mensis. That's when I stumbled onto this place.

"I was a lot like you when I was younger, Corey. I was angry about the way things were run. I was probably close to your age when I discovered the truth about Dusting. It was purely by accident too.

"I overheard Nick Henniger tell his son, Curtis, that only the President of Mensis could live and rule for as long as he wanted. They were the only ones with the option to go to Dusting when they felt they were ready. When his son questioned him about why everyone had to retire at fifty, Nick told him that they didn't have a need for old people. He said old people were a burden on the system, so they were incinerated quickly and painlessly. Of course, I confronted Nick right away when I heard this. He wanted to buy me off to keep my mouth shut, but I wouldn't hear of it. I felt the people should know the truth. Nick threatened to kill me if I didn't keep my mouth closed, so I left. As I said, it took me a lot of years to come to grips with my guilt."

Corey listened to the old man speak. He figured the man must have been pretty lonely here all those years with no one to talk to.

"So, I've been here for the last sixty years, living in peace since I've laid my demons to rest."

"Did you ever come up with a solution?" Corey asked.

"Unfortunately, I decided to run away from the problem rather than try to change it. I thought, what could one person do against a whole system? But the people have more power than they know, especially collectively. If all the people decided to stop pedaling, would it all collapse? You bet it would, but it's up to them to make that decision. Changes are made from within, not from without."

Luther took the dishes back to the sink. He pumped a handle up and down to build up pressure in the small water tank he had designed years ago. He turned on the tap and ran some water over the dishes.

"If the whole system went down," Corey mused aloud, "the people would have to stop pedaling."

"Yes," Luther said, as he turned to face Corey. "I've thought of that many times. I was always pretty sure I could create a computer virus that would infect the system, but you don't just walk into Peddlers and ask someone to lend you their computer." The truth of that statement struck them both at the same time and they stared at one another. A small smile started on their faces then blossomed into full-blown laughter.

"So," Corey said when he could speak again, "when would you be ready to leave?"

Bear and Sunshine walked together toward the workhouse from the monorail. They joined Moonbeam and Lucky, who stood waiting by the retaining wall. They greeted each other solemnly. It seemed when Corey left, he took the spark out of their lives. Each one was worried that he would never return.

"I've decided I'm not pedaling anymore," Bear stated. His friends looked at him as though they had never seen him before. It was so unlike him not to pedal. "I've decided it's time to start spending all the credit that I've been accumulating. The pedaling is not going to get me any closer to where I want to be, so why should I pedal every day when we know it's to no avail?"

Moonbeam had explained the truth of Corey's arrival to Sunshine yesterday after she had found Corey's white tuxedo hanging in the closet. She had no need to ask Bear now about foregoing his ambitions of reaching Dusting before retirement.

"I've pedaled enough electricity. Now I want to spend my credit. I have every right to do that." Bear figured if he couldn't go to the Dome to retire, then he would just take some time off here. He could practice his karate and maybe even find a lover for a change. It would do him good to relax.

"Well, I'm not changing my routine," announced Moonbeam.

"You're being awfully quiet today, Lucky. What's your opinion on this?" questioned Sunshine.

Lucky hadn't been following the conversation. He was thinking back to his date with Chip last night. Lucky had been working in surgery when Chip had called and invited him over for supper. It had been more than just a date. They had decided to renew their old romance. There was a subtle difference in their relationship that neither of them could identify. The time they had spent apart had given them more understanding of their previous relationship and the feelings they had for one another.

Lucky had made plans to meet Chip after work today. It was his last night of work this week. Unfortunately, psychiatry was the most exhausting.

"What do I think?" he said, "I think I'm wasting my time standing here when I could be on my monocycle."

"Have fun, guys," Bear said, as he turned around and headed back to the monorail.

They set out a few days later, with Corey carrying supplies in his backpack. Whenever Luther would slow, Corey would call a halt. They traveled along the shoreline, where ten kilometers of white sandy beaches headed south toward Peddlers. Corey kicked off his shoes and shuffled through the fine powdery sand. He collected a few seashells along the way and left his name etched in the sand. The sun was shining brightly overhead, putting them both in a good mood.

It took the better part of the day, but finally, they arrived on the shores of Peddlers. Corey carried Lu through the waters around the electric fence, then placed him down gently.

"Well, this is it! We made it!" exclaimed Corey. The sun was just making its descent when they made their way through the Park. "It might be a good idea to hide your face, Lu." Corey remembered how the Peddlers all stared at him on his first night for just wearing a white suit. Luther raised the hood on his coat to conceal his age.

"I never realized Peddlers was so huge, or I might have come sooner. I thought it was going to be just a bit bigger than Willowdown."

"This is just the east end. Are you up for walking another hour, or should we take the monorail?" Corey looked down at Luther.

"I don't have a tattoo code, so I guess we're walking."

Corey pointed out various buildings as they went along. He had only known Luther for three days but had come to treasure the comradeship that had been built between them. Luther had taken the place of the grandfather that Corey had never known. He realized his own grandfather would have been about fifteen years younger than Luther. *Everyone should know their grandparents*, Corey thought. There didn't seem to be the same communication problems with Luther as he had experienced with his dad.

Somehow the enthusiasm of youth and the wisdom of age went hand in hand. It seemed to Corey that his father, Zane, was energetic and knowledgeable, but maybe too much of both to be understanding. Zane had still felt responsible enough for Corey to want to control his actions.

It took just under an hour for them to walk to Corey's apartment. They found Sunshine and Moonbeam just finishing supper in the kitchen.

"Welcome back, Corey! It's so good to see you. We all missed you terribly." Moonbeam pumped Corey's hand enthusiastically.

Sunshine threw herself into Corey's arms. She was so glad that he was alive and safe. Tears sprung to her eyes, and she was too choked up to speak.

"You found him!" exclaimed Moonbeam, as Luther walked in. "You found Sandpebble!"

Luther threw back his hood just as Corey was saying, "No. This is Luther. Luther Saxon. He knows how to crash this crazy system and stop the Mensis from having any more control over you."

"God willing, I can crash the system. Pleased to meet you." He extended his hand in greeting.

Sunshine and Moonbeam shook Luther's hand tentatively. They had never seen someone so old before. After getting acquainted and ordering some drinks, they all sat in the living room to hear of Corey's adventure.

Lu's enthusiasm for bringing down the computer system was infectious, and before long they were all throwing suggestions into the melting pot of ideas. It was agreed by all that the outcome would be favorable.

Soon it became obvious that Luther was tired, so Moonbeam helped Sunshine pack up her few items. She decided she would move into Sandpebble's place since Corey had failed to find him. They said their goodbyes and left. Corey gave Luther his bed and stretched out on the sofa. He thought about how great it was going to be when the system crashed, the Mensis lost their iron grip, and everyone could just get on living their lives any way they wanted.

Corey met his friends outside of the workhouse first thing in the morning. He greeted Lucky and Chip warmly. Only Bear was missing. He explained Luther's plan to them.

"You're not really going to pedal today, are you?" Lucky looked over at Corey.

"No, and neither are you, for that matter," replied Corey.

"You're absolutely right," stated Lucky. "Why should we pedal when it's all coming down tomorrow?" Chip had come with Lucky to work today. Normally he worked in a different workhouse, but he wanted to be with Lucky and his friends.

"Hey, Corey," called Moonbeam. "I was helping Sunshine move her things into Sandpebble's old place last night. You should see the sort of things he has in there. He's made all kinds of little gizmos and gadgets."

"I'd love to," replied Corey. He turned to Chip and Lucky. "Would you like to come along, too?"

"No, thanks. We have some catching up to do," answered Lucky.

Sunshine linked her arms to Corey's and Moonbeam's. "This way, guys," she said, urging them forward.

They took the monorail to Seventh Street and walked a block to Sunshine's new place. She was starting to feel like a drifter, going from one home to the next.

Once inside the apartment, they surveyed the various items in the rooms. Sandpebble had reconstructed a monocycle inside his apartment. There were wires leaving the monocycle in all directions. Corey followed one of the wires to a lamp that Sandpebble had hooked up to it.

Corey picked up the lamp and closely studied the wiring. He asked Moonbeam to pedal the monocycle. Once Moonbeam had it in motion, the light popped on, scaring Sunshine half out of her wits.

She went into the kitchen, and Moonbeam was shuffling through some papers that had been lying around. Sunshine came back into the living room and gave the guys each a cola.

"Corey, I think you should have a look at this." Moonbeam handed a piece of paper to him. There was a detailed drawing of a generator and instructions on how it could be used with wind or water to produce energy.

Corey moved over to the monocycle and removed the cover off the box that sat where the computer normally did. Inside was a generator with the basic principles of the design. It differed slightly from the one on the diagram that Moonbeam had shown him, but he could see the resemblance. By using magnets and coils, he was able to create a magnetic current. Sandpebble illustrated in his design how to use the natural elements to keep a constant motion going that would spin the turbines attached to the magnetic field.

"This is amazing!" exclaimed Corey. "We can produce our own electricity by using Sandpebble's design."

"I thought we were supposed to be getting away from pedaling," said Moonbeam.

"We will be because we can use the tides of the ocean or the wind to produce energy." Corey wondered why the Peddlers spent so much time pedaling when they could have created a better system for electricity. He realized that with a generator system, they could produce heat as well as light.

Obviously, there had to be several generators located somewhere in Peddlers that would allow them to channel the energy that they pedaled. Perhaps they needed more electricity than the wind or water could produce? Corey wondered if they would be able to produce enough electricity to accommodate their needs.

What would happen to Havanna if they stopped pedaling? Would the Dome collapse, as he had once thought?

Sunshine held up a piece of paper. "I just found Sandpebble's password. Should we access his information and find out how much credit he has?"

"It can't be very much," explained Moonbeam. "He never pedaled in the workhouses. He used to get by on the trading chips he would receive for his inventions."

Sunshine stood in front of the computer and punched in his number and password. Sandpebble's function list appeared on the vidscreen. She accessed his personal information category.

"I don't believe this!" bellowed Sunshine. "Sandpebble has over three million points of credit!"

"What? I have to see this." Moonbeam nudged Sunshine aside to look at the vidscreen. Sandpebble had amassed 3,065,457 points of credit. "I don't believe it! He never even pedaled."

"Well, he did manage to hook up his computer to the monocycle in the living room. Every time he pedaled it probably accumulated more credit for him." Corey also glanced at the vidscreen. "I'll bet this is why the Mensis took him away."

"Most people retire after they have a million points of credit. I still don't understand why Sandpebble never went to Dusting. He certainly had enough points," Sunshine said.

"Sandpebble was never like everyone else. He was more interested in designing inventions than retiring to Dusting." Moonbeam had gotten to know him quite well as a regular customer at the Trade Center.

"Let's just be glad he didn't go to Dusting. At least this way there is the slim chance he might still be alive." Sunshine and Moonbeam looked at Corey. It was the first time anyone had mentioned the fear they all had for their friend.

Luther stood up from the table where he had been busy writing code all day. His back and knee joints were aching from the long hours spent sitting at the table. He usually woke up in the morning feeling pretty good, but as the day progressed, so did his pain. He normally took walks around the town to exercise his muscles, but today he had been busy with his program for the Peddlers' computer system. He was also doubly sore from his long walk to Peddlers yesterday.

It feels good to be back in the land of the living, Lu thought. He had never noticed how lonely he had become. It was like the first sip of water after a long thirst he had never known he had. He had always felt that it was better to live alone and not have to get involved in other people's problems. He realized now that his lack of action was part of the problem

"How's it coming?" asked Corey, walking through the door. He looked at the gibberish Luther was writing.

"By golly, it's been years since I wrote code. I just hope the language hasn't changed. I've noticed that they are using a 440hz frequency for their programs, which is not a beneficial vibration for people. I'm changing it to 432hz, so when the computers are rebooted, it'll change the frequency. I just need to write a few more strings, then I'll have to go over it again with a fine-tooth comb."

"Can we upload it by tomorrow?" Corey asked, hopefully.

"With any luck, my boy. With any luck."

"We found some diagrams at Sandpebble's apartment that will help us create our own electricity so we won't have to pedal."

"That's great, my boy. Now, let me finish this while it's fresh on my mind, then I'll have a look at those designs. First, we change within, then without." He sat back down.

Corey couldn't stop thinking about how easy all this seemed to be. Was there something that he was overlooking? Certainly, if it was this easy, someone would have done it before. All the people he had spoken to about it seemed supportive, and Luther welcomed the change, so what could be wrong? What could he have not taken into consideration?

These questions weighed heavy on Corey's mind as he lay still on his sofa that night. He couldn't shake the feeling that there was something very wrong, even though he couldn't quite put his finger on it.

The last time he had that feeling was just a few days before he was exiled. He knew then that something was wrong, and he sensed it now, too. He would have to be careful and keep his eyes open for any signs of trouble.

Could it just be my fear coming back to me, he pondered? Was he seeing trouble where none existed? Wasn't it his own actions that caused the problems the last time? He knew that was partly true, but there had been more to Havanna than met the eye. Was that what was bothering him? Thinking that there was more here than what he was seeing? He realized he was still bothered by the discovery of the little generator in Sandpebble's monocycle.

It seemed to him that there was something more complicated to the pedaling system than he knew. Corey fell into a fitful sleep, tossing and turning all night. He kept waking up feeling like he'd forgotten something important.

After ordering up egg and sausage muffins for breakfast, which Luther claimed didn't taste anything like eggs or sausage, they were ready to upload the virus into the computer.

"Shouldn't we have let the people know that the computers will be going down?" Corey asked. He was starting to suspect that was where he went wrong.

"They're likely to find out pretty quick," replied Luther. "I can place a message on their computer screens saying, "Damn the Men."

"That's good! What do you think they are going to do?"

"Go home, I imagine." Luther looked up from the keyboard. "Are you ready?"

"Let's do it."

Luther keyed in a few more strokes, then sat back. "There, done! We should know if it worked in about…" Just then the computer went blank, the lights shut off, and they could hear nothing but silence from outside.

Of course, it didn't take long for the Peddlers to realize the situation. For the first time in over fifty years, the power was out, which meant there was no work. A mass parade of people filed out of the workhouses and into the streets. It started slowly, but it gained momentum. The cheers and excitement were palpable, as everyone released years of pent-up suppression and fear. The Peddlers were not concerned about why it had happened, only that they were free from pedaling.

The riots started in the north but spread quickly all over. The windows in the workhouses were the first to be smashed, but the destruction escalated until half a dozen of them were on fire. With the power out, the automated sprinkler systems did not deploy, and the fires raged all night.

Anne Chaffe went to the Medicure building for an early afternoon appointment. She entered the office and registered her code into the waiting list. There wasn't anyone else there, so she knew she wouldn't wait long.

Thoughts of Corey had still not left her mind. Lionel had been displeased with her behavior on the day of their mating ceremony, and he claimed she had disgraced him in the eyes of his peers. Lionel had proven to be a good husband, though, and honored the wedding customs. He was considerate of her decisions and treated her well. They tried to avoid talking about Corey. Anne knew, as much as Lionel denied it, that he missed his friend.

Somehow, they each became the link to Corey that they both missed. Anne could sense Corey in the phrases Lionel used, and Anne questioned life much in the same way Corey had. Anne often wondered how Corey was doing. *Had he adjusted to his life on Peddlers?* She had gone up to the observation deck once to see if she could see him pedaling. There had been so many buildings along the shoreline. She could see thousands of people, but couldn't make out their faces.

The computer called Anne's name just as Betty Brooke, now Betty Jordan, left the office. They passed a polite greeting before Anne entered. She sat down in the Medichair.

"Good afternoon, Anne," said the gentle voice of DOCTOR. "What seems to be the problem?"

"I have not received my menstrual cycle this month."

DOCTOR instructed her to strip from the waist down and place her ankles in the braces. The mechanical arm swung down and started its examination. The braces didn't release their hold this time as they usually did when it was over.

"Congratulations Anne, it seems that you are pregnant."

Anne felt conflicting emotions. She was excited to be having Corey's child, but she feared what her husband would say or do, knowing that their marriage had not yet been consummated. Was it possible that DOCTOR would discover the child didn't belong to Lionel? Could they tell these things by blood samples? What would happen to her if the truth was discovered? Would she be exiled too?

"Since you are the first candidate pregnant from the class of 2169, I am required to ensure you have twin boys. It is too soon at this time to tell whether you are pregnant with a male or a female, but we will proceed with the operation nonetheless."

"What will happen if they turn out to be female?"

"I am sorry, Anne, but the rules are very clear about that. They will be removed, and you will have until June of 2170 to produce a male. Please relax now. I will be putting you to sleep to perform this operation. You will be free to go home later this afternoon."

Before Anne knew what was happening, her body felt as though it were floating. Within seconds, her world faded out.

Corey could see the fires starting all over town. His dream was going up in smoke. Everything he had done was in vain. He had given the people of Peddlers false hope. It was supposed to be a time to rejoice, not riot. Anger rose inside of him, filling him with adrenaline.

"I'll be checkmated if I'm going to sit here while they burn down the city," he told Luther. Corey jumped to his feet and exited his apartment. Lucky and Chip were just opening the apartment building door by the time Corey reached it. "Where's everyone else?" he asked, without preamble.

"We saw Moonbeam, Sunshine, and Bear two blocks from here trying to stop some people from setting the Church on fire."

"Let's go," Corey said, as he started to run. They had to dodge other people running in all directions.

By the time they reached the Church, the crowds had turned away. The Church was certainly an impressive-looking building. He walked up the red brick stairs and pushed open the carved oak doors, which creaked on their hinges. He glanced up at the stained-glass windows before noticing the pews were filled to capacity.

The mass had already begun. Corey joined his friends who stood in the back with a few other late arrivals. A choir of people was singing songs unaccompanied by instruments. Their voices blended beautifully. Corey could distinguish four different octaves. When the song ended, there was a quiet rustling of feet and whispers.

The High Priestess walked to the podium, wearing a red silk robe over her Red-Level jumpsuit. A large heart hung on the wall behind the altar. She stood behind the podium and turned to face the congregation of people.

"I love you," she called out while raising her arms.

"I love you, too," responded the crowd.

"Let us not lower our vibration with the chaos that surrounds us this night," commenced the High Priestess. "Let us choose peace and love for all those who have descended into fear. Hold the light, as we all know that this too shall pass."

Corey and his friends slipped quietly out of the Church as the choir struck up another song. Once back on the street, they headed for a quiet alley to talk.

"I'm sorry. I had no idea. We should have warned everyone."

"Corey, how could you have known?" asked Moonbeam.

"You knew about this?" enquired Bear.

"My friend Luther and I released the computer virus," confessed Corey. "We were trying to free the people…"

Before Corey could finish his sentence, Bear sucker-punched him in the face, knocking him down, then turned on his heel and left. At once, Sunshine was at his side, dabbing his mouth with her sleeve.

"I'll go after him," suggested Moonbeam.

"No, let him go. He needs to calm down," said Corey.

"Come on, Corey. Chip and I will walk you home. I suggest we all go home and stay safe. Besides, I have a terrible headache."

Lucky held out a hand to help Corey rise. They headed back to Corey's place while Sunshine and Moonbeam went the other way.

Anne opened her eyes and looked around the dark office. Only the emergency light shone over the door. She sat up, feeling a little dizzy. What had happened to the power? When had the power gone out? Had DOCTOR had time to operate?

She walked unsteadily out of the office. The streetlights were out and she could hear screams coming from the skytrain. She realized that people had been trapped when the power went down. Some were even attempting to climb down the 120 feet to ground level.

As she neared the Forum, she could hear people gathered inside. She walked in to find hundreds of people sitting in the stands talking with one another. She found her friend Becky and her husband, Peter Farrell, clinging tightly to each other.

"What's happening?" Anne almost felt as though she were dreaming. Her head felt light and everything seemed unreal.

"The power's gone out," exclaimed Becky, "and the Dome is collapsing! We're all going to die!" Becky broke out in tears as Anne stood facing her. She couldn't believe her ears. Was it possible for the Dome to collapse? She had to find Lionel.

"Have you seen Lionel?"

"I haven't seen him in here," said Peter, holding his wife. "You might want to check the Stadium."

Anne ran from the building. If the Dome was collapsing, then they would be susceptible to outside contamination. Without power, DOCTOR wouldn't be able to help them. Anne instinctively held her arms protectively over her stomach. She didn't want to lose her baby… or babies. She now had a piece of the man she loved, and she didn't want to give that up. She had become very fond of Lionel, but she knew in her heart that Corey was her true love.

Lionel had been at the men's club playing chess with James when the power went out. The doors had automatically opened when the computer went down. The emergency lights flicked on as he made his way outside. People were running frantically in all directions.

That's when Lionel looked up and noticed the Dome was deflating. He felt his whole world was crashing in. He followed the crowds to the Stadium building. Where was Anne? Was she safe? Lionel knew that if the Dome collapsed, none of them would be safe. How was this possible?

Lionel met up with Corey's father, Zane, who was sure it had to be a computer malfunction. Lionel thought of all the times Corey had questioned him about who operated the computers and who would fix them if they broke down. Suddenly, Corey's silly questions didn't seem so dumb. He should have listened more closely when Corey gave his theories on how to make Havanna a better place.

Zane found Helena wandering around in the crowd. He pulled her close to him and kissed her cheek. Things had not been going well for Helena since Corey was exiled. She often cried at night and sometimes didn't leave the house for days. Tanya had taken the news hard, too. She had always loved her brother and had not had a chance to say goodbye.

They were not sure how long the power would be out. Zane realized how much they depended on the computers to keep Havanna running. Without BUDDY, they wouldn't have food, or electricity for the skytrains, or even be able to enter their homes.

Zane jumped up on the stage to calm the people down. He suggested that they all just sit and wait for power to be restored. There would be no point in panicking.

Anne entered the Stadium as Zane was leaving the stage. She followed him to where he sat and found her husband with him. Lionel jumped up to hug Anne.

"I was so worried about you, sweetheart," he lamented. Anne sat down next to him and told him where she had been.

"Lionel, I'm... pregnant."

Lionel didn't comprehend the significance of this statement at first. He smiled at her. "That's wonderful! When... I mean how..." Then his face took on an incredulous look. They had never consummated their marriage. Even though Lionel knew what the answer was going to be, he still had to ask. "Who's the father?"

Anne started to cry. "It wasn't supposed to work out this way. He promised we would be married at the ceremony. How could I have known that I would get pregnant?"

Lionel grabbed Anne by the shoulders. "Who's the father?" he demanded.

"Corey... Corey," she sobbed.

Lionel got up and walked away. He had felt guilty about Corey's exile and felt indirectly responsible for Corey's plight. Now he understood the reasons for Corey's behavior. Anne rightfully belonged to him. Lionel cursed himself and all that had happened.

If only they could turn back the clock and start again. He missed Corey's friendship terribly. If he had known that Corey had been exiled, he would have never been so hard on him. He felt bad that their last encounter had been so violent.

Lionel realized that Corey should have married Anne. He had wanted to prove himself a man that day, but all he did was prove what a jerk he was. His decision had caused his best friend to be exiled, and his wife would never love him the way she should. And now she was having Corey's child.

The day after the power went out, a computer operator checked his charts a second time by the light of the emergency backup system. He couldn't believe what he was seeing. His monitors indicated that the collapse of the entire energy grid originated in Peddlers. *There must be a malfunction in the computer system*, he thought. He would have to bring this to the President's attention right away.

The computer operator wiped his sweating palms on his suit pants, then accessed the red vidphone. Never in his life did he think he would need to use the emergency vidphone, which had a direct link to the President's office. The line rang twice.

"President Henniger speaking."

"Sorry to bother you, Mr. President, but I believe I have found the source of the blackout."

"I'll be right there." President Curtis Henniger disconnected the vidphone in his office. "Damn," he muttered while leaving his desk. He walked out of his office, which was dimly lit with candlelight. "Hold my vidcalls," he said to his secretary.

Cindy Chalmers had been working for Curtis for fifteen years. Her mother had been the secretary of Curtis's father, Nick, for the last few years of his reign, and into the first twenty-two years of Curtis's. Cindy took over her mother's position when she retired to Dusting. No one was quite certain how old Cindy was, but they assumed she was in her late thirties. Only her heart-shaped glasses didn't match her usually conservative dress.

Curtis walked the three blocks to the Mensis Monitoring Station, careful not to step in any puddles in his new dress shoes. The computer operator signaled Curtis over to his monitors.

"Good afternoon, Mr. President."

"Good afternoon," Curtis grumbled. "So, what is it you want to show me?"

"The energy grids are offline, and it seems to have originated from the computer system in Peddlers."

Curtis snatched the chart away from the operator, and without another word, he left the building. He headed straight for the Ministry of Defense and pulled General Russ Fletcher from a meeting with his soldiers. Once they were seated in Russ's office, Curtis explained the present situation.

"I'd like you to take about thirty soldiers, Russ, and head into Peddlers. I'll have my good-for-nothing son drive the medical truck to the outskirts of town. I want him to ride in with you. It's about time he started taking some responsibility, so let him run the show. Just be sure that your soldiers are well informed of their mission before they go in. Only counteract Jason's decisions if he endangers the troops.

"The power is out everywhere. We're running really low on backup power as it is, and we need to keep the other Mensis Phases supplied, as per our contract. Get that computer system up and running and the people back to work. Do whatever it takes, Russ. Whatever it takes."

Russ listened intently. His last trip into Peddlers had gained him the title of General, and he got the extra stripe sewn onto his red uniform sleeve. Curtis had been pleased with the speed with which he had tracked down Sandpebble. It was the position he had dreamed of when he entered the military as a cadet. Russ knew it took hard work to maintain this title, and he was prepared to do what it took. Even if it meant taking orders from Jason.

"Understood, sir. You have my utmost co-operation and trust."

"I expect you to be saddled up and ready to leave first thing in the morning." Curtis left Russ to head back to his office. *That kid's nose is so brown*, thought Curtis, *but nonetheless, he always gets the job done.*

Curtis called Jason from his office vidphone. Jason was sitting behind his desk at the bank, going over statements. His father had given him the position of bank president as a formality more than as an employee. He accessed the visual on the vidscreen.

Jason hid his true feelings behind a smile as his father's pockmarked face appeared on the vidscreen.

"Hello, Pop, what can I do for you?" Jason was thinking, *more like, what am I in trouble for now?* He picked some lint off his navy-blue suit jacket.

"Will you be home for supper tonight?"

"Not likely. Why, what's happened?" Usually, when his father wanted him home, Jason knew another catastrophe had struck.

"We've located the source of the blackout. The computer system is offline in Peddlers, and I need you to reboot the entire system. I want you to head an excursion tomorrow morning to look into it."

"Ahh… do I have to? You know I like to sleep in."

"That's exactly why I want you to go. How long do you think you can keep drinking every night and carrying on till all hours? One day, heaven forbid, you'll be President. Do you think people are going to have respect for an alcoholic playboy who shirks his responsibility?"

Jason gave his father the finger under his desk so he wouldn't see. Why did his father always have to manipulate his life?

"Alright, I'll do it," he sighed.

"I want you to talk to General Fletcher sometime tonight. You'll be in complete charge of this expedition, so think with your head for a change. If you have any questions, consult with Russ. He'll know what to do."

"I'm sure he will," Jason retorted. He had never liked Russ.

"I want you to take this seriously, Jason. Take the medical truck as far as the border, just in case. Have Russ saddle up an extra horse for you, and wear one of the uniforms. You can ride in with the rest of them."

"Is that all?" said Jason, exasperated.

"Yes. I'll be in contact by radio. See you when you return."

Jason disconnected the vidphone. *Why did he get all the shit jobs?* He decided to head over to the defense building right away. *Might as well get the meeting with Russ over with*, he thought.

Jason Henniger reluctantly left his bed at 5:00 a.m. He was still hung over from last night's party. He splashed cold water on his face, put on the red uniform, and called to Lightfoot, his valet, to have his horse saddled. He headed to the kitchen to grab a homemade oatmeal muffin from Petunia, who had made them fresh that morning.

He got his armored suit from the stables and threw it in the back of the medical truck. The stable hand gave Jason the reins to his horse, Wildfire. Jason attached the reins to the side mirror of the truck and drove slowly to the defense building.

Russ and his men were saddled and ready for departure when Jason pulled up. One of the men took Wildfire's reins and pulled him along behind him. Wildfire was at least two hands higher than any of the other horses. Jason led the troops by driving on ahead and then waiting for them to catch up.

This was the first time, he realized, that Curtis had allowed him to lead the troops alone. Usually, he tagged along behind his father, but they had never gone into Peddlers.

Jason had heard stories about Peddlers, and he knew quite a few of the domestics. They had spoken fondly of their home city. Curtis disapproved of his Peddler acquaintances. He felt Jason was too lenient with them, but Jason couldn't bring himself to treat the Peddlers as his father did. They were real people, after all.

The landscape between Mensis and Peddlers was picturesque. He drove past the pastures of animals and the fruit belt. Jason pulled the truck off the side of the road by a field of flowers. He had ridden his horse down this way once and enjoyed the scene as much now as he had then.

The troops joined Jason at the field by eleven. Jason called his father on the radio to give him their position. Curtis suggested that Jason send in a few men first to scout the area and report the problem. Jason ran a hand through his thick, curly brown hair. Even this far from home, his father was still calling the shots.

Jason instructed Russ to take a few men and find out what was happening. Russ rode off toward the Park with his two strongest soldiers, Michael and Andy. Jason took his time adjusting the straps on his horse. He pulled the armored suit from the back of the truck and had two of the soldiers help him on with it. Twenty-five minutes later, Russ returned with his men.

"We questioned one of the Peddlers, who told us the power went out two days ago and then everyone started to riot. It looks like most of the fires are out now, but we need to get the computers back online."

"Let's move out." Jason mounted his horse and thought how smart they looked, like a streak of fire, as he led the soldiers along the shoreline to the fence.

Corey met up with his friends in the Park, leaving Luther in the apartment. Many people had shown up in the hopes of getting some answers. People had been busy for two days trying to douse the fires and clear the rubble.

Gopher positioned himself atop a grassy knoll and was trying to quiet the crowds. An ear-piercing whistle rang out, silencing everyone.

"I'd recognized Bear's whistle anywhere," said Lucky. He took Chip's hand and headed in that direction. Chip had been feeling dizzy all day.

"Quiet, everyone," Gopher began. "I know a lot of you are scared. Nothing like this has ever happened before, but we must stay calm. I'm sure the power will be restored before long. The best thing to do is stay in your homes."

Some people started to leave the Park, but many stayed. Corey, Moonbeam, and Sunshine slowly followed the crowds out of the Park. By eleven o'clock, dozens of people had taken to the waters. Even Lucky had to admit that the day was unusually hot. He stood watching the people with Chip, but they did not swim themselves. Lucky was the first to hear the horses' hooves pounding the sand as they drew close, quickly surrounding them.

Russ noticed a couple of Peddlers, a Blue-Level and a Green-Level, standing at the edge of the crowd. Lucky and Chip were roped and thrown over the rump of a horse. The people openly cried as the two were taken away.

"These men are being taken to the C Zone as an example of what will happen to the rest of you if you should disobey our orders."

Jason was furious that Russ was taking the initiative in dealing with these people. This was supposed to be his assignment, not Russ's.

"You are to return to your homes," Jason cut in. Russ started to say something but stopped at the last minute. "Please turn around and head back." Some of the people started to move, but most of them were reluctant.

"Move!" Russ yelled. The people sprang into action and headed out of the Park. Jason contacted his father to let him know about their present situation. If his father was pleased, he didn't show it.

"Have you got the conspirators?" Curtis questioned.

"I don't know!" responded Jason.

"I should have known better than to send a boy to do a man's job. Hand the radio over to Russ."

"No. You put me on this damn assignment, and I'll handle it."

"Fine. Find them, debug the system, and get the rest of the people into the workhouses." Curtis paused for a moment, then added, "Jason, if you don't find the people responsible for this by nightfall, don't bother coming back."

Jason held the silent radio in his hand while contemplating what to do next. Would his father really banish him from his home if he didn't find the culprits? Jason had learned long ago that his father was full of hot air; so who knew?

The soldiers combed the streets, behind the buildings, and inside the apartments for the people responsible for the computer virus. They aggressively questioned anyone they could.

Bear stepped out of the bushes and approached Russ and Jason. "I know who did this," he stated. Bear didn't want to see the soldiers kill or incarcerate innocent people on account of Corey. He felt it was his duty as a police officer to apprehend the guilty ones.

"Speak," Russ barked at him.

"You'll find the guilty parties at this address." Bear handed a paper to Jason.

"Take him," ordered Russ. Bear was shackled, then roped to one of the men's horses.

The soldiers proceeded directly to the address Bear had given them. They kicked in the door to Corey's apartment and hauled Luther to his feet.

"Get your hands off me," Luther ordered.

"Sorry, pops, you're going with the rest of them." The soldier grabbed Luther by the shirt and dragged him outside.

Sunshine had been crossing the street when the commotion started. She could see the Mensis soldiers roughing up Luther, who looked lost and overwhelmed. There was so much noise and confusion going on around him, and Luther longed for the peace of his little ghost town. He hadn't even had time to grab his walking cane.

Sunshine frantically looked for Corey and Moonbeam. They had been separated in the panicking crowds. She had seen the soldiers taking Bear, Lucky, and Chip away, and feared now for Moonbeam and Corey. The soldiers urged the people to keep moving toward the workhouses. The heat was unbearable as the horses kicked up the dust from the streets. Finally, she spotted Limpy.

"We've got to get Luther away from the Men," whispered Sunshine to Limpy.

"How? The soldiers watch our every move."

"We need a distraction. I'll make a scene and you take Luther away."

"Do you know what you're doing, Sunshine?"

"No, I'm improvising." Limpy took Sunshine's hands in his own. He looked into her determined eyes. They both knew that the soldiers wouldn't hesitate to kill her, or any of them.

"You're a very special lady, Sunshine. I only hope that we are successful." He kissed her on the cheek and let her go.

Limpy edged closer to Luther, who was being prodded from behind by one of the foot soldiers. He would wait for a chance to sneak Luther behind one of the apartment buildings.

Sunshine ran to the center of the crowd. She started chanting, "Damn the Men. Damn the Men." Before long the crowds were all chanting, raising a ruckus. Sunshine raced through the crowd to the front, encouraging people to chant.

The distraction worked, and Limpy was able to grab Luther under the arm and half carry him behind one of the apartments. They crossed over the backyard to the next block. They ran as quickly as they could, but neither of them noticed the soldier ride up behind them and drop his net. Jumping down from his horse, he gathered the net around the two and hauled them up. They hung suspended from the horse's saddle while the soldier walked the horse to the front.

"Hey, Russ, I found a few runaways." The soldier dropped the net at Russ's feet. Limpy threw the net off Luther and helped him to stand up.

By this time, Sunshine had made her way to the front. Once she stopped chanting, so did the others. Soon the crowd was silent again.

Russ looked at the men on the ground. One of them seemed too old to be a Peddler.

"Kill them," he ordered.

"Wait!" Sunshine burst through the crowd. "You wouldn't kill your own people, would you? Luther is one of you."

"Is this true?" asked Jason, from his horse. That is when he noticed that this man was indeed wearing an old suit and not a jumpsuit.

"Yes. I lived in Mensis when Nick Henniger was President."

"You say lived. You don't live there anymore?" asked Jason.

"No. I didn't like the way the Peddlers were treated then, and I don't like the way they are being treated now," Luther said, defiantly.

Jason could sympathize with the old man. He was not fond of the way the Peddlers were treated either.

"He's a traitor, and I say we should kill him," proposed Russ. He jumped down from his horse and grabbed Luther's arm.

"It's people like you that I was trying to get away from." Luther sneered at Russ.

"Shut up!" Russ backhanded Luther with his metal arm. Luther fell unconscious to the ground. Blood flowed from a gash across his cheek.

Sunshine jumped on Russ, beating at him with her fists. Russ flung her to the ground. He pulled the pistol from its holder.

"Stop right there," Jason commanded. "Put your gun away." Jason liked this girl's spunk. It would be a shame to kill her. He dismounted his horse and pulled Sunshine to her feet. Her green eyes were bright with anger and hate. He was amused by this little wild woman. She could prove to be an interesting playmate.

Sunshine couldn't believe the nerve of these men. Did they think people were animals? What right did they have to push people around? She looked into the eyes of the man in front of her. How dare he look at her like that? Sunshine slapped the smile off his face. For a moment she thought she had gone too far. She went numb with fear as Jason's face registered shock, then anger.

He had never been slapped by a woman before. He thought of hitting her back, but instead, he smiled. She would make a great challenge for him, like breaking in a new horse. She just needed to know who the master was. He was sure he could break this wild woman.

The smile was unnerving for Sunshine. She had expected him to hit her back or yell at her, but how could she defend herself against a smile? What was he really thinking? Jason threw Sunshine over his horse and mounted up behind her.

"Take these people back to the workhouses, Russ, and no unnecessary violence." He glanced at the figure of the old man lying in the dirt. "Take this man back to where you found him."

He took off down the street at a gallop with Sunshine bouncing up and down in the saddle in front of him, screaming to be let down. She was worried about Luther. It looked to her as though the soldier had hit Lu hard enough to kill him. In her eyes, Luther seemed so fragile, and she had not seen him move since he'd fallen.

Jason stopped the horse at the boundary of Peddlers in order to open the gate and let Sunshine slide to the ground. As soon as she was down, she started to run. He dismounted Wildfire and ran after the woman. He caught up to her quickly and tackled her to the ground. Sunshine fought mercilessly, clawing and biting wherever she could. Jason slapped her hard across the face and pulled her to her knees. He was starting to doubt that she could actually become a domestic.

"You have a lot to learn about manners, young lady."

Jason grabbed her by the hair and kissed her. He jerked back quickly as Sunshine bit his lip.

"I certainly won't learn them from you."

Jason pulled her by the wrist back to his horse. He took his radio from his pocket and called his father. "We've found the people and we're bringing them to the C Zone." Sunshine continued to struggle against the ironclad hold on her wrist.

"Alright. I'm standing by to restore power when the system is back up. We've wasted enough time already."

Jason put his radio away, displeased. His father hadn't even congratulated him or told him he was doing a fine job. He tried so hard sometimes to please his father and never did he ever get a pat on the back. *Well, screw him then*, Jason thought. *He can do his own dirty work from now on. I don't need this kind of hassle.*

He needed a drink. Good thing he had been smart enough to stash some booze in the medical truck last night. He pushed Sunshine on top of the horse and mounted up behind her. He loved the smell of her hair as it brushed his face in the wind.

Two of Russ's soldiers brought Luther back to his apartment and placed him on his bed. The soldiers went from building to building, getting people back to work.

Russ looked out toward Havanna. The Dome had almost completely collapsed. Russ was not a big sports fan, so he saw Havanna as a waste of electricity. They could use those people to pedal, but he knew Curtis would never hear of it. Curtis was a big football fan.

He was also angry at Jason for taking off and leaving him with all the work of debugging the computer system. Curtis was not going to be happy with that news. He knew Curtis well enough to know he liked things done right. He never should have left his son in charge. The kid had no sense of responsibility.

After sending the criminals off to the C Zone, Russ instructed his soldiers to work in shifts guarding the perimeter of the fence until dawn. There was no point heading back in the dark. Russ left five men on night watch, while the rest of them evacuated an apartment building. He had a few hours of debugging ahead of him. After many intense hours, Russ had the computer system up and running, and the electricity came back on.

Whoops and hollers could be heard throughout Havanna as the power came on again. The Dome started to re-inflate slowly. The people laughed and talked excitedly, and many sighed in relief. The skytrains started up again. The people started to make their way back home. Lionel had been discussing possible courses of action to take with Zane and Helena Tusk, his dad, Doug Chaffe, and Ginther Rhodes and his son, Zachary, in case the power wasn't restored.

"We need to find out more information about Havanna," suggested Doug. "I can't believe that the power just goes out and on again without some cause of action. We need to discover the cause."

"Perhaps the Peddlers had stopped pedaling," offered Lionel.

"What we need is answers," said Zane. "I think we should look around the Dome and investigate what could have caused the power outage."

"We can split into teams in order to cover more ground."

"That's a great idea, Zachary." Ginther ruffled his son's hair affectionately. They stayed to discuss a plan. They were all feeling vulnerable after the collapse of their Dome.

Zane reflected on the conversations he used to have with Corey. His son had never wanted to accept the obvious. He had questioned their whole survival, and Zane had thought he was ungrateful. Perhaps Corey was right in questioning his surroundings, as Helena had pointed out to him.

"I volunteer to check out Dusting," offered Zane. Helena looked at him strangely. Was she to lose her husband now, as well as her son?

"No one has ever returned from Dusting," Helena expressed.

"Don't worry, love, I'll be fine. You should go home and rest, Helena." He wanted to finally be able to answer Corey's questions about Dusting.

"I'll go with you, Zane." Doug got to his feet.

"You're not going without me." Ginger stood up and placed her arm in her husband's. Lionel was proud to see his parents taking part.

"Anne and I can go to the observation deck and look in on Peddlers. We might find a few clues there."

Ginther threw his arm around Zach. "Looks like that leaves us to look around the Dome. We can start with the Stadium and make our way around to the Medicure building."

"Maybe you can discover the mystery behind BUDDY. There must be a reason why the computer failed as it did," Zane remarked.

"Alright, we'll spend what's left of the day looking around, and we'll reconvene here tomorrow morning with our reports."

They headed in their separate directions. Zane urged Helena to go home and get some sleep. She numbly kissed her husband goodbye and left. As he watched her walk away, he had a feeling that he would never see her again. He shook his head to dispel the unreasonable emotion. *What could go wrong?* he thought. *It's not like I'm going to leave the Dome.*

Lionel and Anne took the elevator to the observation deck. They were both quiet after their talk in the Stadium building yesterday. Anne had expected Lionel to be angrier than he was. Perhaps he was more understanding than she thought.

It was almost dark by the time they reached the top. The lights of Peddlers lit up the sky. Anne brought one of the telescopes into focus on the workhouses, but it was too dark to see much. A part of her still hoped to see Corey in one of the windows. Lionel came up behind Anne and encircled her in his arms.

"I really am happy that we're going to have a baby."

Anne noticed that he had said *we*, and not *you*. She turned to face him, kissing him softly on the lips. "You are such a sweet man."

Lionel didn't feel he deserved the praise. The least he could do for Corey was to give his son a good home. "I'll love him like my own, Anne. You are my wife, and this will be our child."

"Or children. DOCTOR said he would ensure that I had twins. Remember Zachary telling you about BUDDY's instructions about replacing Corey with twins to keep up the proper rotation of people?"

Lionel let go of Anne as he started to laugh. *Life was nothing if not full of irony,* thought Lionel. If only Corey had known that his own sons would be the ones to replace him. It seemed to Lionel that his whole life was so intertwined with Corey's even though he was no longer here in the Dome.

"What's so funny?" enquired Anne.

"Nothing," replied Lionel. He took Anne in his arms again. "Do you know how much I love you?" It was not a question requiring an answer. Lionel brought his mouth down to meet hers.

Zane, Doug, and Ginger approached the entrance to Dusting. The door seemed to be locked from the inside. Their codes didn't work to access the lock.

"We're going to have to force it open," said Doug.

"You two wait here, and I'll find something to pry it open." Zane headed off. What could he use? He walked past the ball courts toward the mini-golf. *That's it*, he thought. *I can use a putter.* The fence wasn't locked when Zane reached Joey's Mini-golf, but it would only be a few more minutes before lights out. He pulled one of the clubs from the rack and headed back to his friends. The power went out as he was walking. The streets were dark now, and Zane had to watch where he stepped. He glanced up at the watch tower. It was the only source of light guiding his way. The clock read 2202 hours.

He met up with Doug and Ginger standing in front of the entrance to Dusting. Zane and Doug took turns trying to pry open the door with the club.

"I think I got it!" exclaimed Doug. The door swung open, leading down to a dark staircase. They stepped in cautiously.

"Welcome to The Highway to Happiness!" exclaimed Zane. His voice sounded eerily loud as it echoed off the walls. Ginger giggled nervously.

They reached the bottom of the stairs, then turned left. In the dimness of the emergency lights, they could see a skytrain on the platform. They made their way forward until the platform ended. Their footsteps were the only sounds audible to them. Only Zane took note of the other staircase leading down to the platform.

"Looks like the easy part is over," commented Doug. They jumped down onto the tracks in front of the skytrain. Zane led the way down into the dark, damp tunnel until the lights from the station no longer illuminated their way. By an unspoken acknowledgment of their fear, they held hands to avoid losing contact. Toward the end of the tunnel, Zane could see some light up ahead.

"We're almost there." He quickened his pace. The tunnel opened up into another station. Zane climbed up onto the platform and then helped his friend's wife. Doug followed suit, brushing the dust off of his sweat suit.

"There's some light up ahead. Let's go check it out," suggested Zane. They reached the entrance to the tunnel in the center of the platform. It was dimly lit by emergency lights. The tunnel seemed to go on forever. Zane had never expected the entrance to Dusting to be so bleak.

"I feel like a little girl again," giggled Ginger.

"I know what you mean," agreed Doug. "I guess it's because we've never been up past lights out." They started to laugh, releasing the fear and excitement they felt.

"Come on, I'll race you down the tunnel," challenged Ginger.

"You want a head start?" teased Doug. Ginger started running. She was laughing and looking behind her. Doug and Zane gained on her quickly. Doug grabbed his wife around the waist and twirled her around as Zane continued running forward.

Zane slowed to a stop when he came to a yellow line painted horizontally across the floor. He wondered what purpose it served. He could hear his friends running up behind him again. He turned to talk to them just as Ginger crossed the yellow line.

A bright flash of blue light blinded their eyes. Doug had just been approaching her when she disappeared. He reached out his arms to her. The blue flash sparked again. Doug looked down to see that both of his arms were missing from the elbow down. He uttered a small cry, then fell forward. Zane covered his eyes against the flash that he knew was coming. When he pulled his arms down, only Doug's feet were left intact.

Overhead, the speakers boomed in BUDDY's voice, "LASERS IGNITED. SUBJECTS DUSTED."

Zane stumbled backward, away from Doug's feet. He reached out a hand to support himself against the wall as he started retching. He had never witnessed such a horrible and grotesque event in his life. *Is this what really happened to people trying to reach Dusting?*

"LASERS OFF. SWEEPING CAN NOW COMMENCE."

Why hadn't he listened to Corey when he questioned the existence of Dusting? Was this the only way out? Was the other staircase he saw The Road to Ruin? Had Corey suffered the same fate when he had been exiled? Did that mean that Corey had been dusted as Doug and Ginger had?

Dropping to his knees, Zane started to wail for the loss of his son, the loss of his friends, and the loss of all the people who had come through the tunnel seeking eternal life and peace. He never heard the sweeper coming up behind him, as it knocked him down to the ground.

Jason brought Sunshine back to the medical truck. He helped her down and dismounted. The surrounding land was barren. It looked like a desert to Sunshine. There was nothing but sagebrush and dry dirt.

After tying Wildfire to the truck, Jason brought out a bottle from under the seat. He took a long swallow of the potent liquid. He loved that burning sensation as the liquor traveled down. Already he could feel his nerves calming down. He offered the bottle to the Peddler woman.

Sunshine took a swig and studied this strange man. He was quite handsome, with bright blue eyes and curly brown hair. He stood a foot and a half taller than her.

"What's your name?" she asked.

"Jason," he said, as he removed his armor and threw it in the back of the truck. There was no point in sticking around. Russ would make sure the people would return to their work. He felt confident in knowing that things were restored to normal. There was only one way to keep the system working, and that was to keep the Peddlers pedaling. It was the way it had always been, and it was the way it always would be.

With his things put away, Jason now focused his attention on the woman standing next to him. He thought that she was perhaps the most beautiful woman he had ever seen. He took back the bottle of whisky.

"What did you say your name was?"

"Sunshine."

"Sunshine?" Her eyes looked frightened, but they also held a look of defiance. He wasn't used to women being bold and outspoken. He was sure this little wench would be a real wildcat in bed. Jason grabbed Sunshine around the waist and pulled her close to him. Sunshine almost gave in to the kiss that followed, but pulled back and spit in his face.

"Stay away from me, you scum," she hissed. What did he expect from her? Did he think she would fall into his arms after destroying their hopes for freedom? Was she supposed to be happy that he took her away from her home and her friends?

Jason cocked an eyebrow in amusement and wiped the spit from his cheek. He was going to have fun with this one. "You don't know what you're missing, girl. Once you do, you'll be begging me for it."

"You have to be the most arrogant man I have ever had the displeasure of meeting. And I don't care if my friends are in the C Zone, they'll come back for me. You'll see."

Jason laughed out loud, which only infuriated her more. He knew that was impossible. No one escaped the C Zone. He took another swig from the bottle, then put it away. He gently pushed Sunshine into the truck, then got in and started it up. They drove slowly in silence towards Mensis while Wildfire trotted along beside them.

Sunshine was still sulking, but inwardly she was excited to be riding in this strange vehicle. The landscape entering Mensis was beautiful. She realized that under different circumstances, she might have been having a great time.

He drove as far as the fruit orchards, then pulled the truck over to the side of the road. Sunshine flew from the vehicle and pulled an orange from a tree. She tore the peel from the fruit and bit into it. The juice poured down her chin.

Jason had never seen anyone enjoy an orange so much before. He pulled the bottle out from under the seat and took another swig. He got out and leaned against the hood as Sunshine came back to the truck with an armful of oranges, sidestepping Wildfire, who was grazing on the grass. She placed the oranges on the seat, then went in search of some cherries. She had never tasted fruit so sweet and fresh. Would she eat like this every day? Was all their food in Mensis fresh? She filled the pockets of her Blue-Level jumpsuit with cherries and headed back to the truck, eating a handful of the plump juicy fruits.

Jason watched her devour the cherries. She was a mystery to him. He supposed that was why he was attracted to her. He had never yet met a woman who hadn't thrown herself at his feet. She would be no exception. She just needed a little persuasion. He grabbed her in his arms and kissed her hard on the lips.

Sunshine beat her fists against him, but to no avail. He would not let her go. He was too strong. His tongue darted in and out her mouth, melting her resolve to hate him. Her pulse raced wildly through her veins. Her head suddenly felt dizzy, and her knees went weak. How could she feel this way about a man she disliked? How could her body betray her emotions?

Jason felt the fight leave her. He knew she would come around. Now that it seemed he had broken her, he didn't want to break free. Her kisses were soft, promising more than he had expected. He pulled her closer to him, feeling the contours of her body pressing up against his. Jason was caught up in the heat of the moment, the warmth of her lips and body. He had not expected to feel this way. He had only wanted to break her.

Their bodies melted together, moving in a way neither of them had expected. Their eyes locked, a mirror image of each other's surprise and desire in them. Jason moved his hand up to caress her voluminous breast. Sunshine was shocked at her own reaction to Jason's advances. Suddenly she was angry again. Angry at herself for letting him get to her this way and angry at him for taking advantage of her. Forcefully, she broke free.

"Take your filthy paws off me!"

Jason was taken aback by her response. Had he thought she was sincere when she had only been teasing him? She had made a fool of him, and he would make her pay.

"You'll do as I say, wench, or—"

"Or what?" she demanded. "What could you possibly do to me that could be worse? Even death would be more favorable than letting you have your way with me."

Jason grabbed her wrists, dragged her to the back of the truck, and threw her in. He couldn't figure her out. One minute she was as gentle as a lamb, and the next she was like a wildcat. He was confused about the power she seemed to hold over him. He had never let a woman get the better of him, but this woman had.

Alone in the back of the truck, Sunshine was disturbed by the way she was feeling. When he had kissed her, she felt she was riding on a wave moving toward a distant shore. How could she feel excited about a man she disliked and distrusted? If only he didn't look so strong and handsome in his red uniform, but she knew it was more than that. Her body wanted him, but her mind hated him. She curled up on the cot along the wall. She would have to avoid looking into his eyes. She had to keep away from him. Before long, she drifted off to sleep.

MENSIS

Zachary and Ginther made their way from building to building, looking for anything out of the ordinary. Some of the buildings had been locked during the power outage, such as the bars. The buildings they did have access to were the ones not requiring their tattoo codes to enter.

After looking around the Stadium building, they walked on. Everything checked out fine in the Forum and the residential area. Nothing was amiss at the pool or the ball courts. They couldn't enter the Girls' School or the girls' residential area, and at last, they came to the Medicure building.

The door was open, and they fumbled around in the dimly lit room. They looked through the medical supplies, the cabinets and drawers, but turned up nothing.

"Looks like we hit another dud," sighed Zachary.

"Shh... I think I hear something," whispered Ginther. They could hear someone whistling. It sounded as though it was coming from the other side of the wall. They pressed their ears to the wall, and sure enough, they could hear footsteps.

A hidden panel swung open and there stood a man with his arms full of medical supplies. His green eyes widened in surprise, as he caught sight of the two men standing in the examination room. Ginther and Zachary knocked the intruder to the ground. The sterile blankets and medical supplies flew out of his arms.

"Who are you? What are you doing here? Where did you come from? How did you get in here?"

"Slow down, Dad. Give the guy a chance to answer." Zachary held the man's hands behind his back.

"My name is Arthur Waters and I come from Mensis," he blurted out.

Zachary pulled the guy to his feet. Arthur was an older man with a receding hairline. He wore a pair of faded blue jeans and a blue T-shirt that hung over a slightly protruding belly.

"Where is Mensis?" questioned Ginther.

"It's about fifty kilometers northwest from here. Let go of me!"

They pushed him into the Medichair. Arthur sat there rubbing his arms. These men had taken him totally by surprise. He had been delivering supplies to Havanna for seven years, but he had never expected to encounter any of the patients. Havanna had the reputation of being one of the best mental institutions around. His mother had been brought here when she had been inflicted with Alzheimer's disease.

"How did you get in here?" Ginther repeated.

"There's an underground subway that connects the Dome to the outside." Arthur wondered why they could not remember how they had entered the Dome. It seemed strange that these people had no recollection of Mensis at all.

"How can you travel without being affected by the contaminates in the air? How can you enter the Dome without contaminating it?"

Arthur realized that this man suffered from extreme paranoia.

"It's been almost a hundred and twenty years since any viruses have posed a threat to society. Why don't I just call the doctor and he can take you both back to your rooms?"

Zachary glanced at the time on the computer monitor. "DOCTOR won't be operational until 0600 hours. Besides, it's only a computer."

"You mean to say the air outside is not contaminated? How come we're told that it is?" asked Ginther.

"Look," Arthur said, "I don't know who is telling you what, but the air is fine. You must know that from when you lived in Mensis. How long have you been in here?"

"I've lived here all my life. I've never heard of Mensis," replied Ginther.

"Yeah, right!" *These guys are really crazy*, Arthur thought.

"It's true," stated Zachary. "Everyone who lives here was born here. What makes you think that we weren't?"

Arthur looked over at the young man. He seemed too young to be hospitalized, but mental illness could strike at any age. "I know for a fact that Havanna is a hospital."

"That's absurd!" expressed Ginther. "Havanna is our home and has been since before the war. My great-great-grandfather was one of the first settlers into the Dome."

"All I know is that my own mother was sent here about fourteen years ago. They brought her here instead of sending her to Dusting because she needed medical attention and she wasn't yet fifty years old."

"No one has entered or left the Dome since before the war," argued Ginther, "except for the people retiring to Dusting."

Arthur wasn't sure if these guys were for real or not. They did seem to have their story straight, but it was the wrong story. So far, the only thing they had agreed upon was the fact that the people all retired to Dusting. He wasn't sure if they said that because he had, or whether it was true. Surely, they would have sent his mother straight to Dusting if this hadn't been a hospital.

"You," Arthur pointed to Zachary, "I want you to tell me what it's like in Dusting."

Arthur listened while Zachary explained Dusting to him. The idea of Dusting was like the one he knew, but he had never seen anyone taking the subways beneath the Dome before. From the tale the young man told, Havanna didn't sound like an institution at all. The people here even had children.

Arthur had always wondered where they got all the athletes for their sports if everyone was handicapped or ill. He had always thought it was the doctors and nurses who played, but now he realized it was the normal children that were born into the Dome that did. Arthur knew he had to speak to someone in charge for the answers he wanted. If these guys were telling the truth, he wanted to find out where had they taken his mother.

"Hey, Dad, it's almost 0600 hours. Why don't you stay here, and I'll meet up with the rest of them at the Stadium?"

"Sure thing, Zach, but bring them back here."

"There's a long-distance vidcall for you, Mr. President," Cindy said, as Curtis passed by her desk, wearing his favorite gun-metal blue suit.

Curtis hurried inside to his study. A large stuffed eagle sat perched on the corner of his mahogany wood desk, and antlers and fur pelts hung on the walls. Curtis sat in his favorite leather swivel chair and accessed the vidphone. "President Henniger."

"Good morning, Curtis. It's Stanley. How are you doing, you old dog?" Stanley Bell was an old business acquaintance of his. He had become the President of Mensis, Phase Three, at about the same time Curtis came into power of Mensis, Phase One. President Bell was sporting a light-tan suit with a lilac dress shirt.

"I'm fine, Stan. To what do I owe the pleasure of this vidcall?"

"Right to business, eh, Curtis? It's good to see you haven't changed. I'm calling about arranging a possible union between my lovely daughter, Pandora, and your son, Jason." Stanley's dark blue eyes twinkled behind his horn-rimmed glasses.

Curtis sat up in his seat. This could mean big business for the two Phases, and it would also be good for Jason.

"That sounds like an interesting arrangement," Curtis remarked.

"I propose my daughter's hand in marriage, as well as rifles, coffee, tobacco, the finest leather, and an assortment of soaps and lotions."

"I'd be interested in whatever kind of weapons you could send, as well as rifles," added Curtis.

"Sure," Stanley said, reluctantly. "I can throw in a few cases of grenades and a dozen pistols."

"Fine. I'll have some gifts waiting for you here, once I receive my shipment... as well as your daughter, of course."

"We could really use a new automobile and a couple of four-ton trucks. I'd also be interested in a few hundred yards of silk, and all the fresh fruits and vegetables that you can spare."

"Done. Jason will be pleased, and I look forward to meeting your daughter."

After Curtis disconnected the line, he leaned back in his chair and placed his feet on top of his desk. He was pleased with the outcome of the deal. He was sure that Pandora would be a fine girl. Jason needed to start taking responsibility, and this was a perfect way to get him started.

He could recall the time his father had told him of the marriage he had arranged for him. It had been quite profitable. He not only got himself a beautiful bride from Mensis, Phase Two, but a large dowry to go with it.

Curtis fondly remembered the bride his father had presented to him. She had been a beautiful girl of eighteen, and he had fallen in love with her soft brown eyes and gentle ways. His old friend, Luther Saxon had been his best man and had made all the arrangements for their wedding. His wife would have made a great mother if she had lived through childbirth.

Lisa had a terrible pregnancy from the start, and DOCTOR had advised her not to have the child. She refused to hear talk of abortion, even if it meant her life. Curtis had tried to persuade her, but she wouldn't consider it. She died in the medichair giving birth to that good-for-nothing son of his. Jason had robbed him of the only woman he had ever loved.

Lionel woke Anne, who had fallen asleep in the elevator. They had slept after they discovered the telescopes and the elevator were useless to them after lights out. Anne stood up and stretched. She walked around the observation deck to work out the cramp in her calf. The overhead lights came on but did little to brighten the already sunlit deck. Anne took one last look through the telescope. She could see smoke rising from the city.

"Come here, Lionel, and take a look at this." Anne stood back so that Lionel could get to the scope. There were men in shiny suits riding a large animal along the retaining wall. She focused in with another telescope. The riders didn't seem to be doing much other than passing by.

"Who are those men, Lionel?"

"I don't know, but they don't look like Peddlers."

"Where else could they be from?"

"I haven't a clue. More unanswered questions," he commented. "Let's go and see if the others turned up anything."

They left their telescopes and entered the elevator. They rode down in silence. Lionel was pondering the possible meaning of the riders. Could it be connected somehow with the power failure? Had these men destroyed the power or helped restore it? Were they Peddlers?

Anne and Lionel reached ground level and started for the Stadium building. The door leading to Dusting flew open and Zane stumbled onto the street. He looked as though he had seen a ghost.

"Zane, what happened? Where are my parents?" enquired Lionel.

"Gone," Zane whispered, his eyes unseeing. "Gone, just like Corey. Flash! That's it… gone."

Lionel shook Zane by the shoulders. "Zane, snap out of it. Make sense, will you? Gone where? To Peddlers?"

Zane's eyes were unfocused as he spoke to Lionel. "No. They've been dusted."

"You mean they've gone to Dusting?"

"No. I mean one minute they were in the tunnel and then the next, they were dust." Zane's eyes sought and held Lionel's. "Dusting as we know it doesn't exist. I'm so sorry for your loss. Hate me if you will. It was my idea to go."

Lionel let his arms drop from Zane's shoulders. If not for the clarity in Zane's eyes, Lionel could have believed that he was raving mad. His parents were gone? His parents were dust? Grief set in as the shock wore off. Lionel sat on the ground and buried his face in his hands. Anne stood looking from Lionel to Zane. She could see dried blood on the back of Zane's head. She placed her hand on Lionel's shoulder to give him support.

"Zane, if Dusting doesn't exist, then where are all the people?" Anne wanted to know.

"Nowhere. They don't exist anymore. They've been reduced to dust."

"No, I can't accept that." Tears streamed down Anne's cheeks. Mr. and Mrs. Kravitz had just retired to Dusting. Lionel's parents had just been dusted? Could this be true? Was the dusting tunnel no more than a death chamber?

"I've seen it with my own eyes, Anne."

"This defies the whole meaning of life! Why else would we do the things we do if we're not working toward Dusting?" Anne wiped angry tears from her eyes.

"I don't have those answers." Zane sighed heavily. "I don't know how I'm going to break the news about Corey to Helena."

"What do you mean, about Corey?" Didn't Zane say that Lionel's parents had gone as Corey had? *This just keeps getting worse*, Anne thought.

"The entrance for Exiles leads to the same place as Dusting. There's no way that Corey could have survived."

All three of them were crying openly when Zachary arrived on the scene. They quickly filled him in. Zach was shocked at Zane's discovery. How could any of them have suspected that Dusting had only been a tale? They were not prepared for the truth.

Zachary urged them to come with him to the Medicure building. He told them they had found a man delivering supplies. He recounted their conversation with him as they walked.

"Corey once said that as a child he thought he heard people moving around the Dome at night," recounted Anne. She looked fleetingly at her husband.

"That's right! I remember him climbing in bed with Helena and me on a number of occasions, scared out of his wits."

"Is this man wearing a silver suit?" asked Lionel.

"No. Why do you ask?" enquired Zach. Lionel told Zane and Zach of the riders on Peddlers Island. They reached the Medicure building and followed Zachary inside.

Ginther and Arthur had picked up the medical supplies that had fallen to the floor and were now sitting in the waiting area. Ginther introduced Arthur to the others, and they exchanged information about what they had seen. Lionel still hadn't come to grips with his parents' death. But through their death, they had learned the truth about Dusting.

Arthur had come to realize that these people were not crazy, but they were terribly misinformed. He took the news about Dusting hard. He had wanted to believe that his mother was alive and well, and living out her life in peace. He had been betrayed and lied to by his own people, and not for the first time.

"The men on the horses that you saw," Arthur started, "are soldiers from Mensis. They only go into Peddlers when there is a problem. If you lost power here, it's either because the Peddlers had stopped pedaling or the Mensis cut off your power."

"So, it's the Mensis who are controlling the Dome?" asked Zane.

"Absolutely! I still don't understand why I was told that Havanna was a hospital, and you were told the lies about the outside being contaminated. We were all lied to about Dusting, and who knows what else. I'm going to head straight back to Mensis and confront the President myself."

"I'd love to hear what he has to say," expressed Zane. "Can we ride with you, Arthur?"

"You bet your butt."

"If we leave, we'll upset the balance of the population."

"Really, Lionel? BUDDY is lying to us, killing us, and you still want to defend the system?" Zach asked, incredulously.

"You're right. I'm sorry. It's just so hard to take it all in. Screw it! Let's go. Let's find out what's going on."

Limpy was just starting to pull the covers over Luther's face when Corey and Moonbeam burst into the apartment. They'd had to spend the night hiding in a storeroom at the Trade Center.

Luther lay in his bed with his arms folded over his chest. He had a bad gash on his cheek and there was blood on his pillow. Corey reached out to touch him. His skin was cold despite the heat. It was evident that the old man was dead.

"He passed away about an hour ago. I did what I could to make him comfortable, but he never regained consciousness. He hit his head pretty hard when he was struck," Limpy sadly said, with tears in his eyes.

"Thank you Limpy, but it is I who should have been here," Corey lamented. Tears filled his eyes.

Moonbeam stood beside Corey and placed his arm around his shoulders. Corey's heart ached as he stood there crying, his shoulders moving up and down with his sobs. *Why did Luther have to die?* Corey thought. He knew if he hadn't disturbed him, Lu would still be in Willowdown cooking goose eggs on his wood-burning stove. He felt as though he had killed Luther himself. He had caused this poor man's death.

Corey hung his head as guilt gripped him in a paralytic state. *How do I move on from here?* he wondered. *How can any of this be justified? How do I ever forgive myself?* Luther had given his life to right the wrongs of his past mistakes. How could he do any less? He would have to find the courage to carry on, to complete the vision that Luther had for all of them.

Moonbeam led Corey to the table in the kitchen, followed by Limpy. "It's not your fault, Corey."

"Yes, it is."

"You did the best you could," Moonbeam insisted.

Corey looked at Moonbeam and shook his head. "No, I didn't. Luther once said to me, that the only way to win the fight is to be the best player in it. I owe it to Luther, and all the people in Peddlers, to find a way to free them from the Mensis."

"How are you going to do that?" asked Limpy.

"The way I look at it," Corey began, "is we don't know all the rules of the game. What we have to do is find Mensis and learn where they are weak. When we find the hole in their defense, we'll attack." Corey slapped his fist into his other palm. He felt like a team Captain again, strategizing his plan of attack.

"Alright, Corey, I'm with you."

Corey clapped a hand on Moonbeam's shoulder and looked at Limpy. "If you'd rather stay here, I understand."

"You guys go. I'll look after Luther."

Corey grabbed Limpy's shoulder, gave it a squeeze, then nodded at Moonbeam. "Let's go find these bastards and make them pay."

They left the apartment and headed toward the Park. There were five soldiers mounted on horses when they reached the beach. They ducked down behind a bush for a better look.

"How are we supposed to get around them?" asked Moonbeam.

"We're going to have to wait until they leave," replied Corey. "Shh, I hear more horses."

"Behind you," Moonbeam yelled, as he grabbed Corey's arm. They made a run for it, but they were no match for the speed of the horses.

Curtis Henniger's vidphone on his desk rang. He snatched it up. "President Henniger."

Russ Fletcher hated calling the President, but he had no choice. "The system is back up, the Peddlers are working, and order has been restored. Jason is nowhere to be found."

"Very good. Never mind Jason. I'll deal with that. Good job."

"We've just picked up two more suspicious-looking Peddlers," Russ informed President Henniger. "One of the Peddlers' tattoos says his name is Cobra, but facial recognition has turned up a Havannian name."

"Okay, send me the info." Curtis sighed. "What's the name?"

Even as Russ spoke the name "Corey Tusk," he knew something was wrong. He could see Curtis's eyes go wide and a look of confusion crossed his face. The look quickly changed to recognition and then suspicion.

Of course, that's why it sounded so familiar, thought Curtis. *He was the kid at the mating ceremony in Havanna that refused to choose a bride*. Curtis had been overseeing the ceremony, as BUDDY, when Corey had presented him with a great opportunity. He quickly took advantage of Corey's stubborn refusal to finally extinguish the last of the Tusk bloodline.

Curtis's father, Nick, had convinced President Tusk that all his heirs were dead, and so acquired the position of the Presidency for himself. He had fabricated a story about the Dome being contaminated through the war years. The President had believed him when Nick told him his children were dead. He suggested that they use the Dome as a hospital again, as it was before the war.

President Henry Tusk was the first to visit the new Havanna hospital for his arthritis, after the Presidency was signed over to Nick, of course. Nick Henniger hadn't brought Henry to the top floor of the Dome. Instead, he had him brought to the lower subway, straight to Dusting.

Somehow, though, Corey had managed to escape the dusting tunnel and had made his way to Peddlers. He wouldn't be surprised if Corey was the one behind the computer virus.

Curtis's mind was racing, trying to make sense of the situation. He accessed the files for Havanna on his computer terminal. He opened Corey's personal file and pressed print.

The computer printout read:

> Corey Tusk M-1565-M
> D.O.B.: April 22, 2149
> Son of Zane and Helena Tusk
> Address: R-3, R-596
> Exiled July 31, 2169
> Lasers ignited, dusted, and deceased.

According to the computer, Corey had been dusted. Was it possible that he could have survived Dusting somehow? Could it be that the lasers were not working properly? He had received a report that the lasers had ignited three times last night. He had just assumed it was the effects of the electricity coming back online that had caused it, but now he was not so sure.

"Damn it, Russ, too many things are getting out of control. The lasers must not be working properly in Havanna. On top of a Peddler rebellion and a missing delivery man, we now have a loose Havannian. This has got to stop."

"You want him executed?" enquired Russ.

"No, I want him brought to the C Zone." Curtis wanted Corey to suffer. He wanted the great Tusk bloodline to die, broken and beaten. Once Corey was dead, there would be no more heirs, and no more opportunities, slim as though they might be, for another Tusk to ever challenge the rights to the Presidency.

Sunshine blocked her eyes against the light that flooded in through the door of the truck. Jason looked down at Sunshine's cherry-stained jumpsuit. She had forgotten to take them out of her pockets when she went to sleep. "You're a mess, wench."

"Don't call me a wench," she retorted. "It's insulting."

"It's not insulting. It's just a pet name."

"I'm not your pet, and I don't want to be called a wench."

"Yes, Your Majesty," Jason teased. "Will that be all?"

"No, it's not. I want some breakfast."

Jason went to the front of the truck to fetch the oranges for Sunshine. He had never waited on a Peddler before and now questioned his motives. What was so special about this woman? Why should he treat her any different than he did the others? Why was she not waiting on him? Sunshine was pulling what was left of the cherries out of her pockets when Jason came back. He handed her the oranges.

"Thank you," she said, taking them from him.

"Come ride up front," commanded Jason.

Sunshine admired the view as they drove. She was acutely aware of the electricity between them but chose to concentrate on the scenery instead. She couldn't help commenting on the beauty of the pastures and the fields. She could see Peddlers working the land with machines and by hand. Sunshine wasn't fond of the odor of the farms, but she was enthralled by the animals.

They soon left the farms and headed into Mensis. It was not as large as Peddlers, but it was bustling with activity when they drove through. The streets were lined with trees, and the houses had large grassy yards. Great verandas surrounded the homes, and most had a barn or stable.

The women wore long crinoline dresses with matching hats. Behind them trailed their Peddler domestics carrying packages and bags. The men were mostly dressed in three-piece suits and carried briefcases. There was an aura of glamour everywhere Sunshine looked. It showed in the style of their homes, the cleanliness of the town, the structures of their buildings, and in the look of the people themselves. There was an air of opulence.

Jason pulled up in front of a women's clothing store. Sunshine's eyes widened in fascination as she looked at the window displays.

"I can't have my woman looking a mess," Jason commented. "Let's go pick out a few dresses for you."

Sunshine opened her door but hesitated before the store. Jason took her hand in his and led the way in. The store was richly decorated in shades of lavender. Two beautifully clad saleswomen stood waiting for customers, dressed in summer pastel dresses. Sunshine felt small and insignificant. She knew all the credit she owned would not buy her even one of the dresses that hung from the racks.

"Good morning, Master Henniger," cooed one of the saleswomen.

"Good morning, Charlotte. I'd like to purchase a few outfits for my friend."

Charlotte Leon gave Sunshine a forced smile. She was not unaccustomed to men bringing in their playmates, but she disliked the idea of a Peddler woman wearing the same clothes as a lady. She looked Sunshine over and estimated her size. She quickly selected some items from the rack.

Sunshine took the clothes the woman handed her and stepped into the changeroom. She had never worn anything but a jumpsuit. The dresses seemed awkward and uncomfortable as she struggled into them. They fit well and looked good, but they were not as comfortable as her jumpsuit. Jason insisted she show him all the outfits she tried on. He had the saleswomen bring shoes to match the ones he liked.

An hour and a half later, Jason had bought six outfits, three pairs of heeled shoes, a slew of underwear, and a hat. He wasn't sure why he was buying her all these things. Perhaps it was the childlike enthusiasm with which she welcomed it, or perhaps it was the stunning way in which the clothes fit her.

Sunshine was thrilled with Jason's kind gifts. She knew she could soon get used to the ladylike image that the dresses created.

Maybe Jason wasn't so bad after all, she thought. She rather enjoyed looking like a queen. She now wore a white cotton dress with pink lace trim. On her feet, she wore a pair of white, low-heeled pumps. They felt uncomfortable compared to the running shoes she normally wore. She found it difficult to walk as she made her way to the front counter. Jason signed his credit card slip and placed his card back into his brown leather wallet. Sunshine experienced a moment of wicked delight when Jason asked the saleswoman to throw her shoes and jumpsuit in the trash.

Once back in the truck, Jason drove to his Estate southwest of town. He was aware of Sunshine staring at him but concentrated on the road ahead. The Henniger Estate stood on ten acres of land. Sunshine had never seen such a beautiful place. She could not believe it was a house. It was larger than any residence she had ever seen.

Large marble lions sat as sentinels, guarding the entrance. There was also a guardhouse behind one of the lions. It was surrounded by a five-foot-high stucco wall. The stables stood off to the left of the property. The mansion itself was four stories high, with white pillars supporting a veranda. A flag with the head of an African elephant was perched on the roof, and a large limousine sat in front of the huge mahogany doors.

Sunshine was awed by the enormity of it. She realized that Jason must be from a large family unless this place housed many families. Was Jason taking her to live with him here in this beautiful mansion? It was no wonder he could afford to buy her so many nice outfits. He must be rich!

Jason drove to the right by-passing the main house and pulled up in front of a modest-sized cottage west of the Henniger Estate, about a half-mile away. He watched Sunshine's expression change from childlike enthusiasm to shocked anger. He turned off the truck and then turned to face her.

"So, what do you think of your new home?"

It quickly dawned on Sunshine that she was not going to be the lady of the house, but a whore on the side. It seemed just as she had come to think well of him, he betrayed her trust.

"I think you're despicable. I don't want to live in your whorehouse, and I won't wear these clothes." She threw the bag at him with contempt.

Jason was getting tired of her insolent attitude. He had taken her away from her overcrowded, overworked society, offered her a beautiful private house of her own, bought her gorgeous outfits, and this was the kind of behavior he got in return? He got out and slammed his door. Walking around to the other side, he pulled her door open and grabbed her tightly around the wrist. Sunshine struggled to free her hand. He pulled her over his shoulder, brought her inside the cottage, and let her down.

"Listen, wench… you belong to me now, and you'll listen to what I say." He held her shoulders tightly. "Don't make me get rough with you, or you'll regret it." Jason headed for the door. "When I come back, you had better start treating me the way you should, or I'll teach you a lesson you'll never forget."

Sunshine stood there after Jason had slammed and locked the door. Tears rolled down her face as she kicked off the new shoes. Damn him! How could he be so nice one minute and so mean the next? Did he intend to keep her hostage in this house only to serve his own needs? Well, she wouldn't give him the satisfaction of having her or knowing that she was attracted to him. He couldn't know how she felt, or he would use it to his advantage. She had to hold him off somehow until she could escape back to Peddlers.

She looked around the prison that Jason had provided for her. She had to admit it was a beautiful place. The living room was furnished in rosewood furniture with plush beige carpets on the floors. The dining room held a polished wood China cabinet and a large oak table set. The kitchen was spacious and well equipped with every sort of appliance. There was a small bathroom located next to the stairs leading to the second floor. Sunshine couldn't believe all these rooms were just for her.

Upstairs there was a master bedroom decorated in white and pink. A large canopy bed sat in the middle of the room. From the bay window, she could see a pasture out back. Sunshine walked into the other bedroom. It was smaller than hers but still larger than the ones in Peddlers. The only other room was a large bathroom with a soaker tub.

She filled the tub with hot water, as she needed to wash off the dirt and grime of the last few days. She stretched out in it, thinking about the friends she had left behind. She missed Moonbeam's good advice and the comfortable companionship she shared with him. If only she could speak to him now. He would know what she should do about Jason, whose selfish indulgence had made her his captive. He had taken her from her home and expected favors in return. She hated feeling trapped, and she hated Jason for trapping her. If he thought he could buy her with this absolutely beautiful place, he had another think coming.

After lunch, Ginther and Zachary arrived at the Medicure building to find Lionel, Anne, and Zane waiting for them. Zane was thinking of how Helena had broken down in his arms when he had told her the news. She was heartbroken over the loss of her son.

With the arrival of Zachary and Ginther, Zane brought his attention back to their present situation. They knew the minute they set foot into the office; DOCTOR would be alerted to their presence. The vidcam would follow any movement in the room. Arthur had remained in the waiting room, and now they had to figure out how to get past DOCTOR.

"Why doesn't Anne go in for an appointment while the rest of us sneak through?" suggested Lionel.

"No," argued Ginther. "I'll make the appointment. I can't leave my wife, Louise, and she's not well enough to travel with us."

Ginther passed his tattoo code through the computer console, requesting an appointment. The computer called him in right away. The crowd rose to join him. Lionel held Anne back by the arm.

"You'll be safer if you stay here, especially since you're pregnant. I'll be back in a few days."

"No, I want to come with you. I won't stay here and worry myself sick about whether you're alright."

Lionel was touched by Anne's concern. Since the news of Corey's death, Lionel felt a shift in Anne. It was as if she had lost hope that Corey would come back to her one day. Lionel didn't want to upset her, so he agreed to let her come along.

The vidcam followed Ginther as he took his place on the Medichair. The others crept quickly across the room. Arthur quietly opened the hidden panel to let them out. Once on the other side, they followed the dimly lit hallway to an elevator located towards the center of the Dome. Arthur operated the buttons, bringing them to the lowest level of the Dome.

Anne's stomach jumped to her throat when the elevator stopped. She stepped out, feeling a little dizzy. Even though Arthur assured them that the air was not contaminated, she still felt apprehensive. Perhaps he was just used to it.

The elevator opened up onto a platform, where an underground skytrain was ready to take them further. Arthur and Zane entered the conductor's booth, while the others took seats on the skytrain. While they rode, Arthur explained to Zane that the subway train was powered by electricity, like their skytrains, but could exceed fifty kilometers per hour. Shortly, they pulled into another underground station.

Arthur opened the doors and shut down the subway. They followed him onto the escalators leading up to ground level. The escalators were also turned off when not in use.

"Alright," Arthur said, as they reached the top. "I'm going to open the door, but we have to leave quickly. No dawdling in the doorway." They crowded around him.

"Why do we have to leave quickly?" asked Anne.

"We don't want any stray Peddlers finding their way into the Dome. That's one of the reasons we come at night. Okay, are we ready?" Arthur opened the door and they stepped into the blinding sun. The doorway had been cut into the trunk of a tree, leaving no trace of an opening once closed.

"Wow! This is great!" exclaimed Zachary. "How do you ever find the right tree?"

"There are only three oak trees here, and this is the largest one," answered Arthur.

Anne was surprised to discover that the sun was so bright and hot. The colors of the trees and the grass were incredibly vibrant. She had never realized how much the Dome tinted the hues of nature. The air smelled fresh with a sweet, light scent she could not identify.

Arthur led them to the truck he had parked under one of the other oak trees. It was a four-ton supply truck. Extracting the keys from his pocket, he unlocked the back latch. He threw the door up and helped Anne climb inside. Large windows on the sides of the truck gave them a great view outside. Lionel and Zachary jumped in after her, while Zane took a seat in the cab with Arthur. Once they were on their way, Zane slid open the window panel between the cab and the back.

"Arthur says there is a stream not far ahead. We'll stop there for water." The truck was too noisy to carry on a conversation, so Anne sat curled in up Lionel's protective arms. She could not believe that Corey was dead. Could Zane have been mistaken about Dusting? Could he have only dreamed what he thought he saw when he had been knocked out? Anne knew that it just wasn't so. There could be no other explanation for the disappearance of Lionel's parents.

She looked up into her husband's face. His usually smiling lips were now set in a tight frown. His deep blue eyes were clouded with grief. Anne's heart went out to him. How awful he must feel to lose his parents. He needed her now more than he ever had. She traced the square contours along his chin, hoping to settle the constant clenching of his jaw muscles.

Lionel was barely conscious of Anne's fingers on his face. He had been trying to recall the last conversation he might have had with his parents. Doug had been a good father, even if he had been rough with him once in a while. His mother, Ginger, had always been kind to him. He recalled the times he and his mother would conspire to gang up on his father, tackle him down and tickle his feet. Lionel had always believed this was Doug's only weakness.

Zane closed the sliding window to block out the noise from the back. He marveled at how powerful the truck made him feel. "Feels like we're on top of the world," he commented.

"I always get that feeling when I drive this truck like I'm the king of the road. I've been doing this job now for seven years, and I never get tired of being on the open road. I started in military training, so this is a big change for me." Arthur downshifted to pull the truck off to the side.

"Why did you quit the military?" asked Zane.

"Dishonorable discharge. Here's that stream I was telling you about. If you've never seen running water before, then you're going to love this one." With his foot on the clutch, Arthur placed the truck into first gear. He pulled on the hand brake and shut off the ignition. Reaching behind the seat, he pulled out a jug and a funnel.

Zane opened the back door for the "kids," as he referred to them. They jumped out, and they all followed Arthur into the woods. They had never been in a real forest, so they took their time to touch and smell everything they could. Zachary started collecting pinecones, while Anne was busy picking flowers. Lionel watched a squirrel as it made its way up a tree, and Zane stood next to Arthur while breathing in the sweet smells of the forest. The water streamed down from the north, then banked west. There was a small, sandy outlet where the stream turned, throwing waves upon the shore.

Once on the beach, they stripped off their shoes and waded into the cool water, where Zane washed the blood from his hair and head. It was not as hot in the forest as it was on the road, but they were thankful for the cool water. Arthur filled the jug and assured them it was good to drink. Zachary found a small frog on the bank, and he scared Anne half to death with it. The men laughed at Anne's expense, but she took it well. Even Lionel cracked a smile.

Zane had never thought that life outside the Dome could be so sweet. Why had they been kept from leaving, and by whom? What could be gained from keeping the people sheltered in the Dome? He realized the sooner they got to Mensis, the sooner they would have their answers.

Bear worked endlessly, pounding rocks into usable gravel. He thought back to when they had been brought to the C Zone. Nearly fifty of them had been shackled and whipped by the brutal jailers. He had been left bleeding and bruised in a ten-by-ten-foot room with cement walls. He shared the cell with Lucky and Chip. The cold floor had given little comfort to the heat searing through the skin on their backs.

Bear had been scared that Lucky wouldn't make it through the night. His moans were frightfully weak by the early hours of dawn. Chip had cradled his head on his lap and offered what little comfort he could.

The next day, they were led to the mess tent for a breakfast of runny oatmeal and stale coffee. It was painfully difficult to eat, but they knew they had to keep up their strength.

There were approximately seventy-five other Peddler men with them. Bear realized that many of the men he sat with now were men that he himself had sent here. A large burly man by the name of Eagle approached Bear where he sat with Lucky and Chip. Bear had sent Eagle and his band to the C Zone for their attack on Corey in the Park.

"Hey, aren't you the cop that stuck me in this dump?"

"I was only doing my job," replied Bear, tersely.

"So, my friend, we're all D Men now." There wasn't any malice in Eagle's eyes, only an ironic teasing. Bear was not sure if he could trust Eagle, but he knew he didn't have much choice.

"D Men?" enquired Bear.

"We're the Dead Men who work the Contamination Zone." Eagle was not surprised to see Bear here. He had often thought cops had the same proclivity to violence as criminals, except they were on the other side of the law.

Lucky and Chip had been sent to the sand pits to shovel, and Bear had been assigned to the gravel pits with Eagle. The work was hard, the hours long, the food inadequate, and their sleeping quarters were cramped.

Working side by side, Bear and Eagle watched as a dozen more Peddlers were brought into the camp. The day threatened to be another scorcher, as it had been all week. Bear went back to pounding rocks into gravel.

"Bear, check out the new recruits," Eagle said, nudging his arm.

Bear looked up from his hammering and saw Corey and Moonbeam among those being processed by the jailers.

"Eagle, those are some of my best friends."

Bear wiped his dusty hands on his dirty jumpsuit and then let out an ear-piercing whistle. The men all stopped working for a moment and turned their attention toward the newcomers.

Moonbeam knew that whistle anywhere. He was not sure what Bear was doing here, but he knew it was him. Even though the Peddlers had told Corey of the C Zone, he was not prepared for the site of the barren wastelands to which they had been sent. The jailers herded them to one side of the camp. The biggest of the jailers took them one by one and refastened their wrist chains so they each hugged a wooden pole.

"We have to help them," Bear pleaded to Eagle.

Knowing what the jailers were about to do to Corey and Moonbeam tugged at Bear's heart. Lucky and Chip had explained Corey's reasoning to him for releasing the computer virus, and all the things Luther had revealed. They were here now because of him. He was here now because of his misplaced trust in the law and authority. Rage burned in his heart.

Jason Henninger entered the study where his father, Curtis, was going over his affairs. He crossed the room and perched on the edge of his father's desk next to the stuffed eagle. He adjusted the press on his pant leg.

"Don't you ever knock?"

"Your door was open... good to see you again, too, Dad."

Curtis dropped his pen on his desk and looked up to face his son. Jason's bright blue eyes held a mixture of defiance and an age-long challenge. *What made his son so cocky,* thought Curtis? He had given the boy everything he needed, a home, a position at the bank, a cottage for his playmates, a horse... what more did he want from him? Perhaps he had been too soft with the boy.

He realized now that he should have sent him to military school. He had wanted to, but Jason had thrown a fit and finally, he had given the boy his way. Curtis could see that he was no longer a boy, at least not in appearance. It was time that Jason grew up.

"I've received a vidcall from an old friend of mine. He's the President of Mensis, Phase Three. He'll be sending down a shipment for us, including his daughter, Pandora. It is agreed that you will make her your wife."

"I don't want a wife." Jason sprang off the desktop and turned to face his dad. He resented his father meddling with his life. He was old enough to make his own decisions and choose his own bride if he wanted one.

"Don't be ridiculous, Jason. It's to your advantage to marry Pandora. The dowry will include much-needed supplies such as weaponry, leather, coffee, and other fine goods. It's about time you settled down. Think of your future, Jason. One day you'll be President, and you'll need a proper wife. There's no better candidate than the daughter of a President."

"Sounds like it is more to your advantage. All you care about is the dowry," Jason said, lashing out. "You wouldn't care if she was horse-faced. Did you ever once consider how I felt? What if I don't like her? Can I send her back? No, because you weren't thinking about me when you made this deal, you were thinking about yourself. Well, you're not the one that has to marry her or love her."

"Love, Jason? You don't even know the meaning of the word love. You spend your time jumping in and out of women's beds and you think you're in love. I'm talking about a proper lady who will earn you the respect of the townspeople, a woman who will bear your children and raise them to carry on the family tradition in the Presidency. If you want to have your Peddler women on the side, then that's your business, but you need a proper wife."

Jason realized that his father was right. Men didn't marry Peddler women, they married proper women. Without a doubt, Pandora would know how to throw social balls and mingle with businesspeople. She would be well instructed in childcare and horsemanship. These were the kinds of things that a Peddler woman would never know how to do, not even Sunshine.

This thought surprised him. Had he really been comparing Sunshine to a proper lady? Would he have even considered her for a wife if it had been acceptable? An image of Sunshine passed through his thoughts as he perched back on his father's desk. He could almost feel her lips yielding under his, as they had when they had kissed. Sunshine stirred emotions in him that he had not felt with any other woman, Peddler or not. She could bring a smile to his lips as quick as she could flare his temper. There was magic in those emerald-green eyes that bewitched him so.

Jason brought his attention back to the present as he realized his father was still waiting for a response. "I'll agree to meet her, that's all."

Curtis knew at least it was a start. Once he met Pandora, he was sure Jason would change his mind, as he had when his father had introduced him to Lisa.

"Who was that woman you drove up with today?"

"A new playmate that I picked up in Peddlers."

Curtis didn't like the way his son's eyes brightened as he spoke of her.

"Well, get rid of her. You'll have enough to do around here in preparation for your new bride."

"Forget it! What I do on the side is my business. You said so yourself. Besides, I like this one."

Curtis knew better than to antagonize his son into a stand. No doubt by tonight he'd tire of her on his own accord. Curtis picked up a pile of papers on the side of his desk and handed them to Jason. "I'd like you to update these accounts today. Use your expertise to figure out a tax exemption of a few thousand dollars. We'll be needing a return wedding present for Stan."

Jason took the papers and recognized that he had been dismissed. He figured he had enough time to visit Sunshine before heading to the bank. He could almost taste her kisses as he made his way to the cottage. He unlocked the door and stepped into a quiet house. *Sunshine must be asleep*, he thought. He crept soundlessly up the stairs. He could hear humming coming from the bathroom. Jason stopped in the doorway when he saw Sunshine stretched out in the tub. His eyes drank in the unblemished skin and the well-rounded contours of her well-toned body.

Jason's desire for Sunshine was intoxicating as he watched her bathe from the doorway. She was a beautiful woman, with a strong spirit and a sensual way about her. He had never known a woman who had this effect on him. Watching her now filled him with an ache that was as frightening as it was enticing. He stepped quietly into the room to stand over her.

Sunshine could sense his presence near her, as though by thinking of him she could make him materialize. She opened her eyes to find him staring at her with lust in his clear blue eyes. Startled, she sat up quickly and pulled a towel over herself to cover her nakedness. Her cheeks flushed red with the embarrassment of her thoughts, as well as with what she had read in his eyes. She felt her anger rise.

"How dare you sneak up on me like that? What right do you have to invade my privacy?" She had spoken louder than she had intended, but Jason seemed unaffected by her outburst. A smile formed on his lips that left Sunshine totally unnerved.

"Let me wash your back for you." Sunshine was lost in confusion as Jason picked up the cloth. He rubbed her back with soft, gentle strokes that sent tingles coursing through her body. A protest rose to her lips but came out as a moan instead. She was caught in the mounting sensations that threatened to overtake her. Her hatred for him dissolved as her need for him increased. She didn't want to understand, only to feel.

Jason's yearning grew as he rubbed the soft skin of her back. He traced the lines of her neck, moving the cloth down over her breasts. Sunshine arched up to his touch, gently brushing her lips against his. Jason covered her lips with his own. Her mouth opened to welcome the teasing of his tongue. The intensity of her appetite surprised and delighted him.

He pulled her to her feet, and the towel that separated them fell to the floor. For a moment they stared into one another's eyes, neither of them willing to break the spell with words. Jason encircled her in his arms, bringing his mouth to hers once again. Sunshine slipped her arms around his neck, clinging tightly against him. Jason kissed her eyes, her cheeks, her neck, moving ever slowly to her taut, rosy nipples. Sunshine gave a low, throaty moan. Cradling her in his arms, he carried her into the master bedroom and lay her on the pink canopied bed, where they joined their burning desire.

Afterward, he was reluctant to leave her, but there was business to be taken care of at the bank today. Sunshine started to protest as Jason moved away. She was enjoying the warmth and comfort of his body next to hers. She was confused by the change of emotions she felt for him. She ran her hand through the damp curls on his head as he struggled to pull on his socks. He had been loving and gentle with her, bringing out emotions that she was not prepared to deal with. Perhaps she had been wrong in thinking he didn't care.

"Where are you going?"

"I have to go to work." He leaned over and kissed her softly on the lips. He could feel his passion rising again. He wanted nothing more than to spend the day in bed with her, but he had promised his father he would look after his accounts. Abruptly he stood and moved away from her warm embrace. "I'll call you later."

Without another word, he turned and left the room. Sunshine pulled the still-warm blankets around her protectively. She seemed to spend most of her time alone since Jason took her away. Her body still ached for his touch, but she felt betrayed by his quick departure and vague promise.

Arthur knew they were spending more time than they should by the stream, but he was reluctant to end the enjoyment the Havannians seemed to derive from it. The kids sat in the grass, soaking up the sun. Zachary complained it was too hot, but didn't move into the shade with Arthur and Zane.

"Do you mind me asking why you were discharged from the military?" Zane asked Arthur. Zane couldn't picture Arthur as a troublemaker.

"It's a long story. Suffice it to say that the powers that be didn't want me ascending the ranks. I'll tell you about some other time." Finally, Arthur suggested they continue onto Mensis. It wouldn't take long to get there, confront the President, then get home to his wife, Wendy. He was sure she wouldn't mind company for the night.

They got back to the truck and started on the road. They were feeling relaxed and peaceful after their rest by the stream. They drove on into the badlands. Zane could see a haze rising from the pavement. It seemed to radiate from puddles on the road, but as they approached, the puddles disappeared. It wasn't long before they felt hot in their sweat suits again. The land around them was barren, save a few scraggly bushes. The dirt and grass had a brownish look to them, as though they were void of all color.

"Why is the grass so brown, Arthur?" enquired Zane.

"Lack of water," he replied, simply.

Arthur was pleased that the truck wasn't overheating, and before long they were in the heart of the badlands. There was nothing scenic to look at, just the tumbleweeds blowing lazily in the wind, crossing the road ahead. Arthur rolled his window all the way down to bring in a bit more breeze. He couldn't wrap his head around the fact that his mother was gone. He was so sure she had been well looked after at the Havanna Hospital before retiring to Dusting. This was completely unacceptable! *President Henniger was going to have to answer for this, among other things*, he fumed.

"Why is there a fence around the land up ahead?" asked Zane, interrupting Arthur's thoughts.

"Oh, that's the C Zone."

"C Zone? What's the C Zone?"

"That's where they put the criminals."

"What are criminals?" asked Zane.

"You can't be serious. You've never heard the word criminal before? Doesn't anyone break the law where you live?"

"You mean tabu. Sure, if someone breaks tabu, they're exiled to Peddlers Island, or so we thought."

"Well, in Peddlers, the people who break their customs are sent to the C Zone."

"What do they do there?"

"If memory serves me correctly, the C Zone is one of the nuclear burial sites. The old nuclear reactors leak radiation."

"I don't understand. What are nuclear reactors?"

"I'm not sure. I know that they leak a toxic substance into the air that constantly needs to be covered over with new topsoil," explained Arthur.

"It sounds like dangerous work. Don't the men inhale the toxins while they're burying it?"

"Sure. That's why it's called the Contamination Zone. No one cares if these men die. They're the outcasts of society."

Zane was appalled by the lack of concern Arthur had for these poor men. If the so-called criminals had been sent here for things such as Corey had been exiled for, then they were being unfairly treated.

He was surprised but proud when Corey had stood up against BUDDY at his mating ceremony. He hadn't approved of the way Corey chose to try to change things, but he felt exile was a harsh punishment. Even Zane had thought their system didn't allow for individual compatibility. How could you tell by looking at a girl whether you would get along?

Arthur followed the road right as it rounded the corner of the fence. Up ahead they could see another truck pulling out of the C Zone gates. It looked as though it had just brought in a dozen new criminals.

"That's strange," remarked Arthur. The temperature gauge clicked on, indicating that it was overheating. There was smoke coming from the hood as Arthur pulled the truck to the side of the road. "Well, at least we're near some sort of civilization. Perhaps the jailers will have a spare radiator." Arthur turned the engine off and jumped down from the truck. Zane got out and opened the back doors for the kids.

"Are we there yet?" asked Zachary.

"No. The truck's overheating. We may be able to get some help, though."

They followed Arthur toward the front gates of the C Zone. They could see that there were men shackled with chains around their ankles and wrists.

"Oh my gosh! What's going on here?" Anne asked, in dismay.

"This is the C Zone," explained Zane. "This is where they bring people who break tabu in Peddlers."

"See those men with the black-and-white striped suits?" Arthur pointed out. "Those are the jailers. They're a mean bunch of fellows. They're the type of men who like nothing more than to inflict pain on other people."

"That's awful!" exclaimed Anne.

"These jailers are no better or worse than the people who are sent here, then," remarked Zane.

"Unfortunately, that's true. I've seen a few Mensis men beat a small Peddler guy senseless. Then the soldiers would pick up the Peddler and send him off to this place. Sometimes I'm embarrassed to say I'm a Mensis."

They drew closer to the fence to watch the activities inside. Some of the shackled men were shoveling soil, while others were pounding large rocks into smaller pebbles. They moved mechanically, without life or enthusiasm.

It took longer than Jason expected to finish off the reports his father needed. He had falsified donation receipts to a few non-profit research groups in order to free some funds from his father's account. He closed his eyes to will away the tension between his brows. It was only when he opened his eyes again that he realized it was getting late. Quickly, he connected the vidphone to his playhouse. Sunshine picked up after two rings.

"Hi, Sunshine." Jason smiled at the vidscreen in front of him. Sunshine's chin was set in a firm stance, and her eyes sparkled with fire. Jason knew this look only too well, considering he hadn't known her for very long.

"How dare you lock me in the house all day?" She had discovered her plight as she attempted to leave this afternoon. She had decided it was best for her to return to Peddlers. She knew Jason would only exploit her emotions for him and then return her home when he was done. She had attempted to leave her confused feelings behind and return to the safety of the life she had always known.

Jason ignored her outburst. *The very fact that she was angry must mean that she cares,* he reasoned. She obviously wanted to trust him as much as he wanted to trust her. He knew it was not possible yet, but soon she would know her place. He would somehow need to build up her trust in him.

"I'd like to take you out for dinner tonight. Put on your green velvet evening dress," he ordered. "I'll be by in half an hour to pick you up."

Sunshine disconnected the vidphone, annoyed by his lack of concern for her feelings.

Jason sat staring at the vidphone. How was it that the more she resisted him, the more he wanted her? He realized that Sunshine was not the kind of woman he could dominate with force or intimidation. She would fight him every step of the way. He had thought this afternoon that her submission to his advances had calmed her down, but he had underestimated her.

Was it possible that she felt the same strong desire toward him that he felt for her? Was she also scared by the depth of her feelings? He knew then that the key to disarming Sunshine lay in his ability to seduce her. Could he possibly break her with the uncontrollable passion he felt for her, or would it first destroy his control over himself?

Rising from his desk, Jason placed his father's account books back into the safety deposit box and locked the vault. Everyone had long gone home by now, so he slipped out the back exit to the street.

His friends would be waiting for him at the club as they usually did at the end of the day. He wondered now how well he really knew his friends. It seemed to him that he bought his friends' company more than he had earned it. There was not one man in the club that he felt he could rely on or trust.

For the first time in years, Jason didn't proceed to the bar as usual. Instead, he dropped by the antique store to pick up a gift for Sunshine. The shop stood between a vidphone repair service and a music store. The front display windows were crowded with old pieces of furniture, antique books, and other trinkets. To Jason's eye, a lot of the pieces just looked like junk, but a few looked as though they could be of some value.

The antique dealer met Jason at the door and pumped his hand enthusiastically. He introduced himself as Max. Maximillian Bentley was a tall man with a deeply receding hairline and an easy smile. Only one item caught Jason's interest. It was a pair of ivory earrings with the same elephant design as the flag of his Estate. He paid for the earrings, then walked straight home to dress for his dinner with Sunshine.

"Back to work!" ordered one of the jailers. He cracked his whip in the air to scare the Peddlers into motion. When he extended his arm again, Bear nailed the jailer with the head of his hammer. The blow split the jailer's jaw open and raised a ruckus from the prisoners.

The sting of a whip caught Bear on the lower back, causing him to lurch forward. Eagle reached out a hand to steady him before the other jailer could recoil his whip. They turned to face the jailer together.

The jailers were not used to prisoners fighting back. The D Men all knew what a slow and painful death could do to a man. The jailer looked around for backup but saw only the prisoners closing in on him, with picks and hammers in hand.

Lucky had noticed his friends being led into the camp. He feared for the pain they would bear at the hands of their captors. He had given up the hope of ever seeing Corey and Moonbeam again. Then he heard Bear's whistle.

Things were moving so fast now. There was a riot going on at the gravel pits. Looking around him, Lucky realized that the men he worked beside were now going after their jailers with their shovels. He took the opportunity to make a break with Chip for the front gates.

Lionel, Zachary, and Zane broke into a run toward the entrance to the C Zone. How could they stand by and watch these men whip a man, even if he was a Peddler?

Arthur called out to them. "Stop! You'll be in as much trouble as the Peddlers if you interfere with the law."

Zachary reached the gate first. The guard flew out of his booth to intercept the unidentified people. Zachary took him down in a tackle and landed a punch that knocked him out cold. Lionel and Zane caught up to Zach at the gate. They advanced on the four jailers, two of whom were busy whipping the new men and didn't notice the intruders quickly gaining on them. When the two jailers standing guard heard the steps behind them, they turned and reached for the whips tied around their belts.

Before they could free them, Lucky and Chip hit them from behind with the blade of their shovels. They hit the ground hard; whether they were dead or not, Lucky didn't care.

Another jailer turned from the new recruits, hitting Chip in the back of the head with the tip of his whip. The jailer advanced toward Lucky as Chip hit the ground. He then lashed out at Lucky, snagging the handle of his shovel and pulling it easily from his grip. As he recoiled for the next lash, Lionel brought him down from behind. Lucky helped Chip to his feet. Fortunately, he wasn't seriously hurt.

Meanwhile, Zane had come up behind the last jailer, who was flogging one of the new men repeatedly. The man had fallen to his knees and the jailer was ordering him to stand. He turned and quickly recoiled his whip as he saw Zane approach. He hesitated as he knew that this was not a Peddler.

"Who are you? What do you want?" As if he had not noticed before, he suddenly saw that the camp was in a full riot. The prisoners were attacking his men. He noticed that many were already dead on the ground. He could only hope that the front gate had called for backup.

"Free these men! What you are doing to them is unnecessary and inhumane." Zane clenched his fists by his sides. The jailer pulled his arm back to lash out at Zane. Suddenly, a knife landed in the center of the jailer's chest. Zane swung around to see Arthur standing there breathless with his arm still extended.

"I thought you said it was against the law to interfere?"

"It is, but I couldn't let him kill you. I feel responsible for your safety."

The inmates had now moved to the front of the gates. They were shouting and cheering their success. Lucky had snatched the keys from the jailer's pocket and quickly unfastened his own chains. He then proceeded to unlock his friends from around the poles. Lucky started with Corey and worked his way down the line.

Corey backed away from the pole while rubbing his wrist. His back was stinging with the pain of the blows he had endured. Corey had turned to look for Moonbeam when he recognized his father. His heart started pounding wildly in his chest. What was Zane doing here? Had he been exiled too? He approached his father slowly. He was not sure if that was really him. Of course, it had to be! His life in Havanna came back to him with every step forward. He was not sure how his father came to be here, he only cared that he was.

Zane spotted someone heading toward him. It looked like Corey, but how could that be? How could Corey have escaped the dusting tunnel? Perhaps it was someone who just looked... *no, that is Corey's smile and his walk.* Corey must have been in Peddlers for the last few weeks, then. Zane's heart filled with joy and a knot rose to his throat. He had been feeling like his whole world was crashing down around him lately, but looking at Corey now made him feel so proud. He noticed that Corey seemed more grown-up and mature than he had only a few weeks before. He seemed to have more confidence in himself and less arrogance. Zane stood there waiting for him with his arms crossed and a smirk on his face.

"So, you couldn't leave well enough alone. You had to get yourself exiled from Peddlers, too."

"It's nice to see that you haven't changed, Dad." The two men embraced, awkwardly at first, but then with more strength. Zane pulled away and cleared his throat. Corey wiped a tear from his eye.

"How are you, son?"

"I'm okay. How's Mom?"

"She's fine. Sad, but fine." Zane saw no reason to worry Corey. Helena had taken the news of Corey's death hard, but Zane didn't want to upset his son. He wondered what it would do to her now to find out that Corey was alive.

"What are you doing here, Dad? Were you exiled, too?"

"No. The Dome collapsed, so a few of us went out to look for answers."

"How did you end up out here?" Corey wondered if perhaps it had collapsed when he had uploaded the virus in Peddlers. He had never thought to look.

"We met a man named Arthur Waters. He thinks that either the Peddlers had stopped working or the Mensis cut off the power."

"Who's Arthur?"

"Arthur delivers supplies to Havanna. Ginther and Zachary met him while they were looking around the Medicure building. Lionel's parents and I checked out Dusting. I now know why no one has returned to tell us about it."

"I know too, Dad. I was almost dusted myself."

"That's what we thought had happened to you. I was certain you had… down with the Dome and BUDDY and all his lies!"

There was a bitterness in Zane's voice that Corey had never heard before. He knew the last few weeks must have been hard on him. "Does everyone think I'm dead?"

"No, only a few of us know the truth. It was unfortunate that Lionel's parents had to die in order for us to learn the truth about Dusting."

"Oh, poor Lionel. How's he taking it?"

"I think it's affected him more than he shows."

Corey nodded. Lionel had always kept his true feelings to himself. It was amazing to Corey how quickly he slipped back into his old life. Just then Lionel came walking up to them. Time stood still for a moment as he came face to face with Corey. Zane excused himself to allow the boys time to talk.

Corey looked into his best friend's eyes. He could see amazement and disbelief, but no malice or hate. He wasn't angry at Lionel as he once was. He had come to realize that it wasn't his fate to be a happy Havannian. Suddenly, it didn't matter what had happened in the past. Corey was happy to see Lionel, and that was all that counted.

Lionel was too shocked for words. He had assumed Corey was dead. Somehow Corey must have escaped the death that his parents had not. All the guilt he had felt before came into sharp focus as he faced his childhood friend. If only he could set things right between them again. They now had the chance to bury the feelings of the past and start anew. "We all thought that you were dead. How did you ever escape the dusting tunnel?"

"Just lucky, I guess. It's good to see you, Lionel. It's almost like old times." They threw friendly jabs at one another, but the actions caused Corey's back to throb.

"I'm sorry for what happened at the mating ceremony."

"What's done is done. We can't change the past." Corey now wondered, with Lionel standing in front of him, if Anne was also here. His thoughts were interrupted by Bear and Lucky. They hugged Corey carefully.

"I'm so sorry about getting you caught, guys. I just wanted to make things better, put things right," apologized Corey.

"No, I'm sorry, Corey. I should have believed in you," Bear confessed.

Lucky chimed in, "You don't know what you don't know, Corey. We never could have predicted what would have happened."

"We all wouldn't be here now, though, would we? Luther would still be alive, and I wouldn't have given you all false hopes."

"No, you never gave us false hopes, Corey. You gave us something to believe in. *Ourselves!*" answered Bear.

Zachary came up to Corey and grabbed him by the shoulders. "It is true. You are alive!"

"Zach! What are you guys all doing out of the Dome?"

"Looking for the answers to all those stupid questions you used to ask. They weren't so dumb after all."

Corey was beside himself with joy. He was surrounded by his father, his friends from Havanna, and all his new pals from Peddlers. He had assumed he was never going to see any of them again.

"Lionel, Zachary, I'd like to introduce you to Moonbeam, Lucky, and Bear. Where's Chip?"

"Chip is talking with Eagle over there."

"Anyway, these are my two best friends from Havanna."

Lionel and Zachary shook hands with the Peddlers hesitantly. Even though Arthur had assured them there was no longer a problem with contamination and disease, it was still hard for them to put aside all they had learned about the Peddlers.

"You have very interesting names," Lionel was saying. While his friends were getting acquainted, Corey looked around to be sure everyone was alright. The keys to their chains were being passed around, but the free Peddlers were not making a move to leave.

Zane called Corey aside to introduce him to Arthur. "This is Arthur Waters. He helped us to find our way out of the Dome."

"I've been delivering supplies to Havanna for seven years. I was just as surprised to see your friends as they were to see me," said Arthur, while shaking Corey's hand. Then, through a break in the crowd, Corey saw her. She was more beautiful than he remembered. Her long blond hair blew in the breeze as she approached the circle of her friends. Corey drew her eyes toward him until he was looking into their clear-blue depths. Suddenly everything else stood still around them, and they walked toward one another, never breaking eye contact.

Anne was sure she was dreaming. How could this be Corey walking toward her? Surely the heat or the pregnancy was making her hallucinate. Her heart raced in her chest as they drew closer. It really was him!

"Anne."

That single word brought tears to Anne's eyes, and she flung herself into Corey's arms. They held each other tight. Corey had been sure he was never going to see her again. He had thought of Anne often, but only as a memory. Now she was here in his arms, with her bright blue eyes shining up at him with love.

Lionel watched his wife and Corey from the circle of Corey's new friends. It was apparent that their love had never died. Anne belonged to Corey, heart, and soul. She was pregnant with Corey's child, but she was forever married to Lionel.

Anne pulled away from Corey. Her eyes held a mixture of sadness and strength. Corey knew before she spoke just what she was going to say. "Corey, I have never stopped loving you, but I am married to Lionel. As long as we are married, I can never leave him."

Corey said sadly, "I respect your decision, Anne, even though it pains me. You are the only woman that I will ever love."

"Don't, Corey. You're only making this more difficult."

"Corey," Chip called to him as he approached. "Lucky found a first-aid kit in the supply tent. Remove your jumpsuit, and I'll have a look at your back."

Corey slowly peeled the jumpsuit from his upper body. He bent over so Chip could pour some hydrogen peroxide over his cuts and wrap gauze around his torso.

Anne offered to help, and a makeshift hospital was quickly established. Chip, Lucky, and Anne were bandaging new and old wounds. Bear and Eagle were unlocking the last of the men, and Rocky and Wolf were tying up the guard at the front gate. The rest of the Peddlers sat on the ground, waiting for instructions.

"What are we going to do now?" asked Eagle. He had just joined the rest of the men on the ground. Corey was surprised to see that Eagle and Bear had become friends. He clearly remembered that first night in the Park when Bear was ready to kill him. Corey positioned himself to address the men.

"I would like to start out by saying that everyone here is free to go as they please." Corey waited while the crowd murmured and chattered among themselves. "For those of you who do not know, the attempt to change the social structure in Peddlers has failed. The Mensis soldiers have returned everyone back to work." There were angry shouts and gruff remarks from the crowd.

"The Mensis have fooled and repressed us with their lies and deceit. I feel it is time to change things around here. It's time that all people were treated equally. I can't make you any promises, but if you join me, I say we can take back freedom from oppression for everyone."

The men cheered and chanted, "Damn the Men."

The camp cook had been found hiding in his kitchen. Eagle and Bear had him prepare some food. He made them chicken soup with fresh vegetables, as well as hamburgers. There was plenty of food for everyone.

Corey sat at a table with his friends from the Dome. His father and Arthur joined them for lunch.

"Tonight, there will be another supply run," Arthur informed them. "They'll be sending someone else since I haven't returned. If this man sees that the D Men have been freed, he may just turn back and report it to the authorities."

"What do you suggest we do, then?" Corey asked Arthur.

"There's a lake not far from here. We can hide there for now."

"Great. After we eat, we'll pack up the rest of the food supplies and head over," Corey agreed.

Arthur stood and called for everyone's attention. It took a few minutes before the men quieted down.

"Okay, everyone, listen up. We are going to be safer at Crystal Lake than staying here. I want the men at this table to gather the food, the men at this table to gather the bedding, and the men at these two tables to collect the shovels, hammers, picks, or any other weapons you can find. Bring them all to the truck when you are done. We'll be leaving shortly."

The next few minutes were drowned out by chairs scraping against the floor as the men went about their chores. It was amazing to Arthur how quickly his training as a commander came back to him. He missed having a troop under his charge. When the men started moving, Arthur leaned closer to Corey and whispered, "We have the manpower to fight. If we only had weapons, we'd do alright to oppose the soldiers."

"Are you sure you want to get involved, Arthur?"

"These lies involve all of us. I've helped your friends escape the Dome, and I've killed a jailer. I'm committed now. If I go back, they'll kill me."

"Thank you, Arthur. Will your truck hold all these men?"

"It'll hold half, but there's another truck out back that we can borrow." He gave Corey a sly wink.

His manservant welcomed Jason with a note of disbelief in his eyes. He was not accustomed to seeing him home so early and sober. Dressed in the traditional black suit, with a white shirt and red tie, Lightfoot opened the door of the Henniger Estate for his young master. He had been employed by the Hennigers since he was a young man. His father, Willow, had served President Nick Henniger and had trained Lightfoot well in the duties of providing properly for a President's needs. Although Lightfoot was astonished to see Jason home early, he concealed his surprise.

"Shall I set another place at the dinner table for you, Master Jason?"

"No, that won't be necessary, Lightfoot. I'll be dining out this evening. Would you be so kind as to make a reservation for two at the Antler Room for eight?"

"Will do, sir," said Lightfoot, with a slight bow. Jason ran up the grand staircase two steps at a time. He stopped at the top and turned back to speak to Lightfoot.

"Have the horse and carriage readied as well." Placing his hand on the circular carved handrail, he pushed off to sprint down the long corridor as he had done as a child. He realized he felt as giddy as a boy on his first date as he opened the door to his room.

The dark wood paneling of the room was richly masculine. Jason threw his suit jacket on the brass-framed bed under the French windows. The heavy beige drapes were closed to the last rays of the day. Jason peeled off the remainder of his clothes and left them in a heap on the floor for Lightfoot to pick up.

He dressed carefully in a three-piece tailored suit of light tan with a matching green tie for Sunshine's dress. As he set the tie in place, he questioned his motives for treating Sunshine like a proper lady. Could it be he was just trying to gain her trust or was there more to his feelings toward her than he was willing to admit? He shook his head against these confusing questions and headed for the cottage in the carriage.

Jason let himself into the playhouse. A quick sweep of the ground floor level confirmed that Sunshine was upstairs.

"Are you ready?" he called up from the foot of the staircase.

"Quite."

Jason inhaled as he caught sight of Sunshine at the top of the stairs. The flowing green velvet dress fit beautifully on her full, rounded figure. It tapered to snug her small waist, then flared to the floor over the stiff crinoline slip. Jason's eyes were drawn to the low V-neck of the dress. He allowed his gaze to rest on the creamy mounds of her cleavage. Her fiery red hair hung in waves down her back.

She descended the stairs slowly, aware of the effect she was having on Jason. If she could convince him that she could be trusted, he would not have a need to lock her door. A smile crossed her lips, thinking that her victory of escape would not be long.

"You are so beautiful," Jason whispered. He took her hand in his and led her the rest of the way down the stairs. Her green eyes sparkled with such mischief that Jason mistook it for desire. He pulled Sunshine into his arms and touched his lips softly against hers. Her lips were soft and inviting, and Jason contemplated canceling supper at the Antler Room. Slowly, he pulled away and cleared his throat, hoping to also clear his thoughts.

"Your chariot awaits." He led her to the horse-drawn carriage outside. Jason spoke a few words to the driver before climbing in next to Sunshine. The ride through town to the Antler Room was short, and they arrived for their dinner engagement just on time for their reservation.

The maître D greeted Jason warmly and extended a pleasant smile to Sunshine before showing them to Jason's favorite table. It was a quaint table for two set into an alcove. Jason held Sunshine's chair out for her, then allowed the maître D to hold out his. Jason pressed a few bills into the man's hand.

After the maître D had left, they sat quietly reading the menus that he had left for them. Sunshine didn't have a clue what any of the meals were, and Jason had long ago memorized the entire menu. A wine porter approached the table. Jason ordered a bottle of their best champagne.

Sunshine was acutely aware of the stares from the other tables, but Jason seemed to enjoy the attention. He knew there would be much speculation tomorrow about who the young lady was. He had never been a man to sit around idly gossiping with people. He had always been the one to give people something to gossip about.

The wine porter returned to their table with a wine stand, holding the bottle of champagne in a silver bucket. He ceremoniously threw a cloth napkin across his arm and proceeded to open the bottle. The cork eased off gently, sending bubbles over the rim of the bottle. He placed the cloth around the bottle and poured just a taste into Jason's crystal goblet. Sunshine watched as Jason sampled the champagne and then nodded his approval. The porter proceeded to pour them each a glass, starting with Sunshine's. He was careful to turn the bottle so as not to spill a single drop on the lace tablecloth. No sooner had the porter returned the bottle to its cradle did a uniformed waiter appear by their side.

"Shall I order for the two of us?" offered Jason. He could sense Sunshine's uneasiness with the menu, although otherwise, she was conducting herself in a very ladylike manner.

"Yes, thank you." She smiled at Jason.

"We'll start with the escargot au fromage, and for the main course, we'll have the beef wellington with broccoli and cheese. I'd also like a side plate of fettuccini alfredo, and for dessert, we'll have the peach melba crepes." Jason closed his menu with a decisive snap. He knew the selections were an odd mixture, but he wanted Sunshine to taste all his favorite dishes. The waiter accepted his order without question and relieved them of their menus. A busboy immediately placed a fresh loaf of warm bread on their table with whipped butter and glasses of cold water.

"So, are you enjoying yourself?" Jason reached across the table to take Sunshine's hand in his own. His touch sent tingles up her arm and a blush to her cheeks. She pulled her hand away quickly to avoid falling into the swirl of emotions pounding through her chest.

"A toast!" Jason proclaimed, while holding up his goblet and touching it to hers. "A toast to the most beautiful woman in this room." The champagne tasted sweeter than the wine that she was used to in Peddlers, but she welcomed its warmth to calm her nerves. Could Jason have meant what he said? Did he really think she was the most beautiful woman in the room?

The waiter promptly brought their appetizers and lit the small candle under their garlic butter dishes. Sunshine followed Jason's actions on which fork to use and how to break the bread properly for dipping into their dish.

She was amazed to see that he was as much at home here in the confines of the restaurant as he was in the outdoors. He looked incredibly handsome in his three-piece suit. She was pleased to see that he wore a tie that matched her dress. To a casual observer, they might look like a well-coordinated couple.

His deep blue eyes were smiling at her, and for the first time, she realized that he had dimples in his cheeks. They talked about their lives as children. Sunshine found herself opening up to him more than she had planned. She was sympathetic to his problems with his father and sorry that he never knew his mother.

Jason wasn't sure why he told Sunshine as much as he had, but it felt good to talk about it. She neither judged nor criticized what he said, but listened attentively. Jason was seeing a side of her that had never been revealed to him before. She was understanding and patient in a way he had not expected from her. There was more to this woman than met the eye.

Sunshine enjoyed the taste of the dishes that were placed in front of her. She wondered fleetingly if Corey ate food such as this in Havanna. Suddenly she felt guilty for enjoying herself when most of her friends were in the C Zone. She hoped Moonbeam and Corey had escaped capture. She silently prayed that they were fine.

After dessert, Sunshine was sure she'd never be able to move. The food had been delicious, and the champagne had made her giddy. Jason paid the waiter with bills from his wallet, tipping him generously. He would never tip the Peddler waiters as much as a Mensis waiter, but then, the Peddlers didn't work in classy restaurants like the Antler Room. Most of the Peddler domestics that worked in Mensis had been born and raised here. It was just too difficult to take the Peddlers from their home.

There were exceptions, of course, he thought, as he looked over to Sunshine sitting across from him. She had behaved well tonight. He was sure that she wouldn't cause him any more problems. Now that she had a taste of the good life, she would never want to go back home.

Their carriage was waiting for them as they stepped out. Seated side by side, Jason pulled a blanket from under the seat and wrapped it around Sunshine. He placed an arm protectively around her until they reached the cottage. With a wave of his hand, Jason dismissed the driver for the night. He opened the door for Sunshine, but she stopped him in the doorway with a hand against his chest.

"Thank you for the evening, but I really need to rest." She was not ready to cope with the emotions that Jason evoked in her when she was not of sound mind.

Jason pulled her into his arms and probed her lips with the tip of his tongue. He was not going to let her spoil such a perfect evening. He could feel his desire for her rise as her lips yielded under his own. He had never known another woman who could flare his passion so quickly.

Sunshine chastised herself for weakening in his soft, warm kisses. It was not in her plan to feel this way. She knew she had to stop him before it was too late. Suddenly she stepped back and pushed Jason away.

"Stop that. What right do you have to kiss me without my consent? I clearly said that I wished to be left alone."

"Hey, what's gotten into you, woman?" The evening had gone so well; Jason couldn't understand her resistance. "You weren't so frigid this afternoon."

The slap that followed caught Jason totally off guard. She knew he would use her own weaknesses to his advantage. Never again, she vowed, would she let him get near her.

"You're not coming in until I can come and go as I please."

So, she had been playing him for the fool all night, had she? As much as her behavior infuriated him, he had to admire her strength. She was not a woman to be taken lightly. He sized up the determination of her threat and knew that she was serious. He wasn't going to be bested by a woman, especially a Peddler woman. He would show her that her tactics wouldn't work with him.

"You're a stubborn woman, but two can play this game. You'll not have your freedom until I can come and go as I please." Without another word, Jason closed and locked the door that now stood between them. He ignored the threats and curses from the other side as he headed back to the main house.

It was an empty victory, he realized. Neither of them got what they wanted, but he would be damned if he would let a Peddler woman dictate the rules to him.

They found twelve clean jailer outfits and a hand pistol in the jailer's quarters. Rocky handed the pistol to Corey, who placed it in the pocket of his Green-Level jumpsuit. He would have time later to look at it more closely. The food, weapons, and other handy items were packed in the back of the trucks. Arthur and Zane sat up front in Arthur's truck, and half of the men climbed in the back. The others filled up the second truck, with Chip and Lucky riding in the cab. Chip had a bit of trouble with the gears at first but soon got the truck moving. Once the trucks were in motion, the Peddlers started to sing songs they had learned in the C Zone.

Anne stood beside her husband and enjoyed the songs the Peddlers sang. It was difficult to see them as equals, as Corey suggested they should. She had always been taught in Havanna that they were the special, chosen people, superior to the Peddlers. Anne realized how ridiculous it was for anyone to think more highly of themselves. The only way they could see themselves as superior was to believe the lies, they had been told.

When she had helped to bandage some of the D Men that were hurt, she had found most of them to be very polite. In fact, she found the Peddler people fascinating. They seemed to have an easygoing way about them. Even as criminals, they weren't so bad. Anne knew that these men bled the same color and felt the same pain and emotions as they did. If they were different, it was because of the way they were raised and the things they believed in.

It was only a short drive to Crystal Lake, which they made in good time. The men jumped out of the trucks and immediately started collecting the berries that grew wild. Arthur instructed a few men to gather wood and rocks for a fire. The firewood and rocks were set up, but the fire was not started. He thought it would be wise to wait until after the new supply runner had passed. Others pulled long blades of grass, which they used as a foundation for their bedding. The blankets and pillows from the C Zone were pulled out and laid down atop the grass. The food was stored in one truck, with the shovels, picks, and hammers in the other.

Once they were settled into their new camp, the Peddlers went into the lake for a swim. They scrubbed their skin with the leaves of a mullein plant. The day was still young when they had all washed and cleaned. Zachary pulled a long rope from the supply truck and suggested that they have a game of tug of war. The men divided themselves into two separate teams.

After they finished their game, they took the fresh food from the truck. Arthur lit the fire as night was starting to fall. They sat around the fire pit, eating and talking in small groups. Arthur sat with Zane and Corey.

"The men seem to be settling in well. No doubt their absence has been noted by now," Arthur informed them.

"You seem to know a lot about how things are run for a truck driver," said Corey.

"Arthur has had military training," Zane interjected. Corey looked at Arthur with renewed interest and lifted his left brow.

"Yes. Started as a cadet at the age of fourteen, then joined the military at eighteen. Those were some good years."

"What happened?" Zane enquired.

"Russ Fletcher, Kevin Bates, and I were sent to capture some renegade Peddlers on their way north. Things went south and Russ shot the four runaways. A violent argument ensued between Russ and Kevin, and then Russ shot Kevin. Russ insisted that the official report would claim the Peddlers shot Kevin and were shot in turn. He said things could go very wrong for me when he took over the position of General after his father retired, so I had better stick to his official story.

"A few days later, President Henniger called me into his office and held me responsible for the whole affair. He issued me a dishonorable discharge. I tried to argue my point, but he wasn't having it. He took Russ's word over mine. The bastard wouldn't even listen to my side of the story!

"I suppose I should just be glad that they didn't execute me or send me to the C Zone, as I'm sure Russ would have proposed. It was more important to the President to keep good relations with his General than to seek the truth."

"I'm sorry, Arthur. That must have been tough," Zane sympathized.

"Well, I'm tired of burying my head in the sand. Someone has to stand up to these evil people, and now we have the chance to do so."

"Your knowledge and expertise will be invaluable, Arthur," Corey added. "Glad to have you aboard." Corey got up to join his Havannian friends.

After supper, Lucky and Chip took a walk along the shoreline. They held hands as they walked and watched the fading sun sparkle on the waves of the lake. Lucky reflected how his life back in Peddlers seemed like a remote dream now. His short time in the C Zone had given him the opportunity to do some soul-searching. He had discovered that his love for Chip was all that was important to him. He had felt so lonely and lost without Chip's friendship and guidance when they were apart.

Chip felt Lucky give his hand a little squeeze. When their battle was won and they were free to live as they pleased, Lucky vowed to spend that time selfishly with Chip. When they reached the edge of the forest, they sat on the sand. They expressed their love for one another, quenching their fears in the comfort of one another's arms. Words were not needed for what they had to say. It was expressed in their actions and reactions to a familiar touch.

Moonbeam walked the beach alone, thinking long thoughts about Sunshine. He wondered what she was doing back in Peddlers, and whether she missed them. He knew she would be as worried about them as he was for her.

Arthur joined Anne, Lionel, Zachary, and Corey standing around the fire. He turned to Lionel and Anne. "I really didn't get a chance to talk to you earlier. Zane tells me that you're going to have a baby. Congratulations! I've always wanted children myself. You must be excited!"

Lionel had been pleased by Anne's decision to stay with him. He had been so sure she was going to leave him and renew her romance with Corey.

It took a moment for Arthur's words to sink in, but now Corey could understand Anne's determination to stay with Lionel. He should have expected this since it was required for a couple to have their first baby by June of next year, but it took Corey totally by surprise. He felt a little sucker-punched.

"You never told me you were going to have a baby, Lionel!"

"I'm sorry," he replied quietly. He had not known how to break the news to Corey. Lionel had finally decided that Corey didn't need to know that the baby was his. "I didn't know how you would take it."

"I'm very happy for you. A congratulations drink is in order. Come, I think there's still some beer left. I have so many things that I want to tell you about my time in Peddlers and Willowdown." They made their way to the mess truck, throwing lighthearted jabs at one another. For Corey, it was just like old times, even if there was a little pain behind the smile.

Russ Fletcher entered President Henniger's office. "All the prisoners from the C Zone are gone, sir," he said, without preamble.

"How did that happen?" exploded Curtis.

"The delivery man said that when he arrived, the cook was untying the front guard, and all the rest of the jailers were dead. They've taken the food supplies and a few weapons."

"What kind of weapons?" Sweat had broken out on Curtis's forehead, and his leg jerked up and down in a nervous gesture.

"Mostly whips, picks, shovels, and one hand pistol."

"Damn it! I'm counting on you to find them, Russ. This is too important a mission for Jason. Get it done."

"Don't worry. I'm sure they've gone back to Peddlers. I've never known a Peddler yet that didn't try to go back home."

"Make sure of it."

"Yes, sir." Russ Fletcher saluted, left the office, then gathered two dozen men at the defense building. They saddled their horses and donned their armor. Russ drew a map of the area.

"The C Zone is basically central, so they could have taken the road back to Peddlers south by the Dome, or north, bypassing Mensis," Russ explained to his men. "There's also the road west leading out toward the next Mensis Phase, but it is unlikely they would follow this route. It doesn't lead back to Peddlers." Russ decided as a precaution he'd send one of his soldiers in that direction to check it out anyway. President Curtis Henniger expected the utmost care in this case.

He sent Stephen Cowen and Frank Byers to travel the northern route. They would meet up with the rest of the soldiers outside the gate to Peddlers. Russ would ride with the rest of the men south, where he was sure they had gone. He asked John Williams to ride to Crystal Lake.

"The prisoners will be on foot, so we can expect to catch up with them before noon, even if they didn't stop for the night. It is possible that they could find their way quicker through the forest, but we'll decide later whether to pursue that route. If worse comes to worst, we can pick them up back in Peddlers. I want you to shoot first and ask questions later."

Russ double-checked his list, then ordered his men in line. They rode quietly out of town toward their destinations. The only sound that could be heard in the quiet evening air was the pounding of the horses' hooves upon the ground in their search for the fugitives. John Williams rode south with Russ, almost as far as the C Zone, before veering west toward Crystal Lake.

Not long down the road, John spotted a reflection coming from Crystal Lake. Upon closer inspection, he realized it was the glow of a campfire. His first thought was to turn back and alert Russ to the prisoners' whereabouts. Then again, if he could capture the prisoners single-handedly, he would stand to gain a promotion. If this case was as important as he thought, perhaps he could replace Russ as General. *Wouldn't that burn Russ's ass*, he thought.

John had never cared much for Russ as a fellow soldier, but when he made General, he had become unbearable as a commander. It was just as well that Russ often sent him out alone to chase dead ends. It was better than watching him flaunt and abuse his power.

Turning his attention back to the fire, John dismounted his horse. He tied the mare to a tree and crept up close to one of the trucks. He pulled his pistol from its holder and stepped into the clearing.

"Freeze!"

For a moment, everything went still. The men stopped talking and turned their attention toward the lone soldier. Bear started toward the man, with his hands out in front of him. Arthur looked apprehensively at Corey.

"Corey, you better stop your friend before he gets shot."

"Don't worry about it. Bear's got this," Corey said with confidence.

"Maybe I should go up there and talk to him," suggested Arthur.

"Stay where you are. Bear can handle it."

Bear stopped a few feet in front of the soldier. John was waving the pistol unsteadily in his hand.

"Put your gun away and you won't get hurt. I was once a cop myself, and…" Before Bear finished his sentence, he kicked the pistol from the soldier's hand. John rubbed his hand. He had been willing to listen to reason when the kick took him by surprise. Bear quickly dropped the soldier to his knees. He hauled him to his feet and brought him to face Corey. "What would you like me to do with him?"

"You've done well, Bear. I'll take it from here." Corey faced the soldier who now stood before him in his armor. "Where are the rest of the soldiers?"

"They've gone to Peddlers to look for you."

"Are you alone?"

"Yes."

Corey wasn't sure if the man was lying or not. He sent Bear and Moonbeam to scout the area by the road. He instructed the soldier to remove his armor. Bear came back leading a horse. He reported that the coast was clear.

"Moonbeam, find two volunteers to take up watch on the road. I don't want any sneak attacks. I also want someone to stand watch over the soldier," instructed Corey.

Zachary had retrieved rope from the truck and cut off a piece to tie the soldier's hands behind his back. Once he was done, he led the soldier to the circle of the fire. The men extinguished the fire to avoid further detection. Arthur volunteered to watch the prisoner.

Corey was apprehensive about the lone soldier. It didn't seem likely that they would send only one man into their camp.

After talking to their prisoner, Arthur asked Eagle to watch him and went in search of Corey.

"John is an old friend of mine. He says there is a shipment coming in the morning from Mensis, Phase Three," Arthur informed Corey. "Phase Three produces weapons. There are sure to be some rifles in the shipment."

"Interesting," Corey mused.

"This is just the thing we need," insisted Arthur. "They are bound to send their soldiers after us, so now we can defend ourselves."

"Let's get the men together. We have a lot of plans to make."

Corey and Arthur called everyone around the fire to make an announcement.

"Gentlemen, my name is Corey Tusk. Some of you may know me, and some of you may not. I am sure by now you have all heard the rumors about the computer virus that took down the power in Peddlers. My good friend Luther and I uploaded that virus in an attempt to collapse the system. It worked, but we did not foresee the quick response by the Men.

"My friends and I here," he said, indicating to the right of him, "are from Havanna. We've come to tell you that the Dome is not Dusting. It is not a place of retirement. It is our home, and we have also been told we will one day go to Dusting. But it is all lies! The Mensis have been lying to all of us. Dusting is death!"

There were outraged cries from the D Men as they all yelled or spoke at once. "Damn the Men," echoed through the clamor. Corey raised his hands to quiet the crowd.

"I have lived in Peddlers, working for the very credits that they take back from us for the right to live, to eat, to travel, or seek medical attention. I say this is a travesty! I have seen food growing wild in the forbidden zone, and have tasted water so sweet and fresh running freely on the ground. Do you wonder why they don't want you there? They have you working for ten to twelve hours a day to help them control you! I say their day is done. I say we take back our freedom and our sovereignty.

"My friend Luther was eighty-six years old. Eighty-six years old! Can you imagine that? Do you realize how many good years they are stealing from us? Luther lived his life free and independent of Mensis. He gave his *life* trying to give us all a chance to be free. I say we honor that sacrifice. I say we make our stand against those that would oppress us."

The crowd of D Men shuffled restlessly, talking excitedly, or staring intently. Some of them started to chant, "Damn the Men, Damn the Men." Corey held up his hands again for silence.

"My friends here," he indicated to the left of him, "from Peddlers are committed with me to bring justice to not only the people of Peddlers but of Havanna as well. We have figured out how to produce electricity without pedaling. We have figured out how to grow food. We don't need the Mensis. They need us! Will you stand with us this day? Will you stand against tyranny and oppression? Will you, the D Men, stand with us against the Men?"

Jason sat alone in the Way Inn, drinking a scotch and water. He discouraged conversations when people came by to talk. His thoughts were preoccupied with Sunshine. He knew he should be preparing arrangements for his fiancée's arrival, but he couldn't keep thoughts of Sunshine off his mind.

He missed the way her eyes sparkled like emeralds when she was angry. He missed her soft, yielding lips and the sensuous curves of her body. He wished now that he had had the guts to defy his father and take Sunshine as his wife. Did he really want to marry Sunshine? *Yes*, he thought, *I really do*. He decided to go tell Sunshine how he felt.

Jason unlocked the front door of his playhouse, then walked into the dark interior of the front foyer. All the lights had been turned off downstairs, but a faint fragrance of bath bubbles hung in the air. He took the stairs two at a time to the second floor. There was a light on in Sunshine's bedroom.

"Good evening," Jason cooed from the doorway.

Sunshine looked up from the vidpad she had been reading. She had heard him come in but chose not to greet him at the door. She looked at him coolly, not showing the nervousness she felt when he was around.

"May I come in?" Jason walked in without a reply and sat on the chair beside her bed. He was not sure how to approach the situation. If Sunshine had been a Mensis woman, he could have professed his love for her and everything would be fine. Did he really want to tell Sunshine that he loved her?

Yes, he thought, as he looked into her eyes, *I do love her*. Why did there have to be a distinction between classes? Why didn't society accept the Peddlers as real people? Was it fair to restrict someone from loving who they wanted?

Jason knew that his role as the President's son put him in an awkward position. He was supposed to set an example for other people. He realized that being at the top didn't necessarily buy one's freedom. A leader had to be what the people expected of him, whether it was right or wrong.

Sunshine watched Jason fight his own inner battle. She wished he would talk to her so she could help him. Earlier, she might not have spoken to him, but seeing him now looking vulnerable and lost, she felt the need to comfort him. She had missed his company and his smile.

She placed her vidpad on the side table and took Jason's hand in her own. He looked up into her eyes, and instead of finding a challenge, he found a warm, caring look.

"I've brought you something." Jason reached into his suit pocket and brought out a small ivory box with the elephant earrings in it. He handed it to Sunshine, who sucked in her breath. It was the most beautiful jewelry she had ever seen. It was just like the necklace Corey wore around his neck.

"Oh, Jason, they're beautiful!" Tears welled up in her eyes as she held the tiny box. No one had ever given her a priceless gift like this before.

Jason removed it from her trembling fingers, placed them aside, and then wiped a lone tear that fell from her eye. Sunshine took his hand in her own, kissed it softly, then placed it upon her breast. Jason cupped his hand around the softness of her flesh while seeking her lips with his own. Their desire grew until each one needed the other to satisfy the hunger in their souls.

Sunshine gave herself freely to his demanding lips and welcomed the touch of his caresses. She pulled Jason down to lie with her... against her. She encouraged his advances and responded in kind. He pulled away from her to drink in her emerald-green eyes.

"I love you, Sunshine."

Sunshine was not sure how it was possible for her heart to beat faster as he spoke the words she longed to hear, but it did. A new world of feelings opened to her. "I love you too, Jason."

Their declaration of love broke the dam of their emotions and added fuel to the burning desire they felt for one another. Their lips came together this time with a new sense of freedom and urgency.

Russ and his men joined Stephen and Frank outside the gate to Peddlers. Russ had been riding all night and hadn't seen a sign of the prisoners. "Well, did you spot them?" he asked Frank.

"No, we've been here since early this morning and there's been no sign of activity."

"Damn! Where could they be?" Russ radioed to the defense building back in Mensis. John had not returned yet from his search of Crystal Lake. Russ knew that either he had found them and been caught, or he had continued farther toward the next Mensis Phase. Russ scowled while staring into space.

There wouldn't be a reason for John to leave the immediate area, so he must have found them. *Why would they go to Crystal Lake?* he wondered. Then it dawned on him that the shipment from Mensis, Phase Three was due today. The rebels must have discovered this piece of information and were planning to intercept it.

Russ tried to radio Curtis at the Estate. Curtis didn't answer, so he ordered the troops back to Mensis immediately.

They followed the road north through the woods. Russ was certain with every step they took that they must be at Crystal Lake. It was the most logical thing to do. He wished he had thought of it last night instead of wasting their time riding to Peddlers. He spurred his horse on faster.

The first thing he needed to do was to see if the shipment had arrived. If John hadn't returned by the time they reached Mensis, he'd know for sure. He would round up some more men and close in on Crystal Lake.

Corey looked over the hand pistol that Rocky had found in the C Zone. Arthur showed Corey how to load it, cock it, and fire it. Corey took a few practice shots against an old dead tree. He was surprised to see the bark split with the impact of the bullet. He realized how quickly a bullet could kill a man.

Arthur suited up in the armor while some of the other men put on the jailer outfits, Corey included. Once they were ready, they gathered around for some last-minute instructions.

"Listen up," called Corey. "Arthur will ride the horse and scout the road for the arriving shipment. The rest of us will stay in the back of the trucks until we know for sure how many men there will be. I want those with the jailer suits on to be standing outside the truck with the whips on their belts. Don't draw them unless absolutely necessary. Let's go."

Moonbeam had been watching the road, waiting for the shipment. He reported that they had not driven by yet. Arthur spurred John's horse up past the truck. With Bear and Eagle sitting beside him, Chip drove to a natural bend in the road. They wore the jailer outfits that they had taken from the C Zone.

Chip stopped the truck sideways in the middle of the road. Bear jumped out and opened the back door. While the mock jailers stepped out, Eagle took cover in the bushes with John's shotgun.

Not fifteen minutes had passed when Arthur rode back to say that the shipment was coming. He told Corey there were two armored men on horses, a four-ton truck, and a Cadillac.

The two men on the horses arrived around the bend first and stopped when they saw the barricade. They were wearing the blue uniforms of Mensis, Phase Three under their armor. "What seems to be the problem?" asked Raymond, one of the soldiers. He hadn't expected to encounter anyone on the road.

"We have a problem with some missing prisoners, and we have been instructed to search all of the vehicles traveling on this road. May I see your identification, please?" Raymond handed their papers to Arthur, while the other vehicles stopped on the road behind them. "How many people are traveling with you today?" enquired Arthur.

"Let's see, there's President Bell's daughter, and her servant and driver. There are two men in the cab of the truck and one in the back, besides Mike here and myself."

"How many in your party are armed?"

"Just ourselves and the man in the back of the truck."

"Eight people, three armed," Arthur yelled. The D Men emerged out of hiding and surrounded the party. Arthur cocked the handgun and ordered the soldiers to drop their weapons. Chip jumped from the truck and retrieved the discarded rifles.

"What's going on here?" asked Raymond.

"Shut up," answered Arthur. "I'll warn the men that the man in the back of their truck is armed while you tie up the prisoners," he said to Bear.

A group of D Men headed straight for the Cadillac. Eagle pulled the driver from the car and Moonbeam opened the door to the back, pulling one of the women out by her arm.

She wore a beautiful white lace dress and ribbons in her chestnut-brown hair. Her beauty was breathtaking. Moonbeam looked into her frightened yellow-speckled brown eyes. The other woman, dressed in a Blue-Level jumpsuit, hopped out of the car and pulled Pandora Bell protectively away from Moonbeam.

Pandora couldn't understand what the jailers would want with her. It took her a minute to realize that they were under attack from a group of Peddlers. She watched in horror as the scene unfolded in front of her eyes.

The other D Men surrounded the four-ton truck. Corey pulled the door to the weapons truck open and instantly froze as he faced the barrel of a shotgun.

"Corey!" Lionel yelled, as he lunged forward to knock Corey out of the way. The shotgun blasted through the air as Lionel and Corey went down. Before the blue-uniformed man could re-cock his shotgun, Arthur rode up and shot him in the throat. He had been too late to warn Corey of the armed man in the back.

Corey rolled out from under Lionel's weight. It was then that he noticed Lionel was bleeding profusely. He had been shot in the chest as he attempted to save Corey's life.

"Oh no! No! No! No!" exclaimed Corey. He cradled his best friend's head against his chest. Lionel had a look of pain in his clear blue eyes. He gave a little cough and blood flew out of his mouth.

"I'm going, Corey." Lionel's voice was barely a whisper.

"No, Lionel. Hang in there." Corey's eyes filled with tears as he watched the life draining from his friend. "Please, Lionel, don't die!" Corey rocked Lionel in his arms and looked around him helplessly.

Lionel grabbed Corey's hand tightly in his own. "Take care of her, Corey. She's carrying your child." His body stiffened for a moment and then he went limp in Corey's arms.

"Noooo!" Corey cried out. He wept over the body of his childhood friend, whom he had just gotten back. As much as he had wanted Anne, he hadn't wanted it to be this way.

Arthur pulled Corey away from Lionel's body. A few of the men placed Lionel in the back of the Mensis, Phase Three truck with the dead soldier. The other Phase Three prisoners were put into the back of Arthur's truck. They drove back to the camp and brought the prisoners to the campfire.

Moonbeam apologized to the people of Mensis, Phase Three for the loss of one of their men. He explained their present situation and their fight for freedom against the Mensis.

Pandora was sympathetic to their cause, but she didn't want to get involved with political matters.

"This has nothing to do with politics," explained Moonbeam. "It has to do with freedom and equality."

"You mean that if you win this fight, then I won't have to marry the President's son?" Pandora hadn't been pleased with her father's decision, but she respected his wishes. She was sad to be leaving her home to live with a man she had never met. She didn't feel that it was very fair to her.

"You wouldn't have to do anything you didn't want to do, Pandora. So, what do you say?" She realized that this man speaking with her was interested in her opinion. He cared about her point of view. Her own father had never shown her this much consideration. She was just expected to do her duty.

Pandora found the whole situation to be exhilarating. Her life back in Mensis, Phase Three had been routine and sheltered. She had often daydreamed of exciting adventures and wild romances. They were now offering her that freedom.

"I would be delighted to support your crusade."

Pandora's personal servant, Sable, and her driver, Katz, were Loggers, so they identified right away with the plight of the Peddlers. The Mensis in Phase Three treated the Loggers as badly as the Peddlers were treated here. They welcomed the opportunity to join their cause.

Two of the other men were Mensis soldiers and two were businessmen. They were outraged by the idea of changing their system. The four men were tied and led to join John at the back of the camp. Pandora, Sable, and Katz could wander freely.

Corey carried Lionel's body back into the camp. Anne walked toward them. She covered her mouth with her hand and started to sob.

"I'm so sorry, Anne," Corey said, with tears in his eyes. Anne placed her hand on Lionel's cheek while tears ran down her face. He gave her a few minutes to mourn, then placed Lionel's body in the fire and turned to take Anne in his arms.

Anne cried on Corey's chest, letting out all the pain in her heart. Even though she had never loved Lionel as she had Corey, she had come to feel deeply for him. Lionel had been good to her, and she would miss him.

Corey stroked Anne's soft blond hair while she mourned for her husband. The words that Lionel had spoken before he died now played in his mind. *"Take care of her, Corey. She's carrying your child."* Could it be possible that she had conceived a child while they made love under the skytrain station so long ago? They stood holding one another by the fire, each grieving in their own way.

Eagle put the other body in the flames. The stench from the fire was now unbearable. He threw a few more logs on before moving away from the smell. Zane led Corey and Anne away from the fire and out toward the road. The rest of the men milled about, waiting for Corey's next move.

Curtis was sure something had gone wrong with the shipment. He had expected it to arrive first thing in the morning. *They could have had engine problems,* he reasoned. He cursed himself for sending all his men away on a wild goose chase. Russ should have been back by now.

Jason hadn't come home last night, so he could only assume that he had found comfort in the arms of a woman. Curtis was relieved in one sense that the shipment was late. Jason had not shown up yet to greet his new bride. Perhaps he should send Lightfoot out to look for him.

Russ knocked on the study door and entered the room. Curtis noted the look of fatigue in his eyes. "I presume that you have found the fugitives?"

"Yes and no, Sir. I've just returned from Peddlers, and there was no sign of them. I believe they have gone to intercept the shipment of weapons arriving from the bullet train."

"God damn it, Russ," Curtis yelled and slammed his fist down on the desk. "Why the hell didn't you think of this yesterday?" Curtis realized that so far, he had underestimated their every move. He had to admire the courage and cunning of whoever was leading this, but at the same time, they had to be stopped. A shipment of weapons posed a great threat to the people of Mensis.

"Do you realize the implications of this disaster? If those punks get a hold of those weapons, it could mean war, Russ. I'll not be known as the first President to be associated with war since the Big Three. I want you to send every available soldier down there right away. If you don't stop them, Russ, you'll hang for it."

"Yes, sir." Russ held his anger in check while he left the room. Why was it always up to him to think of everything? Why should he be the one to hang? Why the hell wasn't Jason in charge of this expedition?

Russ mounted his horse and rode to the defense building. Most of the men who had ridden with him all night had been showering while he had been at the Henniger Estate. He urged them to hurry. Russ called all available soldiers to report for duty. They needed to reach Crystal Lake before the criminals had time to intercept the shipment.

Once his soldiers were armored up, Russ divided them into two groups. He instructed his two favorite soldiers, Stephen Cowen and Frank Byers, to take eighteen men to cover the road south toward the C Zone.

Russ would take the other fifty men west from Mensis, on the road that met up with Crystal Lake. Russ figured whatever road the prisoners chose; they would be covered. They would be surrounded like sitting ducks.

The group going south left immediately since it would take them longer to reach their destination. Russ and the rest of his soldiers rode through town. They passed the Henniger Estate on their way west.

"Corey, everyone is waiting for your next move." Zane had found Corey sitting alone behind a tree. He noticed that Corey had changed back into his Green-Level jumpsuit. When Corey didn't answer, he sat down beside him.

"It should have been me, Dad. It was my idea to take the weapons, and that shot was meant for me."

"Corey, I understand what you are feeling. I felt the same way when Doug and Ginger died. It had been my idea to check out Dusting, but they were the ones that died. You'll have to justify Lionel's death as I had to theirs. Doug and Ginger's deaths contributed to our knowledge of BUDDY's deceit. It was an unfortunate accident, which provided us with information that we otherwise would have never known. A few must sacrifice their lives for the good of the whole."

"Well, I won't be responsible for the deaths of all my friends. I can't ask them to sacrifice their lives. I can't!"

"It looks to me, Corey, that these people would do anything for you. They believe in you and the cause."

"And I should betray that trust by having them all killed?"

"Have you not sacrificed your life to help others?"

"That's different," insisted Corey.

"Oh, and how is it different? You're taking as many if not more risks than anyone. Do you think Lionel would have wanted you to give up? He died fighting for freedom, not unknowingly in a dusting tunnel. If you give up now, then thousands of people will die every year unsuspectingly in Dusting. Is that what you want?"

"No! I just want to settle this matter without violence. The only way that I can do that is to talk to the President. He alone has the power to change things."

"Then I don't see how you have much choice. Don't let Lionel's death be in vain. Find a way to talk to President Henniger."

"Did I hear the President's name?" asked Arthur, as he walked up stiffly in the armored suit.

"Yes. Corey was just telling me that he wants to see if this matter could be settled without fighting."

"Not on your life! President Henniger will never surrender without a fight. He's a stubborn old man, and he's set in his ways. He'll fight tooth and nail against any new changes. No, I think your original idea to take them by surprise is the best plan of attack. If we hurry, the soldiers might still be in Peddlers, looking for you there," he said.

"No, I won't go through with this until I can at least try to reason with the President." Corey ran a hand through his hair. "I'd like to settle this like gentlemen, not savages."

"I disagree. If you want to waste your breath on him, then by all means go ahead, but I think the rest of us should continue with your original plan to attack Mensis."

Corey knew Arthur was right. It would be better to strike when the soldiers were the least prepared to defend themselves. If taking down their army was the only way Curtis would listen, then that's what they'd have to do.

Corey got to his feet and looked around him. Zachary and Rocky had put on the armor that the two Mensis soldiers had been wearing. Eagle and Moonbeam were watching over the prisoners, and Anne was talking excitedly with Pandora and Sable, the Logger servant. Some of the D Men were pulling the shipment of weapons out of the truck and loading the guns with ammunition. Others were stacking the goods and supplies from the truck just inside the camp.

"Bear," yelled Corey. Bear let out a high-pitched whistle that silenced the men around them. They turned to face Corey.

"Listen up. We're going to make our move on Mensis right away. When we reach our destination, I want you to round up all the people from town and bring them to the Henniger Estate. We will be riding right past it, for those who don't know where it is. If you encounter any soldiers on the way, don't shoot them unless you are fired upon first."

Corey bowed his head in silence for a moment. "I'd also like to honor our friend Lionel, who gave his life heroically for freedom. I won't be accompanying you to town. I'll be heading directly to talk to the President. I hope to have everything cleared up before everyone is brought to the Estate or before any more people die.

"Arthur will oversee the raid through town. He knows the town well and knows where the majority of the people will be. I want you to give him your attention and support. The women and the prisoners will stay here until we return for them. Zane, can I count on you to look after the prisoners?"

Corey had been apprehensive about his father going into battle. This way he could ensure the safety of his father and the women. Zane nodded his concurrence.

"I hope to see each and every one of you back at the Henniger Estate," continued Corey. "Split up between the two trucks. There are enough rifles for everyone. Keep the safety switch on while you're traveling, though. We don't want any unnecessary accidents. I wish you the best of luck."

Anne approached Corey as he attempted to saddle up his horse. He was having difficulty with the strap. Anne came up behind him and encircled his waist. Corey turned around to take her in his arms.

"Don't go, Corey. I couldn't bear to lose you too."

"You're never going to lose me. I've waited too long to be with you. I must do this one last thing, and then I promise I'll never leave you again. I love you, Anne."

"I love you too, Corey Tusk."

"Ah, must we be so formal?"

Corey looked down into Anne's sad, sweet eyes. He turned her chin up and their lips came together for a farewell kiss. These were the lips that he had remembered so well and missed. Corey pulled away and rubbed Anne's belly. "You take care of Taylor."

Anne laughed as she remembered the night they had chosen names for their children. "It just might well be Taylor and Tyler."

Corey gave a whoop of joy and twirled Anne around in his arms. He kissed her one last time, then mounted his horse. He sat on the animal and rocked back and forth. The horse didn't move.

Zane walked up to see Corey sitting helplessly on the horse. "What's the problem? Can't get the horse to move?" he asked.

"It looked really easy when Arthur did it."

"Here, let me help you out." Zane gave the horse a good slap on the rump. Anne and Zane stood there laughing as the horse took off quickly, with Corey bouncing around in the saddle.

Arthur, Rocky, and Zachary rode on ahead of the trucks. The sun was beating down on them, causing both the riders and their horses to sweat. Over the crest of the hill, they spotted a wall of soldiers riding toward them.

"Quick, turn back," yelled Arthur, who expertly turned his horse around sharply and sped on down the hill. Rocky got his horse turned around and followed Arthur. Zachary had to slow to a stop before being able to turn the horse around. The soldiers were now firing shots at him. He felt a bullet enter his lower back and knock him to the ground. He lay there helpless, with no feeling in his legs.

Through the rear-view mirror, Katz could see the other truck falling behind. Chip was having difficulty changing gears as he tried to pick up speed. Katz slowed the first truck to a stop as soon as he saw Arthur and Rocky heading back toward them. He rolled the window down to speak to them. "What's up?" he asked.

"We're under attack. Get all the men out here quickly." While Bear and Moonbeam jumped out to open the back doors of the truck, Arthur went to have a word with Chip in the next truck.

"I want you to pull the truck up alongside the other one. We're going to make a barricade. Quickly, there's no time to lose." Arthur expertly jumped off his horse and indicated where to stop the truck.

Eagle and Lucky jumped out to open the back door of the second truck. The men filed out with their rifles in their hands. It was only the calm authority in Arthur's voice that kept the men in order.

"Take cover around the vehicles, not out in the open. The soldiers will be over the crest any moment. Don't fire until I tell you."

"Damn it, Terry, why the hell did you fire your weapon without instructions from me?" Russ had quickly put an end to the few soldiers who had fired upon the figures at the top of the hill. It could very well have been the soldiers guarding the shipment coming down from Mensis, Phase Three.

"You told us to shoot first..."

"That was last night," Russ interrupted. He dismounted his horse when he reached the armored man lying on the ground. He bent down beside him to see if he was alive. Russ felt his right wrist for a pulse. It was there, but it was weak.

"Are you alright?" asked Russ.

"I can't feel my legs," Zach rasped. Russ was more concerned about the pool of blood he was lying in. If this man was with the shipment, Russ knew that there would be hell to pay.

"Hey, Russ," whispered one of the men, "this man has a tattoo on his arm." Russ looked at the code on the forearm that he still held. This man was not a Mensis soldier. He was from one of the Domed cities.

"Where are you from?" he asked Zachary. Russ watched as the man tried to speak, but went limp instead. Russ knew he could be from Havanna or the Domed City of Ledecca. It didn't make sense to him, though. None of the people in the Domes had any reason to be traveling this road.

Russ pulled out his radio and called the monitoring station. One of the technicians coded the dead man's tattoo through the computer and confirmed that he was indeed from Havanna. Russ was not sure why this man had been out of the Dome, but he was sure that he wasn't with the shipment.

"Alright, men, prepare to attack," Russ called out, as he put his radio away. He mounted his horse, then waited for his men to gather into formation. The soldiers rode swiftly over the crest of the hill toward the trucks parked in the center of the road. Most of them rode without holding the reins so they could fire their rifles while riding.

Arthur watched while a sea of red-clad and armored soldiers drew closer. He knew the Peddlers were not well trained, so he wanted their targets as close as possible before allowing them to fire.

The soldiers were firing at them, hitting a few of the men. Arthur gave the word and they returned fire. Some of the Peddlers had forgotten to lift their safety latches or their aim was so bad that only a few of the soldiers fell.

"Keep firing! Don't stop!" Arthur knew he was losing more men than the soldiers were. They were getting slaughtered out here. He had overestimated the Peddlers' ability to fight in battle. They would need more than just bullets to win this fight.

The soldiers rode on past the barricade on either side. Arthur knew they would gather into formation again and then attack. He only had a few minutes to reorganize the men.

"Everyone to the front of the trucks," he yelled. "The soldiers will be back in a minute. Take aim carefully and keep out of sight."

The D Men moved from their first position to take up ones at the head of the vehicles. As Arthur passed behind the trucks, he swung the door of the first one closed. At the second truck, he realized there were boxes of hand grenades.

"Bear, come and help me with this," he called out. Bear approached Arthur as he was attempting to pull a box out of the truck. The soldiers were in formation now and preparing for their next move. "Help me lift this box onto the top of the truck."

Moonbeam came around to help them hoist the box up. Arthur quickly explained to Bear and Moonbeam how the grenades worked as they lay atop one of the trucks. The soldiers were heading toward them now. Arthur ordered the men to start firing to create a distraction. He knew they would need the cover of the gun smoke to launch their grenades.

"On the count of three, we pull the pins, stand up, and throw the grenades. Got it? One... two... three."

Arthur, Moonbeam, and Bear stood and threw their grenades, but just before they exploded, Bear caught a bullet in the head.

Jason and Moonbeam hit the deck while Bear's body dropped off the top of the truck to the ground.

The grenades exploded then, momentarily shocking the Peddlers into a cease-fire. Arthur realized they had thrown the grenades too far and only the last few riders went down. He could see Russ spurring on his soldiers to ride faster to clear the barricade.

"Keep firing," he yelled. The Peddlers took their aim again against the soldiers, while he grabbed another grenade. "This time we won't throw them so far," ordered Arthur.

"We're all going to die, aren't we?"

"Cripes, Moonbeam! You pick the worst time to ask questions. Just throw the fucking grenades!"

The next couple of grenades landed in the midst of the soldiers, killing about half of them. The soldiers were too close to throw more grenades, so Arthur took up his rifle. The Peddlers managed to kill a few more before the soldiers were out of range and on their way back toward Mensis.

There was an eerie silence in the air now save for the screams and moans of the wounded. There were dead bodies and injured men all around them. The smell of cordite and blood was prevalent. Many horses had been killed or injured and had to be put down mercifully.

Arthur dismounted from the truck, cursing and swearing. The soldiers would head back to Mensis and alert the rest of the troops. Russ would then come back for another attack, or block them at the entrance to Mensis.

Lucky and Chip took it upon themselves to bandage the wounded. Moonbeam was grieving over the body of Bear, and Katz was walking around in a daze while holding his wounded shoulder. Eagle guided him toward Lucky for treatment.

Moonbeam approached Arthur. "I have never experienced anything like this before. I was not prepared for what I saw or what I did."

"I understand, Moonbeam." Arthur put a supporting hand on the man's shoulder. "Violence is never pretty, and is hard to live with later."

Eagle joined them. "What are we going to do about the trucks? One of them has three flat tires and the radiator is shot. No pun intended."

"What about the other truck?" Arthur asked.

"One flat tire and all the windows are missing," answered Moonbeam.

"Alright, we'll replace the tire, then put all the dead bodies in the busted one. We can't just leave them on the road."

Rocky walked up carrying Zach's body.

"Put him in that truck there, Rocky. Hell! Corey's not going to be happy when he hears about poor Zach," lamented Moonbeam.

"Zach was a brave man and deserved better than this," added Arthur.

After gaining control of the horse, Corey guided it through the woods toward the Henniger Estate, as Arthur had instructed him. The woods provided cover from the sun, but not from the heat. He stopped only once by a stream to drink from it, then continued on his way.

When Corey reached the five-foot wall surrounding the Estate, he could see no way to get the horse over it. He continued to skirt the wall, and eventually found his way into a park. He dismounted from the horse and walked it through town toward the Henniger Estate.

As Jason Henniger was leaving the front gates, he saw a Green-Level domestic approaching with a horse. *This must be the mare I ordered from Mensis, Phase Two,* thought Jason. He waved the man over.

"Just bring her in through here," instructed Jason.

Corey realized right away that this man thought Corey was a courier, so he played along. As long as it got him onto the Estate, he didn't care what the pretense was.

Jason patted down the horse and examined its mouth. He rubbed the forelegs and checked its flank. "This is a fine horse. She's a bit warm. Have you been riding for long?" he asked the courier.

"About an hour," Corey replied.

They fell in step heading toward the cottage where Sunshine lived. Jason thought it would be nice for her to learn to ride.

"I haven't seen you around here before. You must have come down from Phase Two with the horse."

"Ah, that's right," Corey lied.

"My name's Jason. Jason Henniger. This is my family's Estate."

"Pleased to meet you. My name is Corey."

"What brings you to Phase One?"

"Curiosity," replied Corey.

Jason laughed. He liked Corey's sense of mystery. "Tell me about yourself," he probed.

"There's not much to tell." Corey realized that he couldn't very well say nothing. "I enjoy adventure and meeting new people, but I don't like lies and injustice. What about you?"

"That's a hard act to follow, Corey. Unfortunately, I spend most of my time drinking and womanizing."

"Why is that unfortunate?" They both laughed.

"My father seems to think that I should be spending my time getting more acquainted with the family business."

"Is he right?" asked Corey. Jason looked sharply at Corey for a moment.

"Yes, he usually is, even though I hate to admit it. He has a habit of manipulating my life. I don't feel that I'm ready to give up my life of partying and take on the responsibilities that come with the Presidency."

"Do you have to become the President?"

Jason thought this to be a strange question, especially from a domestic of Mensis, Phase Two. Corey should know that the Presidency was passed down to the eldest son or the General of the army if a President had no heir.

"I've never really thought I had a choice. I am my father's only son. If I don't take it, then Russ Fletcher will. I wouldn't want a man like him having control of Mensis, Phase One."

"Why are you scared of the responsibility, Jason?"

"I don't think that I'm scared of it." Jason had never really looked at his reasons for evading his duties. He had just resented his father's manipulations. It seemed strange to be discussing these things with a Pumper that he had just met, but Corey had a knack for getting to the heart of a problem.

"Well," Jason conceded, "maybe I am a bit scared. A President must make a lot of important decisions that affect the lives of many people. That's no easy task."

Corey knew only too well the problems a leader could encounter. He had the same reservations about leading the Peddlers into battle, and maybe even into death.

"You can't doubt yourself, Jason. You have to tackle each problem one at a time. Just do the best you can."

Jason didn't know why, but he liked this guy very much. He seemed centered and wise for a Pumper, and yet he still had a boyish charm about him. "Well, that's good advice. Are you staying long?"

"Not long."

"This is the cottage here. Just put the horse in the corral and then come for a drink," Jason offered.

Jason loosened his tie as he opened the door of the playhouse, while Corey corralled the horse. Jason went into the kitchen and found Sunshine trying to roll out some pastry dough. Her hair and face were full of flour, as well as the front of her dress.

Jason put his arms around her and looked for a clean spot on her face to kiss. Sunshine was glad Jason was home early. She didn't know what to do with herself when he wasn't around. She had been teaching herself how to cook today to pass the time. For lunch, she had fried up some fish, which proved to be simple, but this pie was more difficult than it looked.

"I've brought someone home for you to meet."

"Oh, Jason, I look a mess."

"I'm sure he won't mind. Just wipe off some of that flour and bring us in a few beers." Jason kissed the tip of her nose and then went into the living room to join Corey as he entered the cottage.

A few minutes later, Sunshine came bouncing into the room looking neat and tidy in a pretty pink summer dress. She stopped dead in her tracks when she saw Corey sitting on the sofa. The two bottles of beer slipped from her hands and crashed to the floor. Sunshine stood there, wide-eyed, with broken glass at her feet. Corey jumped up to retrieve the broken shards.

"Sorry if I startled you," Corey said, and his eyes told Sunshine to not say a word. He had been equally surprised to see her... and in a dress. He had assumed that she was back in Peddlers.

Sunshine couldn't believe her eyes. Had Corey come to bring her back home? She wondered if Moonbeam was with him. Sunshine was confused now about what to do. She had finally come to accept her life here and her love for Jason.

"Well, it seems you have quite the impact on women, Corey," teased Jason. He could not understand what had gotten into Sunshine. Perhaps it was still too soon to introduce her to people. She lacked the proper training as a hostess.

"I'll help you with this." Corey headed for the kitchen with the broken pieces of glass. Sunshine followed him in with the rest. They placed the pieces in the garbage, then turned to face one another. Corey placed a finger to his lips until he was sure they were out of earshot from Jason. He grabbed Sunshine up in a big hug, twirling her around in a circle.

"How did you find me?" whispered Sunshine.

"Purely by accident. I didn't know until just now that you were here."

"I suppose you want me to come back with you."

Corey noted the sadness in her voice. "Not unless you want to. It's entirely up to you. Are you happy here?"

"Oh, yes! I would really like to stay."

"I understand. Jason is a nice man."

Sunshine nodded. "What are you doing here if you're not looking for me?"

"Looking for answers and justice." Corey's eyes took on a cold glint. "The Mensis have killed Luther. I'd like to see his death avenged."

The news saddened Sunshine, but somehow, she felt strangely removed from that life now. It seemed to her that she had always lived here. It was where she belonged. "I'm so sorry, Corey. I do know who hit Luther, though. It was a soldier named Russ. I remember one of the other soldiers calling out his name."

"What's taking you two so long?" Jason asked from the doorway. He noticed that they were standing awfully close. Startled, Sunshine moved away from Corey and looked from one to the other. How was it that they were so friendly if Corey was here for revenge? For a moment, she feared for Jason's life. She didn't know what she'd do if something happened to him. She opened the fridge and handed Corey and Jason another beer.

Corey sensed Sunshine's uneasiness and flashed her a bright smile. "I was just getting acquainted with your girl."

Jason smiled and wrapped his arm around Sunshine. "This is my girl, alright. Do you like sports, Corey?"

The question caught Corey off guard. Would he give himself away if he said yes?

Jason was turning the power on to a large vidscreen mounted on the living room wall as he walked back into the front room. "This is one of my favorites. The event took place last night, but I haven't had the time to watch it."

The picture on the vidscreen came into focus. Corey's heart skipped a beat as he recognized the scene as the men's night out in Havanna. Thomas Buckineer was announcing the contestants of the rope tying event.

"Tonight's grand event will take place between our current third-time champion, Jude Wesley, and our challenging opponent, Orthello Willis," Thomas's voice rang out over the crowd.

Corey couldn't believe what he was seeing! How could the Mensis have access to the rope tying event? Not even BUDDY knew of it. Corey paled slightly as it dawned on him that the Mensis recorded everything and used it for entertainment, even their secret men's night out.

"Do you want to make a wager on the winner, Corey?"

"Orthello's got it, for sure. There's no doubt in my mind."

"What makes you so sure?" asked Jason.

"Orthello's much stronger than he looks." Corey thought of all the times Orthello had tackled him on the football field.

They turned their attention to the vidscreen. Jude had just lassoed one of Orthello's ankles. Orthello was now on the ground, sprawled on his belly. Jason started to laugh. "Looks like I just won the bet."

"It's not over yet," declared Corey, with a smile.

Orthello tugged on the rope around his ankle and pulled Jude's smaller frame, tumbling to the ground. Jude had made the mistake of holding onto the rope. Orthello held Jude down with one hand and tied a wrist with the other. He shifted his weight onto Jude and pulled the other arm in, tying it to the first. Jude spit and squirmed under Orthello's weight.

As the crowds were going wild, a wide smile crossed Corey's lips. Things were the same back home, and he felt a tug of homesickness in his heart. The bell sounded, signifying the end of the event. Jason slapped Corey on the back a few times.

"Way to go, buddy." It sounded odd to hear Jason call him BUDDY. He wasn't quite sure what he meant by that. Was it an insult or a compliment?

Wolf said a prayer for the dead men in the truck while the others bowed their heads. He had watched his mother, the High Priestess, perform this sermon a hundred times as a child. After the sermon, the truck was set on fire. The Peddlers helped the wounded men into the back of the other truck. Katz, Eagle, and Arthur took seats in the cab.

The death of the other D Men left the Peddlers' spirits low. Arthur had assured them that they had done well for their first time in battle. It was a small consolation in comparison to the lives that had been lost. The cries and moans of the injured men were a constant reminder of what lay ahead.

Lucky wondered how many more of them would die before the day was through. How many more soldiers would they have to fight? He knew the price of freedom was high, but until now, he had not known how high that was. He was haunted by the image of Bear's face as he had helped to lift him into the truck.

They rode toward Mensis, Phase One with the late afternoon sun in their eyes. Katz was traveling quite fast to make up for lost time. He had never expected to be in the position he was in now. His future had seemed tentative to him as a personal driver for Pandora, but now it seemed even more uncertain. He was not sure he would even live long enough to see Mensis, Phase One.

He slowed the truck down almost to a crawl to follow the hairpin turn in the road. The injury to his shoulder prevented him from turning the steering wheel the way he normally did. He had just started into the bend when a shot rang out. One of the tires had been hit, and Katz struggled to keep control of the vehicle.

The Mensis soldiers had set up an ambush and were firing at the truck. A bullet whizzed in through the cab and struck Eagle in the neck. Katz and Arthur ducked their heads while Arthur screamed, "Drive! Drive! Drive!"

They pulled out of the bend, riding on the ruined rim. Katz hit the gas, as they needed to put distance between them and the soldiers. One quick look at Eagle revealed to Arthur that he was dead.

The shots had stopped now, so Arthur assumed the soldiers were mounting their horses. He instructed Katz to stop the truck while he slid open the panel between the cab and the back. Some of the men had been shot through the open windows and the others were huddled on the floor.

"The soldiers will be back any minute. I want you to take cover around the truck, and don't forget to use the grenades." Arthur turned back to the front, opened the door, and let Eagle's body fall to the ground. He grabbed his rifle and fixed himself a position behind the open front door.

The Peddlers that had been wounded stayed in the back of the truck with the boxes of grenades. Moonbeam and Wolf hauled a box to the top of the truck. The others took cover under or around it.

The soldiers came riding toward them in a cloud of dust. Arthur waited until the soldiers were within throwing distance, then ordered the men to fire. The Peddlers kept up a steady stream of bullets while the others launched grenades.

The battle was short-lived as all the soldiers fell in the onslaught of the attack. Unfortunately, a few more Peddlers had been shot. Arthur and the D Men advanced on the soldiers lying dead or injured on the ground.

Arthur approached Russ, who lay facing away from him. Russ swung around quickly and leveled his rifle. It was evident from the expression on his face that he hadn't expected to encounter Arthur standing there.

"What the blazes are you doing here?" Russ had broken his leg when he had fallen off his horse. "You're helping the... I should have known you would turn against your own people. You traitor!" he spat.

Chip saw Russ cock and aim his rifle at Arthur. This was the same man who had sent Bear, Lucky, and him to the C Zone. While sighting him in his own scope, Chip ordered Russ, "Drop your gun." Without a moment's hesitation, Russ swung his rifle toward Chip and pulled the trigger. Arthur watched, horrified, as the bullet entered Chip's stomach, sending him backward.

"You son of a bitch!" he yelled, turning his own rifle on the most hated General in Mensis' history. Russ didn't have time to recock his rifle before he lay dead on the ground.

Lucky came to kneel by Chip's side, with tears rolling down his face.

"Hey, Lucky..." Chip's face contorted in pain as he tried to smile. "He was going... to shoot Arthur," he said weakly.

Lucky took Chip's hand in his own. "You silly, heroic fool."

"I'm so sorry, Lucky... we could have had... a good life."

"Isn't there anything we can do for him?" pleaded Lucky.

"Yes, there is." Arthur walked up to where Lucky was kneeling beside Chip. He withdrew his hand pistol and cocked it.

"Wait! What are you doing?" beseeched Lucky.

"There's nothing we can do to save him. He'll die slowly and painfully. I'm offering him an escape from his suffering."

"Please," Lucky said, holding his hand out for the pistol. "He was a special friend to me. I should like to do it myself." Arthur nodded and handed him the weapon.

The other men who had gathered around followed Arthur back to the truck. Only Moonbeam stayed to say goodbye to his close friend. He wished he had had the opportunity to say goodbye to Bear.

"So long, Chip. I'll think about you all the time." Tears welled up in his eyes as Moonbeam gave Chip's hand a last squeeze. He stood aside to wait so he could help Lucky carry the body. Lucky bent over Chip to whisper in his ear.

Moonbeam could hear Chip's shaky voice say, "I love you, too." Lucky gave Chip a farewell kiss and then stood. With shaky hands, he pointed the gun at him. The single shot rang out loud and lonely in the late afternoon. Lucky dropped to his knees, sobbing for the loss of his special friend. He had never killed a man prior to today, but now he had shot many. His heart ached as never before.

Moonbeam laid his hand on Lucky's shoulder. He waited until the sobs started to subside, then said, "Come on, Lucky. We have to go." He helped carry Chip's body back to the truck to join the other dead men.

The D Men had rounded up the remainder of the horses since they could no longer use the truck. There were just enough horses if they all rode double. Wolf was no longer with them to say a prayer, so Arthur said one instead. His words were not as smooth or as polished as the sermon Wolf had given, but the meaning was the same. They set the truck on fire, then headed out on horseback toward Mensis, Phase One.

After they finished their beers, Jason walked Corey to the door.

"Goodbye, Sunshine," Corey called. She waved back from the doorway of the kitchen.

"It was a pleasure to meet you, Corey. Maybe we'll see each other around town before you head back home." Jason offered his hand.

"You never know what the future holds," said Corey, while shaking hands.

Jason let out a hearty laugh and patted Corey on the back.

Corey could see the Henniger Estate in the distance. As he strolled casually across the wide expanse of the property, he reflected on the events of the last few weeks. He couldn't understand that nothing unusual had happened for over a hundred years until he got exiled. Why hadn't the Peddlers ever left their home before? Why did the Dome suddenly collapse? Why hadn't the D Men in the C Zone ever rioted before? Why did Lionel and Luther have to die?

If he could only make President Henniger see what he was doing to the people, maybe he would let them go. Surely if the man has a heart, he could make him understand the injustice of the situation.

Up ahead Corey could see a cement swimming pool surrounded by palm trees. He walked across the patio stones to the French windows leading off an exercise room. He stepped quietly into the room and closed the door behind him.

Corey crept silently through the house and up the stairs until he reached the office, which had been left open. He quickly entered, then closed and locked the door behind him. He took a deep breath, then crossed to the filing cabinet. Corey slammed his fist down on top of the cabinet when he realized it was locked. He fished through the drawers of the President's desk, looking for the keys. The upper right-hand drawer was locked as well. Corey grabbed the brass letter opener from the desk and pried the drawer open. Inside there was a ring of keys.

Corey brought the key ring to the filing cabinet, patiently trying every key until he found the right one. The first drawer labeled "Industries" held files on all the different industries in the Mensis Phases. Each industry was alphabetically filed, starting with automobiles and ending with wood.

The second drawer was titled "MENSIS, Mega Enterprises Nationwide Sectioning Individual Systems." It held files on the people in Mensis Phase One, Mensis, Phase Two, and Mensis, Phase Three.

The third drawer was titled "Energy Resource Systems." Inside were three separate sections with subsequent titles. The first was "PEDDLERS, Population Experiment District 'D,' Low Energy Resource System." Corey moved on to the next, which read, "PUMPERS, People Using Mechanics, Producing Energy

Resource System." The last file was "LOGGERS, Low Operative Gains; Growing Energy Resource System."

The fourth drawer title, "Domed Cities," drew Corey's attention. He opened the drawer to discover that this file was also separated into three categories. The first file was titled "HAVANNA, Healthy Adults Vaccinated Annually; Non-Nanobot Antibodies." It held files on all the people in Havanna.

Corey was scared to understand the implication of this file. Could the people in the Dome be no more than the result of an experiment? The other two files seemed to confirm this claim.

The second file was titled "DASIGGE, Designer Adults Seeded in Genius Genetic Era," and the third was "LEDECCA, Laser Equipped Devices Eliminating Cancer Cells in Adults."

The sound of a key in the lock startled Corey. He turned around to face President Curtis Henniger standing in the doorway, immaculately dressed in a dark-blue suit with a white dress shirt, and blue tie. Curtis looked to be well into his fifties. He had salt-and-pepper hair and pockmarks on his face. He was smiling as though he had been expecting him. Corey felt as though he had broken tabu and now BUDDY was going to exile him again.

"I see you've found your way into the files already. It's quite a masterpiece, isn't it, Corey?" Curtis had picked Corey up on the surveillance vidcams outside as he had entered the Estate. He knew Corey would head straight for the office, but he hadn't expected he would have the filing drawers open so soon. "Come and sit down. We have a lot to discuss."

Corey hesitantly took a seat in front of the desk while Curtis sat down in his favorite leather chair. They eyed one another like worthy adversaries. "How do you know my name?"

"Facial recognition picked you up on the vidcams outside, but I know a lot about you, Corey Tusk."

Curtis knew that Corey had the genes of a born leader. He had inherited them from his great-great-grandfather, President Tusk. He had only two alternatives with which he could deal with

Corey. The reasonable way would be to make him understand the importance of the present situation. The other alternative, of course, would be to kill him. He had tried twice now to get rid of him through Dusting and the C Zone, but Corey had proven himself to be cunning and evasive. Perhaps they could use a man with Corey's talents to strengthen their defense department. No doubt he would make a better General than Russ. Curtis knew as long as Corey drew breath, he would always fight for what was right. It was up to Curtis to find a way to convince Corey that what they were doing here was right.

Zane stood watch over the prisoners with the loaded shotgun that Lucky had insisted he take. The prisoners sat in the Cadillac with the car windows rolled down and their sleeves rolled up. Zane's eyes constantly wandered toward the women rummaging through the shipment of goods.

The women pulled the soaps and lotions from the shipment of boxes with squeals of joy, savoring the smells. Anne couldn't remember the last time she had washed her hair. She felt dusty after having slept by the fire, and there were bloodstains on her sweat suit. She started pulling apart the braid in her hair.

Pandora and Sable found a box of cotton towels amongst the supplies. Sable had still not recovered properly from the shooting earlier. Her life back in Mensis, Phase Three had been peaceful. She had never seen anyone die before.

"Are you alright, Sable?" Pandora took Sable's hand in her own. She had become quite fond of the Logger woman, as Sable was only a few years older than herself.

"I keep thinking about the shooting. I thought we were all going to die. I don't know how you kept so calm. I was a real basket case."

"No, you did fine! I was proud of you for protecting me. It showed a lot of courage."

"Courage? I was so scared that they would hurt you."

"Now, don't you worry about me," soothed Pandora.

"That's true. You're so beautiful that no one would ever want to hurt you," Sable said, sincerely.

Pandora patted her hand and smiled. "You have nice qualities, too. Take your hair, for example. If you wore it back off your face…" Pandora pulled Sable's hair back into a ponytail. "There! You also have a nice figure. You know, I bet you'd look really pretty in a dress. Would you like to try one on?"

"Oh yes! I'd love to! Then I could pretend I'm a lady." Pandora opened her wardrobe trunk and selected a pale-pink summer dress with small white dots. She handed it to Sable, who fingered it gingerly. "Thank you. It's beautiful!"

"You think so? Then keep it." Pandora wasn't overly fond of the dress, and she was glad to see Sable smiling again.

"Oh my gosh… look at those gorgeous dresses!" exclaimed Anne. She headed over to the trunk. "Are all of these yours?" she questioned Pandora.

"Yes. You're welcome to help yourself to one. Just don't take the red one with the spaghetti straps."

"Are you sure? You don't mind?"

"No, not at all. I have plenty of them. Go ahead."

Anne chose a light-yellow dress with embroidered flowers on the shoulders. They brought the new dresses and the towels and lotions to the lake to bathe. The water felt cool and refreshing as the women plunged in. The day had turned out to be hotter than yesterday.

After their swim, Sable brought food out from the shipment. She cooked it over the fire while Anne braided Pandora's hair.

"Did you say Corey's last name was Tusk?" asked Pandora.

"Yes," replied Anne, distractedly as she braided.

"Is he related to the Great President Henry Tusk, the founding father of Mensis?"

Anne stopped braiding. "Excuse me?"

"At the end of the Waste War, once the air was safe to live above ground again, it was President Tusk who brought everyone out from the underground bunkers. They had long since lost contact with anyone, and it was thought there were no survivors, as the destruction of the land was devastating.

"It was the Mensis that kept society growing and flourishing. The men of power and wealth became the new leaders and governors of the land. Once radio contact was re-established with two other surviving cities, the leaders discussed future courses of action. It was during these meetings that the three communities joined in a written agreement to become Mensis, Phase One, Phase Two, and Phase Three.

"It became evident, as time went on," continued Pandora, "that many more people than they had expected had survived the war. The Mountain People had hidden in the rain shadow areas and other remote sections that had shielded them. Some of them even had their own fallout shelters built into their homes.

"At first, President Tusk set up the Mountain People to work for him, but as time went on, they needed to establish a place for the nomads to live. It was then that he set up the Energy Resource Systems. So, I was just wondering if Zane and Corey were related to the late President."

"I'm not sure. We'll have to ask Zane." Anne turned and called out to Zane to come and join them for a minute.

Zane walked down to where the women sat on the boxes from the shipment. He carried the gun over his shoulder until he reached the women, then he placed it up against a tree.

"What can I help you with?"

"Pandora was just asking if your father's name was Henry."

"Yes. He was named after his great-grandfather. His grandfather, Roger, was one of the first people to live in the Dome. That was just before the Big Three, as I recall."

"I don't understand this," interjected Pandora. "If you're really the President's heir, then how come you didn't inherit the

Presidency of Mensis, Phase One when President Tusk died? The only reason the Hennigers have it is that all the Tusk clan had died during the war."

"That's a good question because obviously, we are not all dead." This was news to Zane. In fact, he couldn't recall what their own history said about it.

Just then they heard the neighing of a horse as the Mensis soldiers that Russ had sent south rode into camp. Within minutes, the group was surrounded. Zane looked fleetingly toward the rifle he had left propped up against the tree. A soldier caught the movement and positioned himself between Zane and the gun.

"You're a wanted man, Corey. I could, by all rights, have you killed this minute," intimidated Curtis.

"What could we possibly have to discuss if you only wanted me dead?"

"That's what I like about you, Corey, you're perceptive. I won't deny that it was I who had you exiled from Havanna, nor will I deny that I had you sent to the C Zone. I also can no longer deny that you pose a threat to our existing system." Curtis paused momentarily to light a cigar. "I am willing to offer you a deal that I think you will find more attractive than death."

"I don't have to listen to a word you say. Any minute, my people will have imprisoned your people, and you will have to listen to our demands."

Curtis let out a sinister laugh. "Think again, Corey. I sent my soldiers out to Crystal Lake this morning to intercept your people, as you call them. Your merry gang of bandits should all be lying dead on the road about now. Do you really think I would allow you to disrupt the intricate planning of our system?"

Corey stood up quickly and crossed to the window. There were no people around except for the stable hand and the gardener. His men should have been here by now. He gripped the edge of the windowsill as he pictured his friends meeting the same death as

Lionel. He had feared it would come to this. He bowed his head and gave in to the grief in his heart.

Curtis sensed his victory was near. Without the help of the Peddlers, Corey was defenseless and broken. Curtis would sign him up as General to his army, where he could be in a position to help guide Jason once he was President.

Corey slowly turned from the window to face Curtis. "Have you no feeling for the lives of other people?"

"There's so much that you don't know," sighed Curtis.

"Suppose you start by telling me why you keep the people in the Dome? The air hasn't been contaminated for years."

"Have a seat, Corey. Let me explain this to you as simply as possible." Curtis relit his cigar while Corey sat down. "You read the files about Dasigge?" Corey nodded.

"It was the second experimental Domed city to be erected," continued Curtis. "They were experimenting with genetics to produce a superior race of humans. The success rate was phenomenal. The children were highly intelligent, and, in most cases, telepathic. President Tusk decided to leave the experiment in progress during the War.

"Afterward, it was decided that these children, who were now adults, had become too powerful to integrate into society. President Tusk felt it was safer to keep them where they were. Of course, he had to follow suit with the rest of the Domed cities to avoid discrimination and revolt.

"Naturally, there was much controversy on this issue. The other Presidents argued that it would be expensive to keep the Domed cities in food and clothing if they weren't contributing to the rest of society. So, it was decided that the people in the Domes would provide entertainment. Havanna gives us sports, Ledecca gives us theater and music, and Dasigge gives us art. The dehydrated food that they eat is inexpensive to produce as well as nourishing. Of course, the Domes also served to keep the Mountain People working in the hopes of retiring there one day."

"Retiring? Don't you mean Dusting? Why is everyone dusted at fifty? What's the point of anything?"

Curtis looked at Corey with renewed respect. "Well, aren't we the clever one? Dusting was started as a means of population control. It avoided issues of overcrowding in the Domes and of hospitalization for the old, handicapped, and ailing people. It was determined that after the age of fifty, a person is no longer capable of competing in sports with young men. Nor can they work as hard and produce as much electricity. We also adopted this method in Mensis to free the few jobs that were available for the young people."

"What I don't understand," Corey interrupted, "is how do you dust fifty couples? I'm sure they don't just keep walking into the light."

"The Dusting Ceremony is viewed on closed-circuit televisions at the monitoring station. The lasers are only turned on once all the couples have crossed the yellow line."

"If Dusting is monitored, then how come I wasn't dusted?"

"When there is only one person going through, there's no need to monitor it. The lasers are kept on, so the instant that person crosses the line... how did you escape?"

"A rat set off the lasers before I crossed. The computer assumed that it had been me. When sweeping commenced, I made a run for the end of the tunnel."

"So that's how you ended up in Peddlers," Curtis concluded.

"Why do you keep the Peddlers working when you could just as easily use generators?"

Again, Curtis lifted his brows. "Oh, but we do use them. There are massive generators under all the workhouses. The power is then directed toward Mensis by underground cables to our hydro plant. From the plant, we provide electricity to Havanna, Peddlers, and all the other Mensis Phases, as well as to our automobile plants and other factories. In return, we receive wood, water, weapons, oil, and all the other amenities of life. Therefore, it is important to keep the Peddlers working."

"Why do you treat them so poorly?"

"Poorly? After the war, the Mountain People came from everywhere with nothing. We gave them homes, medical care, and a way to support themselves. We put in as much work here to keep Peddlers running smoothly, as they work to provide us all with electricity."

Curtis stood up to open a locked closet in the corner of the room. "If the Peddlers don't seem to have as much as we do, it is only because they started with nothing. The people of Mensis were well off financially before the war ever started."

Curtis pulled out an old-world globe and placed it on the desk in front of Corey. He gave it a spin. "This is what the world used to look like before the Waste War. Each colored section represents a different country. Unfortunately, the countries fought one another over land, resources, and food."

Curtis pulled out a sheet of paper from the drawer in his desk and handed it to Corey. "This is what our world looks like now."

The paper in Corey's hand was a detailed drawing of the location of the three Mensis Phases. Each Phase contained a Domed city and a working-class society. It was a far cry from the vast populations that had once ruled the land.

"Each Mensis Phase needs the others to provide it with the essential resources to survive, namely water. Fresh drinking water is perhaps the single-most-important resource that keeps humanity alive. The Loggers in the north work hard to break down the ice in the arctic regions. The Pumpers work hard to pump the water down to us so that we can have drinking water to survive and grow food, which in turn benefits them as well. The Peddlers work hard to produce electricity so that we don't have to use the water to generate power. We are working together to help one another, not working to destroy each other."

"What about food? How come only the Mensis have a continuous supply of fresh food?" enquired Corey.

"It costs a lot of time, space, and money to produce fresh food. We use it mostly as a tool of trade between the Mensis Phases. We sell it to the other Phases for equally important goods such as paper, soap, clothes, and alcohol." Curtis crossed to the bar to fix himself a drink. "Would you like a drink? Brandy perhaps?"

"No, thank you." Corey couldn't understand why Curtis was being so polite. Could it be that he had only lied about sending out his soldiers to Crystal Lake?

Curtis returned with his drink and took his seat behind the desk. He sat with his hands steepled in front of his face as he studied a worthy opponent. He realized that he had great respect for Corey. The lad was brave, intelligent, and definitely more suited to the Presidency than his own good-for-nothing son would ever be.

"Are you ready to listen to the proposition that I am willing to make to you?"

"What kind of proposition?" asked Corey, skeptically.

"I know that you're unhappy about the way things are run around here, but bringing down the system is not the answer. I'm willing to forget about the past and start anew. I believe you now understand the reasons that the people had to be deceived. It is important that things remain the way they are so that we can prosper together. If one link in the chain becomes weak, then all the Mensis Phases will perish, including the workers and the Domed cities.

"I'm offering you the chance to make the changes that you see fit. Upon my death, the Presidency of Mensis, Phase One will revert back to the Tusk clan, under one condition. You must keep the system running as it is. If you want to give the Peddlers more credit for their work or supply the Dome with more fresh food, then that's your business. But you cannot let the people out of the Domes or do away with Dusting. Is that clear?"

"What if I refuse?"

"I'll kill you and nothing will change, and, heaven forbid, the Presidency might end up in the hands of Russ Fletcher."

At the mention of Russ's name, Corey's eyes narrowed. What might a guy like that do if he oversaw everything? He was the one who had killed Luther, and Luther was the one who had constantly reminded Corey that changes were made first from within, then without.

"Allow me to show to you a video of the people in Dasigge, Corey, and then you tell me if we should be opening up the Domed cities after that."

Zane sat in the front seat of the Cadillac with his hands bound with rope. He glanced over his shoulder to make sure the women were alright. They looked a little frightened, but otherwise, they were fine.

John Williams slowed the Cadillac as they approached the burned-out remains of a four-ton truck. There were also many dead horses along the side of the road. He pulled the car alongside Stephen Cowen, who had just inspected the interior. "What's in the truck?" he asked.

"You don't want to know." Stephen shook his head to clear it from the grotesque sight and smell of the burned bodies.

"Of course, I want to know. You don't think I recognized some of those horses back there?"

"It was really hard to tell who was who, but I would say there were more Peddlers than soldiers."

Anne knew that the men had taken two trucks with them to Mensis. The fact that there was only one must mean that some of them were still alive. *How had the soldiers found them so quickly?* she wondered. She was glad Corey hadn't ridden with the rest of them. She knew it was selfish to think only of Corey's welfare, but she couldn't bear the thought of losing him, again.

Pandora was more upset about having to go through with marrying the President's son. She hadn't realized how much she hated the idea until she was free of the choice, even if it was only for a spell. Her possessions and the shipment of goods were left at Crystal Lake until a truck could be sent to bring them back to Mensis, Phase One.

Zane was worried about Helena. No doubt she would think he was never coming back. He started to wonder himself whether he would ever make it back home. He had never expected life to be so complicated outside of the Dome.

It wasn't long before they approached the other burned-out truck on the side of the road. They all knew it was the last vehicle the men had taken. There were fewer dead horses on the road, implying that the soldiers had won the battle.

Stephen felt a moment of elation as he realized the soldiers had conquered the fugitive Peddlers. He knew what he'd find if he looked inside the truck, and the thought of it made his stomach turn. Instead, he ordered his men to keep riding.

Arthur stopped his horse under a willow tree just outside of the city limits. The men dismounted from their horses and walked around to stretch their muscles, as the Peddlers were not used to riding. Eventually, they gathered around Arthur, who was sketching a rough layout of the town in the dirt. Most of the populated areas were within walking distance of the Henniger Estate.

"I want you guys to spread out and round up all the people you can find. We won't bother with the factories and plants on the outskirts of town. They're too far away and it's mostly automated. Try to do this peacefully, please. These people are not armed, except maybe the soldiers. Reassure them that you will not hurt them if they do as you say. We only want to make a statement, not kill off half the population. Are there any questions?"

None of the men spoke up, so some of them mounted the horses and the others walked. They headed in separate directions into town to take over Mensis, Phase One. There was little or no resistance from the mild-mannered residents and their Peddler servants. The children treated the situation like a fire drill while the adults seemed more inconvenienced. There was soon a parade of people walking down the streets toward the Henniger Estate.

The D Men on horseback, led by Arthur, quickly surrounded the army barracks. They rounded up the remaining soldiers, who had not expected to be in danger, so had not been armed when the Peddlers entered the building.

The monitor operators insisted that at least three people stay on to look after the needs of DOCTOR. Arthur conceded and allowed a few to stay with an armed guard.

Curtis and Corey could hear the voices of adults and children outside the window. They had been sharing a brandy to close the deal they had both just signed. They were exhausted from their hours of discussion and bargaining.

They welcomed a change of scene as they approached the office window. Curtis was astounded to see what looked like the whole town spread out below him. His eyes took in the Peddler men on horseback with rifles in their hands. He was disappointed to see that these inexperienced men had beaten his own well-trained soldiers. With a shrug of his shoulder, Curtis quickly dismissed the thought. He didn't need his army to settle this matter. He had control of their leader. He was back in command of what could have been a disastrous situation.

A smile played on Corey's lips as he realized that it was his men who had herded this crowd here, as planned. They were not all lying dead on the road after all. In retrospect, he realized he should have insisted that his men wait for the outcome of his conversation with Curtis.

"Come with me to the balcony," Curtis suggested. "We can talk to the people from there." Corey followed Curtis out of the office and up the wide staircase to the upper front balcony. Curtis threw open the doors, and the two of them stepped out into the sunlit day.

An eerie silence fell upon the crowd as the people of Mensis saw their well-dressed President step out with an unkempt man in a rumpled, Green-Level jumpsuit. Curtis shot a quick glance toward Corey, who stood calm and composed before he addressed the crowd gathered below.

"Please do not be alarmed by these men who have brought you here today. I have talked at length with their leader, and we have come to a peaceful conclusion."

There was an audible sigh of relief from the crowd before they broke into cheers and laughter.

"It has been brought to my attention," Curtis continued, "how lucky we are to have the things we do. I'm sure you all appreciate what we have, but it is good to be reminded of those who are less fortunate than ourselves. As a result, we have agreed to ship more fresh food to the Domed City of Havanna and to increase the wages of the Peddlers."

Arthur couldn't believe how Corey could just stand there and listen to this bullshit. Whatever happened to equality among all the people? What happened to the ideals they had fought so hard for, like honesty and truth?

"It has also been agreed," Curtis continued, "that the mandatory age for retirement change. A person now has the choice of retiring to Dusting anywhere between the age of fifty to sixty-five. Dusting ceremonies will be held every Saturday at noon."

The crowd burst into applause and talked excitedly together. *It was clear that Curtis had full control as he promised them dreams,* thought Arthur. No doubt it was a plot to disarm the Peddlers and then restore things to normal. He knew from past experience that President Henniger could not be trusted.

"I apologize for any inconvenience to you this afternoon. This demonstration has been a peaceful one, and I feel we should invite these gentlemen to join our community." Curtis had almost spit out the word "gentlemen," but his diplomatic sense kept his true feelings from showing. He couldn't very well kill the Peddlers, nor could he allow them back to their homes. He decided that they would make a fine bunch of soldiers to replace the ones he had lost today.

"Listen to me," commanded Arthur, to the crowd. "Everything he tells you is a lie. He keeps everyone ignorant while he alone knows the truth."

"Arthur! Still causing trouble, I see. The truth of the situation is that your leader has signed a treaty," replied Curtis.

"Bullshit! Corey wouldn't make any decisions without first consulting the rest of us."

"Believe what you will." Curtis gave a dismissive hand gesture.

"I will not believe a word of this until I hear it from Corey himself."

Curtis stepped aside and motioned for Corey to step forward.

"Look," Corey reasoned, "what we believed in and fought for were idealistic notions, but it really doesn't have a place in the scheme of things. What we had proposed to do was just not plausible, or intelligent. Changes come from within, not from without. Curtis and I have spent many hours discussing problems and solutions. We have come to an agreement that holds acceptable terms for everyone."

Arthur couldn't believe what he was hearing. This was not the same Corey that he had spoken to this morning. What about all the people who had died trying to change the system? Had everything they'd done been pointless and meaningless? Curtis stepped forward again to address the people.

"I apologize for this interruption. Let's not quarrel amongst ourselves. Please, you're all free to leave." The crowd burst into applause.

Stephen Cowen and John Williams had first been alerted to the fact that something was amiss when they entered the town.

The streets were deserted and carriages had been abandoned, but it was the silence that was most disturbing. Halfway through town, they could hear people cheering. The sound seemed to be coming from the Henniger Estate.

John brought the prisoners to the Police Station while Stephen and the soldiers crept up to the scene. *It was evident that the Peddlers had forced the people to come here at gunpoint,* thought Stephen. He had not expected to encounter any more Peddlers armed with rifles.

He set his men up for an ambush and waited for the right moment. An opportunity presented itself when the crowd broke into applause. Stephen gave the signal and the soldiers rode in quickly. The first few shots went virtually unheard. It was only the motion of a few Peddlers falling from their horses that had drawn attention.

A woman in the crowd started screaming and the crowd started running wildly in all directions. A few people fell and were nearly crushed by stampeding feet. Arthur hardly noticed the commotion going on around him. His glare was fixed upon the President standing on the balcony. *I'm not going to let you railroad the situation again,* thought Arthur. He raised his rifle to his shoulder and fired a single shot. He was going to end this evil once and for all.

Curtis was stunned by the impact of the bullet entering his chest. His hand went down to cover the hole as he sought out his assailant. His eyes rolled back and his body fell forward, void of life.

Stephen caught sight of a figure in an armored suit firing at the President. He sighted the man on the horse in his scope. He did not recognize his friend Arthur until the second he pulled the trigger.

Stephen jumped down from his horse and raced to his friend's side. Arthur was sitting on the ground, holding his bloody arm.

"Good thing for me you are a lousy shot," he teased his friend.

"Dammit Arthur! I took you for a rebel. What are you doing?"

"Setting things right, my friend. Setting things right. Now get me something to stop the bleeding, will you?"

"You haven't answered my question. What are you doing? You shot the President for Pete's sake!"

"I told you. I'm setting things right," Arthur grunted out through the pain.

"That's not good enough, Arthur." He raised his rifle again. "One more time, what were you doing?"

"Hold up." Stephen turned at the sound of Corey's voice. He had made his way down as soon as he realized that Arthur had been shot.

"Who the blazes are you?"

"Your new boss," replied Corey. Stephen was taken aback for a moment until he saw that Corey held President Henniger's will. He snatched it from Corey's hand.

"It states here," Stephen read from the will. "I, President Curtis Henniger, being of sound body and mind, hereby bequest upon my death that Zane Tusk, descendant of the Great President Henry Tusk should take his rightful place as President of Mensis, Phase One. I leave to him the Estate and all its contents."

AFTERWORD

THREE MONTHS LATER, JASON ENTERED THE STUDY WITH THE monthly statements of the other two Mensis Phases. Corey was busy sorting through paperwork that never seemed to end. Even though Curtis was dead, Zane had still felt compelled to stick to their signed agreement. He understood the importance of keeping the system operating as it was. After all, he too was shown the top-secret video of Dasigge. Zane vowed to change the things he could without disturbing the original arrangement.

The news of losing Zachary, Bear, Chip, and all the good D Men in the battle for freedom weighed heavy on Corey's heart, but their sacrifice had helped to secure a better future. He missed Luther and Lionel the most and was glad that Curtis was dead. They now had a chance to make changes that would benefit everyone. The report that he had just been reading showed that morale was up in Peddlers, even though production was down. He looked up when Jason entered the office and approached the desk.

Zane had given Jason the deed to the playhouse, where he and Sunshine preferred to stay. Jason wasn't overly upset about the outcome of the events. He knew in his heart that Zane would make a better President. The prospect of so much responsibility had never appealed to him. He was content with his position at the bank. The pay was good, and the hours were short.

In his role as administrator, Corey had sent out memorandums to the other Mensis Phases regarding changes to their system.

Corey was not sure how the other Mensis operations would react to his suggestions, but he had decided to take the Dome by storm. He knew Jason now held the results of those memorandums.

"Don't keep me in suspense, Jason."

"It seems that your suggestions were well received. Both the other Mensis Phases will be raising the workers' wages and making retirement optional up to the age of sixty-five. They also agreed to supply more fresh food to the Domed cities."

"That's wonderful! What about eliminating capital punishment?"

"Mensis, Phase Two has agreed to the terms, with the exception of the criminally insane."

"Excellent. Did Pandora and her workers get home alright?"

"Yes. President Bell was also pleased with the shipment we sent up for his troubles."

"Now, what about Mensis, Phase Three?" asked Corey.

"They are dead set against abolishing capital punishment."

"Why?"

"They claim they have no other way to keep the criminals in line. They don't have a nuclear burial site in their area."

"I see." Corey rubbed his chin.

"They said some nonsense about not wanting to break with tradition. Which brings me to my next point. They were both against the removal of class distinction and intermarriage."

"That's unfortunate, but we won't press the issue right now. Let's give them some time to think about it. We can't beat the system by trying to beat the people. We can only change things from within and lead by example."

"Is that why you signed the deal with my father?"

"Yes. Changes come from within, not from without, as Luther was fond of reminding me from time to time."

"Speaking of which... as you know, Moonbeam and Rocky are very pleased with their new jobs, and Sandpebble is happy in the experiments lab, but..."

"But what?"

"Lucky really wants to go back to Peddlers. He says he's not happy as a chauffeur, and he's mourning Chip. He says he's feeling called to go back to Peddlers. His words, not mine." Jason held up his hands.

"Did you explain to him why he cannot go back?"

"Yes, and he says he wouldn't tell a soul of anything he knew. I figure he can say he escaped from the C Zone."

"It's plausible, but what guarantee do we have that he'll stick to that story? Do you realize the consequences of what could happen if the Peddlers learn the truth about Dusting?"

"We can tell him that if word gets back to us that he's said anything, we'll send him back to the C Zone. I don't think he'll be too fond of that idea."

"I hate to issue threats, but I don't see that I have much choice. I don't like to see my friends unhappy either. Alright," Corey decided. "Will you see to it personally, Jason?"

"Sure thing. I'll do it right away." Jason turned to go.

"Could you also extend an invitation to him for supper tonight at the Estate? We'll throw a going-away party for him. Let the other guys know and tell them to bring their dates."

"Speaking of dates, Sunshine and I have finally set our wedding date."

"That's wonderful! I thought Sunshine was against the idea of marriage?"

"She was until she found out she's pregnant. We're going to have a baby!" Jason was smiling from ear to ear.

Corey stood and extended his hand out to him. "Congratulations, Jason! I'm very happy for you."

"Of course, Sunshine and I aren't going to have a big wedding like you and Anne. We'd like to have a quiet ceremony at the cottage."

Corey fondly reflected upon his wedding day. His mother had arrived from Havanna the night before. She looked pale and thin, but her eyes shone with a light that Zane said he had not seen since before Corey's exile.

Helena claimed that Mensis was everything that she had thought Dusting would be. She was sad to leave her daughter, Tanya, but she was happy to be with Zane and Corey. She had assumed that she would never see either one of them again. It was quite a shock for her to realize that she was now the First Lady.

Their wedding had been held on the Tusk Estate grounds toward the cooler part of the day. Anne looked spectacular in her white chiffon dress, embellished with beads and ribbons. Corey had been pleased that he hadn't had to share that special day with forty-nine other couples.

Many of the townspeople showed up and mingled politely with the Peddler friends of the new President's son. Sandpebble had been excited to see them all again but was sad to hear about Bear and Chip.

The couple was showered with gifts and well wishes. The present that Anne most cherished, though, was the ivory elephant earrings Sunshine had given her. She squealed with joy when she opened the box to find the matching jewelry to her necklace.

Corey was glad that Jason had finally set a date for their wedding. He had become like a brother to Corey in the short time they had known one another. It might have had something to do with the close friendship he had with Sunshine. *Luckily, Anne and Sunshine hit it off right from the start, and now that they were both pregnant, they'll probably be inseparable,* thought Corey.

With the death of Zachary and Lionel and the disappearance of Anne from the Dome, it was necessary for Corey to advance two more boys and a girl to keep population quotas on par in Havanna. He also had to ensure twins were born to the first four couples this year.

It was confirmed by DOCTOR that Anne was indeed pregnant with twin boys. Helena and Anne spent most of their days readying a nursery in the west wing for the new arrivals next year.

"DOCTOR says Sunshine is going to have a girl. So far, we have not agreed on a name. Sunshine wants a Peddler name, and

I'd like a more traditional Mensis name. How did you and Anne decide on names?"

"I wisely let her pick the names." They both laughed.

"It's nice to see that Arthur has recovered from his gunshot wound," said Jason as he gathered up his papers.

"I'm glad Dad chose him to be his General. Arthur can instruct him on the ways of Mensis better than I."

"True. Are you happy with the way things turned out, Corey?"

"As you know, I wanted more extreme changes to the system, but Zane thought it wise to maintain the status quo. Believe me, we've had some real drag-down, knock-out fights about this. But as Dad is fond of reminding me, he is the President, not me. He has agreed to let me implement some changes to the system, but insists that it's working fine the way it is."

"Sorry, Corey. I have to agree with your father. This system has worked well for over a hundred years. I'm okay with the changes you are making, but overall, I think the system is as perfect as it's going to get."

"Perhaps. Time will tell. You know, Jason, I've spent most of my life questioning and bucking the system. It just feels strange to me to now be the one implementing it." Corey shook his head. "It just feels like I'm compromising my beliefs for comfort and peace."

"What's wrong with peace and comfort? Isn't that what everyone wants?"

"Yes, but does everyone have it, or just us?" questioned Corey.

"You know, there comes a time when you just have to make a decision and then be happy with it. You have a beautiful wife, and twin boys on the way. What more could you want? Enjoy what life has given you, Corey."

"Maybe you're right, Jason. Life is good right now."

"You'll see. Everything will turn out fine," confirmed Jason. Corey hoped he was right, but deep down in his gut, he had a bad feeling.

Preview to *Havanna*

The red emergency vidphone on his desk rang. Corey Tusk connected it right away.

"President Tusk." It still felt odd to Corey to name himself so, just as it was strange to be wearing three-piece suits instead of sweats or jumpsuits. It was amazing how life had changed so much, so fast. Five months ago, he was living in Havanna, playing sports and hanging out with his friends. Now he was President of Mensis, Phase One, running the whole shebang.

His father, Zane, had passed on the Presidency to him after ruling for only four months. Zane had not been comfortable with the responsibilities and pressures that came with the position. He felt Corey was better suited, and more enthusiastic, for the role.

"Hello, President Tusk. This is President Mark Brennan of Phase Two. I hate to bother you, but we have a problem, and I will need some soldiers to assist us."

Corey noticed the worry lines on President Brennan's brow, which seem to contrast with his youthful appearance.

"What kind of problem?" enquired Corey.

"Residents of Dasigge have been spotted outside their Domed city."

"Yes, I understand how that could be a problem." Corey remembered only too well the vidtape he had seen in President Henniger's office of the Domed City of Dasigge. It was one of the deciding factors for Corey in accepting the agreement with President Curtis Henniger.

"Actually, the problem is that there is a growing number of people gathered outside the Dome. They're coming in from everywhere, Townies and workers from all Phases. We are pushing the people back, but we need more soldiers."

"How many soldiers do you require?"

"I was hoping for about fifty or more if you can spare them."

"Fifty? Why so many?"

"Well, to tell you the truth, we're really not sure what we are dealing with. One of my soldiers panicked and shot a Dasiggean. As soon as he did, the person vanished into thin air. It gets weirder. We never found a body, and all the others with him disappeared as well."

"I see." Corey rubbed his chin. "That is a bit of a situation, for sure."

Corey thought about things for a moment before answering. He was not sure what to make of the situation, but he knew letting the people out of Dasigge was not a good plan. He would have a better idea of the state of affairs once he had seen it for himself.

"I can be there in three days with as many soldiers as I can spare."

CPSIA information can be obtained
at www.ICGtesting.com
Printed in the USA
JSHW061356210822
29486JS00001B/7

9 781039 132009